The Convenient Groom

Denise Hunter

the
Wedding
Machine

Beth Webb Hart

Thomas Nelson
Since 1798

NASHVILLE   DALLAS   MEXICO CITY   RIO DE JANEIRO   BEIJING

The Convenient Groom

Other novels by Denise Hunter include

Sweetwater Gap

Surrender Bay

Finding Faith

Saving Grace

Mending Places

For Jesus, my tower of strength,
my shelter in the storm

Dear friend,

I'm so glad you chose to embark on this journey to Nantucket. I hope you'll enjoy your brief visit to the quaint New England island and the characters who inhabit this story.

While this series was still in its conception stage, God laid a very meaningful scripture on my heart: Zephaniah 3:17.

> *The Lord your God is with you,*
> *he is mighty to save.*
> *He will take great delight in you,*
> *he will quiet you with his love,*
> *he will rejoice over you with singing.*

As I breathed in the comfort and peace the verse offers, I couldn't help but notice that these characteristics of God's are some of the qualities a woman looks for in a man. As that thought jelled, it struck me that a love story between a man and a woman could be a beautiful allegory, showing the depths of God's love. At that moment, this series was born.

One of the things I love about Jesus' parables is the way those stories, subtle as they are, allow us to see a familiar truth with fresh perspective. My goal with this series is to show aspects of God's character through the relationship of the hero and heroine and to trust you, the reader, to make those connections yourself.

Zephaniah 3:17 is so rich I decided to break up the verse and show one characteristic of God in each book. *The Convenient Groom* takes the second line: *He is mighty to save.* What if you had a God that would push through all obstacles for you, his beloved? This story plays out that theme through the characters of Kate and Lucas.

After you've read the story, I hope you'll take the time to read through the discussion questions as a way of digging a little deeper into the story's layers. Most of all, I hope this simple love story will enable you to see Christ's love in a new and exciting way.

Yours in Christ,
Denise

"The LORD *your God is with you,*
he is mighty to save.
He will take great delight in you,
he will quiet you with his love,
he will rejoice over you with singing."

Zephaniah 3:17

⤝

Let your face shine on your servant;
save me in your unfailing love.

Psalm 31:16

Dating is like shopping for a garment. Everything looks great in the display window. Once inside the store, some of the dazzle disappears.

—Excerpt from
Finding Mr. Right-for-You
by Dr. Kate

Chapter One

The red light on Kate Lawrence's cell phone blinked a staccato warning. But before she could retrieve the message, her maid of honor, Anna Doherty, waved her pale arms from the beach, stealing her attention.

Anna's smooth voice sounded in her headset. "Kate, can you come here? We've got a few glitches."

"Be right there." Kate tucked her clipboard in the crook of her elbow, took the steps down Jetty Pavilion's porch, and crossed the heel-sinking sand of the Nantucket shoreline. In six hours, thirty-four guests would be seated there in the rows of white chairs, watching Kate pledge her life to Bryan Montgomery under a beautiful hand-carved gazebo.

Where was the gazebo anyway? She checked her watch, then

glanced toward the Pavilion, where workers scurried in white uniforms. No sign of Lucas.

She approached Anna, who wore worry lines as naturally as she wore her Anne Klein pantsuit. Anna was the best receptionist Kate could ask for. Her capable presence reassured the troubled couples she ushered through Kate's office.

Right now, Anna's long brown hair whipped across her face like a flag gone awry, and she batted it from her eyes with her freckled hand. "Soiree's just called. Their delivery truck is in for service, and the flowers will be a little late. Half an hour at the most."

Kate jotted the note on her schedule. "That's okay." She'd factored in cushion time.

"Murray's called, and the tuxes haven't been picked up except for your dad's."

Bryan and his best man had been due at Murray's at nine thirty. An hour ago. "I'll check on that. What else?"

Anna's frown lines deepened, and her eyes blinked against the wind. "The carriage driver is sick, but they're trying to find a replacement. The Weatherbys called and asked if they could attend last minute—they were supposed to go out of town, but their plans changed."

Kate nodded. "Fine, fine. Call and tell her they're welcome. I'll notify the caterer."

"Your publicist—Pam?—has been trying to reach you. Did you check your cell? She said she got voice mail. Anyway, your book copies did arrive this morning. She dropped this off." Anna pulled a hardback book from under her clipboard. "Ta-da!"

"My book!" Kate stared at the cover, where the title, *Finding Mr. Right-for-You,* floated above a cartoon couple. The man was on his knee, proposing. Below them, a colorful box housed the bold letters of Kate's name. She ran her fingers over the glossy book jacket, feeling the raised bumps of the letters, savoring the moment.

"Pam wants a quick photo shoot before the guests arrive. You holding the book, that kind of thing. You should probably call her."

Kate jotted the note. While it was on her mind, she reached down and turned on her cell.

"Ready for more great news?" Anna asked. Her blue eyes glittered like diamonds. The news had to be good.

"What?"

"The *New York Times* is sending a reporter and a photographer. They want to do a feature story on your wedding and your book."

Fresh air caught and held in Kate's lungs. Rosewood Press was probably turning cartwheels. "That's fabulous. They'll want an interview." She scanned her schedule, looking for an open slot. After the reception? She hated to do it, but Bryan would understand. The *New York Times*. It would give Kate's initial sales the boost it needed. Maybe enough to make the bestseller list.

"Here's the number." Anna handed her a yellow Post-It. "That tabloid guy has been hanging around all morning, trying to figure out who the groom is. I told him he'd find out in six hours like everyone else. The rest of the media is scheduled to arrive an hour before the wedding, and Pam's having an area set up over there for them." Anna gestured behind the rows of chairs to a square blocked off with white ribbon.

"Good. I want them to be as inconspicuous as possible. This is my wedding, and a girl only gets married once, after all."

"One would hope." Anna said. "Is there anything else I can do?"

Kate gave her a sideways hug, as close to an embrace as she'd ever given her assistant, her fingers pressing into Anna's fleshy shoulder. "You're a godsend. I don't know what I'd do without you."

"Oh! I know what I forgot to tell you. The gazebo. It should have been here by now. I tried to call Lucas, but I got the machine, and I don't have his cell number."

"His shop's closed today, and he doesn't have a cell." The man didn't wear a watch, much less carry a phone. She should've known better than to put something this crucial in his hands. Kate checked her watch. "I'll run over and check on it."

❧

The drive to town was quick and effortless, but Kate's mind swam with a hundred details. She jotted reminders on her clipboard when she stopped for pedestrians, occasionally admiring the cover of her book. She called Pam for a quick recap about the *New York Times* reporter, and by the time she hung up, she was pulling into a parallel slot on Main Street, in front of Lucas's storefront.

The sign above the picture window read "Cottage House Furniture." On the second floor of the Shaker building, the wooden shingle for her own business dangled from a metal pole: "Kate Lawrence, Marriage Counseling Services." She needed to remind Lucas to remove it; otherwise he'd leave it hanging for another year or until someone else rented the space.

Kate exited her car and slid her key into the rusty lock of the shop's door. Once inside, she passed the stairs leading to her office and walked through the darkened maze of furniture to the back, where she hoped to find Lucas. She bumped an end table with her shin. *Ow!* That would leave a mark.

The high-pitched buzz of a power tool pierced the darkness, a good sign. "Lucas?" She rapped loudly on the metal door with her knuckles. The noise stopped.

"Come in."

She opened the door. Lucas Wright looked up from his spot on the cement floor at the base of the gazebo, his too-long hair hanging over one eye. He looked her over, then turned back to the spindle and ran his thick hand over it as if testing the curves.

"Aren't you supposed to be at the beach?" he asked.

Kate crossed her arms. "I could ask you the same thing."

He stood, agile for his size, and backed away from the gazebo. Sawdust from the floor clung to his faded jeans and black T-shirt. "I was just finishing."

"You were supposed to be there an hour ago. The gazebo needs to be put in place before the sound system, and the florist has to decorate it, and there are people waiting to do their jobs."

He faced her, looking into her in that way of his that made her feel like he could see clean through her. "Today's the big day, huh?" Putting his tool on his workhorse, he dusted off his hands, moving in slow motion as though he'd decided tonight wouldn't arrive until next week.

Kate checked her watch. "Do you think you can get this down to the beach sometime today?"

Walking around the piece, he studied it, hands on his hips, head cocked. "You like it?"

For the first time since the week before, Kate looked at the gazebo—the white lattice top, the hand-carved spindles, the gentle arch of the entry. At the top of the arch, a piece of wood curved gracefully, etched with clusters of daisies. The gazebo's simple lines were characteristic of Lucas's work, but she'd never known him to use such exquisite detail. The piece had an elegance that surpassed her expectations. He did beautiful work; she'd give him that.

"I do. I love the etching." She sighed. Just when he irritated the snot out of her, he did something like this, caught her off guard. She always felt like she was tripping down the stairs when she was with him.

Focus! "It needs to find its way to the beach. Pronto."

"Yes ma'am." His salute was unhurried.

Before she could offer a retort, her cell phone pealed and buzzed simultaneously, and she pulled it from her capri pocket.

"Hello?"

"Kate?"

"Bryan." Turning away from Lucas and toward the door, she eyed a crude desk with a metal folding chair that bore countless rusty scratches. "Good morning." A smile crept into her voice. It was their wedding day. The day they'd planned for nearly two years. "Did you sleep well?" She hadn't. She'd rumpled the sheets until nearly two o'clock, but that was to be expected.

The silence on the other end, however, was not. "Bryan?" Had she lost the signal?

"Um, Kate, did you get my message?"

There'd been a blinking red light this morning. She'd assumed it was Pam's voice mail and hadn't checked. Suddenly, she wished she had.

"No. What's wrong?"

"Are you sitting down?"

"No, I'm not sitting down. Just tell me." An ugly dread snaked down her spine and settled there, coiled and waiting.

"I'm on my way back to Boston," he said. "I left a message this morning. You must've had your phone off."

Kate's stomach stirred. She stared at the wall in front of her—a pegboard with a zillion holes, metal prongs poking from it, tools and cords everywhere. "What happened?" Some emergency, maybe?

What emergency could trump our wedding?

"I can't marry you, Kate."

The words dropped, each one crumbling under its own weight. The stirring in her stomach intensified. "That's not funny, Bryan." It was a terrible joke. He'd never been good with jokes. His punch lines left you leaning forward, waiting for the rest.

"I'm in love with someone else."

Pain. A huge wooden spoon, tossing the contents of her stomach. Her legs wobbled, trembling on the wedge heels of her sandals, and she clutched the cold metal of the folding chair. "What?" Was that her voice, weak and thready? Someone had vacuumed all the moisture from her mouth, sucked the air from her lungs.

"I'm so sorry," Bryan was saying. "I know this is awful. You don't deserve this, but I can't marry you. It happened slowly, and I didn't realize what was going on until recently. I tried to put it out of my mind, but I just can't. And I can't marry you knowing how I feel. I'm so sorry, Kate."

"What?" It was the only word her mind could form at the moment.

"I know there's no excuse. I should have told you before now, but I thought it would go away. I thought I was just having cold feet or something, but it's more than that."

"We've been together for two years, Bryan."

It was a stupid thing to say, but it was all she could think of. Memories played across the screen of her mind in fast-forward. The day they'd met in line at Starbucks in downtown Boston when Kate had gone there for a conference. Their first date at the Colonial Theatre. The long-distance courting and weekend visits. The e-mails, the phone calls, the engagement, the book. It all whizzed by, coming to a screeching halt here, at this moment. Here, in Lucas's dusty workshop. Here, in front of the special gazebo they were to be married in.

"I've already called my family and told them. I know there's a lot to do, and I'll help any way you want me to. And then there's your book . . . I'm so sorry."

Sorry. You're sorry? She pictured the precise rows of white chairs, the tent being erected as they spoke, the photographers.

The *New York Times*.

She closed her burning eyes. Everything would have to be cancelled.

At that thought, humiliation arrived on the scene, sinking in past the pain of betrayal. The weight of it pushed at her shoulders, and she grabbed the hair at her nape. *Think, Kate! This is no time to lose it.*

"Stop, Bryan. Just stop and think about what you're doing. Maybe you're letting your issues with your parents' divorce affect your decisions. This kind of fear is perfectly natural before a wedding, and maybe—"

"No, it's not that—"

"How do you know?" She forced reason into her tone. Used her soothing voice—the one she put on when things got heated between one of her couples. "We love each other. We're perfect for each other. You've said it a hundred times."

"There's something missing, Kate."

She wobbled again and steadied herself with a hand on the chair. "Something missing"? What was that supposed to mean?

As her mind grappled with that seemingly unanswerable question, she felt a hand at her back, leading her into the chair. She was sitting, her head as fuzzy as a cotton-candy machine, her emerald-cut engagement ring blurring before her eyes.

"What do you mean there's something missing? The only thing missing is the groom. For our wedding that starts in five hours. Five hours, Bryan." Now she felt the hysteria building and took a full breath, nearly choking on the way the oxygen stretched her lungs.

"I'll help in any way I can."

"You can help by showing up for our wedding!"

Her mind ran through the list of people she'd have to call. Her dad, the guests, her publisher. She thought of the money Rosewood Press had spent on this elaborate beach wedding. They'd flown in friends and family from all over the country, paid for the photographer, flowers, caterer, the wedding attire. Kate had only wanted a simple wedding, but with the release of the book, the marketing department had other ideas. "An elegant wedding and a surprise groom just as the book releases. Think of the publicity, Kate!"

A knot started in her throat and burned its way to her heart.

"I'll always care about you," Bryan said.

The words fell, as empty as a discarded soda bottle on a deserted beach.

Enough.

The adrenaline coursing through her veins drained suddenly, leaving her once again weak and shaky. She couldn't talk to him anymore. She wasn't going to break down on the phone, wasn't going to beg him to come back. It wouldn't accomplish a thing anyway. She'd heard this tone of Bryan's voice before. He was a man who knew what he wanted. And what he didn't want.

And he didn't want Kate. She suddenly knew that fact as surely as she knew tomorrow would be more impossible to face than today.

She cleared her throat. "I have to go."

"Kate, tell me what I can do. My family will pitch in too. I want to help fix things."

She wanted to tell him there was no fixing this. There was no fixing her heart or the impending collision of her life and her career. Instead, numb, she closed the phone, staring straight ahead at the holes on the pegboard until they blended together in a blurry haze.

He was leaving her. The man she loved was walking away. This wasn't supposed to be happening. Not to her. She'd been so careful, and for what? A hollow spot opened up in her stomach, wide and gaping.

Instead of the headlines reading "Marriage Expert Finds Her Mr. Right," they would read "Marriage Expert Jilted at the Altar."

Kate had never considered herself prideful, but the thought of facing the next twenty-four hours made cyanide seem reasonable. How could this be happening? To her, of all people? She'd written a book on the subject of finding the right mate and had managed to find the wrong one instead. By tomorrow the whole world would know.

Impulsivity is the enemy.
Intelligent relationships require
careful, thoughtful planning.

—Excerpt from
Finding Mr. Right-for-You
by Dr. Kate

Chapter Two

Lucas watched Kate snap her phone shut. Maybe he should've left when he heard the gravity in her voice, but he couldn't. Like a pedestrian gawking at a car accident, he'd watched Kate receive the news. When he realized what Bryan was saying, he'd wanted to hunt the man down and pummel him until he felt the same pain as Kate. Instead he'd ushered Kate to the chair, wishing he could pull her into his arms and tell her it was going to be okay.

But that was the last thing she wanted.

Now she faced the wall, unmoving. Her glossy black hair hung straight, almost to her wilted shoulders. He'd never seen her so motionless. She was always on the go, steady as a clock; he'd been mesmerized by that the first time they'd met. Now, her stillness seemed unnatural.

He took a step toward her. "Kate?"

She must have forgotten about him, because she jumped slightly, then ran her hand across her face before turning partway. Her hair, always tucked behind her ears, had come loose. Her eyes only made it to his knees.

"Lucas." She studied the floor as if the paint and varnish stains were one of those abstract paintings to be interpreted. "I guess you heard."

Her voice was small. But he watched her straighten her back and turn to look fully at him. A scared little girl in a woman's body. Her eyes went past him to the gazebo for a second before flittering back.

"I . . . I guess I won't be needing that. I'll pay you for it, though. It's really beautiful." Her voice choked on the last word.

"I'm not worried about that."

He half expected her to cave in then, but instead she shot to her feet and began to pace, her heels clicking across the floor. "I have to think," she muttered. "I have to think."

Ka-clack, ka-clack, ka-clack, spin. *Ka-clack, ka-clack, ka-clack,* spin.

Lucas wasn't sure what she meant. Was she trying to figure out how to win Bryan back? Or giving up—making a mental list of everyone to be notified. He couldn't imagine the mess.

But if anyone could wrap her hands around the task, Kate could. He'd watched her patch up marriages that were dangling by a thread, juggle her syndicated column with her counseling service, and write a book in her spare time. Kate was an incredible woman. Bryan was an idiot if he couldn't see what he had.

Kate jerked to a stop and pressed her fingertips to her forehead. "He left me. I have no groom. The newspapers, the media, my publisher. My career. It's over."

She looked fragile and out of place in his expansive and dusty workshop, her short pants and white blouse immaculate, her black belt encircling her tiny waist. But then Kate always looked as if she'd been snapped straight from an ironing board.

"I thought he loved me," she whispered, her words wavering.

Lucas took a step toward her, then stopped, anchoring his hands in his pockets. "It's going to be okay." It felt lame but it was what he always told his baby sister, and it made Jamie feel better. Kate, however, was not Jamie.

"It is not going to be okay." She leveled a look at him. "I've been dumped five hours before my wedding. Everything is riding on this wedding, both personally and professionally. My Mr. Right left me. Do you not understand the irony?"

Maybe he wasn't your Mr. Right. It was on the tip of his tongue, but he caught it in time. He watched Kate's hand tremble against the side of her face. He hadn't known Kate was capable of trembling.

"I'm supposed to be an expert. Not just in relationships, but in finding the right mate. People write me for advice and trust me to give them answers. I wrote a book to help people make good matches, and I can't even make one myself." She looked away and dragged in a shaky breath. "I'm a failure."

"You're not a failure. Your fiancé made an idiot decision; that's not your fault."

The metal chair creaked as she sank into it, the sound echoing in the quietness of the room. "That's not how everyone's going to see it."

He reckoned she might be right about that. People could be judgmental, especially if the media put a nasty spin on it.

"I've got to do something," she mumbled through her fingers. "How can I fix this?"

Lucas didn't think it was possible. She had guests, a slew of media, and all the wedding fixings. Everything but the groom, and that was most important.

Everything but the groom.

The words ricocheted around his head until, one by one, they fell into place like tiles in a Scrabble game.

Everything . . . but . . . the groom . . .

He rubbed the back of his neck, walking toward his work station. It was crazy. Crazier than crazy. It was insane. She'd laugh if he said it out loud. That thought tightened his gut.

Her phone clattered, vibrating on the metal desk. He watched it do the jitterbug.

"I can't answer," she said. "I can't deal with it right now. I don't know what to say." She crossed her arms, and her shoulders scrunched up as though she wished she could cover her ears with them.

Together they watched the phone. *Ring-bzzzzzzzz . . . Ring-bzzzzzzz . . .* When the noise stopped, there was a palpable relief.

Kate drummed her fingers on her lips, quickly at first, then slowing. Her lips loosened, turned down. Her stubborn chin softened. "It's hopeless."

The phone rang again, chittering across the desktop. Kate glared at it, looking as though she might throw it across the room.

"I'll answer." He reached for it.

Kate stopped him with a hand on his arm. Her grip was surprisingly strong. "What'll you say?"

He met her gaze: wide, olive-brown eyes too vulnerable for words. "I'll just take a message."

After a moment, she released his arm, and he picked up the phone, snapping it open.

"Hello?"

A pause. "Is Kate there?" A woman's voice, out of breath.

"She can't come to the phone right now. Can I take a message?"

"Is this Bryan? Don't tell me she's letting you see her before the wedding."

"No. This is a—a friend." That was stretching it. He turned and leaned against the desk.

"Okay, well, tell her to call Pam. No, wait, she won't be able to reach me for a while. Tell her I have good news. This is really important, so be sure and tell her right away. The *Dr. Phil* show called, and they want her to make a guest appearance next month."

Great. Lucas met Kate's eyes, glanced away. Just what she needed.

"Did you get that?" Pam asked.

"Got it. I'll let her know." He closed the phone and set it on the desk. He could feel Kate watching him. Maybe he didn't have to tell her just now.

"Who was it?" Was that hope lilting her voice? Did she think Bryan had changed his mind?

"It was Pam."

She stared at her manicured fingers, clenched in her lap. "Oh."

She'd actually gotten on the *Dr. Phil* show. He'd known her popularity had grown nationwide with the column and book and all. But *Dr. Phil.* That was a whole new ball game.

"What did she want?"

Her knee brushed his leg as she shifted. He crossed his feet at the ankles and gripped the ledge of the desk. "It's nothing that can't wait. She wants you to call her back."

Her upturned face and searching eyes melted him. Have mercy, she was beautiful. He looked away.

"She said something, didn't she? Something you don't want me to know."

Restless energy pushed him away from the desk. He should've known she wouldn't let it go. He shouldn't have answered the phone. Her type A personality required her to know, even when she already had more than she could handle.

"Excuse me, but my life is hanging in the balance right now. Could you please just spit it out?"

Kate had straightened in the chair, her hand grasping the rounded edge of the back. Her left hand. Lucas watched the diamond engagement ring twinkle under the work lights. "She just wanted to let you know about an interview she set up, is all. You can call her later when you—"

"Who's it with?" Her tone demanded an answer.

He exhaled deeply. She was like a ravenous dog with his last meaty bone.

"I know it must be big. She wouldn't have called me today if it wasn't. And stop looking at me like that."

"Like what?"

"Like you feel sorry for me. Who's it with?"

Fine, Kate, fine. You win. "Dr. Phil."

He watched her mouth slacken, watched her blink and swallow, watched her eyes change, deaden. He hated it. Hated he'd had any part in bringing that look to her face.

She was still again, and he hated that too. Maybe it wasn't too late to chase Bryan down and knock him flat on his face. He should be here picking up the pieces, making things right. But he wasn't. Lucas was there, and what could he do?

Everything but the groom.

The words flashed in his mind like a lighthouse beacon, teasing him. *It's crazy.* And even if it wasn't, it was self-serving.

You could save Kate's wedding. Her reputation. Her career. It's an honorable thing.

But I would also be getting what I wanted. Is that selfish?

You were willing to let her go, because you thought that was right. Was that selfish? She needs you now. And you're in a position to help her.

"What am I going to do?" Kate asked

She turned her doe eyes on him, looking at him, needing him. It was heady. He wanted to protect her, to gather her close, the way a hen gathers her chicks under her wings.

"How am I going to face everyone? What am I going to tell the media? My publisher?" For the first time, her lip trembled, and she caught it between her teeth. "They paid for everything; did you know that?"

Should he say it? Should he offer himself? Could it even work? "Maybe it could."

"What?"

He didn't know he'd said it aloud until he heard Kate's response. Well, he was in just deep enough, he figured he might as well dive in headfirst. "I have an idea. It's a little crazy."

Surprisingly, she breathed a wry chuckle. "My whole life's a little crazy at the moment."

He studied her. She was actually looking at him with something like hope in her eyes. "Way I see it, the only thing missing is a groom."

Her laugh was sharp. "A necessary ingredient, I think you'll agree."

He nodded once, hoping she'd put two and two together so he wouldn't have to say it. "What if there was a different groom?"

Now she reared back slightly, blinking. *Great. She thinks I'm nuts.*

"I don't exactly have a waiting list, Lucas."

He shuffled his feet, then leaned against the workhorse, not sure if he was ready for what came next. *Just say it. The worst she can do is laugh in my face.* "What if I stood in for Bryan?"

He scuffed at the white paint on the tip of his right tennis shoe as silence closed in around him. A long silence. An uncomfortable silence. If he could've caught the words and pulled them back, he would've. Instead, he glanced at Kate. The expression on her face reinforced his wish.

"Why would—" She cleared her throat. "Why would you do that?"

Why would I do it? Because I love you. But he couldn't say that. Why hadn't he thought this out before he'd opened his big mouth?

He lifted his shoulder. "To help you," he said.

Her brows pulled together. "We're talking marriage here, not some little favor."

Favor. What if he made a bargain with her? What if she could do something for him in return? "I'd want something in return." *What? What do I want in return?*

At that, her eyebrows slackened as her lips took up the tension, pressing together. Her glare was direct and meaningful, and he immediately knew what she was thinking.

"Don't flatter yourself," he said.

She shook her head as if dislodging a distasteful picture. "It doesn't matter. It wouldn't work. Even if the rest of the world doesn't know who I was marrying, my dad does. And so does Chloe, my editor, and Pam and Anna. Not to mention Bryan's family."

A definite glitch, but was there a way around it? Now that the idea had settled a bit, it was growing on him. He shrugged. "Would they keep quiet?"

She gave him a double take. "Keep quiet?" Her fingers found the high collar of her blouse. "You're actually serious."

His heart was a jackhammer gone wild under his rib cage. He scratched at the dried paint on his thumbnail. "Would they?"

She turned away, her black hair swinging saucily. "You can't— you can't just marry me. Marriage is permanent. At least to me it is. You don't just make a willy-nilly decision to marry someone. People don't do that." She faced him again. "I don't do that."

No, Kate didn't do that. She planned every step days in advance, every detail in order, everything in its place.

At least she hadn't laughed at him. He straightened and shrugged as casually as he could, given that he felt like a man whose date had turned her head when he tried to kiss her. "Suit yourself."

He began wrapping the cord around the sander. It was a stupid idea anyway. He could only imagine his mom's reaction if his parents returned from their trip to find their son not only married, but married to Kate Lawrence. He'd never hear the end of it. And neither would his dad.

Nonetheless, it didn't do much for his ego to know Kate would rather see the death of her career than marry him. He stuffed the ache further down and set the sander on the shelf next to his favorite drill, waiting to hear the click of her heels as she left the shop.

Instead, Kate's voice broke the silence. "The people who know Bryan was the groom . . . what if one of them leaked it? Besides, there's the marriage license and the tuxes. Something could go wrong, and if everyone found out, it would be a bigger disaster than what I have now—if that's possible."

Okay, already, I get it. "It was a stupid idea." She'd made that plain enough. "You should get out your little notepad and make a list of things to cancel."

"Wait. Just wait a minute; I have to think." Apparently she did her best thinking while pacing.

Whatever. He turned back to his tools. He didn't see what there was to think about. At this point it was just a matter of facing the music. He didn't envy her that. But if Bryan was loser enough to jilt her at the altar, he wasn't good enough for her.

He kept silent while she pondered her situation. By the time she spoke again, every tool was put away—something that hadn't happened since he'd installed the shelving unit.

"I think I could arrange to keep everyone quiet. My editor and Pam certainly wouldn't say anything. I can trust Anna and my dad implicitly. I have a couple of distant relatives here, but they'd keep it to themselves."

She was thinking out loud, not even looking at Lucas. "Bryan's family is small, and they're mostly from the Boston area. There were eight relatives here, plus his best man. He could surely convince them to keep quiet. He owes me that at least." Her eyes softened for a moment as if the thought of him made her ache.

Kate was actually considering it. He'd never known her to do a spontaneous thing, and here she was, thinking about marrying him at the last minute. *She must be desperate.*

Kate looked Lucas over from head to toe; he squirmed, feeling he'd somehow failed the examination. "The tux won't fit. You're taller; your shoulders are broader. We'd have to get you fitted quickly. Mr. Lavitz is a good friend of yours, isn't he?"

"Well, yeah . . ."

"The marriage license might be a problem." She tapped her foot and chewed on the side of her lip, her eyes searching the buzzing fluorescent fixtures for answers. "And we'd need an exit strategy. Maybe a year? Give my book time to succeed and give me time to get another book going. We could get a quiet divorce . . ."

Her eyes closed. "I can't believe I'm talking about marriage like this. Like it's a cheap business arrangement."

Lucas watched her face as she wrestled with her principles. "He backed you into a corner. It's not like you have so many appealing options."

She looked at him suddenly, her brows pulling together. "Why are you doing this again?"

Why? Why? How could she help him? She was a marriage counselor, but he wasn't married—yet. His parents' marriage was solid enough, though they loved to fuss at each other. Everyone knew it was just who they were, but an outsider might think . . .

"Lucas? I'm running out of time here."

"My parents' marriage. If you could help them."

Her eyes brightened. Ah, he'd hit the bull's-eye.

"It's in jeopardy?" she asked.

He cleared his throat. Stuffed his hands in his jeans pockets. "They fight a lot lately." He needed more, but he didn't want to lie. "My mom left for a few days last month." On a girl's weekend trip, but Kate didn't have to know that. "Jamie—she's my little sister— said Dad enjoyed her absence." He'd actually said he enjoyed having Jamie all to himself. But that was close enough, wasn't it?

"And you want me to counsel them?"

"No." The word came out a little sharp. "They're both leery of all that psychobabble stuff." Her eyebrows rose, and he rephrased. "You'd have to be sly about it. Get to know them. Get them to open up. You can handle it."

"That's it? That's all you want?"

He wanted much more, but it was a start. "It's my parents' marriage."

"Of course. I didn't mean to make it sound trite." Kate steepled her fingers and tapped the tips together. "I don't even know if this is possible. I think there's a waiting period on the marriage license."

He hadn't thought of that. Maybe the plan was dead in the water. But hadn't his friend Ethan gotten married at the last minute? "I think it can be waived. Nancy Rallings is the town clerk, and I furnished her house. I'll see what I can find out."

He couldn't believe she was considering it. He could be marrying Kate in a matter of hours. In front of friends, family, and media. His legs suddenly quaked as he remembered the article in the paper spelling out the details. The wedding was going to be a media circus. They might want to interview him.

His mouth felt like it was stuffed with sawdust. "No interviews," he said.

It took Kate a moment to hear him, lost in thought as she probably was. "What?"

"I'll let the media snap all the photos they want, but I won't give interviews."

She shrugged, eyeing him. "I agree—we don't need to complicate things. What about your family? How are they going to feel?"

That gave him pause. His mom had been urging him to move on since Emily died five years ago. Kate, however, was the last person his mom would want him moving on with. If he told his mom the marriage was temporary, she would be rude, scare Kate off for good. But if she knew he loved Kate, she'd have to make an effort, wouldn't she?

"My parents are out of town right now, but my brother and sister are here. I'll call my parents afterward and tell them we got married. And I don't want them to know the particulars. As far as they're concerned, it's the real thing." Besides, if it worked the way he hoped, there'd be no exit strategy needed. He held out his hand. "Deal?"

His breath caught and hung below the mass in his throat.

Kate stared at him, her eyes a mixture of fear and resolve. Then she put her hand in his. "Deal."

There's no such thing as Mr. Right.
But there is a Mr. Right-for-You.

—Excerpt from
Finding Mr. Right-for-You
by Dr. Kate

Chapter Three

If Kate had to explain the change one more time, she was going to pull every last hair from her head. The horror etched into the eyes of Anna, Chloe, and Pam had been enough to start the second-guessing. They'd run over the pros and cons, quickly, more for their benefit than anyone's. Kate had covered that ground a dozen times already.

Her dad had listened silently, with shoulders squared and back straight, his only parental concession the lone worry line stretching across his squeaky-clean forehead.

It'll be okay, Dad. I know what I'm doing.

He'd taught Kate to think independently, and he never questioned her decisions. Even now, the most he'd said was, "Kate . . ."

When she'd called Bryan with her announcement and demands, she'd been met with a long silence. She'd almost enjoyed his obvious shock and unspoken, *You're what?* Just when she thought he might have gone unconscious behind the wheel of his car, he asked her to repeat what she'd said. She'd ended up going through it three times, until he eventually assured her his family would keep it quiet. She supposed he wasn't eager for word to get out that he'd jilted Dr. Kate at the altar.

At least one group hadn't needed explanations. Lucas had introduced her to his brother and sister, Brody and Jamie. Brody, a lanky, curly-headed version of Lucas, was home from college on summer break, and Jamie was a teenager with dark hair and braces. They accepted the news of their brother's impending matrimony with friendly smiles before exchanging a silent glance Kate didn't have time to decipher.

Now, four hours, one wedding license, and countless moments of stark terror later, Kate stood in her white gown, feet poised at the foot of the aisle. The media cameras clicked in machine-gun fashion, capturing a three-quarter view. She curved her lips upward and forced a twinkle into her eyes.

Thirty feet down the aisle, waiting in the gazebo, was Anna; Lucas's best man, Ethan; the justice of the peace; and Lucas.

Lucas. Is this really happening?

The musicians started the wedding march. Kate curled her arm around the stiff material on her dad's arm and took the first step. A gentle breeze blew off the ocean, ruffling her hair and veil and feathering her strapless A-line gown against her legs. She'd finally found the satin dress at a boutique in Boston after scouring numerous magazines and shops. Now what did it matter that the gown was perfect or that the hem hit the floor precisely?

How had it come to this? Bryan was supposed to be waiting at the end of the aisle. They matched. They were a fit according to everything she knew about personalities and relationships. They had so much in common—their love of exercise . . . organization . . . punctuality . . . loyalty . . .

Well. She supposed she'd have to rethink the loyalty part.

She passed her Aunt Virginia in the second row, wearing her trademark cherry-red lipstick. Her brown hair coiled above her puffy white face like thick chocolate shavings on a pile of whipped cream.

The groom's side was half-empty, but what did she expect with last-minute invitations? Jamie sat on the first row beside Brody, her brown hair caught up in barrette. Two part-time employees from Lucas's shop sat on the next row, straining to see around a tall, spindly man she recognized from someplace.

She imagined how upset Lucas's parents would be at missing the ceremony. And at finding out about the wedding after it was over . . . But it was what Lucas wanted, and it was his decision. They'd have to smooth things over later.

They . . .

She was going to be joining another family. The thought struck her hard and quick. She didn't even know these people—she barely knew the groom!

What am I doing?

She didn't meet Lucas's eyes until she nearly reached the gazebo and then realized her mistake. A bride would be gazing adoringly at her groom. Was she smiling widely enough? Her dry lips stuck to her teeth.

Lucas had cleaned up well, even shaved his perpetual five o'clock shadow. His long hair was combed back from his face. The hairstyle, combined with the formal suit, gave him the look of a nineteenth-century nobleman. His eyes met hers, pulling her in—a solid lifeline in what felt like a turbulent storm.

They reached the foot of the gazebo, and her dad stopped and kissed her cheek, then took a seat on the first row.

She was on her own now.

What am I doing? . . . What am I doing? . . .

She stepped into the gazebo as the last strains of the wedding march rang out and drew to a halt between Anna and Lucas. Her bare arm brushed his. In the distance, whirring clicks of cameras captured every second of the event, and she knew the best photos would grace the pages of tomorrow's newspapers. But as the justice began talking, all Kate could think about was the way the heat from Lucas's arm seeped clean through his tux and settled against her skin like a thick fog.

"Marriage is commended to be honorable among all men," the justice began. "And therefore is not by any to be entered into unadvisedly or lightly—but reverently, discreetly, advisedly, and solemnly." He emphasized each word, his bushy gray eyebrows inching upward disapprovingly. When Kate had told him Lucas was taking Bryan's place, she'd been half-afraid he'd refuse to perform the ceremony. But he'd only pressed his lips together and nodded formally.

Now he continued. "Into this holy estate these two persons present now come to be joined for life."

Joined for life. She turned her head a fraction of an inch toward Lucas as the ugly scent of fear filled her nostrils, mingling with the tangy, salt-laden air. Life? She hardly knew him!

What am I doing?

She dragged in a breath and slowly released it, careful to keep her expression neutral. *There's no going back now. Focus. Just get through the ceremony.*

Was Lucas afraid too? Was he asking himself what he'd gotten into, wishing he were back in his shop, sitting in a thin layer of sawdust? Was that his arm trembling against hers? He had every right to panic. He was giving up a year of his life. He was being thrust into the public eye.

What if he backs out? Right here in front of everybody? Jilted twice in one day. Had it ever happened before? She imagined the headline. *"Dr. Kate Jilted at Altar by Two Grooms."*

The justice stopped talking, and the moment's silence sent alarm scuttling through Kate. Instinctively, she slid her right hand from her bouquet and reached out, searching for an anchor. When her fingers touched Lucas's hand, his encircled hers. It was warm and strong, and—oddly—confident. *It's going to be okay,* his grip said.

Mrs. Petrie began her solo, her warbly, butterfly soprano wafting on the breeze, and Kate's mind wandered. The song had seemed perfect for her and Bryan. How could she have been so wrong? Who was it who had stolen his heart? Just the night before, he'd held her close and kissed her good night at her apartment door. What was it he'd said? *"I guess I'll see you soon."*

Had there been something in his tone? In his expression? Some warning she'd missed? She'd been too flushed with excitement to notice. And just like that he was gone.

And now she was marrying Lucas. Committing a year of her life to a man she didn't love. Good grief, most of the time she didn't even like him. Not that he was a bad person. He was just so . . . irritating sometimes. Vexing. The way he was late and careless and so laid-back she wished she had a remote control so she could push the fast-forward button.

She couldn't think of a man less suited for her.

Mrs. Petrie finished the song and returned to her seat. The justice began talking about the seriousness of the vows they were about to take. Kate wanted to plug her ears. She was a proponent of life-long marriages. It was her life's work to help couples stay married. And now she was making a mockery of the process.

I'm a hypocrite. A fraud. What would my readers think if they knew?

The justice turned toward her, and Kate focused her attention on him as he announced the reading of the vows. She was supposed to face Lucas. She handed her bouquet to Anna and turned toward Lucas. She wasn't sure if she was capable of breathing, much less speaking.

Then she saw the corner of Lucas's lip tilt up ever so slightly, his eyes soften. Instinctively, she relaxed.

I can do this.

The justice read the vows, and Kate repeated them. "I, Kate Lawrence, take you, Lucas Wright, to be my husband, to have and to hold from this day forward, for better or for worse, for richer, for poorer, in sickness and in health, to love and to cherish, from this day forward." Kate swallowed hard. "Until death do us part."

The last words were rushed, but she'd done it. Now the justice prompted Lucas.

He repeated the vows, and he did it well. His eyes said as much as his voice. The way he looked at her . . . It was the way every bride yearned to be looked at. Like she was precious. Like she was his chosen one. His voice was low, as if rumbling up from the deepest part of the ocean. It was more than credible. It was convincing.

The justice said a prayer and ended it with an amen. "It is tradition to exchange rings as a symbol of the love between a man and a wife."

Rings! Kate felt something akin to a tidal wave inside her. Bryan's best man had her ring. Lucas wouldn't have a ring to put on her finger. She turned a desperate look toward the justice, but he was looking at Lucas as he spoke. ". . . representing the unending love of your union." He cleared his throat as if the words had left a foul taste.

Kate stared hard at the justice, hoping mental telepathy would work just this once. *There are no rings!*

But then Lucas turned to Ethan. When he faced Kate again, he held a ring in the hollow of his palm. He'd taken care of it. Relief washed over her, and she smiled her gratitude.

He took her left hand in his and slid the ring onto her finger until it rested beside the glittering diamond. "With this ring, I thee wed." The look in his eyes burned the words into her heart.

The band was white gold, elegant in its simplicity. When had he had time to buy a ring? And how had he known her size?

The justice was prompting her to get Lucas's ring. She turned to take the ring from Anna. There was no way Bryan's ring would fit Lucas. She hoped it would at least slide over his knuckle. Maybe no one would notice.

She took the ring from Anna's palm . . . but it wasn't Bryan's white-gold band with diamond-shaped cuts. This one matched the one Lucas had put on her finger. She turned toward him and took his hand in hers. The ring slid easily onto his wide, tapered finger and looked bright against the darkness of his skin. "With this ring, I thee wed," she said.

Lucas caught hold of her hands, and the justice gave his closing thoughts. Kate was aware of nothing except Lucas's hands holding hers, his fingers rough and calloused against hers. She noticed that he was almost a head taller than her five-foot-five frame. One strand of his hair had come loose and fallen over his forehead, rogue-style. Her gaze fell to his eyes. He looked straight at her, into her, anchoring her.

The justice was making his closing statements. "By the power vested in me by the State of Massachusetts, I now pronounce you husband and wife."

The relief she felt brought a smile to her face. *It's done. I made it through.*

"You may now kiss the bride."

Her eyes flew back to Lucas. In all the commotion of last-minute changes, she hadn't even thought about the kiss. Had he?

One of his eyebrows quirked as if challenging her.

She leaned toward him and felt his hands go to her waist. She brought her fingers to his jaw just as their lips met. His mouth was soft against hers. His lips moved slowly, deliberately, as he pulled her closer until their bodies nearly met . . .

Oh my . . . goodness . . .

It was over in seconds, but it left her rattled. Good grief, he was a great kisser. Who would have thought?

He was watching her, most likely noting her newly flushed cheeks. His eyes twinkled as if he could tell the kiss had left her shaken. She drew her shoulders back and tilted her chin as the justice said his final words.

"I now present to you Mr. and Mrs. Lucas Wright."

Expectations can make or break a relationship.

—Excerpt from
Finding Mr. Right-for-You
by Dr. Kate

Chapter Four

"In honor of the first man in her life," the DJ announced from the makeshift stage, "The bride would like to have the first dance of the evening with her father."

Kate disengaged herself from Lucas's friends and wound her way through the circular tables to the parquet dance floor, where her dad waited with extended hand. She went into his arms with the first notes of "Unforgettable" playing behind her. It was the only part of the day going according to plan. Everything else had been turned on end, but sharing this dance with her dad was exactly the way it was supposed to be. Kate closed her eyes and relished the normality of it, unwilling—unable—to think past this moment.

"You're holding up well."

She looked up at her father. His face had aged the last couple years, and Kate realized she hadn't visited him in Maryland enough. Phone calls and letters didn't allow the same connection, and she'd spent most of her spare weekends with Bryan in Boston. And for what?

"Really?" She felt as transparent as Saran Wrap and just as fragile. Making rounds with Lucas had been hard. Everyone wanted to know how they'd met and how they'd kept it a secret. Lucas's eyes had said it all. *We didn't.* The two of them had a million details to work out. She didn't know how they'd remember everything they'd come up with on the fly tonight.

"What do you know about this guy?" Her dad shuffled stiffly, leading more like a boot-camp drill sergeant than a dancer. His hair—what was left of it—was combed neatly to the side in a part not quite deep enough to be a comb-over.

What did she know about Lucas? Not even enough to fill a pen cap. "He makes furniture, and his shop is right below my place on Main Street. In fact, he owns the building. I was renting my office space and apartment from him. He did the renovations."

She'd let Lucas know months ago that she was moving out this month. Little had she known she'd be moving into his home. She realized she didn't know where he lived.

"What else?" A benign smile hid his concern.

"He's a nice man, Daddy. Harmless."

She glanced over her dad's shoulder at Lucas. He stood with Ethan, hands resting in his vest pockets, his jacket long since discarded. His white shirt was crisp and fitted, tapering from broad shoulders down to narrow hips. Maybe "harmless" was overstating it.

"I'm not leaving until morning, so if you need anything tonight, call me."

Kate laughed. "Not the words most fathers say to their daughters on their wedding night."

"This isn't most wedding nights."

Kate sobered. No, it wasn't. She didn't know how she was going to survive the honeymoon at the White Elephant, much less the next year.

"If anyone can do this, you can." Her father squeezed her hand in a rare gesture of affection. Behind him, the vocalists belted out the chorus, the lead singer's face reddened from the strain.

"Thanks, Dad."

They danced quietly for a few moments before her dad broke the silence. "I know your mom and I had our disagreements, but I wish she could be here tonight."

Kate didn't want to think about her mom, tonight of all nights. "You're here. That's all that matters." They took one last turn as the band wound down the song and the crowd applauded.

Lucas approached as her dad stepped away. "May I cut in, sir?"

Kate knew he'd scored brownie points for the honorific title. Her dad smiled cordially, but the look in his eyes warned that the points wouldn't carry far.

The band struck up the song she'd selected for the bride and groom's "first dance," and her heart stuttered. "When a Man Loves a Woman" had been their song. It had played on the radio the first time Bryan kissed her. A constricting knot lodged in her throat as Lucas's hands came to her waist. She felt his eyes on her, and she worked to steady her smile. There were people watching. Always people watching. She had to hold it together.

As if sensing her need to hide, he pulled her close. She laid her cheek against his chest, away from all the faces. Above the swelling music and chatter, she could hear the waves swooshing the shoreline with rhythmic certainty. The consistency of the sound soothed her.

"It's gonna be okay, Kate," Lucas's voice rumbled next to her ear. "You'll see."

Her eyes burned, threatening to spill, and she blinked. *Breathe, just breathe.* She needed to think about something else, anything else, but the thoughts wouldn't budge: *"I'm in love with someone else."* Were harsher words ever spoken?

"I'm glad we have a minute alone," Lucas said. "Because I have a question for you."

She swallowed. "What's that?"

"Are we going on a honeymoon?"

Her laugh was feeble. "I'm sorry." She pulled back enough to look at him. "We have reservations at the White Elephant for the week. Is that okay?" He had his work, after all. But if they didn't take a honeymoon, people would wonder.

"I have a couple jobs to finish up this week, but I'll get them pushed back." He pulled her closer. "The White Elephant, huh? Your publisher went all out."

She moved her hand down his shoulder. "The hotel offered an unbelievable rate. They'll get a lot of publicity."

"Surprised you didn't want to go to Hawaii or something."

She shrugged. "Nantucket's done so much for me. I wanted to do something to help the community. The publicity is good for the island." She smoothed the stiff lapels of his jacket. He'd put it back on for the dance. For the photos that were being snapped.

He'd been a perfect gentleman all evening. She was beginning to wonder why he'd gotten on her nerves before. "Thanks for not shoving the cake in my face," she said.

His lips tilted. "Wouldn't dream of it."

The singer crooned the chorus, but Kate kept her eyes on Lucas. They were supposed to be the "happy couple." It was harder than she'd imagined; the pretending was wearing her out.

"So when does this shindig end?"

Not soon enough. "The band has to stop at nine thirty."

Lucas started to look at Kate's watch, but she grabbed his hand and kissed it. The hairs on the back of his hand tickled her lips. "You're dancing with your bride. Time is meaningless."

His eyes clouded, and he settled his hand at her waist, looking away.

"When the band winds down, we'll make our exit," she said. "There's a carriage scheduled to take us to the White Elephant."

It hit her how deceiving appearances could be. For all that this looked like a fairy-tale wedding, a true marriage, it was a farce. Empty and fake, it was an elaborate mansion, gutted on the inside.

"I haven't packed." He spun them around, surprisingly graceful.

"That's taken care of."

The flash of a bulb flared just off the dance floor. She gave Lucas her "adoring bride" smile, letting her eyes rove lovingly over the planes of his face even though she was seeing black spots, as the photographer snapped half a dozen more photos. When he stepped away, she continued. "Anna is going to grab some things for you tonight. That is, if you don't mind her riffling through your stuff. You can pick up the rest of your things tomorrow."

"Not sure how I feel about a stranger riffling through my underwear drawer."

She could tell by his tone that there'd been a shift in Lucas's mood, though she had no idea what had caused it. Of all the things to fuss about. He'd married her at the last moment, but the underwear drawer stopped him cold? What else could they do? They couldn't send his family after his things and have them knowing he hadn't planned for his honeymoon. Even Lucas wasn't that disorganized.

"Do you have a better idea?" she asked.

He looked over her head now, wearing an insipid smile. "Fine. Just send Anna."

Kate opened her mouth to respond, then changed her mind. The last thing she needed was an argument on the dance floor.

⤝

Kate faced the mirror in the bathroom of the White Elephant's Shoreline suite. Her dark hair, caught up on the sides, disappeared beneath the triple-layered veil. Her makeup still looked fresh, her dress stunning. Her shoulders, carefully tanned over the past month, looked every bit as lovely as she'd hoped.

Only none of it mattered now. Bryan loved someone else, and she was married to a man she barely tolerated.

Ah, but my career is salvaged. At least I have that.

She set her heavy bag on the marble counter and opened it, resting the floppy lid against the beveled mirror. The zipper clanged against the glass.

The carriage ride to the hotel had seemed to take forever even though it couldn't have been more than ten minutes. She was tired of pretending. Which didn't bode well—the entire next year would consist of nothing but pretense, and just one night of it had worn her to the bone. Her feet hurt, her head ached, and all she wanted was to slide between the sheets and pull them over her head.

Maybe it wouldn't feel so awful in the morning. The sun would come up, it would glitter off the harbor, and the fresh air would remind her it was a new day.

At least she wouldn't have to move from Nantucket. It had been the one thing she'd dreaded. She pictured Bryan's apartment in downtown Boston and sighed at the thought. She'd never go there again. Never sit on his couch and eat popcorn while they watched CNN.

She turned her attention to her suitcase. Her clothing, carefully rolled to avoid creases, was packed in colorful bins all lined up in rows. She scanned the pieces and realized the satin and lace article she'd planned for tonight would hardly suffice. Instead, she pulled out a shirt with a mock turtleneck and a pair of knee-length shorts. It would have to do.

She looked in the mirror, noting her drawn expression, and willed herself not to cry. Then, with a sigh, she began the tug-of-war of releasing herself from her gown.

Lucas was sitting in the armchair when she reentered the room, his elbows braced on his knees. His gaze flickered over her, and she realized he must be eager to change.

"Anna should be here soon with your things."

He nodded.

"Sorry she couldn't get them over sooner."

He nodded again.

Well, don't go getting all chatty on me.

Giving up, Kate began hanging up her clothing, one item at a time, trying to ignore the fact Lucas was probably staring at her backside. They steadfastly held on to their silence until a few minutes later when a tap sounded on the door. Kate practically leapt across the room to let Anna in.

"Is everything okay?" Anna whispered with a hug.

"Sure." Kate summoned up one last smile. She would've offered more, but Lucas was hovering, obviously wanting to change.

"Here you go," Anna said to him.

He took a paper bag and a noisy cluster of keys from her.

"I couldn't find a suitcase or duffel bag."

"That's okay. Thanks for going to the trouble."

Anna looked at Kate. "Well . . ."

"Well . . ." Kate's brain raced, trying to think of a reason for Anna to stay. *Perhaps she'll notice the slightly manic look in my eyes and take pity.* But with a wave and a quirk of her eyebrows, Anna was gone.

Traitor.

Rather than run screaming after her assistant, Kate continued unpacking, stashing her socks and underclothes in one of the armoire drawers while Lucas disappeared into the bathroom. He returned in record time.

Wearing only a pair of shorts.

Oh . . . Kate's gaze skittered away. As if things weren't awkward enough already.

She was acutely aware of his appraisal as he sat in the armchair. What was he thinking? More specifically, what did he expect from this marriage? If it were Bryan, she'd ask—or likely, she'd already know. How many conversations she and Bryan had had about their expectations. They'd been as prepared as an engaged couple could be.

Feeling him watching her, knowing she was procrastinating, Kate placed her alarm clock and Day-Timer on the nightstand, then stowed her suitcase in the closet. When she could delay no longer, she returned to the bed and pulled the covers down, glancing at the pillow on the other side.

Just what does Lucas expect tonight?

Does he think . . . ?

She sat on the edge of the bed, facing the wall and a framed print of a lighthouse, back rigid, heart racing. She wasn't naive. Men expected sex on the honeymoon.

She and Lucas were married now, and, technically, it was his right to expect it. But . . . it seemed wrong. Theirs wasn't the typical marriage. There was nothing typical about this honeymoon. And there was no way she was offering her body like some . . . some ancient temple priestess.

Still, this was a conversation they should've had before the wedding.

She didn't want to fret over it all night either. She glanced at him, still sitting in the chair. He was leaning back, his head turned toward her. The room was big, and he seemed far away. A good, safe distance. But she could hardly yell across the room.

Kate forced her tired legs to support her weight and walked toward him.

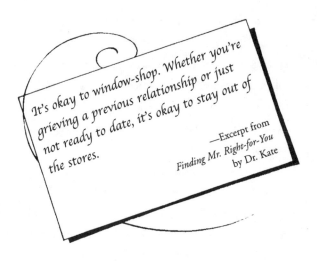

It's okay to window-shop. Whether you're grieving a previous relationship or just not ready to date, it's okay to stay out of the stores.

—Excerpt from
Finding Mr. Right-for-You
by Dr. Kate

Chapter Five

Lucas watched Kate sit on the edge of the couch, perching like a robin on the rim of its nest, alert for the first sign of danger. He wanted to put her at ease, let her know she was safe with him. He wanted to protect her. He would never hurt her. *You are so precious to me, Kate.*

My bride. He savored the word on his tongue.

Kate wrapped her arms around her stomach. "It occurs to me there are some issues we haven't addressed. Perhaps we can discuss the most imminent one now."

So formal. He half-expected her to produce a twenty-page document, spelling out the lay of the land for the next 365 days, and insist he sign it.

"What's on your mind?" He folded his hands on his bare stomach.

She licked her lips, her eyes flashing down to his bare chest for the briefest of moments before she stared at her tanned knees.

"Sleeping arrangements." She cleared her throat. "I appreciate what you did today by stepping in for Bryan. I don't know what you expected from me tonight, but—"

Her cheeks bloomed with color.

"I don't know what you expected from me tonight, but I have no desire to sleep—or do anything else—in that bed with you." He imagined the words she didn't say. Was that what was worrying her? Making her clutch at the nun-high collar of her shirt, making her face turn a dozen shades of pink?

What kind of jerk did she think he was, expecting to be compensated after she'd just been jilted at the altar by the man she loved? As if he'd want her like that—still pining for someone else. After the tenderness of his previous thoughts, the idea sickened him.

"Believe it or not, Kate, sleeping with you is the last thing on my mind." It came out sharper than he'd intended, but blast it all if it didn't tick him off that she thought so lowly of him.

"I was planning to take the couch," he said. "The bed's all yours."

Her gaze bounced off him, and she stood, nodding once. He watched her go without a reply, long legs extending from knee-length beige shorts. She flicked out the bedside lamp before slipping into bed.

He turned out the other lights and settled on the sofa. Grabbing one of the puffy throw pillows, he turned on his side and drew up his knees so he'd fit.

Does she really think so little of me?

His thoughts returned to the first time he'd met her, when he'd shown her the space above the shop. She'd worn white slacks, a blazer, and fancy heels that made him wonder how she climbed the stairs without falling flat on her face.

"It's a large space," she'd said. "I didn't realize it would be wide open."

He looked around at the scuffed white walls and wood floor, dulled by a layer of dust. Except for the small office and restroom at the back of the building, it was an open space. "Used to be a photographer's gallery. You said something on the phone about making it a living space and an office of some kind?"

She walked the room, her skinny heels clacking on the floor. "I'm a marriage counselor. I'd need a small lobby area and a private room for counseling. I was hoping to make my living space up here too. It's big enough, I think."

With rent so high on Nantucket, it made sense to combine the two. She moved toward the back of the building, jotting something on a clipboard, and he walked to the front of the room, giving her time to look around undisturbed. Outside the front windows, dead leaves sailed on a gust of wind. A handful of tourists walked the brick sidewalks.

"What's your policy on renovations?" Kate was making her way toward him, her silky black hair swinging. She was all business, straight to the point. He wondered if she was good at what she did. She didn't seem warm enough to be a therapist. Then again, what did he know about it? Or about her?

"How long were you planning to stay?" He didn't mind renovations so long as she'd be there a while.

"It depends on the terms of the contract."

The space had been empty for two months. The summer people

were gone for the season, and with winter coming he'd have a hard time renting it to a merchant. "If you cover cost of materials, I'll see to it the renovations are done."

She nodded, glancing around at the space as if she was trying to envision it completed.

Now that the season was over, he'd have extra time. Too bad Brody was back at college or he'd ask his brother to help.

"How soon would you need it done?" he asked.

Kate wrote something on her paper while he noted that she had a tiny mole on one side of her pointed chin and lips full enough to beg a man's attention. "I'd like to get my business up and running as soon as possible. The living portion is less urgent. I can sleep in the office back there or even in my new office until it's finished."

It was an awkward time of year to open a business. She seemed a little citified, and he wondered if she'd ever wintered on the island before. Oh, well. Wasn't any of his business.

"Give me a day or so to think it over, and I'll get back with you," she said, extending her hand and shaking his.

The next day she signed the contract and moved her luggage into the old office at the back of the building. They agreed to meet that afternoon to go over renovation plans. She was waiting for him when he arrived, and he realized he was probably a tad late. She checked her watch before sitting at a padded card table she must've brought.

"The builder's coming, isn't he?" She set a manila file on the table and folded her long, slender fingers on top of it.

Did she think he was hiring a crew or something? "I'm the builder." He took a seat opposite her.

Her eyes widened, and she blinked twice, her black lashes fluttering. "But—but I thought you built furniture."

Her eyes were a bewitching mix of green and brown. He wondered what color her driver's license said they were. "I do build furniture. But I've done plenty of carpentry and plumbing and wiring. I built my house, and I've done room additions."

"Do you—Are you a *licensed* builder?"

He found her tight little smile amusing. Did she think his walls were going to collapse or his wiring was going to burn the building down? "I'm licensed. If you want to check out my work, I did all the renovations downstairs. It was an open space like this when I bought it."

"Oh. Well, your shop is very nicely done. I just didn't realize you'd be doing the work, that's all."

Ever since that first meeting, ruffling her feathers had served as a cheap form of entertainment. He knew she'd been pleased with his work, though his pace seemed to aggravate her. She even tried to put him on a schedule at one point, telling him when he should have the drywall completed, when he should have the bathroom and kitchen plumbed. The woman lived and breathed by the agenda she had with her at all times.

Still, there was something about her.

Now, as he lay staring toward the shadowed fireplace in the darkened room, he realized all her plans had blown up in her face. He wondered what she would've thought if he told her that first day that she'd marry him three years later. She probably would've laughed in his face.

And yet here they were, on their honeymoon.

Yeah, I'm on the couch. She made it real clear she wants nothing to do with me.

And he'd made it just as clear he wasn't interested. Too clear, maybe. He hadn't exactly been the picture of loving-kindness.

He heard a sound coming from the general direction of the bed and lifted his head. A sniff, muffled by a pillow or the bedspread. A quiet hiccup, then another sniffle.

With a sigh, he lay his head back down and closed his eyes. He was a dog. Why had he snapped at her like that? She was grieving. She hadn't had time to recover from the shock of being dumped before she'd found herself married to another man for the next twelve months.

His hands fisted, clenching the pillow until his fingers ached. He wished he could put his arms around her and tell her it was going to be okay.

He wished it was him she loved so much.

❧

Kate felt another sob rising and muffled it with the pillow. Two years with Bryan. Two years spent getting to know him, investing in the relationship, coming to love him. How could he leave her so suddenly, so cruelly? The betrayal was almost too much to bear.

Had his lack of commitment been present all along? Is that why he'd never come to the island, except once, early on in their relationship? She'd made the trip to Boston out of respect for his job. Her hours were more flexible than his, and they were able to spend more time together when she traveled to see him. If it had been up to him, maybe he wouldn't have made the long trips.

Their weekends together had been special to her. They holed themselves up in his apartment, talking and just being together. Bryan turned down invitations to events and get-togethers so they could have time to reconnect. He'd seemed committed.

She was so confused! Kate reached out into the vacant space of the bed where Bryan was supposed to be, her fingers sliding across the cool, empty sheets. Her heart felt as empty.

She pulled the other pillow into her stomach and remembered all the grieving women she'd counseled. Women who'd poured their life into a relationship only to have it jerked from under them at a moment's notice. She hadn't known it felt like this. Seeing others endure it and suffering through it yourself were two different things.

A memory flashed in her mind. It had been shortly after her mom kicked her dad from the house. Her mom's reddened eyes and baggy clothing had become part of her identity, and Kate couldn't remember the last time she'd seen her smile, much less laugh.

Kate entered the tiny living room where her mom sat curled on the couch, staring at the TV, though Kate didn't think she was watching. Kate picked up the remote and flipped through channels. If only she could find something to cheer her mom up. Something to make her forget. Something to make her smile again.

When Kate flipped to *Roseanne*, she turned up the volume. Her mom always laughed at that show. Sitting beside her, she pulled her knees to her chest and yanked her nightgown over them, stretching the thin pink material to its limits.

The show's audience laughed at something Dan said, but a glance at her mom dampened Kate's spirits. Her face was blank, the light from the TV glazing her deadened eyes. Why was she so sad? If she missed Daddy, why didn't she ask him to come back?

Kate felt her own eyes burning, watched Roseanne's living room blur. She missed her dad, and her mom obviously missed him too. Why wouldn't she let him come back?

Her mom popped to her feet. "I'm going to bed, pumpkin." Her words sounded squeezed from her throat, as if a scarf was wrapped too tightly around her neck.

"Good night," Kate answered, but her mom was already down the hall, closing her door. The light in the room flickered as the scenes on TV changed. Kate watched the room glow white, then blue, then white again.

From down the hall the sound of her mom's muffled weeping reached her ears. Kate had grown to hate the sound that escorted her to sleep each night. She turned up the volume and lay on the itchy tweed couch, then pulled a pillow to her ear . . .

Now, Kate turned over and dried her face with the sheet. She hadn't thought about that night in years. Not until now, when her own life seemed to have taken over exactly where her mother's had left off.

A sound reached her ears, and she lifted her head from the pillow, listening. A second later, she heard it again—a long, loud snort coming from the direction of the couch. *Great. Just my luck.*

Her new husband snored.

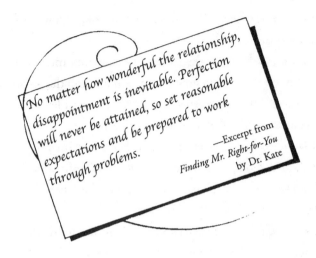

No matter how wonderful the relationship, disappointment is inevitable. Perfection will never be attained, so set reasonable expectations and be prepared to work through problems.

—Excerpt from
Finding Mr. Right-for-You
by Dr. Kate

Chapter Six

A distant clattering woke Kate. She stirred, stretching her limbs, before opening her eyes. The room was dark, and she tried to get her bearings as the events of the day before emerged, rising like a tsunami out of a still sea.

She'd married Lucas.

She was on her honeymoon.

Kate closed her eyes, wishing for the oblivion of slumber again. Maybe she could fall back asleep. For a year.

Another noise, a quiet clinking, disrupted her efforts. Apparently Lucas woke before the break of dawn. She rolled over and tugged the duvet over her head, but moments later the rich aroma of brewing coffee beckoned her. *Aaahhhh . . .* She pushed the cover down and sat up against the heap of pillows, untangling her legs from the sheets.

"Sorry," Lucas whispered from the wet bar. "Didn't mean to wake you."

Kate rubbed her eyes. Her lids felt heavy and swollen. "You're forgiven. Especially if you made enough for me." She needed it right now just to keep her eyes open.

He turned on a light over the bar. "How do you take yours?"

"Cream and sugar." What she'd really like was some good espresso, but the coffee should be decent in a fancy hotel like this. "Do you always rise so early?"

She heard the splash of coffee into the cup. "Yep."

Great. She hoped he didn't expect her to talk in the morning.

Before she could make her legs work, he brought her a mug. "Thanks."

He'd apparently already showered and dressed. His wet hair hung in strings beside his face. The five o'clock shadow was back.

She took a sip. It was good for regular coffee. Strong enough to wake her at least. For the rest, they had cappuccino and lattes at the restaurant. She'd made certain of that before she'd made the reservation.

As she sipped the brew, her mind kicked into gear. She thought about the wedding and Lucas's family. She thought about the media and the articles coming out in today's papers. What would they say?

Then she thought about Bryan. Was he planning to marry this other woman? Why hadn't she asked who it was? Maybe he'd realize he made a mistake and break up with the mystery woman. Why hadn't Kate told him this marriage with Lucas was temporary? Maybe she and Bryan could still be together someday.

"What's on the agenda today?" Lucas's voice startled her.

She sipped her coffee. "What makes you think there's an agenda?"

He gave her that lazy half smile. "Because you're Kate Lawrence." The smile faltered. "Well. Guess you're not anymore."

She was supposed to be Kate Montgomery. She remembered the way she used to jot her name with her boyfriends' last names when she was a teenager. She'd say the name out loud, testing it on her tongue. She hadn't even thought of her married name with Lucas until the justice pronounced them man and wife. *Kate Wright.* It sounded strange.

Lucas studied her from across the room, and she remembered he'd asked a question. The itinerary. She had it memorized. "We were supposed to go to the beach today, surfside. Bryan wanted to—" Why was she rambling about Bryan? "Anyway, it would give us time to make plans, if you're up for it." He didn't seem like a beach person, but she could be wrong.

He shrugged. "Sure. I'll need to swing by my house and pick up my things first."

He'd need to know what she had planned in order to pack accordingly. She rattled off the agenda, noting the whaling museum, the day trip to Martha's Vineyard, and the other points of interest she'd planned to take Bryan to.

The more things she listed, the higher Lucas's brows went.

"What?" Kate asked.

"There any room for spontaneity on that list?"

"Spontan—what in the world for?"

His crooked smile was slow. "Tell you what. I'll do everything on your agenda if you'll allow one day of spontaneity."

Kate frowned. What was the point? She'd included everything a person could want from one week on Nantucket. She studied Lucas skeptically. "What would we do?"

His head cocked. "Planning kind of ruins the point."

She sighed. She supposed it was his vacation too. "Oh, all right. One day." Her hollow stomach let out a growl. "I'm starving." She hadn't taken more than two bites at the reception.

"Room service?"

She was ready to sit down to a big, hot breakfast. "I was thinking the restaurant."

He leaned against the back of the sofa, hands in his shorts pockets. "Won't that seem odd?"

Odd? Oh. Newlyweds would still be in bed at this hour. For several more hours, at least. She felt her cheeks grow warm. "Maybe you're right. Will you order something while I grab a shower?"

He gave a mock bow. "Your wish is my command."

Kate refrained from rolling her eyes.

~~~

While Kate showered, Lucas called room service and placed their order, then puttered around the room awhile, procrastinating.

He couldn't put it off any longer. The last thing he wanted was for his parents to read about the wedding in the paper before he told them. As it was, it wasn't going to be much fun.

He picked up the phone and dialed his mom's cell. "Hi, honey," his mom greeted him. "Hang on a second. I need to plug in the phone."

A moment later she returned. "Ah, there we go. My battery was about to go, and I didn't want to lose you. Everything okay there?"

"Everything's fine. I just called with some news." He gulped, ambled across the room, and leaned on the armoire. "It might be a little, uh, surprising. Are you sitting down?" It didn't matter if she was. When she heard the news, all the miles between them wouldn't seem like enough.

"I'm in the car, Lucas. What's wrong?"

"Well, you won't believe it, but I—" *Just say it.* "I got married last night."

The silence betrayed her shock. Three seconds dragged by. He heard the clock on the wall ticking them off. Then . . .

"Mar-ried!" His dad said something in the background before his mom spoke again. "Who in the world to? I didn't even know you were dating."

Neither had he. "Well. We kind of kept it under wraps. Low-key." Nonexistent key. *I have to tell her; there's no way to soften the blow.* "It's Kate, Mom. Kate Lawrence."

It sounded like his mom sucked the air from the hotel room through the phone line. But he didn't have to wait long for her to recover. "Kate Lawrence. Kate Lawrence?" She jabbed each syllable at him. "Lucas, how could you?"

"I know. I know, Mom. I knew you'd be upset. That's why I didn't tell you until now."

"You mean until it was too late to do anything about it!"

"There's nothing you could've done about it anyway. I'm a grown man, and I make my own decisions. Especially about whom I marry."

"You didn't even invite us to the wedding." She sucked in another breath. "The wedding! She was supposed to have some big production with the media!" His dad mumbled in the background again. "For heaven's sakes, how did it look that we weren't there? The whole country is going to know we missed our son's wedding!"

"It was actually a small, intimate affair, Mom, and I'm sure—"

"This is awful!"

"I know you're shocked, and I don't expect you to be happy about Kate. But I want you to remember one thing." He waited until she stopped huffing. Then waited two beats beyond that. He needed her to hear what he said, take it to heart.

"I love her, Mom. Regardless of the past—which, incidentally, she's not responsible for—Kate makes me happy."

He could almost hear his mom's frustration, her emotions torn between her unresolved anger and her son's happiness.

The shower in the bathroom kicked off. He wanted to be off the phone before Kate returned.

"Were Brody and Jamie there, at least?" His mom's words sounded as though they'd been squeezed from a lemon.

"They were there. My identity was kept a secret from the media, you know. Nobody knew it was me until last night."

"Well, you could have told us."

His dad's words were muffled. "Let it go, Susan. What's done is done."

Sage advice, but easier said than done, and probably not welcome coming from the man she blamed.

❦

Kate left the foggy bathroom, feeling somewhat refreshed, though still sleepy. She should have asked Lucas to order a latte. She walked into the room, where the breakfast food was set out on the coffee table. Lucas sat in the armchair, waiting to dig into his home fries, over-easy eggs, toast, and stack of crispy bacon. In front of Kate's seat was a plate of fresh melon, granola, and yogurt. Her stomach protested.

She put her dirty clothes in a plastic laundry bag, settled on the couch, and stabbed a berry with her fork, sliding it into her mouth.

"What's wrong?" Lucas loaded his fork with potatoes and took a bite of bacon.

"Nothing." The berries were good. Sweet and juicy. Healthy.

"I didn't know what you liked."

Of course he didn't. It wasn't like they'd dated. He didn't even know how she took her coffee or that she liked to sleep in. "This is fine. It's good." She took a bite of granola to prove it. It was homemade, crunchy and sweet. Just not what she'd been in the mood for.

"Here." Lucas scraped an egg and half his potatoes and bacon onto the plate his toast had been on.

Her mouth watered. "I'm fine, Lucas."

He slid the fruit to the side and pushed the plate in front of her. "Eat up."

They ate quietly, and by the time Kate set her fork down, she'd made up for the meal she'd skipped the day before.

"I went out and got the paper while you were getting ready."

"Which one?"

"The *Mirror* and the *New York Times.*" He produced sections of the papers from the coffee table's shelf.

Her insides were an ocean buoy in the wake of a speedboat. "Did you read them? What did they say?"

Oh, please, please.

She grabbed the *Times* first. There they were, her and Lucas, on the cover of the "Style" section. A photo of them dancing. They were looking into each other's eyes, and the photographer had captured Lucas's smile.

"See for yourself," he said.

Her eyes flitted to the article. Its heading read "*Dr. Kate Marries Mr. Wright.*" She smiled. "Clever."

"Thought you'd like that," Lucas said.

She read aloud. "'Syndicated columnist Kate Lawrence, known to audiences as Dr. Kate, married Nantucket native Lucas Wright in a ceremony last evening on Jetties Beach in Nantucket. The wedding was scheduled to coincide with the release of Dr. Kate's book *Finding Mr. Right-for-You*.

"'The identity of the groom was kept secret until the ceremony—part of the publicity campaign surrounding the book's release.

"'Lawrence said she met her Mr. Wright when she rented the space above his furniture shop in Nantucket Town. "He renovated my apartment and my office. Then I guess he renovated my heart."'"

Kate glanced at Lucas, her face warming.

His lip quirked. "I had no idea," he said.

"Dream on." Kate went back to the article.

"'Lucas Wright is a furniture maker, known locally by wealthy vacationers who summer on the island. When asked about their future plans, Lawrence said, "We plan to stay in Nantucket, of course. It's our home."

"'*Finding Mr. Right-for-You* is Dr. Kate's first book. She will appear on the *Dr. Phil* show later this summer, and she plans to continue her column while she works on her second book.'"

Kate put the paper down. "It's all good," she said in wonder. *We did it.* They'd pulled it off—at least, if the *Times* was any indication. "What does the *Mirror* say?" She picked up the next section. The photograph was a close-up of them in the carriage, waving good-bye, the tulle of her veil blowing to the side. It had much of the same information as the *Times*, though presented with a more local approach.

When she was finished, she picked up the *Times* again, noticing the way the paper trembled in her fingers. "Rosewood will be thrilled. I can't believe how relieved I am." Relieved wasn't the word. If she'd gone through with the wedding only to be found out, it would've done more damage than being jilted.

"Did we cover all our bases?" she asked. "We have to be sure those who know aren't going to say anything."

"I told Mr. Lavitz when he fitted me for the tux about the need for discretion. He's an old friend—I know he won't say anything. And you know Nancy and the justice will keep quiet. They're town officers. They know how to be discreet."

"Pam and Chloe and Anna won't say anything. My dad's a given. Who else knows?"

"Bryan's family," he said.

It was the biggest risk of a leak. Had Bryan told them? Kate chewed on her lip. What if one of them read an article and told a friend or two the wedding was a farce? What if they contacted the media?

"Maybe you should call him and make sure." Lucas leaned forward, planting his elbows on his knees, bracing his coffee cup between his palms.

Kate had been thinking it herself, but dreading it all at the same time. It hurt to think about Bryan. She'd been up half the night thinking about him, about how he was supposed to be in bed beside her. *This was supposed to be the beginning of our life together.*

Suck it up, Kate, and move on. You've done it before, and you can do it again. She'd made a lot of sacrifices along the way, and she wasn't giving up now.

"You're right." Her watch said it was just after eight. Late enough to call. *What, am I worried about waking the man?* She should have called him in the middle of the night. He'd kept her awake, after all. It would've served him right.

"Why don't I go home and get my things while you make the call?"

Kate nodded, wondering what to say to Bryan. "What about your parents? You need to call them before they see the papers."

Lucas folded the paper and stood. "Already did, while you were in the shower."

"What did they say?"

Lucas shrugged. "They were shocked, naturally. I told them we'd kept it low-key because of the media."

"Weren't they angry they weren't here for the wedding?"

"Disappointed. They were glad Brody and Jamie were there."

Kate tucked her damp hair behind her ears. "Oh, good. Well, I guess we'll have to make it up to them when they return."

Lucas left, and Kate retrieved her cell phone. She dialed Bryan's number, her heart drumming a syncopated beat.

The phone rang twice before a woman answered. "Hello?"

Kate's words clogged her throat. She was there? In his apartment? In the apartment that was supposed to be *theirs*?

"Hello?" the woman repeated.

Kate took the phone from her ear and started to hang up.

But she had to talk to Bryan, had to make sure he'd spoken with his family. She put the phone back to her ear and heard shuffling sounds, then Bryan's voice.

"Hello?" His voice was morning scratched.

Kate clamped her teeth together. Were they in bed together? What had happened to their agreement to save themselves for marriage? Apparently it had only been Kate's conviction.

"Kate?"

"Yes, it's Kate. I can't believe she's there with you. For heaven's sake, Bryan, we were supposed to get married yesterday."

She heard a rustling noise—sheets? "Excuse me if I'm wrong, but didn't you just spend the night with your new husband?"

His comment made her skin tingle, made the flesh under her arms go hot. "After you deserted me on our wedding day!"

"What do you even know about him, Kate?"

"What do you care?" She stood and paced the length of the room. What was she doing? She had to settle down. It would accomplish nothing to have Bryan angry at her. "I didn't call to argue. I called to make sure you'd talked to your family. Did you make them understand how important it is that they keep their mouths shut?" She could've worded it more nicely, but he wasn't exactly on her favorite-people list right now.

"I talked to them. I told you I would." His voice was tight.

What did he have to be angry about when he had another woman there in bed with him? While she'd been crying over him in their honeymoon bed, he'd been—She closed her eyes and shook her head to dislodge the image. She couldn't bear the thought of it right now.

"My career is riding on this, you know," she said. "Do they understand the magnitude of—"

"Yes, yes, they understand. Do you think I want to be in the spotlight as the jerk who jilted Dr. Kate at the altar?"

"Well said."

The silence was deafening. She should hold her tongue; she really should. She was a counselor, for crying out loud. Where was her control?

"I'll let you go." Perhaps he'd get the double meaning. "I just wanted to be sure things were taken care of."

She hung up before she said something she'd regret later. When she set the phone on the coffee table, she realized her hand was shaking.

Bryan was in bed with her. Kate's Mr. Right in bed with someone else on what was supposed to have been their wedding night. Could life be more unfair?

At least he'd made his family understand the importance of keeping quiet. That was the main thing. And the articles were positive.

Look on the bright side. I'm going to live through this and come out stronger. The year with Lucas would pass quickly, and then she could get on with her life and career.

She realized she hadn't told Bryan the marriage was temporary, but given the situation, she didn't want to give him the satisfaction. Let him think she would be bound to Lucas for the rest of her life. Maybe it would make him squirm just a little.

Eventually something in the display window might compel you to enter the store. Decide first if you're ready. And if you are, shop wisely.

—Excerpt from
Finding Mr. Right-for-You
by Dr. Kate

Chapter Seven

Kate shrugged off her cover-up, took her list from the tote, and lay belly down on the beach towel beside Lucas. She squinted against the sun's reflection on the bright white paper.

"Okay, we need a story. We already told people how we met, but I think we need more details to make it realistic. Your family will probably want to know what we do together. They'll expect us to know things about each other."

"I know you take your coffee with cream and sugar." Lucas leaned back on his elbows a foot away from her. The wind blew his hair away from his face.

"But you don't know that I drink a triple-shot latte every day before work. Or that I prefer showers to baths. Or that I'm allergic to cats."

"Hope you're not allergic to dogs."

"Do you have one?"

He lay back against the towel, folding his arms behind his head, his eyes closed against the sun. "A sheepdog named Bo. You'll love him."

She wasn't much of an animal person, but she supposed she could deal with one dog. Wasn't a sheepdog like a miniature Lassie? She could deal with a little dog as long as he was well trained.

"Found him alongside Milestone Road when he was a pup," Lucas said. "He was missing a bunch of fur on his neck, and I couldn't find his owner, so I kept him."

She jotted down the information. *Sheepdog, Bo.*

"What else should I know about you?" she asked.

She watched his chest rise and fall, glistening under the glare of the sun. His skin was dark, his chest well defined. She wondered if he worked out or if the muscles came from his work.

Stop staring! She sneaked a glance at his face to be sure she hadn't been caught looking. He'd probably think she was checking him out. Which she hadn't been.

Well, not too much.

"I like to sail, watch documentaries on TV, and fix anything broken."

Kate scribbled more notes. "Anything else?"

A muscle twitched in his jaw. "I was married before. I guess you need to know that."

How had she not known? "What happened?"

His eyelids fluttered, and he swallowed, then shifted, clasping his hands together on his flat abdomen.

"Sorry if I'm prying, but—" His family would expect her to know. She wondered if his ex-wife lived on the island. Maybe Kate knew her.

"Her name was Emily. She died five years ago."

Oh.

She studied him. His tone was so soft, it obviously still affected him. Did he still love her? Maybe that's why she hadn't seen him with another woman.

"I'm sorry," she said.

"Her family used to summer here. I met her when she came to the shop for a rocking chair. The business was getting off the ground, and we started dating. The rest was history."

Kate waited for him to finish. The only sounds were that of the waves crashing the shoreline and the laughter of children playing in the shallows. "Is that when you built your house?"

He crossed his ankles. His legs were long and thick, covered in wiry black hair. "No. We lived in a cottage in Cisco after we married. I didn't build my house until . . . until after."

She didn't have to ask "After what?" It was still painful for him to talk about. Kate wondered why he'd married her. Given the way he obviously still felt about Emily, he had to care a great deal about his parents to be willing to sacrifice a year of his life to save their marriage.

She hated to grill him, but she'd be expected to know. She set the pen on the towel and propped her head on her palm. "How did she . . . die?"

She didn't think he was going to answer. She wasn't even sure he'd heard her softly spoken question over the seagulls' cries. But after a moment he sighed.

"It was my fault. Guess that's why it's still hard to talk about."

What did he mean? She wanted to ask, wanted to know the details. Even though Lucas irritated her, he wasn't the type to harm anyone. In fact, he was always helping people. In his own time, but helping them nonetheless.

"She had allergies—lots of them. The environmental ones like pollens were easily controlled with medication, so it wasn't a big deal." He shifted. "She'd tested allergic to peanuts as a teenager, but she'd never had a reaction. She avoided them, though, because her doctor told her to."

Two teenagers behind them tossed a Frisbee, and it sailed over them and landed a few feet away, flicking up the sand. Lucas waited while they retrieved it.

"The week she died, I'd done the grocery shopping. I bought a bag of chips that were fried in peanut oil." He shook his head. "Didn't even think about checking the ingredients. I used to tease her about being overly cautious."

Kate's heart went out to him. Couldn't he see it was an accident?

"I'd been at the shop working on an order I was running behind on, and when I came home . . . it was too late."

She watched his face, the way his jaw clenched, the way his lips tightened. She wished she could console him somehow. "I'm so sorry."

His chest rose and fell. "It was a long time ago."

Five years wasn't that long. He'd been married to the love of his life and now he was sitting on the beach with his counterfeit bride. She wondered how he felt about that.

He turned and opened his eyes, squinting against the glare of the sun. "So that's my story. What's yours?"

She appreciated his desire to change the subject. "What do you want to know?"

Lucas watched Kate turn her head until her cheek rested in her hand. She looked like a little girl, her sun-flushed cheeks bunched up against her palm. He already knew more about her than she was aware. She was twenty-eight, her favorite flowers were daisies, her birthday was November 26, and she color-coded her Day-Timer.

He went for the unknown. "How did you become an advice columnist?"

She smiled. "Friends in high school always came to me for advice, and I was good at giving it." Kate shrugged. "I started on my life plan my junior year in high—"

"Life plan?"

"A plan detailing my short- and long-term goals." She said it as if everyone had one. "Anyway, I realized I had a knack for helping people with relationship decisions. Then I took a fabulous writing class in high school and started my first manuscript." She cocked her head. "It was bad, but I didn't know it at the time. However, I realized I wanted to combine my love for helping people with my love of writing."

"You had all this planned out before high school graduation?"

She flipped onto her side. "Sure. I knew I wanted to get a psych degree from Cornell and go into counseling so I could support myself and gain experience while getting my writing career started."

"You were born on Nantucket, right? Is that why you're here now?"

"My parents grew up here, and, yes, I was born here. We moved to Maryland when I was five because my dad got relocated. Then, when I was in college, a friend invited me here for a week to stay in her parents' cottage in 'Sconset. What can I say? It felt like coming back home."

"So you added Nantucket to your life plan?"

"Are you making fun of me?"

How could he criticize when she'd met all her goals? Except he was sure marrying him hadn't been on that list of hers. "What about the column?"

She stuck her knee out to the side, and he worked to keep his eyes away from the smooth curve of her hips. "I started it at Cornell for the school newspaper. At first I wrote my own questions; then students began writing me, and it all took off from there."

Apparently she set her mind to something and made it happen by sheer will. "Ambitious one, aren't you?"

A wind tousled her fringed bangs. "I like helping people. Initially in my practice I focused on couples with marriage problems."

"You seemed to build up a decent clientele." He was in his shop enough to see clients passing up and down the stairs on the hour.

"The more I counseled married people, the more I began to see that people were making poor choices in the spouses they selected. They'd come to me, polar opposites, wanting different things out of life, and wonder why they couldn't get along. I started putting together a plan to help people make better choices about who they marry."

She made it sound like it could be boiled down to cold, hard facts. "What about love?"

"Well, of course, there has to be love. But by choosing to date the right people, you limit yourself to those who are best suited to you."

He turned on his side, mirroring her position. "How do you know if they're suited to you until you know them? And once you know them that well, aren't you likely to have fallen in love with them already?"

Her breath huffed out. "What is this, an inquisition?" She rolled onto her back, propping her head on her bag, and closed her eyes. "My plan is detailed and well thought out. If you want to know more, read the stinking book."

She'd gotten snippy in a hurry. Maybe she felt defensive since her fail-proof plan hadn't turned out to be so fail proof.

Which reminded him of her ex-fiancé. Lucas wanted to ask if she'd called him, but judging by her set little chin, maybe now wasn't the time.

Something at the corner of his vision caught his attention. A man in dress clothes sat on the sand down the shore, holding a camera with a zoom lens. He looked as out of place as a diamond in a toolbox.

Lucas looked at Kate. "I think we have company."

She didn't bother opening her eyes. "Who?"

"One of the photographers from the wedding. Down the shore a ways."

She opened her eyes.

"Don't look."

Kate looked at Lucas instead. "Is he looking this way? Does he have a camera?"

"Yes and yes."

"Which one is he?"

"I don't remember. He was at the wedding, though. The one with spiky hair and artsy glasses."

She sighed. "He's from *Cosmo*. I guess they wanted some honeymoon shots for the article."

"They could've asked instead of sneaking around like the paparazzi."

"They can't. I made it clear to my agent the honeymoon was off limits. Did he see you looking?"

"No. But he has a zoom lens that can probably see the amber flecks in your eyes from a hundred feet."

She tucked her hair behind her ears. "Great. I guess we haven't exactly looked like newlyweds, have we?"

He rolled on his stomach next to her, their sides brushing. Her skin was warm, and the feel of her smooth skin against his leg stoked a fire in his belly. "We could consider that our first fight."

"Wasn't much of one." She smiled.

She was probably thinking they made a much better photo now, lying so close and gazing into each other's eyes. But all Lucas could think about was what her sun-warmed lips would taste like. The wedding kiss seemed like a distant memory and Kate had been shell-shocked. What would a slow, lingering kiss feel like here on the beach, under the sun with the salted breeze stroking their skin?

"Why are you looking at me like that?"

Because I want to pull you in my arms and give that man a lensful. "We're honeymooners, remember?"

She pulled her lip between her teeth. "Oh. Right. And we just had our first tiff. Maybe we should kiss and make up."

With the sun shining into her face, her eyes ran more toward rich brown than olive. Like melted caramel. "It's a thought," he said.

"Okay, go ahead." She tilted toward him. Her eyes skimmed his face and fell on his lips.

He grinned, leaning over her until his shadow blocked the sun from her face. "I have permission now, huh?"

She touched his jaw. "What?"

"Are you sure it's on the list for today?" he teased.

She twitched her eyebrow. "You sure know how to ruin the mood." Was her voice a little breathy?

"There was a mood?" Before she could answer, he closed the space between them and kissed her slowly, reveling in the way she reciprocated. His hand settled on her side where her silky bathing suit clung to the curve of her waist.

For a moment he let himself forget she was only responding for the camera. He remembered every time he'd seen her leaving her office, every time he watched her walk down the sidewalk, hair swishing with each step. Every time she knocked on his shop door late at night to complain about the noise.

All those times I wanted to grab her and kiss the living daylights out of her.

Kate pulled away from him, breaking his thoughts. "There. He should've gotten plenty of good photos."

The cold wave of her words doused the mood. Trying for non-chalance, he turned onto his back and closed his eyes, hoping she couldn't see his heart thundering against his chest wall. He'd wanted the kiss to be more than show. He wanted it to be real.

You got yourself into this, man.

"Is he still there?" she asked.

They'd only started playing the game, and already he'd tired of it. "I don't know." And he wasn't going to look.

"I guess we shouldn't look."

He felt her hand, delicate against his own.

She's just pretending. Don't forget that.

"Let's talk about your parents. I need to know anything that will help me understand their problems."

Lucas was tired of the whole thing. Right now he wanted to blurt out that his parents didn't have a problem, that he'd married her because he loved her. But that would only scare her away.

He swallowed. "I'm not sure what's wrong between them. They just fuss a lot."

"You said your mom left for a while. Did they have a fight?"

This was going to be harder than he thought. "I don't know. I really don't know what the problem is. That's why I need your help."

Her fingers intertwined with his, and he felt the wedding band.

"Don't you feel you can talk openly with your parents?"

He cringed. He was getting himself in deeper and deeper. "I'm not a talker—you know that much about me." The seagulls cried out, and another wave hit the shore. "I'm just not good with words, and I don't think they'd want me interfering anyway."

He needed to make sure Kate was subtle with his mom. Otherwise Kate would find out it was all a ruse. "You'll need to get to know my mom before expecting her to open up." *Good luck with that.* He couldn't imagine anyone his mom would be less likely open up to.

An instant later panic struck. What if his mom confronted Kate about her mom? No. As soon as the panic hit, it evaporated. His mom didn't confront people. She killed silently with subtle digs and innuendos, God love her.

"That goes without saying."

"And leave Jamie and Brody out of it. I don't want them stressing about our parents." Or setting Kate straight about their fussing.

"If they live with your parents, they know what's going on. Even young children pick up on conflict. It affects them more deeply than you realize."

Her voice held a tone of sadness. He looked at her, but she turned onto her back, withdrawing her hand, and closed her own eyes. Lucas had a feeling there was a load of hurt backing up that statement, and he wondered if Kate would ever trust him enough to share it.

⌒⌒

Lucas took Kate's hand as they climbed the steps of the White Elephant. The week had passed quickly. It was hard to believe tomorrow it would be over. His Spontaneity Day with Kate had proved to be a challenge. She seemed unacquainted with the idea of letting things happen and had spent most of the day trying to figure out what they were doing next.

Now, she looked tired and sun drained, her cheeks reddened from their walk through 'Sconset. Maybe he'd order room service so she wouldn't have to go back out for dinner.

They entered the lobby floor and passed the registration desk. Kate stopped suddenly by a woman at the desk, withdrawing her hand from his.

"Mrs. Hornsby?" Kate touched the woman on the shoulder, and she turned. The woman might have been attractive if not for her puffy eyes and tight, bronzed lips.

"Dr. Kate." Mrs. Hornsby straightened and turned her lips into a semblance of a smile.

"Are you okay?" Kate asked.

Lucas stepped away to give them privacy, inspecting some literature on the desk. He couldn't help but hear their conversation.

"I'm fine." The woman said, but her words crumbled like a soggy cookie.

Kate took her arm and pulled her away from the desk. "What are you doing here? Did something happen?"

Lucas heard the woman restrain a sob. "Earl is having an affair. I have proof this time. I just—just couldn't stay there."

"I'm so sorry." Kate's tone softened. She rubbed the woman's arm. "Do you want to talk?"

Mrs. Hornsby laughed feebly, wiping her eyes. "Oh, honey, no. It's your honeymoon. Besides, you're not even counseling anymore." She withdrew a tissue from her beige purse and dabbed her eyes. "I'll be fine."

"Don't be silly," Kate said. "Are you finished checking in?"

The other woman held up a key card. "Yes."

Kate squeezed her rounded shoulder. "I'll be right back."

She approached Lucas, and he put the brochure for a whaling tour back into the holder.

"Would you mind having dinner alone?" Kate asked, then lowered her tone. "She's a former client, and she could use someone to talk to."

"Of course not," Lucas said. "Want me to order you something from room service?"

"Thanks, but I'm not sure how long I'll be."

A moment later, Lucas was alone.

Look very closely at his family.

—Excerpt from
Finding Mr. Right-for-You
by Dr. Kate

Chapter Eight

"Start slowing down," Lucas said. "That's it. The one with the truck out front."

Kate navigated her car down the street. It ran parallel to the shore and was lined on both sides by cottages, generously separated by wide grassy lots.

Kate braked and eased into the drive, the tires slurping through the thick layer of gravel. Lucas's house sat off the road about a hundred yards, and behind it, the ocean provided a deep blue backdrop. The nearest house on his side of the street was a couple hundred yards away, the second story barely visible above a rise in the ground.

Kate stopped behind a beater Ford in the drive. *I married a pickup man.*

That thought was barely out before she surveyed the cottage.

Instinctively she liked its character. Gray, weathered shingles covered the small cottage. The trim and porch railing sported bright white paint, and orange flowers of some kind lined the front beds.

She put her car into Park and slid out. "It's nice." Small, but new. There appeared to be a main part of the house and a small addition of some sort.

She popped the trunk and had just grabbed a bag when she heard a shout.

"Welcome home!"

Four people scampered down the hill from the house next door. She recognized Brody and Jamie. The other two must be Lucas's parents. A huge, hairy dog led the pack, and Mrs. Wright trailed the others by several yards, her slender body stiff, her arms stagnant at her sides.

Kate waved and smiled for their benefit. "What is your family doing here?" She wanted to get settled in the house. She was tired of being on public display. The photographer had left them alone after that first day at the beach, but even eating out they'd encountered stares and whispers.

"They live next door," Lucas said. "Didn't I tell you?"

Next door? Maintaining her smile was no easy feat. "You neglected to mention that detail." He was going to get an earful later.

"Hey, guys," Lucas called as his family approached.

The dog leaped on Lucas. It was the size of a bear.

"Hey, Bo." He ruffled the animal's floppy ears.

That is not Bo. She considered the size of the house and the size of the dog. What was he thinking? She nearly expressed her thoughts, then remembered his family would find it odd she hadn't seen Bo before. They probably wondered how they hadn't seen her there before, living right next door like they did.

Roy Wright approached first, wearing jeans, a Nantucket polo, and a genuine smile. "Welcome, welcome." He hugged Kate first, patting her shoulder as if to burp her. He had a thick head of gray hair and a tan that leathered his skin. His clear green eyes angled downward at the sides.

"Thank you," Kate said. Her eyes met Susan Wright's as the woman came to a stop at the edge of the gravel driveway. "Hello."

Susan nodded, her rose-colored lips pulled back into what didn't quite pass as a smile. "Kate." Her mushroom-shaped hairstyle framed her narrow face and high cheekbones.

"I wanted to get some pictures." Jamie held up the camera that was around her neck. Her smile revealed braces with purple and pink bands. "Did you have a wonderful week?"

Kate felt like she was trapped in a *Raymond* episode. In real life the situation wasn't so amusing.

"It was perfect," she said as Lucas embraced his mom. Brody shook her hand, an apology in his eyes, if not on his lips.

What kind of man built a house next door to his parents? Apparently she'd not only married a pickup man, but a momma's boy as well.

Lucas and his parents caught up briefly before Lucas asked them inside.

"No, we're not staying," Susan said pointedly. "Are we, Roy?" She set a fine-boned hand on her husband's arm.

"Of course not; we just wanted to welcome you home, welcome Kate to the family."

"And take a picture of Lucas carrying Kate over the threshold," Jamie said.

Kate had forgotten about the tradition. A stupid tradition. She didn't want to be cast into the helpless maiden role. "How thoughtful."

She was tired of smiling. She didn't want to smile for the next week.

"Don't pressure them, Jamie." Susan eyed Kate up and down. "Besides, Lucas might not be up to it."

Score one for the mother-in-law. Kate smiled through clenched teeth.

"No doubt," Brody whispered to Lucas, wearing a sly smile. "Bet you're exhausted."

Lucas elbowed his brother. "Far be it from me to deny tradition."

"Pick her up, Lucas!" Jamie said. "This is so romantic." She clapped her hands.

"Scrubbing the floor would be romantic to you," Brody said.

"Shut up." Jamie whacked him in the gut with the back of her hand while Bo barked loudly and circled around them as if sensing the excitement.

"I'll get your bags," Brody said, walking toward the trunk.

Before Kate could move, Lucas swept her off her feet. She grabbed him around the neck, latching onto his shoulders as he walked toward the cottage and up the three steps. The camera clicked several times.

"You could have warned me," Kate whispered in his ear. First the next-door in-laws, then the big hairy dog, and now another photo op? Who'd started this dumb tradition anyway? She felt like a worthless sack of beans in his arms.

"Just sit back and enjoy, Mrs. Wright." His breath hit her cheek. Another photo snapped. "Don't call me that."

He shifted her and pulled open the screen door, then twisted the knob on the wooden door. She should probably help, but wasn't in the mood. She heard yet another click as Bo brushed by, squeezing his enormous mass past them.

Kate clenched her jaw. *Please let this end!*

"That's enough, Jamie," Susan said. "For heaven's sake."

Once inside, Lucas set Kate down and she stepped away, relieved to be on her own feet again. Brody had followed and now handed Lucas their luggage. They stood awkwardly for a moment, Brody looking from one to the other with a grin.

"Well, guess you two love birds want to be alone."

Lucas looked at Kate. "Guess so." Kate refrained from responding.

Brody hugged Lucas exuberantly and, after a slight hesitation, did the same for Kate. He clattered down the steps to his waiting family.

"'Bye, kids!" Roy waved.

"I'll print these out soon and bring them by," Jamie said, holding up the camera.

Susan merely nodded and turned back toward her house.

"Thanks," Kate called.

She stood watching her new in-laws through the screen door as they made their way back up the hill, Brody and Jamie arguing the whole time. Then she turned and narrowed her eyes at Lucas. "You are so dead."

Before he could respond something caught her eye. Her gaze left him to scan the room. "What in the world . . . is all this . . . stuff!"

She stared in horrified amazement at piles and stacks and layers of stuff. Clothes, boxes, magazines . . . The phrase "Early-American Junkyard" came to mind. Was that a shovel leaning against the TV? And what was that smell?

And through it all, Bo wove in and out, his enormous backside wagging. The dog hit a leaning tower of newspapers, and it toppled.

Lucas is a messie. She'd married a messie.

"Sorry about that." Lucas kicked a sack aside and closed the front door. "Didn't have time to clean up before the ceremony."

There had been clues on the honeymoon. Socks balled up and left lying on the floor, toiletries spread across the marble counter, wet towels left on the couch.

But this . . .

She felt trapped, and she wasn't even a claustrophobic. What was the floor even made of? She could hardly see it through the stuff. Anna could have warned her, for heaven's sake.

Bo bumped up against her, knocking her sideways. Lucas steadied her. "No, Bo. Come here." He rubbed the dog's head and Bo sat. "Settle down, boy."

Kate picked up her bag. Maybe the whole house wasn't like this. "Where can I put my things?"

Lucas grabbed a few articles of clothing from the back of the sofa and draped them over his shoulder. "Let me show you around."

Bo was up again, circling them, panting happily. Kate glared at him and then at Lucas. Lucas appeared to get the idea.

"Come on, buddy." He let Bo out the front door, where the dog sat facing the screen and barking. "He's just a little excited."

Scooping up a Pepsi can and an empty bowl with a sticky-looking spoon, Lucas led the way down a short hall.

"This is the bedroom."

Bed unmade, clothes heaped on the dresser.

"Yours?"

He opened a dresser drawer, shoved the clothes from the living room inside, and pushed it closed. "Uh, yeah. You can put your bag here." He pushed the heap of clothes to the other side of the dresser, having the grace to look sheepish. "I'll make room in the drawers and closet for your things."

"I was planning on taking another bedroom." *Hopefully a cleaner one.*

He set down the can and bowl and took her suitcase, setting it on the dresser. "I'm afraid this is it."

Kate let this sink in as she watched him attempt to make the bed. He pulled the blue quilt up over the pillows, leaving the sheets in a wad underneath. "'This is it'? What do you mean?"

He pocketed his hands. "There is no other bedroom."

This was getting worse by the minute. "You built a house with one bedroom?"

He lifted his shoulders. "There's only one of me."

How could he be so casual? So indifferent? Wasn't he at all concerned about his space? "Well, now there's two of us, in case you haven't noticed."

One side of his mouth turned up. "I noticed."

"Who builds a home with one bedroom?" And who was going to sleep on the couch? For a whole year.

"I was planning to add on later."

Well, there you go. The answer to their dilemma. How long could it take to build a bedroom? He could add a room on the other side of the house by the living room.

"Uh-uh," he said, watching her face. "Do you know what my family will think if I add another bedroom?"

That they were sleeping separately? Or no—that they were planning to start a family. Why else would they need another bedroom? Jamie would probably start knitting baby blankets and booties. Strike that idea.

"Look. We're grown adults," Lucas said. "The bed's a double, plenty big enough for both of us."

She looked him over. He was easily six feet, maybe an inch or two more, and he was broad. He'd make the bed feel like a twin. The thought of sleeping so close to him left her feeling hot and itchy.

She cleared her throat. "I'll just take the couch." She took the handle of her luggage.

He set his palm flat on the suitcase. "Don't be ridiculous. You can't sleep on the couch for twelve months."

"Sure I can." Especially if he wasn't going to offer. She pulled at the suitcase, but it went nowhere under his grip. "Let go."

"What'll my family think?"

"They won't think anything. They won't even know." She would put her blanket and pillow away first thing every morning. She supposed she'd have to keep her clothing in the bedroom, though.

"You turn in early, Kate. I'm a night owl."

She hadn't thought of that. How could she fall asleep on the sofa if he was watching TV until midnight? She checked the bed out, wavering.

Lucas leaned against the dresser and crossed his arms over his chest, looking smug. "You afraid or something?"

Kate crossed her own arms. "Don't be ridiculous."

"I'm not the one getting all hot and bothered about sharing a bed."

"I'm not—" She ground her teeth and smothered a growl. Why did he have to say things like that? It was like he took pleasure in getting under her skin.

It's just a sleeping arrangement, nothing more. What am I so afraid of? It'll be like sharing a bed with a friend on a girls' outing. Her eyes swept over Lucas's solid frame, down to his hairy legs and sandal-clad feet. She swallowed hard. *Okay, not quite like that.*

I don't have to . . . do anything in that bed except sleep. In fact, I'll be asleep by the time he comes to bed anyway. And he rises before me. I'll hardly notice he's there.

Resolved, she met his eyes square on. "Fine. We'll share the room."

Know what you're looking for before you begin dating. As with a spontaneous shopping spree, if you don't have a goal in mind, you'll come home with the wrong thing.

—Excerpt from
Finding Mr. Right-for-You
by Dr. Kate

Chapter Nine

It was dark by the time they unloaded Kate's belongings in the cottage. She plugged in her treadmill, which they'd squeezed into a corner of the living room. From here she had a good view out the front window and could watch the news too.

As she contemplated her surroundings, Bo brushed against Kate's legs as if trying to guide her toward the sofa.

"He wants you to sit down and pet him," Lucas said.

"Why is his fur discolored under his mouth?"

Lucas rubbed Bo behind the ears. "Drool yellows the fur." He disappeared into the kitchen, Bo plodding behind him.

Kate grimaced. *I had to ask.*

She turned on the treadmill, making sure it worked, then straightened the square pillows on the couch. She'd tried to tidy up a bit, and now that the floor was clutter free, she saw the nice rug that covered the oak floors. Too bad it was covered in dog hair.

Bo ambled back and plopped down by the fireplace, watching her, his huge, shaggy head cocked. His white hair hung like a dirty mop over his eyes. At least he didn't smell.

"You didn't tell me Bo was so big," Kate called.

"He's a sheepdog," Lucas called from the kitchen, as if that explained it.

"I thought that was like a miniature Lassie. I wasn't expecting a"—there was no call to be rude—"a large dog." Kate stepped past Bo and surveyed the room. Even clean, it felt tiny. The treadmill looked mammoth against the sand-colored wall.

"That's a Shetland sheepdog. He's an Old English sheepdog." Lucas was in the kitchen doorway, two steps away. He extended a cut-glass vase filled with white daisies. "These are for you."

Kate didn't know what to say. "What for?"

He rubbed the back of his neck. "Our one-week anniversary." Was that a flush climbing his cheeks? "It's silly."

The gesture took her aback. "No, it's very . . . sweet." The petals were satin smooth, the stems and leaves clean and groomed. She wondered where he'd gotten them. And when; they'd been together most of the day. "Daisies are my favorite."

"I know."

Kate was sure she hadn't mentioned it on their honeymoon. Even Bryan had always sent orchids for special occasions just because they were most expensive.

Lucas gestured toward the flowers. "You always have them on your desk at work."

She stopped at Flowers on Chestnut for a fresh bouquet every Monday morning after getting her latte. Having fresh daisies perked up the office and inspired her. Strange that he'd noticed. She remembered the daisies he'd etched on the gazebo. She'd thought it a coincidence.

"Well, thank you," she said. "I'll set them on the kitchen table between the salt and pepper shakers."

"I'll do it."

As he returned, Kate yawned. It was getting late, and there was no delaying bedtime. Besides, if she hoped to be asleep when Lucas retired, she needed an early start.

"I think I'll turn in now," she said.

Lucas sank into the recliner and flipped on the TV. Bo curled up at his feet. "'Night. Let me know if you need anything."

Kate stood awkwardly for a moment, but it looked as if Lucas was engrossed in what he was watching. *Well, okay then.*

After completing her beauty regimen and brushing and flossing, Kate changed into her pajamas. She surveyed the bed and felt something cold wedge between her ribs.

I can do this. I can. No big deal. She snorted at the thought. *Yeah, right. I'm about to climb into the bed of a man I barely know. And he's going to climb in later.*

Her eyes fell on a worn quilt crumpled between the bed and wall. She retrieved it, spread it across the bed, then rolled it like a giant burrito. Next, she laid it down the center of the bed as a barrier between the two sides. *There, that should do it.*

Kate clicked off Lucas's lamp and rounded the bed, settling on her side. The sheets were soft and cool against her skin, the mattress giving slightly to her weight.

She turned her face into the pillow and immediately regretted it. It smelled faintly of Lucas, all musk and woodsy. Even here, she couldn't escape him.

She thought of the daisies and chided herself for thinking ill of him. He was trying. It wasn't his fault they were so different. Or even that they were stuck together for a year. In fact, he'd saved her life, and she should be grateful. He'd salvaged her book and her career.

She'd called Pam twice from the White Elephant, and Rosewood was thrilled with the wedding publicity. Several cable network shows wanted Kate to make an appearance. Rosewood was talking about a possible book tour, and Pam had scheduled numerous phone interviews with radio shows and newspapers. Kate wondered how she'd keep up with her articles and find time to write another book.

No matter, though. If the publicity sold book one, it would be worth it. And at least she would still have her office space to work in since Lucas hadn't rented it out yet.

She thought of Lucas's family and wondered how she was going to find time to help his parents' marriage. She'd sensed the tension between Susan and Roy. Maybe she could find an activity to do with Susan. It would give them time to talk.

Kate turned and pulled the quilt over her chilled shoulder. It was quieter here than in town. If she listened closely, she could hear the water hitting the shore, and a clock ticking somewhere. The TV program Lucas was watching barely filtered into the room, and a slit of light from the living room underlined the door.

What time would he retire? She hoped he kept to his own side of the bed. Judging by the rumpled sheets she'd found upon her arrival, she had her doubts. He was used to having the whole bed.

Kate was too, but she planned on hugging the edge all night.

If I ever fall asleep. She rolled over again and resituated the pillow. She'd already made a to-do list for tomorrow, which usually freed her mind to sleep. She was tired, so that wasn't the issue.

As it had all week during quiet moments, her thoughts turned to Bryan. Kate hadn't called him again, nor had he called. She supposed there was no reason to expect him to. She shouldn't even want him to.

But feelings didn't flip off like a light switch. She wondered if he'd seen the photo and article in the *New York Times*. Part of her regretted not telling him her marriage was temporary. The other part hoped it sowed seeds of jealousy.

He's not jealous; he's with another woman. I'm the one who's jealous.

She didn't want to dwell on it anymore. The sound of the woman's voice when she'd answered the phone, the rustling of covers before Bryan spoke. It was torturous.

Think about something else.

Kate turned her thoughts to her book and upcoming *Dr. Phil* appearance. Ten seconds later, she was thinking of the daisies on the kitchen table. *Ah, we've come full circle.*

And I'm still awake.

Kate was about to shift when the door opened. She lay still, not daring to open her eyes. She heard the whoosh of something dropping to the floor. Then another whoosh.

He was *not* undressing!

Seconds later, the mattress sagged under his weight. The force of it nearly pulled her to the center, but she braced herself on the edge. The bed shimmied, and the covers shifted as he slid under them. His foot brushed hers, and she fought the urge to pull away. How had it gotten past the barrier?

Breathe deeply. I'm asleep.

When he finally stilled, the only sound was the ticking clock and the waves. And her own breath. She could even hear her heart. Her arm, pushed under her pillow, ached, but she didn't move. How awkward would it be if he realized she was awake and started a conversation? What was he wearing over there, anyway? She was afraid to know.

Kate opened her eyes and stared at the big lump beside her. He was facing the other way, and already his breathing had evened out. Not fair. How long would she lie awake? Why couldn't she go to sleep?

She tried to think about her book, about next week's article, about anything other than the very male body inches away. Her skin prickled with heat, and she wished she could throw off the covers.

A few minutes later, a quick snort pierced the silence. Three seconds later a long grating snore sounded.

And he's off to the races.

Kate closed her eyes on a sigh.

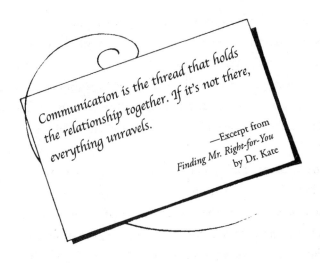

Communication is the thread that holds the relationship together. If it's not there, everything unravels.

—Excerpt from
Finding Mr. Right-for-You
by Dr. Kate

Chapter Ten

Lucas pushed open his parents' door, and Kate entered the bright two-story cottage. She could only hope his family didn't enter his house as freely. They were seventeen minutes late—a fact that didn't seem to bother Lucas at all. How a man could be late when he'd done nothing but piddle around all morning, Kate had no clue.

Inside the door, an oval braided rug covered aged wooden planks, and daylight poured in from the transom over the door. Voices and clattering pans sounded from the back of the house, and the smell of fried chicken beckoned.

"We're here," Lucas called, shutting the door.

Jamie scurried into the cozy foyer and hugged Kate first. "Hi, Kate. Hi, Lucas."

They followed Jamie into the cheery yellow kitchen where Roy drained skinless potatoes in a strainer over the porcelain sink. Susan, her tiny frame wrapped in a lavender apron, turned from the stove long enough to give a brisk nod and say hello.

Jamie disappeared, and for the next few minutes Lucas made small talk with his parents before Roy shooed them from the kitchen. "Go on up and get settled. The kids are already up there."

"What should I get you to drink?" Susan asked Kate.

"Whatever you have is fine . . ."

Susan's penciled-in eyebrows hiked, clearly indicating she was waiting for a better answer.

"She likes tea, Mom, sweetened." Lucas stared pointedly at his mom, giving Kate a moment's gratification. He was actually taking up for her. Strangely, the notion lifted her spirits.

He took her hand, and Kate followed him through the foyer and up the stairs. The banister was thick and swirled at the end. "Why are we going upstairs?" Kate asked halfway up the flight.

He made the turn at the landing and continued. "We eat on the widow's walk."

A mental picture of the two-story house formed. Kate vaguely remembered a large widow's walk on the top, an historical feature of many Nantucket homes dating back to the whaling days.

Her legs wobbled, not from exertion, and her fingers tightened on the banister. "You eat on the roof?"

They reached the second floor and he took another flight of stairs, this one narrow and steep. Their feet thudded on the hollow wooden steps.

"It's tradition."

Tradition. That explained it all. He could have mentioned that little detail earlier. Didn't he know she was—

The dark stairwell opened to bright blue sky. And vast views of the island. High, vast views. Kate stepped to the side, keeping to the brick chimney chase.

Jamie and Brody greeted them from a round table, set for six, and centered on the square wooden platform. A spindled railing encompassed the perch. Lucas pulled out a chair for her on the other side of the table.

"I think I'll sit over here if you don't mind." Kate smiled at Lucas's sister. "By Jamie." As if that was her sole reason.

Lucas sat beside her. "Good idea. This is where the view's at."

For the first time, Kate looked outward. Her only thought had been keeping the solid brick of the chimney at her back, but now that she looked up, all she saw was open sky and the ocean spread out far below, disappearing into the horizon. She put her hands on the table and twisted the rings on her finger.

"Can I see?" Jamie asked, gesturing toward her wedding set. Okay, not a set exactly since Bryan had purchased one and Lucas the other. Luckily they were both white gold.

Jamie touched the emerald-cut diamond with her index finger. "Pretty. I didn't know Luc had such good taste."

"Or that he would part with that kind of cash," Brody said.

Kate and Lucas traded a look. "She's worth it," Lucas said.

"I read all your columns," Jamie said. "I can't believe you married Luc."

Lucas's chair creaked as he shifted. "Thanks a heap, sis." He tugged at his sister's high ponytail.

"You know what I mean," Jamie said.

Kate leaned back until her hair snagged on the brick behind her. "Shouldn't we help your parents? I feel bad just sitting here." Actually she felt bad about sitting up here period, and helping downstairs would get her off this bird perch. *And put you in the ring with your new mother-in-law.*

"Mom likes to wait on everyone," Jamie said.

"If you go down, Dad'll just shoo you away." Brody shook his curls out of his eyes.

"How did school finish up this year?" Lucas asked.

"He's thinking of switching majors again." Jamie snickered.

"Shut up, squirt." Brody elbowed her. "Mom and Dad don't know yet," he warned them.

The wind blew across the roof, ruffling the red plastic tablecloth, and Kate grasped the arms of the lawn chair. What kind of family ate on the roof?

"What do you want to switch to?" Lucas asked.

Brody planted his elbows on the table. "Architecture."

The sound of approaching footsteps halted the conversation. Susan entered, balancing a tray that held a pitcher of iced tea and six glasses. Lucas took the tray and set it down for Susan to pour the drinks. The ice cubes crackled as the tea splashed over them.

Susan set Kate's glass down. "Thanks." Kate let go of the wooden arm long enough to take a sip.

When Roy brought up the food, everyone passed the dishes, helping themselves. Kate couldn't believe the trouble they'd gone to. Fried chicken, mashed potatoes and gravy, buttered noodles, and coleslaw that looked homemade.

She picked up a drumstick and bit into the crispy breading. *Heaven.* "This is delicious."

"Thanks," Roy said.

"I wish you wouldn't fry it." Across from Kate, Susan picked the breading from a wing with a fork. "I keep telling him to bake it skinless. I swear when you get to be our age, the very smell of food causes weight gain."

Kate didn't see a spare ounce on Susan's petite frame.

"You'll walk it off this week." Roy spooned a heap of mashed potatoes onto his plate and covered them with a ladling of gravy.

"Your arteries are clogging as we speak," Susan said. She took a tiny portion of potatoes and set the bowl on the side table.

"I'll die a happy man." The look Roy sent Susan didn't seem happy.

"Suit yourself," Susan said. "But for heaven's sake, could you at least wipe the grease off your chin so we don't have to look at it?"

Lucas gave Kate a pointed look. Yes, there was tension between the Wrights.

"Would you like the pepper, Kate?" Roy asked.

Kate slid her fork into the slaw. "No, thank you. Everything is perfect. You're a walker, Susan?" She hoped to ease the tension between them.

"I have to be if I want to stay slender. You should try it."

Kate felt her temperature soar as heat singed her cheeks. Maybe she wasn't as small-boned as Susan, but she kept her weight well under control.

"She does," Lucas said. He looked at Kate. "Mom walks every day too. Maybe you could walk together."

Kate's eyes narrowed, but she refrained from outright glaring at the man. Besides, she had to spend time with Susan if she was going to keep her end of the bargain. She just wasn't sure every day was necessary.

Lucas scooted his chair closer to the table and Kate could have sworn the whole platform shook. Her hand tightened on the metal fork.

"Actually, I use a treadmill," she said.

Susan poured Brody a second glass of tea. "Well, that's certainly easier."

Kate chewed a bite of food, then swallowed the dry lump. "On second thought, walking outdoors might be a nice change of pace from my incline training."

She wasn't willing to give up her treadmill time, but walking with Susan would give Kate time to figure out how to help their marriage. If she could stand being with the woman that long.

"It's settled, then," Susan said.

"Look, the Porters have their boat out."

Kate followed the line of Jamie's finger and saw a bright yellow sail on the water. The view made her dizzy and she focused on her slaw.

Roy was addressing her. "What did you and Luc do on your honeymoon?"

"Roy, for heaven's sake." Susan took a bite of white chicken meat.

"Well, I'm not asking for juicy details. I'm just making conversation."

Kate wanted to crawl under the table.

"We went to the beach." Lucas smoothed things over. "And to the whaling museum. Kate had never actually gone."

"We took a boat to the Vineyard and went shopping," Kate added.

"*You* went shopping?" Jamie asked Lucas.

Roy set his chicken thigh down and wiped the grease from his fingers with a paper napkin. "It's amazing the things a man in love will do."

He said it as if to get a dig in on Susan, though Kate wasn't sure what it meant.

"Well, I wasn't surprised Lucas was in love with you," Jamie said. "The way he spent all that time renovating your apartment and refurbishing your floors. I knew he was falling for you."

Kate tried to catch Lucas's eyes, but he seemed intent on his food.

"And all the time he spent on the gazebo," Jamie continued. "We should have known there was more to it. He worked on it forever."

Kate wondered about the mottled blush that climbed Lucas's cheeks. She hadn't known he was so easily embarrassed. Well, Jamie could think whatever she wanted so long as she bought their story.

≈

Tourists and locals alike clogged the cobblestone surface of Main Street. Lucas took Kate's hand and led her through the Fourth of July throng. They'd watched the watermelon- and pie-eating contests and gotten soaked during the water fight between the fire departments. Now it was time to find a spot on the beach for the fireworks.

When they neared Jetties Beach, Lucas adjusted the blanket and picnic basket in his arms and ushered Kate through the Pavilion. The place looked different than the night of their wedding. Had it only been two weeks? He wondered if she was remembering too.

All day they'd run into friends and acquaintances. Kate had constantly had her hand in his or her arm wrapped around his waist. Having her at his side made him stand taller. At one point, they found themselves standing by Selma Bennett, an editor at the *Mirror*. Lucas had leaned down and pecked Kate on the lips. Her eyes widened before she leaned into him for the briefest moment.

Now they exited through the back of the building and crossed the sand where people were spread out across the beach, lounging on blankets and beach chairs. When they found an empty spot, Lucas shook out the piecework quilt, and they ate their turkey sandwiches and Doritos, then snacked on fresh strawberries.

Lucas popped one in his mouth and leaned back on his hands, his legs stretched out to the edge of the quilt. Smoke from firecrackers and salt from the ocean blended together in a unique concoction that reminded him of Independence Days long past. Laughter and chatter filled the darkness, punctuated by the sharp pop of firecrackers, as the crowd waited for the public display to begin.

"Nantucket knows how put on a Fourth of July shindig," Kate said.

"Can't believe you've been here three years and haven't come."

She shrugged. "I've always been out of town." She didn't have to say she'd been visiting Bryan.

Two blankets over, Bryce Webber, who ran an online community and discussion forum, saw them and waved. They returned the greeting, Kate leaning into Lucas's side as if suddenly realizing they were still on display. He sat up, draping his arm across her shoulders. He could get used to this.

When Kate plucked a strawberry from the Rubbermaid container and looked into his eyes, he wanted to claim her mouth then and there. But she touched the strawberry to his lips instead. Lucas opened his mouth, accepting the offer, and her fingertips brushed his lips. *Have mercy.* The tang of the fruit didn't compare to the sweet taste of her lips.

The first firework exploded, drawing Kate's attention to the sky over the barge where the fireworks were shot from. A red glow, a reflection of the firework, blossomed over her face. Lucas already had fireworks going off inside. The big booms were only an echo of his heart.

With Kate nestled into his side, they watched the display. He could've lain there the rest of the night, her fingers tucked inside his. But all too soon, the fireworks ended, and they were packing their things and heading to his truck.

Lucas felt a disconnect between them as soon as they left the traffic and turned toward home. The ride was quiet. Kate sighed deeply and crossed her arms against the coolness of the night as the truck bumped along the street, jangling his keys. He itched to reach across the expanse and warm her hands in his.

"Quite a day, huh?" he asked.

Kate leaned her head against the passenger window. "Mmm."

Lucas turned off the air and adjusted the temperature. "What'd you think of the fireworks?" They might not compare to Boston's, but he'd always thought Nantucket put on a pretty good display.

"They were good."

Lucas felt his spirits deflating like a punctured inner tube. They'd been close all day. Kate seemed to enjoy his company, even his touch. Her eyes lit when she laughed at the things he'd said. Somehow he'd let himself believe it was real.

But it wasn't real. Her affection was for appearances. And now, feeling Kate disengage from him was . . . hurtful. He wanted it back, the way they'd interacted, the way she'd looked at him, touched him. How could she turn it off like a spigot?

How had he not realized how difficult this was going to be?

❧

Lucas shut the door hard behind Kate. She set her purse on the sofa table as he brushed by her and disappeared into the bathroom. Ten seconds later, the shower kicked on.

Was it her imagination, or was something bothering him? Kate took the picnic basket into the kitchen and tossed the trash. It had been a good day, but tiring. She'd seen everyone she knew, it seemed, at some point. With everyone congratulating them, she felt obligated to play the happy honeymooners, and it had worn on her.

Not that Lucas was hard to be affectionate with; he'd played along beautifully. But she was tired of being on display. By the time the fireworks ended, she was ready to hole up at the house where she didn't have to pretend.

As Kate finished putting away the picnic supplies, the shower went off. Good. She could use a rinsing herself. Though the weather had cooled after dusk, the sun had been hot and bright overhead all day. Besides, she wanted to wash the sand out of her hair.

Kate gathered her things from the bedroom and headed for the bathroom, her mind on her plans for the next day. When Lucas rounded the corner, she nearly smacked into his bare chest. He wore a blue towel that barely closed around his waist.

Kate stepped aside, averting her eyes. "Do you mind?" She pulled her own bundle of clothing into her chest as she passed.

"Nope." His tone was uncharacteristically sharp.

Kate stopped, ready to return and ask him what was wrong. But when she heard the unmistakable whoosh of the towel dropping to the rug, she darted into the bathroom and shut the door behind her.

Every relationship you try on won't fit. Don't try to squeeze into it. Put it back on the rack and look for a better fit.

— Excerpt from
Finding Mr. Right-for-You
by Dr. Kate

Chapter Eleven

Lucas watched his mom and Kate cut across the beach, their bare feet kicking up sand, their evening shadows stretching behind them. He hoped his mom behaved herself.

The warm breeze ruffled the corners of the newspaper in his lap as he thought over the past two weeks. He'd enjoyed having Kate around, grown used to it. It felt good seeing evidence of her presence in his house. Her robe on a hook behind the door. Her toiletries a neat row in the medicine cabinet. Her shoes lined up by color inside the closet. He didn't see the point in that one, but whatever.

There'd been a learning curve too. Earlier that week, she'd exited the bathroom, a look of strained patience lining her lips. "I appreciate that you shaved, but would you mind rinsing out the sink since we only have the one?"

He shrugged. "Sure."

She hadn't mentioned the wet towels until the third morning and by then they were a knee-high blue pile in the corner.

What was it with Kate and order? It was like a god she worshipped. Why did everything have to be perfect?

Lucas opened the *Mirror* and shook his head. It did tickle him to watch confusion shadow her face when he cooked. He'd thought everyone dumped the whole package of bacon into the frying pan until he'd seen the way she'd done it, one tedious strip at a time, all neat and tidy.

The woman kept a record of her workouts, for crying out loud. He'd looked at the clipboard one day after she'd exercised, made notes, and disappeared into the shower. She marked the miles, the speed, the incline, and the time she'd walked, down to the minute.

But as much as her librarian ways amused him, he wondered what had her so tightly wound. She lived as if life could be boiled down to one big list. As if by keeping everything in order, somehow she could control things.

You'd think she'd have learned by now that some things were beyond control. If Lucas hadn't known that before Emily's death, he knew it now.

"Hey, Luc." Jamie stepped onto the covered deck and sat in the Adirondack chair beside him. Her lanky legs, already summer brown, extended from a frayed pair of denim shorts.

"Hey, sis. How's summer going?" He gave up on the paper, folding it and dropping it onto the deck.

"Okay, I guess." Jamie twirled a purple flower in her fingers. "Mom and Kate went for a walk?"

He closed his eyes and let his weight sag into the chair. "Yep."

"The gazebo looks good there," Jamie said.

Ethan had helped Lucas move the piece to his backyard over-looking the beach. It was as though it had been built for the spot.

For a while they sat in silence, listening to the sound of the water licking the shoreline. Lucas wondered what Kate was saying to his mom. More important, he wondered what his mom was saying to Kate. What if Kate figured out his parents were fine? He felt bad she was spending so much time on a fictional problem, but he'd had to use some excuse. He could hardly have told her the real reason he'd married her.

"How do you know when you're in love?" Jamie's voice cut through his thoughts.

Lucas looked at his sister, only fourteen, still in braces, and wanted to tell her she shouldn't be thinking about love at her age. But he'd been fourteen once, although it seemed a lifetime ago. Emotions had felt bigger than life then.

"Who is he?"

Jamie wrapped the flower's threadlike stem around her index finger. "His name is Aaron Brinkley, and he goes to my school. I've liked him forever, but he was going out with a girl named Liz." She rolled her eyes.

"Don't like her much?"

"She's a snot. I don't know what he saw in her. But he's been at the beach all week, and Meredith said he broke up with Liz. He asked me to play volleyball today."

Lucas propped his ankle on his knee and clasped his hands on his stomach. "Did you?"

Jamie flicked sand off her shorts. "Yeah, but I beat him."

Lucas laughed. Jamie was a starter on her team and the best player, if he did say so.

Jamie slugged his arm, and the flower went flying. "It's not funny. I think he's mad at me."

Lucas stifled the laugh. "What makes you say that?"

"He didn't talk to me after that." She wrinkled her little nose.

"Were his friends around?"

Jamie's face fell. "I should have let him win." She crossed her arms and chewed on her lip.

"He'll get over it. Trust me."

"What do I say when I see him tomorrow? I really like him."

"*You're* worried about finding something to say?"

She shrugged. "I get tongue-tied with him. I'm afraid I'll say something dumb."

"Be yourself. If he likes you, he'll like you for who you are."

She rolled her eyes. "You sound like Mom."

Maybe he wasn't helping. But given his own love life, he wasn't sure he was qualified to give advice. "What are his interests? People like to talk about themselves. Especially teenage boys."

Her face brightened. "He likes the Red Sox, and I know he's into sailing, so we can talk about that. What else?"

"What do you mean?"

"Duh. I mean, do you have any other advice?"

If only he could condense everything he'd learned about relationships and pass it like a baton. Unfortunately, life didn't work that way. "Just don't be afraid to let him know you like him. He asked you to play volleyball, so it sounds like he's interested. Guys have a lot of pressure to initiate things. It'll make it easier if he knows he's not going to get rejected."

"You think he's nervous too?"

Lucas clasped his hands behind his head. "Trust me, the nerves go both ways."

Jamie was gone by the time Kate returned. The back door fell closed with a smack, and she cornered him in the living room.

"*What* is the deal with your mom?" Her damp bangs clung to her forehead, and her ponytail swung like a pendulum.

Lucas folded the paper again and set it on the table. "What do you mean?"

"I mean she can't talk to me for two minutes without getting in a dig. There's all this subtext going on, and I think it's more than that she missed our wedding. You want to fill me in?"

It was only fair. He should have already. "It's not you. There's some history you don't know about." Maybe her mom had told her the story, and she didn't realize who Susan was. "Your mom was my mom's best friend years ago. They went to high school together. Did your mom ever talk about that?"

Kate shook her head. "What happened?"

It was all ancient history, but to his mom it was the unpardonable sin. A woman scorned, and all that, he supposed. "When my mom and dad were engaged, your mom was supposed to be her maid of honor, only—" How to put it delicately?

"What?"

He sighed. "I guess your mom had a thing for my dad. Something happened the week before the wedding. I don't know the details, but your mom slept with my dad. My mom cut her out of the wedding and refused to talk to her again."

Kate's eyes widened slowly, her jaw following suit. Then she pressed her lips together and jabbed her hands onto her hips. "Why didn't you tell me?"

"I didn't think it mattered."

"It matters to your mom." Kate walked to the window and turned. "How am I supposed to help your parents when your mom hates me?"

"She doesn't hate you. She doesn't even know you."

"She'll never trust me now."

He supposed Kate was right, but he'd been hoping his mom would come around. It wasn't Kate's fault, and it had been more than thirty years ago. "I'm sorry. I should have told you, but I was hoping she'd get to know you and realize you're not to blame."

That seemed to quench the fire in her eyes. "She probably thinks I'm just like my mom. Not only am I guilty by association, she's probably worried I'll betray you just like my mom did her. She's worried I'll hurt her son."

Funny, he was worried about the same thing. But he hadn't considered his mom might be worried for him. "Being a therapist must come in handy."

Kate gave him a wry smile. "I have a feeling I'm going to need all the expertise I can get."

⌒✦⌒

Two days later, Lucas was remembering his conversation with Kate when a knock sounded on his shop door.

Ethan, his friend and his best salesperson, opened the door. Lucas turned off the sander.

"There's a lady here who's interested in a few custom pieces." Ethan pushed up his wire glasses with his middle finger.

Lucas set the sander on the plywood table. "Be right there."

He removed his goggles and brushed the sawdust from his skin and clothing before entering the showroom. He found Ethan and the customer by his collection of Shaker-style bedroom furniture. The woman had auburn hair that fell in waves past bare, slender shoulders.

"Miss Delaney, this is the owner, Lucas Wright. Lucas, this is Sydney Delaney. She recently purchased a home on Madaket Harbor."

Lucas shook her hand. "Pleased to meet you. That's a nice area."

Though she was tall enough to intimidate most men, her movements were fluid. "I love your work." Her fingers caressed the footboard of a queen-sized sleigh bed made of maple and finished with a caramel stain.

"Thanks. Ethan said you're interested in some custom work."

Another couple entered the store, and Ethan excused himself.

"I love the Shaker style. It's simple but elegant."

It was Lucas's favorite as well. There was something about the old-fashioned simplicity of the lines that drew attention to the beauty of the wood.

"I see a lot of things I like." Sydney gave Lucas a coy look. "But I have some specific pieces in mind for the living room that would need to be custom-made."

"I'd be happy to come and take a look at the space. You could show me what you have in mind."

She cocked her head and smiled slowly.

Lucas realized she'd read too much into his words. He crossed his arms, making sure his left hand showed. "I'll need to take measurements; then I can give you an estimate, and we'll go from there. How does tomorrow at ten a.m. sound?"

"Perfect." She gave him her address and phone number, then hitched her tiny purse on her shoulder. "I can't wait to see what you come up with."

He walked her to the door, but she stopped on the threshold.

"Oh, I hate to be a bother, but I'm looking for a fudge shop I've heard about. Aunt something . . . I have a terrible sweet tooth." Her smile flirted.

"Aunt Leah's Fudge—down on Straight Wharf." He followed her out the door and pointed east. "If you follow Main Street, you'll find yourself on the wharf. It's on the left. You can't miss it."

His brother entered his line of vision, walking up Main Street, his stride slow and loose.

"Hey, Lucas."

Lucas was about to introduce Sydney, but Brody stepped around him and opened the door. "Is Kate upstairs?"

The question caught Lucas off guard. "Sure." He wondered what Brody wanted with Kate.

Lucas watched his brother until Sydney placed a hand on his arm.

≈

The sound of feet thudding up the wood steps of her office pulled Kate's attention from the letter. A glance at her watch told her it was too early for Lucas. They'd begun eating lunch together on Mondays, Wednesdays, and Fridays. Strictly for appearances' sake.

Sun-blond curls appeared first, followed by the lean frame of her new brother-in-law. He wore a pair of bright orange and blue Hawaiian-print trunks and a white T-shirt.

"Brody." Kate folded the "Dear Dr. Kate" letter and set it on the desk next to the other letters she'd waded through. "This is a pleasant surprise."

He stopped at the top of the stairs and stuffed his hands in his pockets, a move that reminded her of Lucas. "I should've called."

"No, come in. Have a seat. I'm just reading through some letters."

Brody surveyed her desk. "That's a lot of letters." He glanced around the room—what used to be the lobby of her practice. She'd moved her desk to the front so she could take advantage of the natural daylight that streamed though the windows.

"I haven't been up here since Lucas renovated," Brody said.

Kate appraised the room with fresh eyes. The shiny wood floor, the soothing green walls that set off the maple color of the wood trim. She'd found an area rug in shades of green, navy, and beige that tied the colors of the room together.

"He did a nice job," she said. "He's quite the carpenter, your brother." Never mind that it had taken forever to get it done.

Brody sank into the waiting-room chair with a sigh. "I know."

Kate wondered what had brought him here. She set her elbows on the swivel chair's wooden arms and leaned back against the plush leather. Brody crossed his legs, propping his right ankle on his hairy knee. Gravity pulled at the heel of his worn flip-flop.

"So, to what do I owe the pleasure of your visit?" Kate teased.

"I was wondering if you'd help me with something." His eyes darted around the room, settling nowhere.

"I'd be happy to help in any way I can." Kate felt sorry for him in his awkwardness. "Is it a girl problem?" That she was accustomed to. People often sought her advice—not just in letters, but on the street sometimes.

"No, not girls. I got a handle on that." His cocky smile lasted a short second. "It's . . . school." The word dropped like a fifty-pound bag of sand.

"Ah," Kate said. "The switch in majors?"

"Yeah." He shook the bangs from his eyes. "I can't decide what I want to do. I mean, I'm three years into college and I still don't know what I want to be when I grow up." He tucked in the corner of his mouth at his joke.

He was still young at twenty-one, but Kate understood his frustration. "What was your major when you entered college? University of Massachusetts, right?"

"Yeah. I started as an education major. That lasted for a year and a semester."

"What made you decide on education?"

"I thought I could come back here and teach high school. Maybe middle school. I don't know. I did well in school and I thought it would be fun to teach."

"What did you change to?"

"Art." He rolled his eyes. "I know—it's like, what am I going to do with a career in art?"

"Are you good at it?" Kate watched his face, looking for some sign of passion.

"Sure, I guess. My professors thought I was."

Outside the front window a truck braked, the squeal piercing the wall. "What made you change?"

"Does the term 'starving artist' mean anything to you? After a couple semesters, I realized how hard it would be to support a family with an art degree. Megan—she was my girlfriend at the time—thought I should switch to computer science."

"Is that what your major is now?"

"Yeah. I like computers and everything. I get good grades, and I know it would be a good career, but . . ." He punctuated the sentence with a sigh.

Kate waited. She had yet to see him talk about anything that ignited a fire in his eyes.

"So now you're thinking of architecture?"

Brody looked out the window. "It's kind of in the art field, but I could make a decent living."

"Let's talk about things you like to do. Lucas said you play baseball for UMass?"

"I'm shortstop. But I'm not pro material, if that's what you're thinking."

"I'm just trying to get a feel for the things you enjoy. What else? What do you do in your spare time?"

"I spend a lot of spare time at the beach. I surf a little. I wait tables at the Even Keel in the summer to supplement the money my parents give toward college. I've helped Lucas with construction, but I don't have a knack for it like he does."

Kate's legs ached from sitting. She stood and crossed the room. "Any other jobs you've held or volunteer positions you've enjoyed?"

"I enjoy working, so I've liked all my jobs. I was a lifeguard at Cisco beach for a couple summers. When school is in session, I tutor a couple local middle schoolers for extra money. That's rewarding. One of my students is a boy with a learning disability. His parents were really frazzled about his schoolwork. I tutored him last year starting after Christmas break, and his grades went from, like, Ds and Fs to Bs and Cs."

"You must be quite the tutor."

"Nah, Jared just needed some encouragement and help getting organized. He's a bright kid—he just had trouble remembering his homework and focusing." Brody lifted a shoulder. "He's a huge Giants fan and I found ways of relating that to his schoolwork."

"Have you considered changing back to education?"

Brody tucked his chin, and his eyebrows hiked up. "Not really."

"Why not?"

He looked away. "I don't know."

"You seem to like kids and know how to motivate them."

"There's not much money involved in teaching."

"You get summers off . . ."

Lucas grinned. His even white teeth reminded her of Lucas's. "Good point."

The bright sunlight from the window beckoned Kate. "Well, it's something to consider. I wouldn't fret about changing gears with your major. This is the rest of your life you're talking about, so it's important to follow your passion. The main thing is finding out where your passions lie."

"Too bad I can't major in girls."

Kate looked out over the street where tourists meandered down the brick sidewalks. A movement below caught her eye. Lucas stood in front of the shop with an auburn-haired woman. She wore a sleeveless ivory sweater and ivory slacks. The woman placed her hand on Lucas's arm, letting it linger. Her head tilted toward Lucas like she would live or die by his next words.

". . . give it some thought," Brody was saying.

Kate peered though the old, wavy pane. "Who's the woman outside? The one talking to Lucas?"

She heard Brody stand. "The leggy redhead? I don't know her. They were talking when I got here."

Kate felt a twinge of something unpleasant. It struck her as odd at first. She tried to rationalize it as common sense. After all, Lucas was wearing a wedding band, and the way Red was hanging on his arm was hardly appropriate. She glared down at the woman. *Boundaries, lady. Have you heard of them?*

Before she could help herself, Kate took a step toward the stairs with the thought of putting the woman in her place. Then she stopped. She imagined Lucas's amused brow, quirking upward, his crooked smile as Kate staked her claim. She wouldn't give him the pleasure. Besides, what did it matter if Red flirted with Lucas? It wasn't as if Kate had feelings for him.

She was *not* jealous, and there was no way on earth she was going to let Lucas think she was.

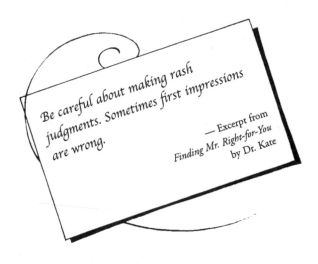

Be careful about making rash judgments. Sometimes first impressions are wrong.

— Excerpt from
Finding Mr. Right-for-You
by Dr. Kate

Chapter Twelve

Kate slipped from the bed shortly after four o'clock and felt her way across the floor. From the floor on Lucas's side of the bed, Bo shifted. As she pulled her thin robe from the hook and tiptoed from the room, she heard his toenails clicking across the wood floor. Kate saw no way of making him return without disturbing Lucas.

The house was dark and quiet, except for the living room clock ticking off time. In the darkness she made her way to the back door and opened it quietly, keeping Bo inside. A warm breeze tugged at her cotton robe, and she gathered the belt, tightening it around her waist before sitting.

The dream that had awakened her surrounded her like a thick wet fog. In it, Bryan had come to her office, climbing the stairs with purposeful steps like Brody had. But Bryan wasn't there for advice.

He took her in his arms and proposed to her. When they left the building, they weren't on Main Street, but at Jetties Beach for their wedding. As Kate approached the altar, he turned. But it wasn't Bryan. It was Lucas.

Now, Kate watched the moonlight flickering on the surface of the shadowed water. She closed her eyes and leaned against the wooden back. The oscillating sound of the waves washing the shoreline didn't soothe her. Inside she felt as jolted as she had in the dream when she realized Lucas had replaced Bryan.

It happened for real too. Kate sighed. She wished she could fast-forward through the year and get her life back on track. How had she gotten so far off course? What was she doing in this house with a man she barely knew and hardly liked?

That's not true, her conscience corrected. *He might grate on the nerves sometimes, but Lucas has his good qualities.* And the last few weeks had been better than she expected in terms of getting along with him. It was just that her life was careening out of control like it hadn't since she was a child. She felt shaken and vulnerable.

A vision of her mom surfaced from the dusty corridors of her mind. Kate had been eleven and had just returned from her best friend's house. She often went to Mackenzie's house just to escape her own. But Mackenzie was mad because Kate never invited her over, and Kate had run out of excuses.

Kate closed and locked the front door before removing her snow boots and wiggling her numb toes. "Mom?" she called, not knowing whether or not to expect an answer. Sometimes she found her mom doing laundry and humming game-show tunes, and other times Kate wished she hadn't returned at all. It was the uncertainty she hated most. Even at eleven she knew it was true.

There was no answer on this night, so Kate set her heavy book bag on the rocking chair, flipped off the lights, and climbed the creaky stairs. Maybe her mom was asleep. She crossed her fingers on the banister as she ascended.

The bathroom light glowed in the darkness. She opened the door and found her mom on the green shag carpet next to a mystery stain they'd inherited with the house. One of her mom's sweater-clad arms draped over the tub ledge, and the other hugged a clear bottle of alcohol. The room smelled sour, and Kate turned on the fan.

"Mom," Kate whispered. She shoved aside the fuzzy pink slippers her dad had sent for her birthday and knelt on the carpet. "Mom."

Her mother stirred as Kate slipped the empty bottle, still warm from her mother's hand, out of her grasp. "Katie, baby." She licked cracked lips and opened her eyes to glassy slits, reaching toward Kate with her delicate white hand. It didn't quite make it and instead thumped on the carpet beside her leg.

"Come on, Mom. Let's get you to bed." Kate helped her mom stand, wrapped an arm around her gaunt waist. Propping her mom's arm around her own shoulders, Kate led her next door to the bedroom. Her mom wobbled and staggered, bumping her bony hip into Kate's and stepping on her cold toes.

When they reached the bed, Kate helped her mom out of her sweater and black slacks. She tugged a nightgown over her head, turned back the covers, and guided her mom into the bed, then pulled the woolly blanket over her. Her breath reeked of vodka.

"Katie . . ." If her mom wanted to say more, it was swallowed by oblivion.

"'Night, Momma," Kate whispered before extinguishing the bedside lamp and leaving the room.

It hadn't been the first time Kate put her mom to bed and it wasn't the last. If her dad had known how bad things had gotten for her mother, he would've gotten custody of Kate. But Kate couldn't stand the thought of leaving her mother all alone, so she kept their secret and spent her childhood feeling anxious and ashamed.

Now, as Kate curled her leg under her, she realized life felt as out of control as it had during those days. And just like then, there was nothing she could do but wait and hope things improved.

Only they never had. Her mother had died an alcoholic.

She tried a pep talk. *You made a better life for yourself. Look how far you've come from that cold house on Stinton Street. You have a successful career, a promising book, and you get to help people for a living. Help people that otherwise might be swallowed whole by their problems, like your mom.*

But regardless of all my planning, I lost Bryan to another woman, and I'm married to a man I don't love.

Only for a year, Kate. Bryan will come to his senses when he realizes his mistake. This other woman is just an outlet for his fear of commitment. Once he realizes that, he'll be back.

What am I saying? I can't believe I still want him back after what he did.

Beside her, the door clicked open, and Bo barreled through, with Lucas following. In the dark, his silhouette revealed tousled hair and a shirt that hung open at the front. Kate looked away.

"You okay?" Lucas whispered.

Bo licked the back of her hand, leaving a warm, wet film on her skin. Kate wiped her hand on her robe and crossed her arms.

"I'm fine. I didn't mean to wake you."

Lucas sank into the chair next to hers and silence settled around them. His presence changed the atmosphere. The masculine scent, the warmth of his large frame only inches away, the sound of his quiet breaths. Before it had felt empty. Now it felt . . . alive.

Kate shifted in her chair. Why had he come out here? He was an early riser, but not this early. Even the birds still slept and there was no light yet on the horizon.

"My family treating you all right? My mom didn't say something to hurt your feelings?"

"Your family's fine." Strange but fine. She hadn't gotten far with Susan, but it was early. First Susan had to like and trust Kate. Then maybe she would open up. And given the history between Susan and Kate's mom, that was going to take time.

"Mom can be tactless sometimes."

Tactless she could handle. It was the crazy that unnerved her. Lucas was probably wondering when Kate was going to keep her end of the bargain. Maybe he didn't understand that subtlety took time. "We're getting to know each other. I'm hoping in the next month or so I can introduce the subject of marriage. I'll let you know how it goes and keep you up-to-date on any progress."

The chair creaked as Lucas shifted. A cricket chirped from someplace under the deck. "Not worried about that."

Kate wondered why he brought it up. Oh, well. She was too tired to figure Lucas out.

She wondered if Bryan was still in bed. She wondered if he was alone. There were things she missed about him—mannerisms. Did Bryan set his hand in the small of the woman's back when he escorted her to the car? Did he hold her pinky on the console as he drove?

A yawn started, and she stifled it. The dream that had chased her from bed kept her from returning for fear that it would resume. Her only hope of escaping it was to stay awake. And even that wasn't working.

Lucas felt Kate move in the darkness. The smell of her hair, a blend of sunshine and citrus, wafted over on a breeze. Did she know how maddening it was to be so close, so *married*, and yet have none of the normal privileges?

No, of course she didn't. From her perspective this was a business deal. Lucas's presence was a means to a goal. She had no idea how much he craved her. How he loved her slightly pointed chin and her almond-shaped eyes, loved the way she brushed her hair behind her ears when she was intent on something.

His advice to Jamie replayed in his mind: "*Don't be afraid to let him know you like him.*" What a hypocrite he was.

Bo rubbed against his leg, and Lucas set a hand on his furry head. His situation was different from Jamie's. Kate didn't have feelings for him. She was still in love with Bryan. Was probably thinking about him right now. Maybe that's why she wasn't sleeping.

He remembered the nights after Emily had died. Lying awake until his eyes ached. Turning a dozen different ways on the bed. Feeling for her empty pillow and pulling it to his chest. If Kate was going through anything close to that, he needed to give her space. And time to get to know him.

"Go for a walk?" he asked. Bo perked up at the word, but Kate only looked his way.

"I'm in my robe."

He scooted to the edge of his seat. "Come on. We'll be back before light."

"But what about—"

"Who cares?" he said. "It'll clear your head." He extended his hand, wondering if she could see it in the moonlight.

She was going to say no anyway. What was he thinking? Kate wouldn't go for a walk unless she'd penciled it in a week ago.

"I guess I can go. I'll have to change first, though." She was inside before he could reply.

When she returned, they stepped off the deck and into the grass. Somewhere in the distance a dog barked, and Bo stopped to listen, his bulk a shadow in the dim light. Then, satisfied the other was of no importance, he led the way down the path toward the water.

When they reached the beach, they turned away from town. The wet, packed sand was cool and spongy under his feet. Lucas wondered what Kate was thinking. He remembered his advice to Jamie and started there.

"How's your column going?"

A wave washed up under their feet. Kate sucked in her breath at the coldness of the foamy water and scampered a few feet up the beach. "I've decided on the letter for my column. The woman wrote a four-page saga, so tomorrow I'll boil it all down to a one-hundred-word question."

He had no idea what went into an advice column, and he started to ask how she'd become syndicated, then thought again. Maybe she didn't want to talk about work at four thirty in the morning.

Bo ran ahead of them, trotting through the intermittent waves that washed ashore, then turned toward them, a still, shaggy silhouette. The moonlight offered enough light to see by. It washed gently over Kate's features, highlighting the bridge of her nose, the bow of her lip. Lucas looked away.

A wind blew across the water, and Kate shivered. "I didn't expect it to be so cool."

Lucas shrugged out of his shirt and placed it over her shoulders.

"Thanks." She put her arms through the sleeves, and he thought her eyes lingered on his bare chest for a moment.

Kate pulled Lucas's shirt tight, overlapping it like a robe. The material was still warm from his skin and smelled like him. The gesture had surprised her, but he'd done many small things that surprised her. Pulling out her chair at dinner, pouring her coffee every morning . . . And she had to admit he was trying to mend his messy ways. He'd even been hanging up his wet towels.

She wondered how Emily had coped with his disorganization. But maybe Emily had been like Lucas. Or maybe she'd considered Lucas's homemade meals and good manners a fair trade-off. Kate wanted to ask, but he never mentioned Emily. Bringing up his late wife would feel as if she was trespassing on sacred ground.

She wondered how Lucas felt about their pretend marriage after having had the real thing. It must feel hollow. Kate could hardly believe even now that he'd done it. That he'd stepped in at the last moment and rescued her.

Then again, he was getting something in return.

"Tell me about your dad," Kate said. Susan was guarded, but maybe Kate could get a fuller picture by learning about Roy.

They caught up with Bo, and he ran ahead of them down the shore, a giant lumbering fur ball.

"He's a man's man. Always liked to work with his hands. His dad was a criminal lawyer, and from what I understand, was disappointed when Dad didn't follow in his footsteps."

"Your dad held his ground?"

"Yep. Dad got a job working for a builder on the island. He framed houses and eventually started his own company."

"Is that how you got involved with wood?" Another wave washed over Kate's feet, tickling her with foam.

"Dad had me using tools by the time I was four."

"But you didn't want to build houses?"

He shook his head. "I like the detailed work. Knew it the first time I made a mantel for a house we built."

"When did your dad retire? And what happened to his business?"

Lucas picked up a shell, examined it, then tossed it into the water before answering. "A few years ago he started having some trembling in his hands. A while later he was diagnosed with Parkinson's disease."

Kate's stomach knotted. How come she hadn't known this before? Neither Lucas nor Susan had mentioned it, and she hadn't noticed any trembling. "I didn't know."

"He decided to sell the business. He was set for retirement anyway, and the work wasn't good for him in the long run.

"What's his prognosis?" She knew a little about Parkinson's, but how quickly did it progress?

"It's a degenerative disease, but its rate of progression varies. Eventually he'll be completely incapacitated, but he's only stage one. There are five stages, and he's progressing slowly."

"Do you think the diagnosis played a role in their marriage problems? It must cause a lot of stress." Why would Lucas worry about them divorcing when his father was ill? Surely Susan wouldn't leave him now. But then, how well did she know Susan?

"They were devastated when they found out. We all were."

No wonder she hadn't known about the disease. Maybe the family was in denial. How would they cope as his condition worsened? "It's lucky you live so close. Your mom will need help." Eventually Roy would be bedridden, and Susan wouldn't be able to handle his weight.

"That's why I built next door."

Kate met Lucas's gaze in the darkness. A glimmer of moonlight shone in his shadowed eyes. "Oh. I thought—" Kate looked away, embarrassed. She'd thought he was a momma's boy. There was no kind way to say it. It hadn't been kind to think it. Especially when his real reason was so unselfish.

"After Emily died, I couldn't live in that house anymore." He seemed about to say more, but stopped.

Kate wanted to know more, but what right did she have to pry? After finding Emily dead in the house, Lucas probably couldn't put the image from his mind. Who could blame him for moving on, starting over? But instead of choosing his own place to live, he'd built beside his parents, to be available for them, and instead of starting over with a new love, he'd stepped in and rescued her. The more she learned about Lucas, the more she realized she hadn't known him at all.

Once you know what you're looking for in a man, don't settle for less. And most important, make sure the man you're dating meets your qualifications before you become emotionally invested.

—Excerpt from
Finding Mr. Right-for-You
by Dr. Kate

Chapter Thirteen

"Let's go sailing," Lucas said as Kate stepped off the treadmill the following Saturday, toweling the sweat from her forehead.

He'd just returned from walking Bo, and the dog trotted over to Kate and nudged her toward the bathroom as if to escort her to the shower. Like she needed help deciding where she was going. She stopped at the doorway and pushed Bo with her knee, glaring at the dog.

"I can't," she said. "I need to clean and catch up on laundry and prepare for a phone interview. Plus we need groceries, and I need to run to the bank."

"I saw your list." Lucas filled a glass with tap water. "We can do those things tomorrow. I'll help." He gulped down the water.

"The bank is closed tomorrow."

"We can run by the bank on our way to the harbor."

"My phone interview—"

"Can wait until tomorrow." He set the glass on the countertop. At her look, he opened the dishwasher and set it inside. "Any more excuses?"

They weren't excuses. Well, not exactly. She just wanted to get her list done. But she'd never seen Lucas's eyes lit like they were now, and he'd done so much for her lately in return for so little.

"Come on. It's seventy-five degrees, the sky is clear blue, and there's a good steady breeze."

"I've never been sailing," she said lamely, hoping he'd rescind the offer.

"Doesn't matter." His Colgate smile illuminated his face. "Get your shower, and I'll gather supplies."

Two hours later, Kate watched Lucas from a bench seat on the boat. He hadn't stopped since they'd left the harbor, pulling on this line and that, tying them off on their cleats.

"Can I do anything?" She tightened the strap on her bulky orange life vest.

He pulled up a sail, his muscles straining under his red tank. "Nope," he called over the wind. As he turned the boat with the tiller, the sails fluttered like gulls' wings, and he adjusted them with one hand. He continued doing what seemed like three things at a time, handling the jobs with the ease and dexterity of a man who'd done it a thousand times.

Soon, he turned the boat slightly into the wind and pulled the white sails tight. Kate dug in her satchel for sunglasses and joined Lucas where he steered the vessel. The deck felt unsteady under her feet, and she grappled for a hold.

"Having fun yet?" he asked. His eyes hid behind his own sunglasses, and she saw herself reflected in them.

"I had no idea there was so much involved in sailing."

He smiled, clearly in his element. "It's a blast. I sail a couple times a month at least. More, if I have time."

"Who taught you?" Kate thought it'd take her years to learn everything he'd just done, but then she wasn't a mechanical person. And she could tell already sailing wasn't going to become her favorite pastime. Being at the mercy of the wind was unsettling. What happened when it changed directions? How did you go back where you came from if the wind was blowing the other way?

"Mom. Dad knows how, too, but Mom's the expert. Want to take a stab at it?" He moved to the side, offering her steering privileges.

Her legs shook at the thought. "No, you go ahead."

He shrugged. "Suit yourself. There's soda in the cabin if you get thirsty. Otherwise, just relax and enjoy."

Kate took the bench nearby and grabbed the railing. The hot sun beat down on her face, and she was glad she'd applied sunscreen before they left. Lucas hadn't applied any and she wondered if he'd burn. His sandal-clad feet were braced a shoulder width apart, and his dark hair and T-shirt fluttered behind. He seemed unconcerned about the lack of sunscreen and life vest.

In the distance, other sailboats dotted the ocean. She looked down at the water rushing by and wondered how deep it was. Just then the boat tilted. She gasped and gripped the metal rail. A glance at Lucas hinted nothing was awry, but her nerves jangled just the same. What if they tipped over? The idea of floating in the middle of the ocean made her palms clammy. Maybe she'd feel better below deck, where she didn't have to see the wide expanse of water.

She stood, steadying herself with whatever she could grab. "I think I'll get a soda," she said.

Lucas nodded, lost in apparent nirvana, oblivious to her discomfort.

"Okay, then."

Rolling her eyes, she took the steps down to the galley. Below, the room was dark and cool after the brightness of the sun. Sliding her glasses up, she noted the tiny galley and a booth; beyond that a bed consumed an entire room. The cabin was pleasantly tidy, but she supposed it had to be; otherwise things would bump around.

As if reading her thoughts, the boat turned, and Kate sank onto the soft blue cushions of the booth. A fake plant was anchored to ivory Formica, and Kate smoothed her hands over the surface, appreciating the solid coolness against her palms.

She hadn't known sailing would disconcert her. She hoped she didn't get motion sickness. *Just my luck I'll be hurling over the side of this thing while Lucas laughs at me. Gee, how fun.*

Was her stomach feeling unsettled now, or was she imagining it? She swallowed compulsively as the boat turned again. Was he zigzagging? *For heaven's sake, can't he just point the thing in one direction?*

She remembered the soda Lucas had mentioned and walked carefully across the galley, grabbing a Sprite from the fridge before falling onto the bench as the boat heeled once again.

How long would Lucas want to be on the water? Was this an all-day thing, or would a couple of hours suffice? She checked her watch and wondered if she'd have time to finish her list once they got home. She didn't want to spoil his fun, but there was nothing to do down here, and she hadn't brought a book to read or writing materials to work. What did people do on boats? She didn't see anything in the small cabin to occupy herself, but the thought of going up on deck was enough to weaken her legs.

Suddenly, the boat slowed, its change in momentum bottoming out her stomach. Had something gone wrong? She wanted to go see but couldn't make herself leave the booth's security. Instead she sipped her Sprite, then realized her stomach felt worse. *Please don't let me puke!*

Footsteps sounded, and Lucas entered the cabin, ducking under the header.

"Is something wrong?" Kate asked.

He grabbed a soda from the fridge, then a brown bag, which he dangled in front of her. "Thought you might be getting hungry."

"You packed food?" He intended to be out here awhile. Her spirits sank.

"Just sandwiches. You hungry?"

Kate's stomach protested, but the sooner they ate, the sooner they could return. "Sure."

He put the food on paper plates with sides of potato salad and chips and headed up the steps. "Coming?"

She wanted to eat there in the enclosed cabin where she could almost pretend she was on dry land. But Lucas was already on deck. The last thing she needed was to give him one more reason to tease her. She stood and followed. The next time he suggested sailing, the answer would be a flat no.

Outside the sun was too bright. Kate pulled down her sunglasses and followed Lucas to the bench she'd vacated earlier. The wind drove the boat, and it rocked gently in the waves.

Lucas handed her a plate. "Beautiful day," he said around a bite of sandwich.

The heat of the sun made her skin prickle, and its glare on the water hurt her eyes. "That it is."

She started on the turkey and bacon sandwich. Would they head back after they ate? She could only hope. She scanned the horizon. Land was nowhere to be seen. With that knowledge, a sudden dizziness overtook her, and she focused on her plate. Did Lucas know where they were, how to get back?

"Love the sounds out here, don't you?"

The water splashed against the boat's side, and the wind billowed the sails. A seagull, on its way somewhere, called out. Maybe she was just a city girl, but she liked the sound of people, vehicles splashing through puddles, and the scrape of sandals on the sidewalk.

Ugh. Her stomach stirred uncomfortably. Maybe she shouldn't eat. The boat dipped. *Be still!* she thought, as if she could stop it. She set her sandwich on her plate and sipped her Sprite.

"You okay?" Lucas cocked his head, but she couldn't see his eyes past the sunglasses.

"I'm fine." She smiled to prove it and bit into a salty chip.

When the wind gusted and the boat dipped again, she steadied herself with the first thing she could reach: Lucas's leg. "Sorry." She removed her hand as quickly as she'd placed it.

The second chip went down. On the third, she stopped. There was no getting around it: her stomach was definitely threatening to expel her lunch. Kate couldn't take another bite. Her head spun, exacerbated by the boat's movement, and she grasped her plate with both hands.

"Kate." Lucas took her plate, tugging it from her tightened grasp. He set it on his other side. "What's wrong?"

She closed her eyes, but that made her head and stomach feel worse. "I'm not—feeling so well." She swallowed, reminding her stomach that things were supposed to go down, not up.

"Oh, honey, why didn't you say something?" He helped her up. "Come over here."

She pulled toward the cabin. "I just want to lie down. I'm sure I'll be fine." *If I don't die first.* She hadn't felt this bad since she had the stomach flu in the seventh grade and vomited all over Miss Heinschneider's white leather Reeboks in gym.

"Lying down is the worst thing you can do." He guided her to the center of the boat and turned her toward the ocean. She didn't want to look at the water. And there was no place to sit. She was willing to sink to the floor, but there wasn't room. Instead she grabbed the railing and leaned over it. She was beyond pretending she was fine. Pride had fled, leaving desperation it its wake.

Lucas put an arm around her middle and pulled her against him. "Look at the horizon. It'll help."

Kate had read something about that, but given the condition of her stomach, she was skeptical. She followed his directions anyway.

"I don't think we have any medications aboard," Lucas said.

Her head fell against his chest, and she smothered a moan. How had she lived this long and not known the body could feel so bad? At this point, she wished she could just get it over with, Lucas's presence notwithstanding.

"Are you watching the horizon?"

His stubbly chin rubbed against her temple, a welcome distraction. She nodded. The horizon was a fuzzy line against the blue sky. She focused on that line like her life depended on it.

"I'm sorry, Katie." His hand moved up and down against her side. His stomach was like a solid wall against her back. "I should point us toward shore. The sooner you're on dry land, the better you'll feel." His arms loosened, but she clutched them, fearing dizziness would overtake her.

"Wait," she said. If only she could sit down.

He tightened his arms, supporting her, and she stared at the horizon. Was the dizziness improving?

"I shouldn't have let you go down to the cabin earlier. You probably would've been fine."

She hadn't been feeling right before she'd gone down, but she didn't have the strength to say so.

"There are saltines and Coke in the cabin. Will you be all right for a minute if I get them?"

Kate wasn't sure she'd ever feel all right again. She wanted to say no, hesitant to stand without the strength of his support, but she nodded anyway and realized she must have a shred of pride left. She leaned forward on the railing, wishing she'd vomit while he was gone and get it over with.

No such luck. He returned a quick minute later and handed her a cracker. "This'll help."

Kate bit into it and followed the cracker with a sip of the Coke he'd brought while he rubbed her shoulders. It seemed her infirmity had granted him touching rights, but it was a welcome distraction. So welcome, she leaned against him moments later and his arms came around her again.

The saltines were working a little magic, and for the first time since she'd eaten, Kate began to believe lunch might stay put. Relief flowed through her and she relaxed against Lucas's chest. She became aware of his breath at her temple, the heat of his arms against hers. Gradually, relief morphed into self-consciousness. She felt silly and vulnerable. She wanted her strength, her dignity back. Yet, the security of his embrace comforted her.

"Feeling better?" The closeness of his voice startled her.

"I am, actually." Her stomach still rebelled; her head still swam. *But at least I'm not wishing I was dead.* It was an improvement.

"Good." He squeezed her and let go. "I'll get us back to shore as quick as I can."

He left, and the wind brushed the heat of her back where he'd been, chilling her skin. She watched him walk away, his long, steady legs navigating the deck. The wind tousled his hair as he adjusted one of the sails.

For some reason it was harder than she expected to look away. She rested her forearms on the railing and turned toward the horizon.

Later that night, Kate lay in bed alone, grateful to feel human again. Dry land was a wonderful thing. She didn't plan on leaving it anytime soon. After they'd docked, Lucas had brought her straight home, even though she felt better. He'd left with her grocery list and returned with a half dozen bags of food, then scolded her for cleaning while he'd been gone.

She smiled against the feather pillow. She hadn't figured on him being a mother hen. Then she remembered the feel of his solid arms around her and the roughness of his jaw at her temple, and something inside her stirred. Had he called her "honey" earlier?

What is wrong with me? I love Bryan. This isn't a real marriage, but a business arrangement.

And good thing. You couldn't find a more polar-opposite husband. Lucas is everything you need to avoid in a permanent relationship.

If she were to receive a Dear Dr. Kate letter spelling out her own circumstances, her advice would be to run. *"Don't get involved with someone ill suited to you; it's an invitation for disaster,"* she'd write.

But moments later, when the bed sank behind her with Lucas's weight, she couldn't stop her heart from speeding or her breath from catching. The covers shifted, and she felt the mattress dip down, felt his body almost touching hers.

Then she felt something else. A kiss pressed to the crown of her head.

Everything stilled for a moment as she waited . . . hopeful? Fearful? She wasn't sure what emotion made her heart stutter.

The bed quivered again as Lucas settled on his side, and her heart's pace slowly returned to normal as her eyes searched the darkness.

Love is a precarious creature, sometimes appearing when we least expect it.

—Excerpt from
Finding Mr. Right-for-You
by Dr. Kate

Chapter Fourteen

Kate's feet pounded the pavement beside Susan's as they turned the corner and headed toward their homes. She'd decided she would bring up Susan and Roy's marriage today, but if she didn't hurry, Susan would be giving her a curt good-bye and striding up the grassy hill to her house.

Kate checked her watch. She had a scheduled meeting with Mr. and Mrs. Hornsby in an hour. Mr. Hornsby had broken it off with the other woman and they were trying to put their marriage back together. Even though Kate wasn't officially counseling them, she knew they were counting on her help.

She would need a shower before the meeting, so there was no extending the walk.

Their breaths slowed as their strides shortened. Kate tried to find the words. She had to be subtle so she didn't come across like a know-it-all counselor interfering in her in-laws' relationship.

Silence had settled between them; now would be the perfect opportunity to say something.

"Susan, can I ask you something?"

Her mother-in-law stepped over a crack in the pavement. "All right."

"Well," Kate took a few breaths. "I've been thinking lately about conflict in marriage. Well, really, conflict resolution. When you and Roy have a disagreement, how do you handle it? How do you resolve it?"

She stopped, afraid she'd put her foot in her mouth if she continued. Truthfully she wondered if the couple even employed conflict resolution the way they picked at one another.

Susan quirked a brow. "I'm surprised you're asking."

Kate stiffened. "Why do you say that?"

Susan flipped her hair from her face. "Well. You're the expert."

Why did the woman have to rub her the wrong way? "I know. It's just—" *Just what? Tell her I'm taking a poll or something?*

"I suppose studying relationships and actually being in one are two different things," Susan said.

Kate wasn't sure where Susan was going, but she nodded.

"Marriage isn't easy. Conflict is a normal part of it, though. You're lucky Lucas is so easygoing."

Susan must think—Oh, great. She thought Kate and Lucas were having problems. She'd probably made the woman's day.

A yappy little dog scurried down a gravel driveway but stopped short of reaching them.

"Roy used to give me the silent treatment for days when he was upset. Sometimes I didn't even know why he was mad and by the time we talked about it, he'd blown it all out of proportion." Susan shook her head. "I used to get so mad when we argued that I'd storm out of the room or even take off in the car."

"Really?"

Susan launched into a story, and Kate realized she'd hit pay dirt: Susan thought Kate needed advice, and she certainly had no trouble offering it. Finally, Kate had a way to get Susan to open up. Of course, Susan was coming at it from the wrong angle, but still . . . Maybe now Kate could finally get some real insights into Susan and Roy's marriage. And finally begin fulfilling her promise to help Lucas.

That evening Lucas was fixing a broken lamp when a knock sounded at the back door. Kate, who was in the kitchen loading the dishwasher, opened the door. Lucas heard his sister's voice. "Is Lucas home?"

"Of course," Kate said.

Jamie entered the living room, and Lucas saw tears sparkling in her eyes. He set the lamp on the table. "Hey, what's wrong, sis?"

Jamie plopped beside him and crossed her arms over her T-shirt. "I just got back from Meredith's house and she said—" Jamie sniffed as a tear escaped. "She said Aaron said I was a loser."

"Now why would she say that?"

Jamie flicked the tear off her cheek. "When we were at the beach last week, you know, after I talked to you, I went up to Aaron and sat with him. We talked and I tried to, like, show him I was interested like you said."

Lucas's stomach sank. He hoped he hadn't given her bad advice. The last thing he'd do was hurt her.

"I thought things went pretty well, but he didn't come to the beach anymore that week, and I haven't seen him since."

"And then you went to Meredith's today?"

"Yeah. We were having a good time and everything, and then she just brings up Aaron and says that he called her a few days ago after I sat with him on the beach, and that he called me a loser!" Jamie wept into her hands. "I made such a fool of myself!"

"Oh, honey, come here." Lucas wrapped his arm around Jamie, and she turned in to his shirt.

"I flirted with him and everything." Her hands muffled her voice. "I practically threw myself at him."

Lucas rubbed Jamie's shoulder. Across the room, Kate loaded a plate in the dishwasher and met his glance, a sympathetic smile on her face.

Lucas returned his attention to Jamie. "Now, hang on. Why did Aaron call Meredith?"

"What?"

"You said Aaron called Meredith and he said you were a loser. Why was he calling her?"

She uncovered her mottled face. "I don't know."

"How do you know she's telling the truth?"

Jamie sniffled. "Why would she lie?" Her eyes widened.

"Well," Lucas said. "Relationships can be complicated. For instance, what if Meredith likes Aaron? What if she's jealous?"

Jamie straightened a bit and wiped her face with the back of her hand. "I guess that could happen. But if Aaron called her, he might like her and not me."

"That's possible too. I'm just saying you should think it through and not necessarily believe everything you're told."

Jamie tilted her head and stared at the stone fireplace. "He did seem interested at the beach." Jamie ran her finger along the couch's trim. "He even said I have pretty hair."

Lucas smiled. "That doesn't sound like a boy who thinks you're a loser."

"I know. I thought he'd call, but it's been almost a week, and he hasn't been at the beach either."

Lucas squeezed her shoulder. "Give it time. Maybe he doesn't want to appear too anxious."

"I guess."

Jamie and Lucas talked until she felt better, and when his sister left, she hugged him before sliding out the back door.

⁂

Kate changed into pajamas and opened the closet door, peeking at the suit she'd bought for her appearance with Dr. Phil. It was a dove-gray Ann Taylor with a structured jacket and streamlined pants. The classic white oxford under the jacket was a good contrast for her skin tone and black hair.

She ran her fingers down the soft material of the suit coat, feeling anxiety work into her fingers. She'd been invited on the show to advise an engaged couple who was having difficulty merging their personalities. What if she said the wrong thing? Worse, what if Dr. Phil disagreed with her advice?

Relax. You're trained for this. You're an expert.

Except in my own relationships, where I'm the epitome of disaster.

Nobody knows that. As far as they're concerned, you married your Mr. Right.

But what if the media attention from this appearance invited scrutiny of her marriage? What if someone figured it out? What if one of Bryan's relatives saw the show and leaked the truth?

Kate closed the closet door. She could only hope for the best. She'd already taken preventative measures. Maybe one more call to Bryan, asking him to check in with his family, wouldn't hurt.

But maybe that was just her wanting to talk to Bryan. She was suddenly tired, though it was only nine o'clock. She approached the nightstand, ready to set her alarm, when she noticed a box on the new nightstand Lucas had brought home.

The box was wrapped in pale pink paper with a white bow. She picked it up. "To Kate," it said on the tiny gift tag in Lucas's left-handed scrawl. She pried open the piece of tape, unwrapped the package, and pulled out a navy-blue velvet box.

The hinge creaked as she opened the lid. Inside, a delicate pair of earrings were nestled side by side. Elegant in their simplicity, they were the same silvery tone as her wedding band.

"Hope you don't mind." Lucas's voice startled her from the doorway. He looked boyishly shy, and she couldn't keep from smiling.

"What kind of woman minds getting jewelry?"

He shrugged, walking toward her. "You don't wear much jewelry. I just thought . . . Well, it's been a month today."

Their anniversary, such as it was. Lucas stopped at the foot of the bed. She watched a blush creep into his cheeks.

"It was very thoughtful. Actually, they're perfect for the *Dr. Phil* show."

What did the gift mean? Flowers was one thing, jewelry another.

Was Lucas trying to make their relationship appear real? Or was there more to the gesture? Her insides fluttered at the thought. She remembered the way he'd laid a kiss on her head. It had been sweet. It made her feel . . . protected.

She glanced at the box in her hand. "I'm sorry. I didn't—"

Lucas waved her off. "I didn't expect you to. I saw those in the window at Pageo's and thought of you."

He was making nothing of it. Maybe it didn't mean anything, but it had been a thoughtful gesture. Lucas had some irritating qualities, but he could be awfully sweet when he wanted to be. Carried away by the moment, Kate reached up and kissed him on the cheek. Her lips tingled against the roughness of his jaw.

When she pulled back, she saw something in Lucas's eyes and wondered if she'd crossed some invisible line. But then he rubbed the back of his neck and turned away. "You heading to bed?"

She closed the lid of the box, watching him go. "Yeah, I'm beat."

He turned as he pulled the door. "'Night,"

"Oh, I forgot to tell you I talked with your mom this morning. The subject of conflict came up and I asked her about her and your dad."

Lucas stilled, his hand on the knob. "What did she say?"

Kate sighed and rolled her eyes. "She thought I was asking her because we were having trouble. Like I wanted her advice on how to handle conflict."

Lucas chuckled. "That's rich."

Kate frowned at him. "It's not funny. She must think I'm a lousy counselor." *She's wondering what kind of idiot her son married.*

"Relax. She's just doing what moms do."

Well, then. How would Kate know that? In her experience moms didn't give advice and nurture. They went out and came back unexpectedly and left you wondering what would happen next.

"Anyway," she said. "I wanted to tell you I'd gotten the ball rolling, that's all." She sat on the bed. "Good night."

After Lucas pulled the door shut, Kate threw the wrapping paper in the trash and tucked the jewelry box inside the top nightstand drawer. She flipped off the lamp and crawled under the covers, but it was a long time before she drifted to sleep.

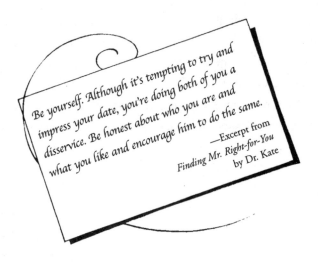

Be yourself. Although it's tempting to try and impress your date, you're doing both of you a disservice. Be honest about who you are and what you like and encourage him to do the same.

—Excerpt from
Finding Mr. Right-for-You
by Dr. Kate

Chapter Fifteen

Kate stepped from the fog of the bathroom and toweled off her wet hair. She could smell bacon frying and hear it sizzling on the griddle. She'd come to expect Lucas's big breakfasts on Saturday and had decided it was a nice start to a weekend. As long as she stayed out of the kitchen while Lucas cooked and she didn't have to see the counters splotched with pancake batter or the cracked eggshells in a pile near the sink. If she faced the wall as she ate and didn't have to see the mess, she could almost put it from her mind.

Kate was shoving her towel into the bedroom hamper she'd bought when the phone rang. By the time she entered the kitchen, Lucas had answered.

"Who's calling?" he asked, setting the greasy spatula on the counter. "Just a minute." He handed her the phone, wearing an inscrutable expression.

"Who is it?" she mouthed

"Bryan." Lucas turned and stirred the pancake batter.

Kate's adrenaline spiked like she'd had three shots of espresso. Why was Bryan calling? She walked toward the back door and put the phone to her ear.

"Hello?" Her tone was cool and collected.

"Hi, it's me."

It rankled that he could still say that. *It's me.* Like they were still so close he needn't identify himself. Had he forgotten he'd dumped her for someone else? Kate stepped out the back door and closed it behind her, keeping Bo inside.

"Bryan. How are you?" There was nothing in her voice to make him think she actually cared to hear the answer.

"I'm good. Better than I've been in weeks."

"Wonderful. Is there something I can help you with?" Polite. Friendly, but not too friendly. It unnerved her that it was such a strain. Was it just barely over a month ago that he'd kissed her good night on the eve of their wedding day?

"Kate, I'm so sorry. It's killing me to hear you like this. Like we're strangers or business acquaintances."

Did he have any right to tell her about his pain?

"I called to say I was wrong," he said. "I know that now."

Kate stared toward the horizon and leaned against the square column that supported the roof.

"Things are over with Stephanie." He said it like he expected her to shoot off fireworks in celebration.

Stephanie. So that was her name. It was no one Kate knew. She was glad for that.

The pause was deafening. Emotions twisted in her like vines around a tree. She wasn't sure which was strongest.

"Kate, did you hear me?"

What did he want from her? Now that he'd dropped his other woman, was Kate supposed to fall in his arms again? "What am I supposed to say?"

"I know. I know," he said. "I—" Kate could hear the frustration in his voice. She imagined him running his hand through his blunt cut.

"I was a fool," he continued. "It was just like you said. It was nothing more than a fear of commitment. I was afraid and looking for an outlet, and Stephanie was convenient."

"Your outlet was costly."

Costly wasn't the word. It had changed her life, changed their future. It was a little late to realize he'd made a mistake. Did he think he could fix it so easily?

A seagull cried out overhead and swooped over the beach, soaring with wide wings. Kate wished she could leave all this behind her and soar over the landscape of her life as the bird did.

"I miss you, Kate."

The words, spoken softly, pried at the door of her heart. Kate closed her eyes. *I will not tell him I miss him.* He didn't deserve to hear it, and she wasn't even sure it was true. Her feelings for him were muddled, blurry, like the line between the ocean and sky. How could that be when she'd been so certain of her feelings for him only five weeks ago?

"I'm married, Bryan." It gave her no pleasure to say it. She'd heard the pain in Bryan's voice, and even though he'd hurt her terribly, she didn't wish to hurt him.

"I know." He swore. It was the first time Kate had heard him swear. Why had he called? He didn't know her marriage was tempo-rary, though he must realize genuine feelings weren't involved. Did Bryan think she'd divorce Lucas the moment he returned?

"Who is he, Kate? Do you know what it's doing to me, imagin-ing the two of you together?"

"Yeah, actually, I do," she snapped.

"I'm sorry. Of course you do." He sighed. "I don't know what I'm saying. I'm just—I'm just going crazy over here. My whole life has been so planned, all my ducks in a row, and now I just feel like it's all exploded in my face."

Have you forgotten you're the one who lit the fuse? She wanted to say it out loud, but what good would it do? What was done was done. She had to stay married. The media would have a heyday if she divorced Lucas and married Bryan. She shook the thought from her head. It was ludicrous to even entertain the idea.

"You don't love him, do you?"

Kate grabbed the hair at her nape and squeezed. To tell him yes would be a lie, but to tell him no felt like a betrayal to Lucas. She let the silence grow. She wanted to ask if he'd loved Stephanie, but what did it matter now? The other woman's journey with Bryan was over, and she had nothing but a foiled wedding as a souvenir.

A bolt of fear struck her thoughts. *What if Stephanie leaks the information to the media? What if she told them Bryan was supposed to be my husband and that I'm nothing but a fraud?*

"Bryan, how did things end with you and Stephanie?"

The pause seemed to last a lifetime. "What do you mean?"

"How did things end?" she asked sharply. "Did you break it off? Was she upset?" She grasped the phone tightly, wanting to wring the answer from it.

"I broke it off," Bryan said. "She was upset. Why, Kate?"

Kate descended the deck steps and crossed the sandy grass toward the shoreline. "What if she goes to the media and tells them everything?" She felt like swearing herself. She didn't know what kind of a person Stephanie was. Was she the vindictive sort?

"She wouldn't do that," Bryan said.

"How do you know?" She wanted proof. Or better yet, a reason Stephanie wouldn't want the news out that she'd broken up Dr. Kate's marriage. Maybe she detested being in the spotlight or had a career that would be damaged by the gossip.

"She's not like that. There would be no reason for her to do it."

"You said she was upset."

"Well, she was, but I think she'd—"

"You *think* or you know?" Kate kicked a hill of sand and took a breath.

"I'll call her if it'll make you feel better. I'll do whatever I have to do to protect you, I promise."

His tone was sincere, but the last promise Bryan had made ended with her at the altar saying "I do" to another man.

⁂

Lucas turned off the griddle and scooped the bacon onto a plate. It clanked as he set it too hard on the table. He opened the oven and removed the warming pancakes.

He had no idea how long Kate would be on the phone, but he was going to eat while it was hot. He scooted his chair back and sank into it. Bo, knowing better than to beg for food, settled on the rug beside him.

When Bryan had identified himself, Lucas had wanted to ask what business he had calling *his* home on a Saturday morning and asking to speak to his wife. He might have done it, if Kate hadn't been standing there with her wide eyes and tousled wet hair.

She'd gone outside for privacy, but he'd heard every word through the open window.

Lucas grabbed a piece of bacon and took a bite. He'd been relieved at Kate's cool tone even though he knew she was only guarding her heart.

When he heard her say, "I'm married, Bryan," he wondered what had prompted those words. Did Bryan want her back? Is that why he'd called?

The back door opened, and Kate entered. She set the phone in the cradle and joined him at the table. Her face revealed nothing. Was she wishing she'd never married him? Was she wishing it was Bryan at the breakfast table now?

Well, Bryan had left her for another woman. It was Lucas who'd cared enough to follow through. Lucas who'd stuck by her though all those publicity photos. Lucas who got up at the crack of dawn and fixed her eggs over easy, the way she liked them.

Kate picked up her fork, and the diamond on her finger glittered under the kitchen lights. Bryan's diamond. Lucas wanted to slide it off her finger and toss it into the ocean.

He took a drink of coffee and set the mug down hard. It clattered against the saucer and splattered on the table. Without a word he stood and retrieved a towel, wiping up the mess before settling in his chair.

"What's wrong?" Kate asked.

"Nothing." *My wife's ex-fiancé called my home and probably declared his love for her. What could be wrong?* He bit into his eggs.

"Well, something's wrong."

Lucas swallowed hard, trying to suppress words he shouldn't say.

"I don't appreciate your ex-fiancé calling here, is all." He applauded his calm tone. Across from him, he felt Kate still.

"I didn't think—I mean—" She cleared her throat. "It's not like this is a real—"

He looked at her, daring her to say it. Yeah, maybe it wasn't a real marriage in theory, but there were feelings involved. His. And he'd been hoping hers were a little involved. Had he been wrong?

"I just meant—"

"I know what you meant, Kate." Lucas stood and took his plate to the trash, dumping a half slice of bacon and the remainder of his sticky pancakes.

"Bryan was supposed to be my husband. Things ended very quickly and there was no time for closure—"

"I was there, remember?" He rinsed his plate in the sink, washing the yellowed yolk with the scrub brush.

"Of course you were."

She said it so quietly, he almost didn't hear over the running water.

"If you hadn't married me, I'd—I don't know what I would've done. I appreciate what you did. I hope you know that."

Did her voice shake on those last words?

Lucas had too many emotions storming through him. He was still angry, and yet, from her point of view, it wasn't justified. It couldn't be unless she knew how he felt, and it was too soon for Kate to learn that.

"What did he want, if you don't mind my asking?" He shut off the water and leaned on the sink ledge, keeping his back to her. His thumbs curled around the sink's corners.

"Of course not."

He heard her pick up her coffee cup and take a sip. It settled into the saucer with a quiet click.

"He had some unsettling news about the woman he was with. Apparently he broke it off with her and she's somewhat upset."

Lucas steeled himself at her words. What was to keep Kate from going back to him? Her career? Her book? Would she let those things stand in the way if she still loved Bryan?

"I'm concerned that she's going to leak the news to the media," Kate said. "If she's angry enough, it would be a one heck of a way to retaliate."

Lucas heard a scuffle on the deck. Bo? Then he remembered Bo was lying on the rug under the table. That meant . . .

Oh, shoot! He leaned forward and peered out the window far enough to see Jamie running from the house.

"Jamie," he called out the window, but she didn't stop. He rushed after her, opening the door and taking the steps in one leap. Had she heard everything they'd said? "Jamie, wait!"

He caught up with her on the grassy knoll and took hold of her arm.

She jerked her arm from his grip. "Let go of me!" Her chest heaved.

"What were you doing snooping outside my house?"

"I wasn't snooping. I came to talk to Kate and I heard you fighting." She crossed her arms.

"We weren't fighting."

"It's not my fault the window was open."

Lucas stuffed his hands in his shorts pockets and thought back to what Jamie might have heard. They'd said enough. "It's complicated, Jamie."

His sister glared at him. "You lied to us."

Lucas swallowed around the lump of pancakes that seemed to have congealed in his throat. He looked back at the house to where

Kate stood on the deck, one foot in front of the other, as if torn about whether to stay or come. He waved her back. It would be better to handle Jamie alone.

"I don't know how much you heard but—"

"I heard enough to know it's all a big lie."

"That's enough. It's not a lie. Kate was in a fix. Her career was on the line, and I stepped in to help her."

"How could you just pretend to love each other? We all thought she was part of our family, and now you're telling me it's fake."

Lucas turned toward the ocean. He remembered being out there with Kate the week before, remembered the feel of her in his arms when she'd been sick. There'd been nothing fake about that.

"I'm telling Mom and Dad the truth." Jamie turned to go.

Lucas grabbed her wrist. "Don't, Jamie." If their mom knew the marriage wasn't real, there would be no holding back the resentment. She'd scare Kate away for good.

His sister whirled around. "Why shouldn't I? You should've been honest to begin with instead of making us think your marriage was real."

"It *is* real."

"I'm not a baby, Lucas. I know your marriage is real on paper, but it's not real in here." She tapped her heart. "And that's the only thing that counts."

All those romance novels had gone to his sister's head. Sometimes reality couldn't live up to the happily-ever-afters in her books.

"Can you keep a secret?" Lucas asked.

Jamie stared at him, her green eyes squinting against the glare of the sun. She crossed her arms. "You know I don't like secrets."

She was growing up. He remembered a time when she'd collected secrets like seashells.

"This is personal. Like your feelings for Aaron. I'd never tell anyone about that."

He could see her acquiescence in the way she tucked in the corners of her mouth. "What is it?"

Lucas glanced over his shoulder toward the house. Kate had gone inside. "Kate loved Bryan." He rubbed the back of his neck. "She probably still loves him, for all I know. She married me because she was backed into a corner and I was her only way out."

Jamie's eyes softened, and her squared shoulders relaxed.

Lucas turned his face into the wind and let the salty breeze push his hair off his face. "But I had different reasons." Lucas met Jamie's gaze, then took his hand from his pocket and touched his heart. His eyes clung to Jamie's, and he saw hers glaze over.

"It's not a fake marriage." His voice deepened with emotion. "I love her. I'd lay down my life for her if necessary. Do you know how rare that kind of love is?"

Jamie blinked rapidly. "But she doesn't love you?"

Lucas gave her a half smile. "I chose to love her. Whatever she does with that is her decision."

Jamie sniffed. "That's so sad."

Great, now she pities me. "Hey, she's got to come around eventually, right?" He tapped her nose and struck a ridiculous pose. "I mean, what's not to like about this?"

Jamie pushed him, but she smiled around her tears.

"Are we okay now?" Lucas asked. He couldn't stand to have Jamie mad at him.

Jamie nodded.

"I can count on you to keep my secret?"

Jamie kicked his ankle with her flip-flop. "You know you can."

Lucas pulled her toward him and held her there, his hand on her head. He realized it felt good to admit how he felt about Kate. A relief to release it.

Then he heard Jamie's muffled voice. "And to think I was coming to *you* for love advice."

If trust is the foundation of a relationship, honesty is the mortar that holds it in place.

—Excerpt from *Finding Mr. Right-for-You* by Dr. Kate

Chapter Sixteen

Kate clutched her hands in her lap, feeling her palms grow hot and sweaty. Dr. Phil's set looked exactly as it did on TV. She'd already been coached by Pam and Chloe, her publicist and her editor. Her agent, Ronald, had also met her at the studio for emotional support. But now she was on her own. When she'd left the green room, Dr. Phil had welcomed her graciously and congratulated her on her new book.

But now, as the cameras were ready to roll, Kate felt as if her nervous system was on overload. The newlyweds she was to advise sat on stage with Dr. Phil. The crew was placing mikes on their lapels and giving them last-minute instructions. Hope was a cute blonde with a pixie face and good taste in shoes. Ryan had dark hair, well trimmed, and repeatedly pushed his glasses up the bridge of his nose with his finger.

Kate was grateful to be on the first row of the audience rather than under the bright lights of the stage. Beside her was a child psychologist who was there to advise a family in crisis. She'd brought her husband, and they whispered back and forth. On Kate's other side were the parents of the couple Kate was to advise.

Kate straightened her suit coat, making sure the mike was well placed, then twisted the earrings Lucas had gotten her.

Be still, Kate. It's not live, only tape. And they can edit if anything goes wrong.

Oh, please, don't let anything go wrong!

She wished she had someone beside her to tell her everything was going to be okay. At that thought, Lucas's image flared in her mind like a Fourth of July firework. And just as quickly she reared back in surprise. *What is with me? I'm an independent woman.* She was accustomed to being on her own, and no one needed to tell her she didn't need a man to be happy. She'd been dispensing that advice for years.

But her thoughts returned to her last few moments with Lucas at the airport the day before. He'd managed to get her there on time and had insisted on walking her to the counter where she checked in. Then he walked her to security. Among the people being herded through security, Kate recognized Dahlia Stevens from the Chamber of Commerce, setting her bag and laptop in a gray tub. She waved at Kate and Lucas.

"Our first night apart," Lucas teased, setting her bag down.

"I'm not sure I'll be able to sleep without your snoring."

"I don't snore."

"Hah!" she said, and he grinned.

There was an awkward moment when they realized it was time to say good-bye. Kate was about to leave Lucas for the first time since their wedding. She was excited about the show, but also nervous. She wasn't used to hiding personal secrets and certainly not from the country at large. Now she would be on national TV, and what if something went wrong?

"You'll do great." Lucas seemed to read her thoughts. "Dr. Phil will probably make you a regular if you're not careful."

"I don't think I'm ready to move to Hollywood."

Lucas smiled. "Good."

Kate glanced at her watch. "I should get to my gate." She pulled her boarding pass and driver's license from her suit pocket.

"Have a safe flight." Lucas looked over her shoulder, and Kate knew he was conscious of Dahlia. He leaned forward and gave her a kiss. The gentleness of his touch tugged at her, even with the brevity of it. Would she ever get used to him kissing her? Wasn't it supposed to become old hat after a while?

Now, as Kate waited for the cameras to roll, she touched her lips, remembering the way they had tingled after the kiss.

Do I have feelings for Lucas? Feelings that go beyond friendship?

Before she could chase the thought, one of the crew gave the signal for taping to begin, and the show was underway. Her couple was up first, thankfully.

Dr Phil started. "Today we have Hope and Ryan. They've been married for eight months and are wondering if they're just too different to make it work. Come on, guys, you're supposed to be in the deliriously happy newlywed stage, so what gives?"

Hope twined her fingers with Ryan's. "The delirious stage lasted about two days for us."

"It was a whirlwind kind of courtship," Ryan said. "I guess we didn't know each other very well, didn't realize how different we were."

"How long did you all date?" Dr. Phil asked.

They looked at each other; then Hope cringed. "Five weeks."

The audience groaned.

"Five weeks!" Dr. Phil's voice rose. "You barely know how he takes his coffee in five weeks."

"I know, I know," Hope said. "It was impetuous, and we regret that we didn't wait longer. I guess I let the whole 'falling in love' thing go to my head. I mean, we are in love, and we want to make it work. But we're so different—we just aren't sure how to find a middle ground."

"Well, they say opposites attract," Dr. Phil said. "Tell us what your hot buttons are. What are the differences that drive you crazy?"

Hope and Ryan eyed each other again. "I guess our spending habits are one of the biggest issues," Hope admitted. "It's not like I go on spending sprees or anything, but I like to dress nicely, and Ryan was raised to be more tightfisted—

"Frugal," Ryan corrected. "I believe in a budget."

"And I think 'What's money for if you can't spend a little?'" Hope wrinkled her nose.

They went on to discuss their differing views on household duties, their differing social needs, and their differing recreational preferences.

"Well," Dr. Phil said. "We brought in reinforcements on this one. Dr. Kate, syndicated columnist and author of the newly released *Finding Mr. Right-for-You* is here to see if we can't help you two make this thing work out."

Kate smiled as the camera focused on her, and the audience applauded. She could feel prickles of heat singeing the skin under her arms.

"Dr. Kate has something else in common with you two—she's also a newlywed, so congratulations on that."

"Thank you." Kate smiled.

"Now, Dr. Kate," Dr. Phil said, "We know you advocate investing the time and energy to make a solid match, but what about situations like this? Are they too different to make it work?"

Kate felt a bolt of energy at the opportunity to help Hope and Ryan. How many times had she advised similar couples in her office? At least this couple hadn't waited until they had years of animosity between them.

"First of all," Kate began, "Congratulations on your marriage and on your willingness to seek help from the beginning. Every marriage is a merging of two personalities—sometimes more if there are children involved. When you're blending two sets of ideals and expectations, there's bound to be conflict. And when you're opposites, there's a greater amount of conflict." *Boy, can I relate to that.*

"The key," she continued, "is to determine which areas need changing and find the middle ground. Pick your battles. Does it really matter that he balls up his socks before he throws them in the hamper? Probably not. Does it matter that you disagree on how much of your income is expendable? Definitely."

Kate swallowed, hoping nobody could tell how dry her mouth was. "Relationships are constantly negotiated," she added. "Opposites can make it work if they're both willing to find the middle ground. And both of you seem willing to make this work."

"We are," Hope said. "But every time we have discussions about our differences, we end up arguing."

Kate jumped in. "It's important to choose the right timing when you discuss your differing opinions. For instance, the arrival of the Visa bill isn't a good time to discuss Hope's spending habits. It's too late, and that leaves Ryan feeling stressed and out of control."

"Exactly," Ryan said. "I'm already angry that she's spent the money without regard for my budget."

Dr. Phil spoke up. "And, Hope, did you sit down with Ryan and work out this budget, or was it foisted upon you?"

Hope nodded. "Ryan did the budget on his own. There is no room for good shoes in that budget."

The audience laughed.

"A woman's got to have good shoes, Ryan," Dr. Phil said. "Rule number one."

He turned toward the camera. "You can read more about how to find a suitable mate in Dr. Kate's book *Finding Mr. Right-for-You.*" There was a close-up of her book cover, then Dr. Phil continued. "All right, next we have a blended family who can't seem to blend." He looked at Hope and Ryan. "And you thought blending two was tough! We'll be right back."

After the show, Kate slid into the black limo for her trip to the airport. In the back of the car, her nerves still jangled. It had been an exciting experience, and she felt giddy with energy. She'd already celebrated with Pam, Chloe, and Ronald in the green room, but now that she was away from the moment, she wanted to share it with a friend. Before she would have called Bryan, but who did she call now?

Anna? No, her former assistant was out of town with her new job.

Her dad? She considered it a moment, then took out her cell and dialed. It rang and rang before going over to voice mail, and she hung up.

She had to tell somebody. What good was exciting news if she had no one to share it with?

Well, I know exactly who I could call.

Well, then, Kate, just do it.

She dialed Lucas's shop, and when Ethan answered, she asked for Lucas. As she waited, she second-guessed herself. Would he find it odd that she'd phoned him when she'd see him at the airport in several hours? Why should he even care how the show had gone? It was her career, her book. In a matter of months, she'd be nothing to him but a name on the divorce papers.

Shoot, why did I call him? Maybe I should hang up. Kate pulled the phone from her ear.

"Hello?"

She put the phone back. "Hi, it's Kate."

"Hey!" He sounded happy to hear from her. "How'd it go?"

Kate relaxed a bit. He didn't seem confused by her call. "It went very well. Quick, but good."

"All your worries were for nothing. I knew you'd do great."

"Easy for you to say. You weren't the one on national TV."

He chuckled, and she realized she missed the warmth of his laugh. "That's why I make furniture and you give interviews."

She sighed, the excitement of the morning giving way to something calmer.

"Where are you now?"

"In the back of a limousine." The driver turned onto the freeway and accelerated.

"Aren't you special. How was the hotel?"

"Gorgeous, accommodating, and pristine. You could have eaten off the floors."

"Hope you didn't get too accustomed to that."

"Don't worry—I'm already anticipating the condition of the house."

He chuckled again, and Kate let a comfortable silence fall as she settled back into the leather seats.

"My flight's running on time. The question is, will you be?" she joked.

"Only time will tell," he retorted.

"Is that supposed to be a pun? It might help if you wore a watch, you know."

"What fun would that be?"

Kate chuckled. He was hopeless. "I guess I'll meet you outside baggage claim. Do you have my flight number?"

"Uh, let's see." She heard crackling, like he was holding the phone between his ear and shoulder. He was probably riffling through his cluttered wallet.

Some things never changed. "Here, let me give it to you again." Kate consulted her ticket and rattled off the flight number and arrival time.

When they hung up, Kate tucked the ticket into her suit coat and looked out the window, watching palm trees and tall buildings go by. In two weeks, the show would be broadcast, and the sales of her book, already good, from what Rosewood told her, might just skyrocket. Would it hit the *New York Times* bestseller list? She could only keep her fingers crossed. It couldn't hurt to have Dr. Phil announcing her title on the air.

But she couldn't quell the niggling fear that national attention would expose her to personal scrutiny. And now that she'd gone so public, what was to stop someone from digging around and finding out the truth? The answer was as close as Bryan and his family. Or, more likely, Stephanie.

Now that she was in the public eye, reporters would jump at the chance to smear her reputation. And, for the first time, she realized it wouldn't only be her reputation that got ruined. What would the exposure do to Lucas and his family? Jamie might already know the truth, but the rest of his family would feel betrayed, and Lucas would suffer the scrutiny and distrust of his own hometown.

What am I doing?

It felt as though she'd been asking herself that question every day for the past month. And she still didn't know the answer.

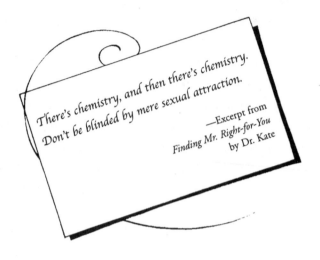

There's chemistry, and then there's chemistry.
Don't be blinded by mere sexual attraction.

—Excerpt from
Finding Mr. Right-for-You
by Dr. Kate

Chapter Seventeen

"Ready?" Kate heard Lucas call from the shop downstairs.

She saved her article and grabbed her purse. When she reached the bottom of the stairs, Lucas was waiting, keys in hand.

"What are you doing?" she asked.

"Taking you home to watch the show."

"Oh." The realization that he wanted to see it sent warmth through Kate. She avoided his gaze as she slid past. "Well, come on, then. It starts in fifteen."

After a quick trip home, Kate flipped on the TV, and Lucas made a pot of coffee. Kate's fingers fluttered like a ship's sails as she waited.

A tap sounded at the front door. Roy peeked around the edge.

"Hello! We're not late, are we?" He entered, followed by Susan, Brody, and Jamie.

"Oh, my goodness, you all came." Kate hadn't expected it to be a family affair.

"We wouldn't miss this for the world, would we, dear?" Roy said. "It's your national debut."

The group of them congregated on and around the sofa.

"Are you nervous?" Jamie asked.

"A little," Kate said. "Which is silly since it's taped."

"I'm sure you did fabulously," Roy said. "I'll bet your book is going to make that bestseller list yet. We have a real celebrity in the family!"

Kate glanced at Jamie, feeling awkward at the mention of family. Jamie withdrew a romance novel from her bag and propped it open on the arm of the couch.

"Coffee, anyone?" Lucas asked from the kitchen.

"Sure." Roy grabbed the remote and turned up the volume.

"Turn it down, Roy; that's too loud," Susan said.

Brody checked his watch. "You better hurry. Two minutes and counting."

Kate sank into the armchair.

"When is your segment on?" Brody asked.

"It's first—if they air it in the order they taped it."

Moments later, Lucas handed Kate and Roy their mugs, then retrieved his own cup and sat on the arm of Kate's chair. Bo settled on the rug beside Jamie and she scratched behind his ears.

"Hey, his icky yellow beard is gone."

Kate had donned rubber gloves the day before and scrubbed the mutt's chin. "I cleaned him up and put cornstarch in the fur under his mouth."

The corner of Lucas lips twitched. "Cornstarch?"

"It's amazing what you can learn when you Google something."

The *Dr. Phil* theme song began. "Be quiet; it's on." Roy increased the volume until Susan glared at him.

Jamie closed her book and leaned forward.

As they watched the opening, Kate's hands grew cold. Lucas's family's attention was rapt on the TV. She was the only reason they'd come. How easily they'd accepted her into their family, counting her as one of their own. Even Susan seemed to be giving her a chance. They couldn't be more supportive if it were Lucas on the show.

I'm a horrible, horrible person.

Dr. Phil introduced Kate, and her face appeared on screen.

"There you are," Jamie said.

"Shhhh!" Brody said.

The room got quiet as Dr. Phil mentioned her newlywed status. Kate felt her face heat, and Lucas set his hand on her shoulder. Kate sipped her coffee.

The segment continued, going exactly as Kate remembered. Her makeup, which had seemed too heavy on the day of the show, looked natural under the lights, and the stylist had done a nice job with her hair.

When Dr. Phil announced the title of her book and showed the cover, Lucas squeezed her shoulder. She'd hoped they wouldn't edit that out.

The segment ended and they broke for a commercial.

"Well done, Kate." Roy said.

"You did great," Jamie said. "How did you stay so calm? I wouldn't know what to say."

Brody elbowed her. "That'll be the day."

Jamie jostled him back.

"It's second nature by now," Kate said. "Though I was nervous since it was national TV."

"I couldn't tell," Roy said.

The phone rang, and Kate jumped up. "It's probably my publicist." She dashed to the kitchen and picked up. "Hello?"

"Hi, it's me."

Her stomach flopped. "Bryan," she said quietly, peering into the living room where Lucas's family continued their conversation. Lucas met her gaze, and she turned away, walking to the kitchen window.

"You were amazing, Kate," Bryan said. "I was so proud of you."

What right did he have to be proud? He didn't deserve to say those words. He hadn't coached her on what to say or driven her to the airport. *He didn't even show up for our wedding.*

Kate hadn't even thought of Bryan watching the show. She didn't think he'd even known it was airing today. Plus it was during work hours, and it wasn't like they were together anymore.

"You weren't even nervous," Bryan said. "And the way he plugged your book. I bet it'll take off now." He gave a familiar whistle. She'd forgotten that about Bryan—that little whistle he did to punctuate his excitement.

"That's the hope."

A long silence followed her words. Kate heard a ruckus in the living room and knew Lucas's family was leaving. Outside the window, the sea oats on the hill bowed against the breeze. Why had Bryan called again? Didn't he realize it was awkward for her?

"I miss you, Kate."

She gritted her teeth. "Stop it, Bryan."

"It's true. I miss the way you leave everything in tidy stacks, and the way you squint your eyes at me when I say something foolish. I miss the way you—"

"Stop it." He was getting to her, and she hated that. She rubbed her eyes. "You have to stop calling me here."

"Your cell was off."

"That's not what I mean. You can't just call me whenever you want now."

Kate heard footsteps behind her, heard the clatter of something being put in the sink. She turned and met Lucas's eyes. He knew it was Bryan; she could see that much in his expression. There was something in his eyes that tugged at her heartstrings. Hurt? Lucas looked away before she could pursue the thought.

". . . where we can talk in person," Bryan was saying.

What had she missed? He wanted to meet?

Lucas leaned against the sink, facing her, his palms braced on the ledge behind him. His stance said, *Talk all you want. I'm not going anywhere.* What did he expect her to do? Hang up on Bryan? *It's not my fault he called. I didn't ask him to.*

"What about it, Kate?"

What about what? She couldn't think straight.

"Or I could come there if that's easier. Whatever you want to do, but I want to see you. I need to be with you. Please." He grated out the word.

Lucas cocked a brow.

Kate's heart beat like a frightened bird's, and she wasn't sure why. She felt cornered. By both of them. She had to get out of here. Away from Lucas's strange looks, away from Bryan's hurt pleas.

"I can't talk right now."

"I'll call you back," he managed to get out before Kate hung up. She set the phone in the cradle. A step away, she could feel Lucas's tension.

"I'm going for a walk." Kate grabbed the doorknob leading to the beach.

"I want him to stop calling here." Lucas crossed his arms over his chest, his right bicep bulging over his left fist. He looked away.

"I'm a little tired of everyone telling me what they want right now." Kate pulled at the door.

Lucas put his hand against it. "He has no right calling my house."

"*Your* house? I thought I lived here too." Kate turned and was surprised to find Lucas so close, his arm extending past her.

"You know what I mean."

Did she really? Was he being possessive of the house or of her? Why did he care if Bryan called? Sometimes she thought she saw something in Lucas's eyes, but right now she thought it had nothing to do with her. It was about possession. Bryan and Lucas were like two wolves fighting over an animal carcass.

And I'm tired of being caught in the middle.

She jerked on the door, but he held it fast.

What was it with men and control? "Let me go." She pulled at the knob again. It didn't budge. "Lucas! Let me—"

"What if I don't want to?"

And just like that, time slowed.

Almost against her will she looked at him. And was caught by his eyes. They pulled her in, held her hostage. She stilled, her anger fading, replaced by something . . . more complicated . . . less welcome . . .

"What if I don't want to?" What did he mean? Suddenly desperate to understand, she searched his face and watched as his eyes darkened into shadowed whirlpools.

She forgot how to breathe.

"What if I want you to stay?" His gaze traveled the planes of her face and stopped at her lips.

"What . . ." He was so close she couldn't think. His thumb grazed her cheekbone, barely a touch, and yet it heated her skin. She shuddered and closed her eyes against the riptide tugging inside her. What was happening? This was Lucas, not Bryan. Lucas, who frustrated her with his lack of organization. Lucas, who annoyed her with his sluggishness.

Lucas, who held you in his arms when you were seasick. Lucas, who stepped in and saved you when you were desperate.

"Open your eyes, honey."

Her stomach tightened at the endearment. She was powerless against the emotion raging inside her. It felt wonderful and terrible and scary.

"Lucas." Nothing more than a whisper.

"Open your eyes," he said. "See what's right in front of you."

She obeyed his request. What was this spell he'd cast? She wanted to fall into the depths of his eyes and get lost. She wanted to touch his jaw and feel the roughness against her fingers.

But before she could follow the impulse, he closed the distance between them. And his lips touched hers, gentle and slow.

Without thought, Kate laid her palm against his face and heard his intake of breath before he deepened the kiss, pulling her closer, making her head spin. His movements were sure and slow, like everything else he did.

It wasn't even their first kiss. But the others hadn't been like this. There was no photographer snapping pictures, no public judging the validity of their vows, no family to convince.

It was just Lucas and Kate. All alone. Exploring feelings she hadn't known existed.

No. That's not true.

Maybe she had known, or maybe she'd been in denial. Maybe she'd been blinded by Bryan's rejection. But she was seeing things now. And feeling them. Things that she'd never felt before, not even with Bryan. The way Lucas made her forget everything except the feel of his lips. Made her want more. Made her need more.

More. She slid her hand into his hair, cupping his head, and arched closer. He was warm and strong. He smelled like cedar and musk. All man.

"Katie . . ." Lucas whispered against her lips.

She didn't think, just felt. The urgency pushed her on. *It's okay, Kate. You're married. Lucas is your husband.* She submitted to the thought, letting her emotions guide her.

But . . . what happens when it ends?

Against her will, the question rose from a deep and distant well of reason. Kate ignored it, let the feel of Lucas's body against hers drown everything out.

But the voice grew louder, more insistent.

What'll happen when the year ends? Why are you becoming emotionally invested in a temporary relationship?

And it had to be temporary. Muddled as her thoughts were, she hadn't lost all sense of reason. She and Lucas were too different—more dissimilar than her mom and dad had been, and look how that had ended. She of all people knew the odds against opposites making a marriage work.

You have to stop. Now!

Somehow mustering the strength, she pushed at Lucas's chest, separating them. Her chest heaved. She was beyond her target heart rate and she hadn't moved. Judging from Lucas's expression, he felt the same. A pink flush mottled his face. His eyes were glazed, his lips swollen. She was tempted to soothe them with her thumb.

Stop it! You have to stop before this gets out of hand. You're too different.

They might be different, but heavens to Betsy, the chemistry was there in spades. She had to escape before she lost her resolve.

She reached for the doorknob and pulled.

"Running, Kate?" The dare emerged, raspy and breathless.

She ignored it, pulling the door shut behind her and dashing toward the shoreline. Yes, she was running. And too afraid to say anything for fear it might reveal too much.

As if her actions hadn't already revealed far too much.

Honesty begins within yourself.

—Excerpt from
Finding Mr. Right-for-You
by Dr. Kate

Chapter Eighteen

Lucas slammed his fist on the counter. He hadn't succeeded in opening Kate's eyes; he'd only succeeded in pushing her away. As he watched her scramble across the sandy grass toward the beach, he feared he'd scared her away for good.

He punched the counter again, then shook his throbbing hand. Bo nudged his leg with his wet nose. "Not now, boy."

Why had he moved so fast? He'd only meant to kiss her gently, to show her how he felt. But then her hand had wound into his hair, and she'd pressed herself against him.

His own hand now raked his hair. His timing couldn't have been worse. Fresh from a phone call from Bryan, she was probably thinking of him. She wasn't over Bryan; that much he knew.

It's too soon to tell her how you feel.

But her response was so—

She was thinking about Bryan. Wishing it was him she'd married.

Lucas left the kitchen and paced the length of the living room as if he could distance himself from the thought. But she wasn't Bryan's wife.

She's my wife . . . Yeah. Temporarily. In name only.

You agreed to those terms, Luc, so stop your whining.

Only he hadn't known it would be so hard. Hadn't known it would make him long for her more. Hadn't known it would hurt so much.

He sank into the recliner and let his head fall against the cushion. What was Kate thinking right now? Would she expect an apology when she returned?

Well, she wouldn't get it. He wasn't sorry, even if she had been thinking about her idiot ex-fiancé while he kissed her.

All I did was lay my feelings out. Nothing to be ashamed of.

So why was his gut strung tighter than a bowline knot?

⚭

By the time Kate returned, the house was empty. Lucas's truck was gone, which meant he must've gone back to his shop. Relieved, but dreading the inevitable confrontation, Kate started dinner.

Her walk had helped clear her head. Obviously Lucas had feelings for her, and Kate admitted she'd grown fond of him as well.

Fond? You were all over him, girl.

She emptied a package of ground beef into the skillet, threw away the Styrofoam platter, and washed her hands. Okay, so maybe she had feelings for him. She had to remember the advice she dispensed in her book. "Once you realize a man is not well suited to

168

you, it's imperative to end the relationship before you become emotionally invested."

Well, she couldn't end the marriage, but she could put the relationship back on track. They were friends. No—roommates. That was all. The sooner Lucas realized it, the sooner they could put this awkwardness behind them.

Bo sat by the back door and turned his big head toward her. She let him out and kept an eye on him through the window while she cooked. The smell of dinner soon drew him back.

The taco filling was hot and bubbly by the time she heard the front door open and click closed. Kate lowered the heat to a simmer and stirred the beef mixture as it sizzled. Would Lucas join her or would he grab a shower? She hated this indecision, this awkwardness. She didn't like walking on eggshells in her own home. She wanted to return to the way things were before.

When Lucas entered the kitchen, Kate gave the beef one last stir and turned. They might as well put this behind them.

Lucas removed a can of Coke from the fridge and popped the tab. He wouldn't even look at her. She wondered what he was thinking, what he was feeling. His expression revealed nothing.

"About earlier," Kate started, then wondered what to say next. Why hadn't she planned something? *Think!*

Lucas took a drink, then shook his head, a barely perceptible movement. "Not necessary."

He moved closer, and Kate pressed her back against the oven. The metal handle dug into her back. But Lucas reached into the cabinet instead. Shaken, Kate turned.

Lucas removed two plates and shut the cabinet door. "It was a mistake," he said as he stepped away.

Kate heard him setting the plates on the table. *A mistake?*

Well, what did you expect him to say?

She wasn't sure, but it wasn't this. Maybe she thought he'd confess he had feelings for her. But maybe he only missed Emily. Maybe he missed the intimacy of their marriage.

"Let's just forget it happened." His voice penetrated her thoughts.

Let's just forget it happened? Forget the way you took my mouth, forget the way you touched me, forget the way you felt against me? She wondered if that were possible. "Right."

Dinner consisted of tacos, avoided eye contact, and stilted conversation. When Susan dropped by and invited Kate on a walk, Kate readily agreed. Because despite her agreement with Lucas, she couldn't seem to eradicate the memory of the kiss.

❧

Kate felt warm and cocooned as she stirred from sleep, only half-conscious. She kept her eyes closed, hoping to fall back asleep. The covers twisted around her legs in a snug knot, but a big pillow, snuggled into her stomach, warmed her.

She wondered about that because her pillow was under her head. Coming more fully awake, Kate opened her eyes. She could barely see by the soft morning light that filtered through the curtains. More important, her arms and face felt the softness of flesh against them and she knew it was no pillow she cuddled with. Her arm curved around Lucas's side and her body spooned into him, her face against his back. Her thighs pressed into the backs of his.

She started to jump away then stopped herself. Maybe he was asleep—completely unaware that she clung to him like a barnacle on a boat. A sudden move would wake him. If she disengaged slowly, he'd be none the wiser. *Oh, please, let him be asleep.*

She lay quietly listening to the sound of his breathing. He wasn't snoring, but that didn't mean he wasn't asleep. His respirations were deep, a good sign.

How had she ended up on his side anyway? Had she had some weird dream about their kiss? Where was her rolled-up quilt barrier? The way the covers tangled around her legs, she or Lucas must've had a fitful sleep.

Okay, time to disengage.

She carefully removed her hand from his stomach. Inch by inch, she lifted her arm until it had no contact with Lucas. Next she lifted her head, moving her face away from the heated hardness of his back.

So far, so good.

The only thing against him now was . . . well, the rest of her body. Her legs tingled with awareness.

Stop that! Good grief, what has gotten into me?

She eased her weight onto her elbow and held her breath as she moved away from him.

Lucas stirred and turned, settling on his back. Kate froze above him. His side pressed into her now and his face was inches away. Thankfully, his eyes remained closed. She lay still, hardly daring to breathe. Was her heartbeat shaking the entire bed?

She glanced at his clock. It was later than she'd thought. The alarm would sound in three minutes. She had to break away.

Kate scooted back, easing away from him. She'd moved only a few inches when she felt resistance. Her pajama top was caught. Lucas had rolled on top of it.

Gritting her teeth, she grasped the material and tugged slowly, watching Lucas's face for any sign of awareness. But it freed without incident, and she sighed quietly. Being careful to steady the bed, she used her feet and right elbow to support her weight and scooted her hips away.

When she reached her own side of the bed, she rolled to her back and let out a shaky breath. Her heart, beating more rapidly than could be accounted for, really was shaking the bed. Thank goodness Lucas had slept through it. There was no telling what he'd think if he knew she'd snuggled up to him like that.

"Next time you want to cuddle, just say so."

The voice from beside Kate startled her. Then the meaning of his words penetrated her mind. He still lay perfectly still, his breathing deep and even. *That jerk!* He'd been awake the whole time and let her suffer.

She yanked the pillow from under her head and swung it at him. But the only response she got was his insufferable laughter.

Fear and its close cousin, jealousy, will do more to ruin a relationship than any other factors.

—Excerpt from
Finding Mr. Right-for-You
by Dr. Kate

Chapter Nineteen

The Wright house was buzzing with activity when Kate and Lucas arrived the next Saturday.

"Come in, kids!" Roy called from where he emptied ice cubes into glasses. He was about to say something else, but Susan turned on a noisy mixer and began running it through a pot of steaming potatoes. In the next room, the TV blared, but Jamie was curled into a fat armchair with a book.

Lucas and Kate greeted them; then Roy took Lucas into the garage to show him the new mower he'd bought. When Susan turned off the mixer, silence settled on the kitchen.

"Can I help with something?" Kate asked.

"No, thank you."

Kate searched for something to say. It was easier when they were walking; she didn't feel the need to fill the silence. For the hundredth time, she thought about addressing the issue of Susan and Kate's mom. Would it clear the air between them if she apologized on behalf of her mom? Would it open the door for Susan to confide in Kate about her marriage problems? Or would it just anger Susan that Lucas had told her?

She was formulating her thoughts on the matter when Lucas and his dad reentered. "You can borrow it anytime," Roy was saying to Lucas as he took a pitcher of tea from the fridge.

Oh well, it would have to wait for another time. "Is Brody around?" Kate asked.

"He's upstairs already," Roy said.

"I think I'll join him, if you don't need any help," Kate said.

Roy shooed her on, and Kate climbed the two flights, dreading the rooftop experience but wanting to catch up with Brody. They hadn't had an opportunity to discuss his majors since he dropped by her office.

She found Brody leaning on the widow's-walk railing, high above the landscape. He greeted her as she slipped into her chair against the chimney chase.

"Great day, huh?" he asked.

Kate forced her eyes from him. The blue of the sky melted into the expanse of ocean, its unending vastness interrupted only by the colorful dots of sails. The sun burned hot, and the breeze chopped at the water's surface. Kate's fists tightened around the chair's arm, its edges cutting into her palm.

"Beautiful." She tucked her feet under the chair. Why wasn't it getting easier to face her fear of heights? She'd thought she could overcome it if she only forced herself up here every week.

Her mind went back to the first time she'd felt the fear.

Ironically, it hadn't been her own life she'd feared for at the time. Her mom, belly filled with alcohol, had climbed out her bedroom window and onto the sloped roof of the porch. Kate had come home from a friend's house to find her teetering on the edge.

"Mom, don't move!" Kate ran upstairs, down the short, narrow hall, and into her mom's bedroom. The wooden sash was thrown open and the curtains fluttered in the night breeze.

"Mom, come here." Kate climbed out the window and took slow steps down the slope. Her mom's blouse rippled in the wind, and for a moment, Kate thought it would be enough to blow her right over the edge. She grabbed her mom's hand. "Come on, Momma."

Kate didn't know how frightened she'd been until they were safely inside the house. Only then did she realize her heart felt as though it was going to burst through her ribs.

Now, her heart pounded in remembrance. Ever since that day, heights had frightened her.

This is not helping. I need to focus on something else.

Brody shifted, drawing Kate's attention, and she remembered her purpose in coming. "I've been wondering about your career path. Have you given it more thought?"

Brody leaned his weight against the railing. Didn't he realize it could give way? If it did, he'd hurtle three floors to his death. Okay, maybe just a broken leg, but still. Kate's palms grew clammy; she felt dizzy at just the thought.

"It's all I think about," Brody said. "Other than girls, that is." He flashed a smile, revealing a dimple she hadn't noticed before.

Kate remembered the passion in his voice when he'd talked about tutoring his little friend. She had a suspicion education was his main interest. The question was, why had he changed majors? What was holding him back?

"When I look into the future," he said, "I can see myself teaching middle school. Maybe art or computers or even science. But—"

Kate waited for him to finish, although she had to look away; the mental image of the rail breaking loose was too much. She watched her oval thumbnail follow the square edge of the chair's arm.

"I don't know. I changed majors for a reason. I keep trying to remember why."

"You switched to art next, right?"

The wind tousled his hair, and he shook it from his eyes. "Yeah. Dumb move."

Kate shook her head. "We make decisions for a reason. Sometimes you just have to dig deep to find them."

She was beginning to think she understood Brody's reasons.

She leaned back, and her chair, its legs not quite even, rocked an inch. She stiffened, clutching the table's edge. Her breath caught in her throat, and prickles of adrenaline flared under her skin.

When she looked up, Brody was studying her. "What's wrong?"

Kate forced her fingers to loosen and crossed her legs. "The chair rocked back and I lost my balance."

Brody's head cocked. "You always sit with your back against the wall, and you never walk around up here." He pointed his finger at her. "You're afraid of heights, aren't you?"

Kate gave a wry laugh. "I'm not afraid of heights so much as I'm afraid of falling."

Brody sat at the table. "You should have said something. We could eat downstairs."

She shrugged. "I don't want to break tradition. Besides, I don't like letting fear rule my life. This little once-a-week trek is my way of telling my fear to take a hike."

Brody laughed, and as he did, a thought struck Kate. There was nothing like fear to change your course. How many people had she counseled whose fear of intimacy kept them from experiencing the very thing they desired?

She leaned back. "Maybe you're a little like me."

"What, me? Afraid of heights? No way. I've been parasailing lots of times and even hang gliding a couple times. Don't tell Mom and Dad. They'd freak."

Kate shook her head, sure she was onto something. "No. Afraid of falling." She watched him, waiting for him to connect the dots.

His head tipped back, his eyes narrowing. "You think I'm afraid of failing."

He was obviously offended, and Kate wondered if she'd overstepped her boundaries. "Only you know the answer to that." She smiled to soften the words. "I'm just putting it out there."

It made sense. Maybe he'd only changed majors because he excelled at many things and couldn't make up his mind. But in light of his passion for teaching, fear of failure made sense. He wouldn't be the first.

The sound of feet thumping up the stairs warned them they had company coming, and the topic was tabled for the day.

⌘

Kate was eating alone at the Even Keel when her agent, Ronald, called with great news. *Glamour* magazine wanted to feature her in a monthly "Dear Dr. Kate" column. They'd seen her appearance on Dr. Phil and had been tracking her career. It had been between her and another syndicated columnist, and she was their first pick.

Kate paid her bill and rushed back to the shop, hoping Lucas was there, wanting to share her good news. She would have been eating with him except he'd canceled because of an appointment.

But what Kate saw when she neared the shop pushed her good news from her mind and stopped her feet midstride. Someone behind her bumped her, treading on her good heels.

"Sorry," Kate mumbled as the tourist passed her with a glare, pulling a golden retriever on a leash. She shifted over, moving closer to the gift shop, out of the stream of traffic, her eyes returning to the scene that had stopped her.

Lucas helped a woman from a silver car. The woman unfolded herself from the compact vehicle, and Kate saw her long red, hair. Lucas shut the door and followed the woman into his shop.

It was the same woman Kate had seen him with the day Brody stopped by her office a month or so ago. Was she the reason Lucas had cancelled their lunch plans? Had he and Red had lunch together?

Something tightened deep in her stomach like a dishrag wrung hard.

Don't be ridiculous. She's probably just a friend. Or a business acquaintance.

From a distance, Kate watched Lucas hold the store's door for the woman. She turned and laughed at something he said, cocking her head.

Kate's lips pursed in reaction. She disliked the way the woman looked at Lucas. She disliked her own reaction to it more.

It's not jealousy. She looked away and watched the tourists and locals walking past her. What would people think if they saw Lucas and Red eating together? Especially if the woman was hanging on him like she had the first time Kate saw them together? He was married to her, Dr. Kate, and she couldn't have people thinking he was wining and dining another woman. As careful as they'd been to make the marriage appear legitimate, she couldn't believe he'd be so careless.

A passing dog bumped her thigh, and Kate straightened. She'd have to say something to him tonight.

He'll think I'm jealous.

Not if you handle it carefully.

Kate hitched her bag on her shoulder and set her feet in motion, her ire rising with each step. Didn't Lucas know she had a reputation to protect? Hadn't he given any thought to how it would appear, him gallivanting all over the island with another woman?

She composed her features as she entered the shop, the bell jangling against the glass door. Soft music greeted her, and the air-conditioning was welcome against her heated skin. But there was no sign of Lucas or the woman on the floor.

"Nice lunch, Kate?" Ethan called from behind the mahogany desk. He adjusted his wire-rimmed glasses.

"Sure." She hesitated on the first step. "Is Lucas around?"

"He's in the back." Ethan leaned over his papers.

Behind her, a customer entered the store, and Ethan stood.

Kate started up the stairs. "Thanks, I'll just . . . talk to him later."

Why would he take Red to the back of the store? There was nothing there but the pieces he was working on and a bunch of tools.

Her heels clicked up the wood steps. When she reached the top, she hung her bag on the coatrack and sat at her desk. Ethan hadn't acted as if anything was amiss. He would know if something was going on between Lucas and Red. Kate was letting her imagination run wild.

Come on, Kate; get back to work. She moved the computer mouse, stopping the screen saver, and the article she'd been working on before lunch appeared. She'd already condensed the letter and needed to formulate an answer for Never a Bride in Albany, whose letter smacked of desperation.

Kate wrote a reply then reread it, editing as she went. The second letter she'd chosen was already succinct, but she edited it down and typed it into the document as well, then formulated her answer. When she was finished with the article, she stood and stretched. Of their own volition, her feet carried her to the street window.

Below, in the parking slot in front of the store, was the silver car. Her heart sank. She checked her watch. It had been an hour. What were Lucas and that woman doing downstairs? What if . . . ?

What if Lucas had been dating Red before they got married? Was it possible he was seeing someone on the side? Was it possible he was in love with the woman?

A space inside her hollowed out.

What do I care? Our marriage isn't real. We'll be divorced in less than ten months.

But the memory of their kiss kicked to the surface of her thoughts.

There is more than a contractual agreement between us.

The confession filled the pit of her stomach with something both pleasant and disturbing. She was relieved to finally admit actual feelings for Lucas were growing like tenacious weeds in a carefully cultivated garden. But like those weeds, the feelings were undesired. They didn't belong; their presence was a hindrance.

Kate's gaze centered on the silver car, and she bit the tender flesh inside her mouth. What possible reason could the woman have for being down there so long? Were they still in the back? Maybe Kate could go down under some pretense.

But what reason could she have? Her mind was a blank screen. She could almost see a skinny cursor blinking on the white space, taunting her.

It would be suspicious if she went down. She never interrupted

Lucas while he worked, and the last thing she wanted was to give him the pleasure of thinking she was curious about Red. Or worse, jealous.

If only she could hear what they were saying. Then she would know if anything—

She remembered something. The vents. Kate walked across the room to her old apartment, the sound of her heels muffled by the rug. The noise from the workshop carried through the heating ducts into her old living room. She remembered all the nights listening to Lucas's sander through the vents. She'd contemplated throttling him some evenings when she wanted peace after a day of listening to people's problems.

She walked to the vent against the back wall, where she kicked off her heels and squatted down, listening. Were they still in the workshop or had they gone back into the store? On the balls of her stocking feet, she balanced with a hand on the wall and stilled.

There were voices, barely audible. She heard the deep tones of Lucas's voice, but couldn't make out the words. Was that a woman's voice she heard now? She couldn't be sure. Kate set her knees on the floor by the register and leaned down further, pressing her palms to the dusty floor. There was nothing now, just silence.

No, there it was, a woman's voice, too quiet to make out.

She needed to get closer. Maybe then she could hear what they were saying.

Kate glanced down at her suit, weighing the dirty wood floor against the notion of letting her curiosity go unsatisfied. Then, with a sigh, she lowered herself to the floor, lying flat on her stomach. The suit was bound for the cleaners now.

As she bent her head, her thick metal earring clanged on the vent's louvered cover and she rose up enough to remove it, then set her ear against the cool metal surface.

There was a screech, like the sound of a chair against the concrete floor. Lucas was saying something. She stilled.

". . . that's what I thought."

Red spoke again, but Kate couldn't make it out. *Speak up, woman!*

It was quiet again, and Kate didn't even dare to swallow in case she missed something.

"What do you . . ." The rest of Lucas's words were muffled, like he'd turned away. Kate heard a creak and knew he'd leaned against his old metal desk.

". . . like the way . . . very nice . . . ." Kate didn't like her tone, even muffled through the ductwork.

The sound of heels clicking on the floor reached Kate's ears. Was the woman walking toward Lucas? Away from him? She didn't hear his footsteps, though his sandals were soft soled.

Then there was nothing but quiet from below. The silence unnerved her. What were they doing down there? Her imagination filled the gap. She imagined Red approaching Lucas, placing her long, slender fingers along the side of his neck. Was he wrapping his arms around the woman even now? Was he kissing her the way he'd kissed Kate the week before?

Heat prickled the back of her neck.

That's silly. If he were seeing someone else before he married me, he wouldn't have married me.

But that doesn't mean he isn't interested in the woman now.

Maybe he'd met her after they married and was pursuing the relationship. Did Kate really have any rights to him? Any say in what he did in the privacy of his own workshop?

He's married to me. Even if it is in name only, he owes me the respect of keeping his vows.

She had kept hers, after all. It wasn't her fault that Bryan called sometimes.

She sighed. Though now that the cramped stiletto was on the other foot, she realized it was unfair to take Bryan's calls. Lucas had been angry last time Bryan called. *"He has no right to call my house,"* he'd said. Maybe it was just caveman tactics that inspired the words, but followed so closely by those other words—the ones she'd repeated in her mind ever since—his anger took on a different meaning.

"What if I want you to stay?"

Had he meant it the way she thought? Did Lucas want their marriage to be real?

That's crazy. Although the notion held more appeal than was healthy for two individuals so incompatible, Lucas had never given any other indication he considered the marriage binding. Except, well, the fact that he'd kissed her. And boy, had he kissed her. Her stomach fluttered now just thinking about it. Maybe he did want more.

Yeah, Kate, that's why he's alone downstairs with that beautiful, leggy redhead.

And why is it so quiet down there? Kate pressed her ear on the vent and listened.

Love doesn't have to be complicated.

—Excerpt from
Finding Mr. Right-for-You
by Dr. Kate

Chapter Twenty

"It shouldn't be too long." Lucas opened the door for Sydney. "I'll call you when it's finished."

"Feel free to call before then if you have any questions." Sydney's smile indicated a call would be welcome, questions or not.

With nothing more than a polite nod, Lucas let the door close and wiped his hands on his jeans. He appreciated the business—she was giving him plenty—but the woman had the subtlety of a shark in a fish pool. He had little respect for a woman who ignored a man's wedding band. Did she even care that he belonged to someone else?

You're only a name on a wedding certificate, man.

His eyes wandered up the staircase to Kate's office. Would she mind if he interrupted her work? He hated to admit it, but he'd missed having lunch with her. Missed the way she wiped her lips after every bite. Missed the way she separated the food on her plate so nothing touched.

Mostly, he missed listening to her talk about her work. At first glance, some might think Kate's career was self-serving. But if they heard her talk about people—heard the excitement in her voice when she helped someone—they'd know differently.

It was quiet upstairs, not even the clacking of her computer keys. Maybe she was taking a break. Lucas took the stairs, glad for the opportunity to shake the cloying cloud of Sydney's perfume.

When he reached the second floor, her office chair was empty. A colorful screensaver danced on the computer, indicating she hadn't been typing for some time. Strange—he knew she was there; her car was out front.

He was about to call for her when he saw movement at the back of the building, through her old apartment doorway. He walked the length of the rug—and stopped. Beyond the coffee table, Kate lay flat as a mat on the floor. Her head faced the wall, ear to the floor—or was that the vent? One hand clutched the hair at her nape, pulling her cream-colored suit coat up at the waist. Her pants hugged the curve of her derrière, and the tops of her feet skimmed the floor.

What in the world? Why would she be lying over the—
Unless . . .

His lips curved into a smile as the wonder of it washed over him, cool and refreshing.

Oh yeah. This was going to be good.

Lucas leaned against the door frame, crossing his arms, biding his time. Finally, when she didn't budge, he cleared his throat.

Kate jumped, turned toward him, letting loose of her hair. The air must have kicked on because a blast blew a strand across her face.

"Looking for something?" He almost felt sorry for her as she scrambled into a sitting position. But the look on her face was too comical, and the feelings her jealousy inspired, too heartening.

"Lucas. I was just—" She dusted her suit coat, working her flattened fingers down the length of her arm in short swipes. "My earring." She held out a circular piece of jewelry lying in her palm. "I was getting my earring."

Who was she kidding? She'd been lying flat on the floor, her ear against the register. She was caught. Nailed. Busted.

"Did it fall down the vent?" He held back a smile, barely.

Her cheeks bloomed with color as she attempted to put the earring in. Even across the room he could see her hand shaking. "Of course not. It just—" Kate tried again to poke the earring through the hole and failed. She gave up and looked at him like a butterfly caught in a net.

He raised his brows, waiting.

At that, her shoulders drew back, her chin tipped. "All right, all right," she snapped. "You made your point."

Lucas approached her, feeling sorry for her now that she knew she was caught. Still, there was that whole jealousy thing that tugged the corners of his mouth.

Kate set her earring on the coffee table and struggled to stand. When he extended his hand, she smacked it away, her eyes narrowing as she straightened. Her crisp white shirt had come loose from her waistband, and her hair was tousled like she'd just awakened. She smoothed it and tucked it behind her ears with quick hands.

"I saw you after lunch with that . . . woman," Kate said. "I was worried about how it might look to other people." She crossed her arms over her chest. "We have an image to maintain, and it's not proper for you to be gallivanting all over the island with someone else."

Her words were so ridiculous he didn't know where to begin. *"Gallivanting?"*

She looked him in the eye. "You know what I mean. People will notice when you're eating with another woman. It's a small island—"

"I didn't eat with Sydney." Was that really what was bugging Kate? What everyone else thought? The notion sucked some of the air from his sails.

"Well, whatever. It's not proper for you to be seen with someone like that." Her lips, free of artificial color, pressed together.

Was she only concerned about her reputation, or was she hiding her jealousy behind its mask? "Someone like what?" he asked, curious to hear her answer.

"Someone like—You know what I mean. She isn't exactly unattractive, and she's . . . clingy."

"Clingy?"

"Like socks out of the dryer," she retorted. She tilted her head. "You know exactly what I mean."

Lucas lost the tug-of-war with his smile. "You're jealous," he said.

Kate turned away, tucking in her shirt before grabbing the earring off the table and walking toward a mirror that hung over the armchair. "I'm concerned about my reputation." She took the back off the earring and put it in.

"And that's why you were spying through the vent?" It didn't wash. If she were concerned about gossip, she would confront him, not eavesdrop.

Her eyes met his in the mirror. "I'm just trying to protect my career."

He walked closer until he was behind her. "Is that what you're telling yourself?"

Her hands fell slowly to her sides. In the light of the window to the side of the mirror, her eyes brightened to a caramel color. He wanted to get lost in there. Better yet, he wanted to climb behind those eyes and see what was holding her back.

Did she love Bryan still? He reviewed their kiss for the hundredth time and felt his confidence climb. A woman didn't kiss a man like that when she was in love with someone else. Maybe she'd never been in love with Bryan.

All Lucas knew was she had some kind of feelings for him.

"Why are you so afraid to be honest with yourself?" he asked.

Kate stared back. "I'm not afraid."

Her bravado seemed to have shrunk two sizes. He wanted to reach out and wrap his arms around her, pull her against him as he had on the sailboat. But he had a feeling he didn't dare move or she'd run.

"Why can't you admit you're jealous? It's not a crime." He found the courage to open up. Someone had to. "When Bryan called last week, I was jealous."

Something in her face softened. Her lips parted to speak. Then, as if she thought better of it, they sealed again.

Why was it so hard to admit something was happening between them? They had almost ten more months together. Would it hurt to explore the feelings?

"There's something here, and you know it," he said.

She blinked, her eyes fastened on his for just a split second before she walked away. "Stop it, Lucas. Leave things as they are." She stopped behind the barrier of the sofa.

Heaven forbid she let her guard down. "All neat and tidy, you mean?"

"What's wrong with neat and tidy? Neat and tidy is simple and clear-cut, and nobody gets hurt."

"Is that what's got you worried?" Was she still nursing wounds Bryan had inflicted? Couldn't she see he'd never forsake her as Bryan had? He always wanted to be there for her. To protect her. To cherish her. To love her.

"Nobody likes to get hurt."

He held the image of her on their wedding night. Remembered the sound of her sobbing in that big empty bed. "I'm not the one who left you at the altar," he said gently.

Kate wrapped her arms around her stomach. "Look, it just—It just won't work between us. We're too different. *Completely* incompatible, for heaven's sake. I've seen what happens too many times."

Did she think feelings were planned? Scheduled and carried out like entries on her color-coded calendar? "There's never been another you and me. You can't compare us to some couple you counseled in your office."

"I don't have to look any further than my parents to strike a comparison."

Something in her tone alerted him. "What about your parents?"

"They argued constantly. Good grief, they were like hot and cold, hard and soft, and whatever other opposites you can think of. I can still close my eyes at night and hear their bickering."

It was starting to make sense now. Her passion for helping others find a compatible mate. Her parents had divorced, possibly damaging her greatly, and now she was out to save the world. "Is that why you do it?"

"Do what?"

"Counsel others. Help people find their soul mate."

She rolled her eyes. "Huh. I don't believe in soul mates. I believe in helping women find a compatible mate whose values and personality line up with hers."

"All neat and tidy."

"We can't all live a messy, jumbled life."

Is that the way she saw his life? Like a chaotic heap of garbage?

"It might not be pretty to look at, but I found love nonetheless."

It was out before he could stop it. His heart skipped a beat.

The look on Kate's face made him glad he'd risked it. The way her eyes widened ever so slightly before she looked down at her fingers curled around the sofa's cushion. Was it awe or joy he'd seen before she looked away?

"I didn't mean to disregard what you had with Emily. I'm sorry."

Emily. She thought he was talking about Emily. The disappointment was keen. Hadn't he shown her his feelings these weeks they'd had together? Even if he hadn't said them. Apparently, he'd been too subtle. Or she just didn't want to see the truth.

She was waiting for his response. "Don't worry about it," he said, feeling like a fool. She didn't want anything between them; she'd made that clear. Maybe he wasn't the kind of man she wanted. Maybe she was waiting to be with Bryan.

For the first time he wondered if he'd ever be able to change her mind.

Don't expect your man to change.
If you want something different,
find it elsewhere.

—Excerpt from
Finding Mr. Right-for-You
by Dr. Kate

Chapter Twenty-One

The phone on Kate's desk rang. She saved her column before answering.

"How's my favorite author?" Pam, Kate's publicist, greeted her.

"Pam! How are you?"

"Good, good. I wanted to update you on a few interviews I've scheduled. I e-mailed them to you a minute ago, but I have a last-minute opportunity, so I wanted to see if you were available. My contact from *Live with Lisa* called a few minutes ago, and they want to interview you tomorrow morning. They probably had a cancellation, and it's a fabulous opportunity for exposure on cable TV."

An interview on the popular program would be a boon. "That's great. Let me check my schedule." Kate pulled out her calendar. There were a couple appointments, but nothing that couldn't be rescheduled. She was almost finished with her column and her *Glamour* piece.

"I can do it."

"They intimated that Lucas would be welcome if he'd like to take part," Pam said.

Kate doubted he would but said she'd mention it to him and get back to Pam.

The discussion turned to the other radio interviews scheduled for several weeks out.

"Is *Mr. Right* doing okay saleswise?" Kate asked. Rosewood had hoped it would make the *New York Times* list, but so far it had only appeared deep on the *USA Today* list. She was afraid they were disappointed with sales, and this far out from the release, it wasn't likely to improve much, although an appearance on *Live with Lisa* wouldn't hurt.

"The book's fine. I know Chloe is eager for a new proposal."

"I'm working on an idea. Once I have it nailed down, I'll send it."

After Kate hung up, she closed her document and gathered her things. She had to get home and pack because her flight would leave that evening. Unless Lucas agreed to participate, they'd be apart another night, but what would it matter? It seemed as if they were on two different planets since their confrontation in her office nearly a month earlier.

❦

"You didn't have to take me, you know." She almost wished he hadn't, since he'd dawdled around for fifteen minutes—after she'd rushed to pack and stowed her suitcase in the car. Now she was arriving later than she'd planned.

Kate grabbed for her suitcase handle, but Lucas reached it first. They walked toward the airport.

"I don't mind."

Her heels clicked against the pavement. After hurrying with the packing, Kate felt as if she'd forgotten something. She mentally checked off the necessary items to assure herself.

After she'd gotten off the phone with Pam, she'd gone to Lucas's shop and told him about the interview.

"They'd like to have us both on, if you'd like to participate," Kate said.

He'd lowered a tool, his eyes widening. The cliché of deer in headlights came to mind.

"Don't think so," he said before picking up a rag and wiping down a chest of drawers with a honey-colored stain.

"Why not? It might be fun." And good for the public to see them together.

He gave the bureau one last swipe and stood back, looking it over. "Talking's not my thing." He set the cloth on the plywood table. "Words don't come easy to me, like they do you."

The more she thought about it, the more she wanted him there with her. Maybe getting off the island, away from the grind of life, would break the stalemate they'd had between them the past month. Ironically, she'd thought she'd wanted distance between them. But now that she had it, she was lonely.

"I'll fill in the gaps," Kate said. "You wouldn't have a thing to worry about."

"I can't."

Did he have work that couldn't be put off? Or maybe he just wanted a break from her.

"Look, something happened when I was a kid. I was supposed

to give a speech in front of my school. In a school assembly." He picked up the rag and twisted it in his stained fingers. "I froze. Forgot everything I was going to say." He wiped the top of the bureau again. "I haven't talked in front of an audience since."

Now, as he walked her to security, she imagined Lucas as a frightened little boy, paralyzed in front of his peers. He seemed so far removed from that little boy, so strong and capable. But she remembered his one request when he agreed to marry her: *"No interviews."* It must've been hard enough for him to be in the spotlight as he had. But he'd done it for her.

And his parents, she reminded herself.

As they approached the security officer, Kate remembered the first time he'd brought her here. Dahlia Stevens had been in line, and he'd kissed her good-bye. Today no one waited in security, and Kate noted the edge of disappointment that pricked her heart.

What is wrong with you, Kate?

What's wrong? I want him to go with me. Want him to kiss me. That's what's wrong.

Lucas handed Kate the overnight case before they reached the balding security officer. "Kate . . ."

She checked her watch before meeting his gaze.

He shifted his weight. "When you get back, we need to talk."

Something hardened in her stomach, gelling into a thick lump. She hated when people did that. Now, the whole time she was gone, she'd wonder what he wanted. The sudden fear that he wanted to end their arrangement left her speechless. What if he was tired of pretending? Tired of the awkward silence between them these last few weeks? She wanted to say she was sorry, but sorry for what?

"Is something wrong?" she asked instead.

Lucas waved her off. "Nothing to worry about." He looked at her as if studying her features. She'd only be gone one night. *What's going on?*

He reached out and rubbed her chin with his thumb.

Kate stilled at his touch, feeling the roughness of his thumb all the way to her toes.

"You had a little something right there," he said.

She remembered the globby grape jelly on toast she'd scarfed down on the way out the door and ran her finger over the spot, rubbing away the feeling his touch had left behind.

He scanned the area around them. Was he remembering Dahlia and wishing for an audience? The airport was quiet as a sepulchre tonight. *Where's the media when you need them?*

Kate wanted to run her fingers along the rough surface of his stubbly jaw. What would he think of that? Would he kiss her then, if she took the first step?

Lucas caught her staring. She was loath to leave him for a night. How had she gotten so accustomed to his company? She remembered how he'd irritated her when he was just her superintendent. How had he found a way through the cracks in her heart? How had she come to expect his presence, depend on it?

He cleared his throat and pocketed his hands. "Well. Have a safe trip."

Kate blinked and looked away, hiking the weighty bag on her shoulder. "Thanks."

When he walked away, Kate realized her feelings for Lucas were rising dangerously high, like floodwaters on the banks of an unprotected shore.

Three cups of coffee and Kate was finally awake. She sat opposite the interviewer, Lisa Evans. A mike had been placed inconspicuously on the collar of her red Donna Karan blazer. The makeup people had done a good job, but the foundation was heavy and felt like it was melting under the hot lights.

The producer gave last-minute instructions, but Kate had heard most of it before. She settled back in the chair and waited while they opened the show with news on the other side of the studio. A copy of *Mr. Right* was propped on the glass cube between them.

Lisa, in a robin's-egg blue suit, reviewed her notes, making no conversation. That was typical. Interviewers liked to save it for the show.

When it was time for their segment, they were cued, and Lisa straightened, smiling toward the camera.

"This morning we have syndicated dating-advice columnist and noted author Dr. Kate. Welcome."

Kate smiled. "Thank you for having me."

"I have to say I read your recent release, *Finding Mr. Right-for-You* and was riveted." Lisa's eyebrows inched up into her blonde bangs.

"Thanks, Lisa. There's a lot of interest lately in compatibility in dating and marriage."

"Which begs the question," Lisa said. "There are numerous Web sites and books on the subject. What makes yours different?"

"Good question. In my counseling with couples, I've found the key ingredient to a lasting relationship to be compatibility. So many times we women get our hearts way ahead of the game. In the book, I teach women to put their hearts on hold long enough to establish compatibility."

"Is that what you did with your Mr. Right?" Lisa tilted her head.

The personal question caught Kate off guard. "Of course. You really can't make a rational decision about someone's suitability when your emotions are clouding your judgment."

Lisa nodded. "We know how emotions can affect good judgment."

Lisa asked several more questions about the book; then they opened the line for callers.

"Stephanie from Boston, you're on the air." Lisa said.

"I have a question for Dr. Kate," the caller said.

"Go ahead." Lisa smiled, her berry lip gloss shimmering under the lights.

"I'd like to know why she married someone else when her real fiancé dumped her on their wedding day."

What? The malicious tone, the ugly words, sent a wave of fear through Kate. She smiled through it. *What was the caller's name?* Had Lisa said Stephanie?

"Dr. Kate?" Lisa asked, clearly confused. "I'm not sure what the caller's referring to."

"I'm not sure either . . ." *Hang up. Disconnect the caller.* Her eyes pleaded with Lisa.

"Her real fiancé was Bryan Montgomery," the voice on the line continued. "And he dumped her the morning of the wedding. I'm not sure where Dr. Kate found her fake groom, but the wedding was phony, and so is she."

This isn't happening. Kate's thoughts seized in a paralyzing spasm. She fought to control her expression. The camera was on her. What could she say? Her mind was a numb void. *Say something. Anything.*

"Dr. Kate?"

Her head buzzed with electrical activity, all of it sparking nothing.

No clever turn of phrase. No smooth transition of subject. The seconds stretched out like a long empty runway.

"My marriage is not fake." She forced a calm tone. "It's legal in every way." *Change the subject!* "The advice in my book comes from years of extensive counseling and research. I have a passion for helping women find suitable partners, and that's what this book is about."

The producer was cuing a commercial. Sure, just as soon as Kate had found her tongue.

But Lisa was ending the segment. When they were off the air, she reached over and placed her hand on Kate's. "I'm so sorry about that, Kate. I assure you it was as unexpected for me as it was for you."

Kate stood on shaking legs as someone disengaged her mike and battery pack. She had to get out of there. She wanted to run someplace far away and hide.

Regret is a bitter friend.

—Excerpt from
Finding Mr. Right-for-You
by Dr. Kate

Chapter Twenty-Two

The same plump woman who'd escorted Kate around the studio since her arrival accompanied her to the green room, where Kate collected her things. Her mind spun, but she feigned a smile and followed the woman to the car that waited at the curb.

Once in the luxury vehicle, she told the driver she was going to the airport. He pulled away.

What now? What should I do? Everyone knows.

Rosewood was going to be turned on its head! She reached for her cell phone and turned it on. She'd missed three calls. Kate didn't stop to listen to the messages. She had to call Pam. They needed damage control. But how could they control damage that was already done? It was live TV, and every viewer watching this morning had heard she was a fraud.

She punched in Pam's cell number. The driver had a talk radio program on in front, so she could talk quietly without being overheard.

Pam picked up on the first ring. "Kate! That was just awful."

"It was Stephanie. The woman Bryan left me for." The shock was wearing thin, revealing a layer of anger beneath.

"I know. I saw the whole thing. This is not good. Not good at all."

"What are we going to do? Did Chloe see it?" Kate's editor might know about her marriage, but she would have to explain it to her boss, who didn't know. *Have I jeopardized Chloe's and Pam's jobs?*

"She called me after the segment. She's pretty upset," Pam said. "Listen, we need to figure out how to handle this. There's going to be a lot of media wanting an interview with you now."

"Sure, there will, but I can't do that, Pam." The idea of exposing herself to that kind of spectacle was unthinkable. *How can I defend myself when it's true?*

"You need to do whatever Paul says." Pam's tone chided, reminding Kate that Chloe's boss was in for a rude awakening. "It's the least you can do at this point."

Of course Pam was angry with her. Chloe would be too, and Kate didn't blame either of them. Rosewood would come off like frauds, same as Kate. Everyone who'd known the truth would pay a price.

Lucas. She closed her eyes and let her head fall against the firm leather headrest. He'd watched the interview; she was certain of that. What was he thinking now? Thank goodness he hadn't come along for the interview. But how would this affect him? How would it affect his family?

What have I done?

"This is bad, Kate. The media will make this into a huge scandal, and we'll have to fight our way through it."

It was a career-busting scandal. Who would want her advice now that she'd proven herself a hypocrite by marrying her complete opposite, a virtual stranger? It would kill sales on her book. And she could probably kiss the *Glamour* and syndicated columns good-bye. How could she face Rosewood after disappointing them so? How could she face her faithful readers?

"I suggest you call Chloe and offer to break the news to Paul. She probably won't let you, but—"

"I will. I'll do that. What else can I do?"

"Don't talk to anybody. You might be getting calls, or worse. Let us get a game plan together before you say anything publicly."

No need to worry about that. All she wanted to do was crawl into a hole and have someone fill it with dirt. "All right. Calling Chloe now."

"Good luck." The sarcastic tone wasn't lost on Kate.

She punched in her editor's cell number, seeing the calls she'd missed on the screen and thinking about Lucas again.

Chloe answered immediately. Her tone was basted in stress. "Kate." She swore. "I guess you know the spot this puts me in."

"I'm so sorry, Chloe. I'll take complete responsibility." And she should, as it was entirely her fault. "Let me call Paul and tell him. He needn't know you were involved."

Chloe raised her voice. "You don't think he's going to ask me if I knew? I'm not going to lie, Kate."

Kate rubbed her forehead. *Why did I do it? If I could only go back and do the day over.* She should have done the honest thing and admitted to the media that the engagement was broken. But how could she have done that at the release of her book? Rosewood would have paid the cost for her personal crisis.

They were paying now anyway. A higher price than before.

"I know. I know, Chloe. Tell me what I can do." She waited, sure Chloe was doing her deep yoga breaths. There weren't enough yoga classes in the world to help ease this kind of stress.

"Just give me time to think. I'll tell Paul when we get off the phone and get back with you. Just—just go home and hole up until you hear from me." She huffed. "You know this is going to be all over the news by tonight. The papers, the news—it's going to be everywhere."

Kate had been hoping it might quietly blow over, but she knew that kind of optimism was unjustified.

Chloe ended the call, and Kate thought again about calling Lucas. She decided to listen to the voice mails first.

The first two were Pam and Chloe. Lucas's was the third. She listened to the familiar deep tone, closing her eyes and wishing he were beside her in the car.

"Kate? Are you all right? I saw the interview." A long pause followed. "I'm just—Call me, okay?" There was another long pause, like he wanted to say something else, before the click came.

Kate exited voice mail. It wasn't lost on her that Lucas was the only one of her messages that sounded remotely sympathetic. He, who had more personally at stake than anyone.

She still had a while before they reached the airport. She checked her watch and punched in their home number. Lucas answered quickly.

"It's me," she said.

"Kate." He breathed her name like he'd been holding his breath waiting for her call. "Are you okay?"

"I'm fine." *So much for honesty.* "Well. Fine as I can be given that my whole career came crashing down around my feet this morning. On national television." Her throat stopped up and her eyes burned. *Not now. Buck up until you're home at least. You still have to face a two-*

hour wait at the airport, and it won't help matters if you're seen crying in public.

"It's gonna be okay." He was only trying to help—she knew that—but they were trite words. Trite and untrue.

"It's not going to be okay, Lucas. The jobs of my editor and publicist are in jeopardy because of me, Rosewood is going to drop me like a rotten apple, and my readers are going to turn on me. What's okay about that?"

Kate rubbed her temple, frustration choking further words.

"I'm sorry, honey."

Now she felt like a slug. It wasn't his fault. He was a victim in this nutty escapade—her short trip down Insanity Boulevard. He wasn't guilty of anything but trying to help her.

She sighed. "It's not your fault. It's all mine." She beat the back of her head against the seat. "How could I have done something so stupid? I don't do foolish, impetuous things, like marry a man last minute."

"You were backed into a corner. Give yourself a break, Katie. We'll get through this."

His soft tone broke her. Kate felt tears welling, and she blinked them away. She had to get off the phone before she lost it. She had a feeling once she did, she wasn't going to come up for air for a while. "I have to go. I'll talk to you when I get home, okay?"

By the time she hung up, they were nearly to the airport. She'd have to call her agent, Ronald, while she waited for her flight. And her dad.

Lucas's words echoed in her head. *"We'll get through this."* But there was no "we" now. No need for them to remain together. No reason for their marriage. Because come tonight, everyone would know their marriage—and Kate herself—was nothing but a fraud.

When problems arise, face them head-on. Every relationship has conflict. It's how you handle it that matters.

—Excerpt from *Finding Mr. Right-for-You* by Dr. Kate

Chapter Twenty-Three

Lucas arrived at the airport, not merely on time, but early. He waited for Kate in a sling-back chair, his elbows propped on his knees. Their phone conversation haunted him. Her tone, so lost and broken, begged him to fix the mess. But there was no easy fix this time. The problem was too big, too overwhelming.

Guilt clung to him like grains of sand on wet skin. The marriage had been his idea. He'd practically talked her into it. He'd only been trying to help. He'd done it out of love, but look what happened. He'd hurt her instead.

When the time came for her flight's arrival, he watched for her. How would she react to him? How did this change their relationship? And he had no doubt it would change their relationship. Lucas regretted wasting the past month. He should have been winning Kate over, showing her his love. Instead he'd given her space.

Well, he was out of time now. Pretense had been the glue that held their marriage together and there was no need for it now.

Kate has feelings for me. I know she does. Maybe it was wishful thinking, but he was sure he'd caught her watching him lately with a certain look in her eyes. And there was no denying the passion of the kiss they'd shared or the jealousy in her eyes when he'd caught her spying on him and Sydney. Was it too much to hope that she might open her heart to him?

Kate appeared down the corridor, and he stood. She walked with her chin up, shoulders back. To anyone else she was the picture of a composed businesswoman in her stylish gray pantsuit. Her hair swung saucily with each step, and her eyes focused on a point straight ahead.

It was only then that he noticed another man walking toward Kate with a pad and pencil in hand. Lucas recognized him as Herb Owens, a reporter for the *Mirror*, and he made a beeline for Kate.

"Dr. Kate, I'm Herbert Owens from the *Mirror*. Would you like to make a comment concerning the allegations—"

"No comment." Kate's mouth pressed together as she looked away, quickening her steps.

Herb began walking toward her, then met Lucas's glare and slowed his steps.

Lucas knew when Kate saw him because her rigid features relaxed the slightest bit, her mouth decompressing, her eyes softening. The fact that his presence had that effect on her buoyed Lucas. He grabbed onto the notion, blew it up like an inflatable raft and took a ride on it.

Get a grip, he told himself. *She's probably just relieved to see a friendly face.* Who knew what she'd faced on the way home.

How should he greet her? They had an audience, but would she want him to keep up the charade? Was it a charade anymore? But as she neared, Lucas forgot about pretense. Kate's eyes looked weary, her face strained. He wanted to ease her worry, soothe it away with a touch.

Lucas took her bag, then set his palm alongside her face, making eye contact. He leaned close and pressed a kiss to her lips. His only thought was to comfort her.

She gripped his arm like it was a life preserver, returning the brief kiss.

When he pulled back, he draped his arm over her shoulder. "Let's get you home." He looked over her shoulder where Herb stood against the wall, watching.

By the time they reached the car, Kate had grown distant, remote. Did she think his kiss was for show? The ride to the house was quiet. Kate, her hands clutched together in her lap, her feet crossed at the ankles, seemed lost in thought. She stared out the window instead of facing him. Lucas felt her slipping away more each second.

"What can I do?" He asked, desperate to help, desperate to keep her.

There was a long pause, and he wondered if she'd heard him through the chaos of her own thoughts.

He braked at a stop sign, then accelerated. Was she shutting him out already? Hadn't they become more than just business partners? They'd shared a life these past three months. A life that meant everything to him.

"There's nothing we can do but wait," she said, still looking out the window where the glaring sun cut harsh shadows across the ground. "And hope the rest of the media won't hop on board and make it into the scandal of the year."

Even so, the news was out. Lucas didn't know much about publishing, only the little bit he'd gleaned from Kate, but it seemed her publisher wouldn't be interested in promoting her career after a scandal. Her readers wouldn't be too keen on her either. It didn't seem fair to crucify her for one decision. Bryan was the one who'd dumped this mess in her lap. Where was he now, when the chips were falling?

Lucas pulled into the drive and turned off the truck. When Kate didn't make a move to exit, he faced her, propping his knee on the cracked vinyl seat between them.

"We have to tell your family." Kate looked over the hill to where his parent's rooftop peeked above the sea oats.

"I already did." His dad had watched the segment. Lucas had gone over and told the rest of them in person.

Kate faced him. "I'm sorry I wasn't here. How did they respond?" Her forehead wrinkled, her eyes puppy-dog sad.

His mom had been angry at first, then seemed to realize she'd proven herself right. *"Kate's just like her mom, Lucas,"* she'd said. *"You're better off without her."* Of course, it was no surprise to Jamie, but Brody was hurt. His dad tried to be understanding, but Lucas could tell by the way he avoided Lucas's eyes that he was disappointed.

"My family will be fine," he said. "Don't worry about them."

A few quiet moments later, she exited the truck. Lucas followed her inside and set the bag in the bedroom. Bo, excited to see Kate, rubbed against her leg and shepherded her into the kitchen, where she started a pot of coffee.

"I feel like I've been run over by a city bus," Kate said.

Lucas pulled two mugs from the cabinet and the creamer from the fridge. "No wonder. What did the people at Rosewood say?"

Kate scooped grinds into the filter. "Right now they just want me to sit tight. I think a lot depends on how widespread this becomes."

Could they go on as if nothing happened? Would the readers who saw the interview conclude that it was an unfounded rumor? Apparently there was nothing they could do but wait and see. It had been so easy to step in and save Kate when her wedding plans had fallen apart. Now, all he could do was wait with her, and that was a notion that didn't set well.

⬧

Kate pulled her knees close, letting her toes dig through the hot surface of the sand to the cooler layer beneath. In the distance, the ferry horn sounded, announcing its arrival to the island. After stalling as long as she could, she'd called her dad and told him about the interview. She could hear his shock in the silence that drew out over the lines. It pulled her spirits even lower.

"Oh boy, Kate," he'd said when he'd found words.

She'd never done anything so careless and never planned to again. How could someone who planned every facet of her life have taken this reckless road?

Once her dad had a moment to think, he begged her to come for a visit. *"Come to Maryland, just to get away for a while. You'll have time to think here. Time to plan your future. Maybe you can open an office in the city."* It was a tempting offer and one she'd give some thought to once she heard from Chloe.

After they'd returned from the airport, Lucas seemed to sense her need for space and had gone back to his shop. But now, as the sun seemed to still in the sky, Kate wished for a distraction.

She'd already finished her column and didn't want to be near the TV after watching it half the afternoon. Two cable news shows had mentioned the scandal, saying they were looking into the allegations. With a scorned woman like Stephanie on the loose, they wouldn't have to look far.

Her cell phone rang incessantly, but she didn't answer the calls.

Two reporters had had the nerve to show up on their doorstep, but she hadn't answered, and eventually they'd gone away.

She'd wait and see if the afternoon papers picked up the story. She imagined that's what Chloe was waiting for. Would the *Mirror* pick up the story? The thought of the locals knowing the truth was enough to put a lump in her throat. They knew her here not as Dr. Kate, but as a friend and neighbor. She ate and shopped and worked among these people. They would feel betrayed when they found out. And Lucas's family, natives of the island, would be center stage.

My life is spinning out of control, and I'm helpless to stop it. It was the same feeling she'd had as a child. Never knowing what to expect or what to feel because she had no control over it.

She pulled her legs closer, set her chin on her knees, and rocked in the sand.

❧

Kate waited to hear from Chloe the rest of the day, but no call came. What was her editor waiting for? The morning papers? She slept restlessly that night. Beside her, Lucas seemed to sleep peacefully, his breaths deep and even in the darkened room.

She hadn't heard a peep from his family. Maybe Lucas had asked them to give her space. Maybe they were relieved she wasn't really part of the family. His mom was probably thrilled.

How were they treating Lucas? Were his dad and Brody angry at him for the deception?

Just when Kate thought it couldn't get any worse, she remembered his parents' marriage. She sighed, regret filling the hole in her gut. *I didn't do a thing to help—haven't kept my end of the bargain at all. Lucas married me for nothing—except all the grief he's getting.*

It's not like Susan wanted your help.

Maybe not, but Lucas kept his part of the deal, and I let him down.

You didn't exactly have the twelve months you expected. You're not a miracle worker.

If only I'd had more time.

Kate faced the wall, turning quietly so as not to disturb Lucas.

Why didn't Chloe call back? Were she and Paul and Pam deciding how to handle things, or was she so angry, she was making Kate suffer? Because that's exactly what Kate was doing: suffering. The waiting was killing her. She couldn't plan her next move until someone told her what to do.

Kate felt the bed shift as Lucas moved. Then she felt his arm settle around the curve of her waist, felt the warmth of his stomach against her back.

He pressed a kiss on the top of her head. Kate's heart sped. In his arms she felt safe and loved—cherished. Like her world wasn't a whirling top, spinning toward the edge of a table. She wanted to sink into his weight and let him be her shelter from the storm. But she was unaccustomed to counting on anyone other than herself. The very thought of sharing her burden made her anxious. *How do I know I can count on him? What if he fails me?*

And why was he holding her? *What is it he wants from me?*

She lay still, tense, waiting. He'd played his part of the game, met his end of the bargain. If anything, he should be angry with her too. Angry, like everyone else.

As moments passed and Lucas made no further move, Kate felt her body slowly sink into the hardness of his stomach. *Just for tonight. It doesn't mean I'm turning over control.* She closed her eyes again. Kate knew she shouldn't let herself find comfort in his arms, but she was too tired to fight the urge.

Healthy couples can weather brutal storms and come out stronger on the other side. This is how relationships grow and deepen.

—Excerpt from
Finding Mr. Right-for-You
by Dr. Kate

Chapter Twenty-Four

The shrill of the phone pulled Kate from slumber. She stirred, orienting herself, then crawled across Lucas's empty side of the bed. The events of the day before crashed in on her like a tidal wave. *It must be Chloe.* She cleared her throat before answering.

A male voice greeted her. "Hi, kiddo. How are you holding up?" It was her agent.

She sat up in bed and looked at the clock. Seven forty-two. "Ronald. I'm doing as well as can be expected." Given that her career was on the line. She'd fallen asleep somewhere around three o'clock, when the rain had started, and had slept fitfully. Thunder cracked outside.

"I haven't heard from Chloe yet." Kate had told Ronald she'd call when she heard something. He must've thought she'd forgotten.

"Actually, Chloe called me this morning," he said.

If Chloe was using her agent as a go-between, her editor was distancing herself from Kate. Not a good sign. "You have bad news."

"I'm afraid so, Kate. It hit the papers this morning."

Her throat constricted. She rubbed the sleep from her eyes and braced herself for the news. "Which ones?"

"*New York Times, Washington Post, Chicago Tribune, LA Times.* The Associated Press picked it up. I'm afraid it's everywhere. Mainly in the entertainment section, from what I can see."

Entertainment. Like her life was a circus meant for the public's amusement. The worst had happened. *I'm a laughingstock. A fraud.* The letters from her disappointed readers would pour in. She'd disappointed so many people. The weight of it dragged her under the choppy water, and she fought for breath.

"Paul and Chloe scheduled a conference call with us at noon to discuss how to handle the media. They'll want your story in detail to determine if there's any way to spin this in a positive light."

"Of course." She didn't see how. For the life of her, Kate couldn't see how they could control the damage. It was all true. She was an expert on finding Mr. Right, and she'd impulsively entered a loveless marriage. A marriage with no real feelings.

That's not true, Kate, and you know it.

All right, maybe she did have feelings for Lucas now, but she didn't have them when they'd married.

"They'll call you on your home phone, and I'll be there too," Ronald said.

"What about my column? What about *Glamour*? Do you think—" She was afraid to pose the question, but she had to know. She pulled at a loose thread on the quilt and balled the string between her fingers.

"I wasn't going to say anything; you've got enough on your plate right now. But *Glamour* has asked you to step down for the time being. Maybe when this blows over . . ."

But even when it blew over, Kate knew the damage left behind would be irreparable. "I'm guessing the syndicated column is in jeopardy too?"

The silence on the other end spoke for itself.

Kate felt her throat closing, her eyes burning. *I can't believe this is happening. How have I fallen so far? So hard?* She was on the verge of losing control of her emotions. She cleared her throat again, hoping for a space to open up. "Listen, I've got to go. I'll talk to you at noon."

After they hung up, she set the phone on the nightstand. In the other room, she heard her cell phone ringing. She'd forgotten to turn it off. She couldn't talk to anyone. She wanted to pull the covers over her head and pretend none of this had happened.

But what good would that do?

Come on, Kate. Buck up. Get out of bed and figure a way out of this hole you're in.

That's what she would do. She had four and half hours to find a way to spin this to the good for Rosewood. Four and half hours to develop a plan.

Kate jumped out of bed, took a quick shower, then dressed. Realizing she detected the robust aroma of brewed coffee, she entered the kitchen, Bo on her heels. A note, scribbled on the back of the utilities bill sat beside the coffeepot.

KATE,
WENT OUT FOR A WHILE.
BE BACK SOON.
L

Where had he gone so early in the morning? It was pouring buckets outside. Maybe he really was having an affair with Red. Maybe he'd gone out to meet her. Maybe he realized the marriage was over now.

She'd no sooner finished the thought when she heard the door open. By the time Lucas appeared, she'd poured herself a mug of hot coffee and added cream.

"Morning." His voice was deep and groggy, a welcome sound. Even the stubble on his jawbone had grown on her.

"Morning," she replied. His navy T-shirt was plastered to his shoulders, and his hair was spiky-wet and tousled from the rain. Or maybe someone had run her hands through it.

She wasn't going to ask where he'd been. It really wasn't her business anyway.

"Don't suppose you heard from your editor," he said.

"My agent called. We have a conference call with the people from Rosewood at noon. The news has hit the press in a big way."

Kate realized this was bad for Lucas. It was his life they were talking about too. Everyone would wonder why he'd stepped in last minute, and he could hardly admit it was because of his parents' souring relationship. She'd put him in a tight spot.

"I saw the papers." He poured himself a cup of coffee and let Bo out the back door.

"Is that why you went out?" She didn't mean to ask.

"I was hoping to bring back good news." He tucked his hands in his pockets.

Kate pulled her laptop from her case and flipped it open. She still had—she checked her watch—almost four hours to come up with an idea. Something that would make the media back off or at least soften the blow.

"Do you have any of the papers?" Kate asked. "I need to see what I'm up against." She pushed the On button and tapped her fingers, waiting for it to boot.

"I left them in the truck." He shifted his weight. "What's the plan?"

Kate plugged her laptop into the outlet under the table. "My plan is to come up with a plan. I need some ideas for my publisher, some way of spinning this so they, at least, don't come off smelling like a pig."

Kate opened the word processor, and a blank document appeared on the screen.

"I'll be right back." Lucas left the room.

There wasn't much Kate could do until she knew what the media was saying. Maybe it was only hearsay, her word against Stephanie's. Though Kate hadn't exactly defended herself on TV. She'd only tried to change the subject. People would see right through that.

When Lucas returned, he carried a thick stack of damp newspapers. He set them beside the laptop and sat across from her. "Sure you want to do this?" His was the look of someone who'd already read the articles.

"Everyone else is going to know what they say; *I* may as well."

The kitchen light was off and the storm outside darkened the room, but there was enough light to read by. She'd start with the Nantucket paper. The *Inquirer* and *Mirror* had tried to call the day before, but she hadn't answered. The paper was already opened to the article. Kate unfolded it and read.

"Famous Local Advice Columnist Jilted at Altar"
In a TV interview on *Live with Lisa*, local resident and famous author Dr. Kate was accused by a call-in listener of marrying a stand-in groom. The caller, who identified herself as Stephanie from

Boston, claimed Dr. Kate's original fiancé, Bryan Montgomery, broke the engagement on the morning of their wedding. A marriage license bearing the names of Montgomery and Dr. Kate was found on record, substantiating the woman's claim. Neither Montgomery nor Dr. Kate could be reached for a comment.

Dr. Kate and local furniture maker Lucas Wright were wed on June 21, the same day as the release of Dr Kate's first book *Finding Mr. Right-for-You*. It is unclear how Wright came to be the stand-in groom.

"I should have tried to eradicate the evidence," Kate said. "I didn't think about the marriage license." Kate set the paper down and sighed. "I'm sorry they mentioned your name. I was hoping at least the local papers . . ." *Who am I kidding? It's not like everyone on the island doesn't already know Lucas is married to me. Now they just know it's a sham.*

"Which one has the Associated Press article?" She riffled through the papers.

Lucas pulled one from the stack and laid it open to the article.

Kate read the headline. "Dr. Kate's Mr. Wright is Mr. Wrong."

"Clever," Kate said, sarcasm oozing from a deeply wounded spot. The article read much like the local one; only the journalist had scored an interview with Stephanie. They cited the marriage certificate as well.

"This isn't good," Kate said, setting the paper down. "I didn't realize they'd find proof so quickly. I hope Pam hadn't planned to deny it, because there's no way I can do that now."

Kate glanced at her watch. She had to think. There must be a way to make this better. She shoved the papers to the other side of the table.

"Let's think this through," Lucas said. "Maybe we can come up with something if we put our heads together." He leaned on the tabletop, his bulky forearms planted squarely in front of him.

Kate didn't want to hurt his feelings, but she was done with depending on someone else for help. She worked better alone. "If you don't mind, I think I need to do this on my own. I need to focus, because I have less than four hours."

He shrugged and gave that half smile that charmed her. "We pulled off a wedding in barely under that."

She smiled wryly. "Seems to me that's what got us into this mess to begin with."

By the time the phone rang at noon, Kate had all her notes on the screen. Lucas was somewhere else in the house. She'd been lost in her own thoughts since he'd left the table four hours earlier, and she hadn't seen him since.

Kate answered the phone.

"Hello, Kate. It's Chloe. Pam, Paul, and Ronald are already on the line."

"Hi, everyone," Kate said.

Their greetings were less than enthusiastic. Hopefully, they'd agree to what Kate had come up with as the best approach.

Lucas entered the room and leaned against the doorway as she opened the conversation.

"Can I just say something first? I want to tell you how sincerely sorry I am for the trouble this is causing. It was never my intention to damage your businesses or careers, and I'm deeply sorry." Kate hoped her tone expressed the depth of her regret. "I'll do anything I can to help rectify this."

"Fair enough," Paul said. "The damage is done now, and we need to figure out how to proceed. Kate, if we could hear what happened, in your words, that might help."

Kate took a deep breath and told the story of her wedding morning: Bryan's phone call, Pam's news of the *Dr. Phil* show invitation, Lucas's offer.

Chloe stopped her there. "You said Lucas was only an acquaintance. Why did he offer to take Bryan's place?"

Kate stopped pacing, her eyes fastened on Lucas's. Could she tell them about Lucas's parents? She wasn't going to hang him out to dry again.

"I agreed to help him on a personal project. That part of the story really has no bearing on this."

"Tell us the rest of the story," Paul said.

Kate finished, explaining the temporary nature of the agreement. "I've done a lot of thinking this morning, and I think our best bet is for me to face up to what I've done publicly. I'm genuinely sorry, and I think once my readers see I was jilted at the altar and made a poor quick judgment, they'll be generous with their grace."

"Let's not overlook the fact," Ronald said, "that any publicity is good publicity. It's quite possible the scandal could increase Kate's sales. It's happened before with other books."

Kate stopped at the back window. Now that was the best news she'd heard in a while. Was it possible this might turn out well for her publisher?

"Keep in mind," Pam said, "that Kate's book is a self-help book, not a novel or a memoir. Her readers are willing to plunk down their money because they trust her advice. That trust has been broken. She might be seen as hypocritical since she advised her readers one direction and took an entirely different direction herself."

Kate jumped in. "That's why I should apologize, offer an explanation. I think my readers would sympathize with the fact that I was jilted at the altar. What woman wouldn't be confused and prone to bad judgment at that point?"

"The fact is, though," Paul said, "you aren't every woman. You are Dr. Kate, expert in love relationships. Your whole book is about finding a marriage partner for a lifelong relationship, and you've entered a loveless marriage on a one-year lease. I'm not going to sugarcoat it, Kate. The media sure isn't."

Kate felt heat flush her neck and cheeks. That was as close to a dressing down as she'd received since her dad scolded her for loaning out her Nikes when she was in fourth grade.

"We need time to digest this," Paul continued. "We'll get hold of you later today and let you know what we've decided. Until then, don't answer your phone."

By the time they disconnected, Kate felt wrung out. More waiting. *I'm tired of waiting. I want to do something.* She leaned against the windowsill. Outside, the landscape looked gray through the blanket of rain.

"How'd it go?" Lucas asked.

Kate shrugged. "They're going to decide how they want to handle it. They'll call back later today. I don't think they were too keen on my honesty plan."

Kate didn't think they were too keen on her either, and she didn't blame them.

Hope is not a strategy.

—Excerpt from
Finding Mr. Right-for-You
by Dr. Kate

Chapter Twenty-Five

Kate searched for ways to stay occupied as she awaited Paul's call. She filled the sink with soapy water and washed dishes. She wiped down the counters and table. When she was finished, she decided the linoleum needed a good scrubbing. Lucas worked on a design for an armoire while she cleaned.

Later, they had a quiet lunch of soup and sandwiches, then resumed working. The phone rang often, but the numbers were unfamiliar. She wished their number was unlisted. At least no one had shown up at the door today.

The storm raged on, rain tapping on the windows like a stranger with bad news. The sea oats bent in submission to the wind, and gulls floated high in the air, riding the gusts wherever it took them.

Lucas was stirring a pot of boiling pasta when the call came. Kate picked up.

"Kate," Ronald said. "I just heard from Paul."

"What did they decide?"

"They want you to avoid the press, kiddo. They're afraid you'll open yourself to all kinds of speculation. People will find out more than they already know, and from what they've heard, it's not good."

"They want me to do nothing?"

Lucas turned from the pot of spaghetti and studied her. As his eyebrows lifted, long lines formed across his forehead.

"Unfortunately, I agree, Kate. As much as I'd like to think this publicity will be advantageous, I think it's going to cause damage. And the more details the media gets, the longer this is going to brew. The best we can hope is that it'll blow over soon and be forgotten."

The thought of doing nothing was demoralizing. It wasn't in Kate to sit back and let things happen. She was a planner, a doer. She wanted to work this out; she wanted to fix it.

"If you're confronted by the press, Paul suggested you say, 'No comment' and keep moving. It would be prudent to tell your family and anyone who has details to avoid the press also."

Thunder cracked in the distance, and the rain pummeled the roof over the kitchen. "Paul asked about Bryan. I didn't see him quoted in any of the articles. They're hoping that's an indication he won't submit to an interview. They want you to confirm that."

"I'll call him," Kate said. Her voice sounded choked. The burden of her mistake weighted her. Her body felt heavy—too heavy for her trembling legs.

As she ended the phone call, her legs buckled, and she dropped on the wooden window ledge. "I have to call Bryan." She wasn't up for it, but that didn't matter. She dialed his home phone. It rang four times before the voice mail kicked on.

"Bryan, it's Kate." She ran her fingers through her hair. *What should I say?* "Can you call me when you get this? Listen, it's very important that you not talk to the press." *Unlike your skanky girlfriend.* Kate gritted her teeth. She needed Bryan to cooperate, and a snarky attitude wouldn't help. "Just call me."

She hung up. Lucas was looking at her with an expression she couldn't read and didn't have the brainpower to decipher. She dialed Bryan's cell and got voice mail again. She left a similar message and hung up.

"What did your agent say?" Lucas asked.

"They want me to stay quiet. Do nothing. Hope it blows over."

"You're not happy."

"I see where they're coming from. They might even be right; they've got more experience than I. It just makes me feel so—"

Helpless. Useless. Like a sitting duck. Like a twelve-year-old girl waiting to see if her mom is Jekyll or Hyde that day.

She walked away from the thought, into the bedroom, but it followed her there, like a persistent shadow. She didn't bother to flip on the lamp, though only remnants of daylight seeped through the curtains. Instead, in the darkness, she paced the short length of the room while rain pounded the roof, a surge of the storm's temper.

Lucas appeared in the doorway. He leaned against the doorjamb, watching her.

"I just—I hate this doing nothing." She whipped around, her hair slapping her on the cheek, and sank on the edge of the mattress. Would this be the way her career went down? With her forfeiting the match; not even putting up a fight?

Lucas approached Kate, aching to comfort her. "Maybe they're right," he said. "Maybe it'll blow over."

And what will happen to us? He wanted to know but couldn't ask. Not now, when she'd been bombarded by everyone else. Heavy clouds seemed to roll in, darkening the room.

"What if they're wrong? What if my readers think I'm a hypocrite?" Her eyes glazed over and she blinked rapidly. "Maybe I am a hypocrite."

He'd never seen her look so fragile, so vulnerable, not even on her wedding day. She looked broken, her always neat hair a disheveled mess, hanging in her face.

"Hey . . ." he said, smoothing the sides of her hair with both hands. He tucked it behind her ears the way she liked it. "Stop talking like that. It's going to be okay." He cupped her face between his palms. "We'll get through this."

A tear escaped, and he brushed it away with his thumb.

"Why did we ever plan my wedding around my book's release? It was stupid. I thought it was a brilliant idea, but it was just stupid. Look where all my planning has gotten me. My career is over, Lucas." Her voice wobbled. The tears chased each other rapid fire.

"Shhhh." He pulled her to him and caressed her hair, letting her cry. Her arms wrapped around his waist, her fingers clutching his T-shirt. She was falling apart, his composed Kate. He hadn't thought it possible.

A bucket of guilt poured down on him like the rain that deluged the ground outside. This was all his fault. He was the one who'd offered to stand in for Bryan. If not for him, Kate would have told the truth. Sure, it would have been hard. It may have ruined her book sales, but it wouldn't have wrecked her career.

"I'm sorry, Kate," he whispered into her hair. He'd thought he was saving her, but he'd ruined her instead. "It's my fault."

She sniveled. "No, it isn't." She shook her head against his chest. "It was my decision."

"It was *my idea*." His arms tightened around her as his thoughts went back to that morning when he'd seen her so shaken, seen her eyes deaden to the reality of her situation.

"I was just trying to—" *Save you. Love you.* His gut tightened.

She pulled away, looking up at him. "Stop it." One last tear trailed down her cheek. "You were only trying to help."

He brushed the tear away, dried her face with his thumbs. Her eyes were sad pools of regret, her lashes spiked with moisture. If only he could clean up the mess he'd made so easily. He had been trying to help that day, trying to wipe that look of despair from her face. He would have done anything to accomplish that.

And yet here was despair again, sevenfold.

"I would never hurt you," he whispered. Did she believe him? It was important that she did.

"I know." Her lips barely moved on the words. A tear trembled in the corner of her mouth. He swept it away, his thumb lingering over the plump curve of her lower lip.

Mercy, did she know how much he cared for her? How much he wanted her to be completely his? Did she know he'd do anything to protect her?

Did she know he loved her? The words hovered on the tip of his tongue, wavering, eager to escape, yet afraid of the consequences. What would she do if she knew? What would she say if she knew he'd loved her from the beginning?

Kate wanted to lose herself in Lucas's eyes, in those fathomless green depths. Something stirred in her. His words replayed in her head. *"I would never hurt you."*

She knew it was true. He would never have deserted her on her wedding day, like Bryan had. Lucas would stand by and defend her, protect her no matter what. Kate had never considered herself the kind of woman who yearned for a knight in shining armor, but just now the notion was appealing. And the look in his eyes was irresistible.

He was so close. She felt the warmth of him through his T-shirt. Kate turned her face into his hand and pressed a kiss against his calloused palm. He was a man's man, a hard worker. Loyal to the death. So many good things. She wanted all of them.

She kissed the curve of his jaw, feeling the coarseness of his stubble against her lips and relishing him for the man he was.

She heard his breath catch, and it emboldened her. With a hand against his face, she turned him toward her. Their lips met gently, and Kate soaked up his response. Her fingers tightened on the cotton material of his shirt.

Lucas pulled her closer, into the strength of his embrace. His stomach was hard against hers, his shoulders like solid rock. He was a sure foundation in a raging storm.

"Katie," he whispered.

The taste of her name on his lips, so desperate and devoted, was sweet and heady.

I want him.

No, I need him.

He deepened the kiss, and she responded in kind, drawing her fingers through his hair. Lucas leaned into her, pressing her back against the bed, the weight of him more welcome than a cool breeze on sun-scorched skin.

What am I doing? The thought had no more than formed than she pushed it down.

But it resurfaced with force. *Is this right? Do I love him?*

He's your husband. You have every right.

She latched onto the thought, clinging with everything in her. *He* is *my husband. He's mine.*

With the thought came complete surrender. She ran her hands along the plane of his back and returned his kiss with fervor.

"Katie," he said, his breath ragged. He pulled back, putting space she didn't want between them. His eyes were deep shadows of longing, a mirror of her own. "Are you sure, honey?"

Kate pulled him close, kissing his jaw and the corner of his lips before he claimed her mouth.

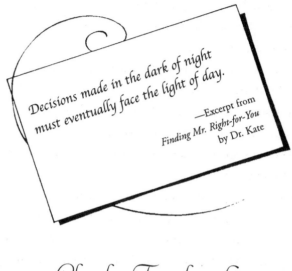

*Decisions made in the dark of night
must eventually face the light of day.*

—Excerpt from
Finding Mr. Right-for-You
by Dr. Kate

Chapter Twenty-Six

Morning light flooded through the windows, piercing Kate's aching eyes. She checked the clock and realized she'd slept late. Yesterday's shirt hung from the cone-shaped lamp shade.

The memory of the night before struck her like a rogue wave. She swiveled her head on her pillow and met Lucas's gaze.

"'Morning," he said. He lay on top of the covers in jeans and a T-shirt.

How long has he been watching me? Her own nakedness under the covers made her squirm. Kate clutched the quilt, pulling it to her shoulders, reality slamming into her hard. *What have I done? We didn't even use protection. What was I thinking?*

She was unaccustomed to waking with him in bed. Un-accustomed to what they'd done the night before. The two realities clashed, ushering in an awkward moment.

"You're still here."

He propped his elbow on the pillow, head in hand. "Just watching you sleep."

She could get lost in those eyes again if she let herself. But she shouldn't. Couldn't. What sense did it make? She looked away under the guise of checking the time.

Daylight had chased away the shadow of desire, exposing the irrationality of her actions the night before. She'd let herself become swept up in her feelings for Lucas.

And yes, she admitted she did have feelings. Strong ones.

But he's all wrong for me. How could I forget that? Me, who wrote an entire book on the subject? Maybe I am a hypocrite.

"Look at me, honey."

Her stomach tightened at the endearment, the same one he'd used just before they'd—

Kate turned her head. Lucas's cheek was pillow creased. She'd kissed that cheek the night before. Kissed those lips, run her hands over the sharp curve of his jaw. *Stop it!*

"What's going on behind those big brown eyes?" He brushed her hair from her cheek.

She flinched at his touch, wary of being swept into the tide pool of longing, and Lucas withdrew his hand, a frown pulling his mouth.

Kate needed time to think. Time to sort through her feelings. Time to get dressed, for heaven's sake. She pulled the quilt to her chin.

"I just need . . . a little time, Lucas. Everything's changing so quickly, I can't wrap my brain around it. I need time to figure things out."

The sparkle left his eyes. She wanted to say something that would light them again, but it wouldn't be fair to offer false hope.

"Right," he said.

She should say something. Something to soothe the hurt on his face, but nothing came to mind. Nothing honest. Not when her mind was a riot of confusion.

Lucas got up, the bed shaking in his wake. He cleared his throat. "I have errands to run anyway." At the foot of the bed, he slid on his sandals.

"I didn't mean for you to leave."

He walked toward the door without looking back. "It's okay."

Moments later she heard the door open and shut. His truck roared to life outside, and Bo entered the room, his paws clicking to a stop beside her.

What had she done? As if life needed to get more complicated. *What was I thinking last night?*

She'd been thinking with her heart, that's what. The way he'd touched her, like she was the most precious object in the world. Even now, she shivered in remembrance. She'd never felt so cherished, so . . .

Loved.

Lucas doesn't love you. He was a man, wanting what a man wants.

But it hadn't felt that way. Hadn't felt that way when she'd awakened and caught him watching her.

Stop it, Kate. You need to think with your head, not your heart. Be smart. Listen to your own advice.

Forcing herself to move, Kate got up and showered, dressing in her favorite jeans and her royal blue shirt. It was Sunday and she wondered if Lucas's family would welcome her to their family meal. Maybe she shouldn't go. But she had to face them eventually, even if only to apologize.

As she poured her coffee, she heard a car pull into the driveway. Her nerves immediately clanged, like the wind chimes on the back porch on a windy day. She didn't know what to say to Lucas yet. What they'd shared had been so intimate, and yet now, in the light of day, she knew it was a mistake. How could she tell him that?

Maybe he's thinking the same thing.

The thought disturbed her. Hurt her feelings—which was ludicrous considering she felt the same way. She couldn't even agree with herself.

Maybe a walk on the beach would clear her head. Through the kitchen window she saw the weather had calmed. It was no longer storming, just overcast and gloomy. The ocean was gray and choppy, its waves striking the shore with white foam fingers.

One thing she knew: she had to escape the island. There was no reason to prolong the marriage, and staying was too difficult emotionally. Obviously her feelings for Lucas had grown into something beyond her control. *If only we weren't so different. If only we weren't completely incompatible, we could make it*

Her heart ached for the chance to try.

But the memories of her parents' arguments, their vicious battles over every little thing, stopped her, even if her experience as a counselor didn't. She wasn't going to waste her life forcing a round peg into a square hole. She'd watched too many people try and fail. She'd watched her parents try and fail. That wasn't the life she wished on anyone.

A knock sounded at the front door.

Kate set down her mug and walked into the living room, peering through the window in the door. She prayed it wasn't another reporter coming to get the scoop on her private—

No.

Through the glass, the top of a head was visible, but she would've recognized that neatly clipped brown hair anywhere. She paused, gathering her thoughts a moment before she pulled open the door.

"Bryan." She hadn't seen him since the eve of their wedding day. He looked older. Tired. Wrinkles and creases covered his dress shirt and slacks, like he'd slept in them. "What are you doing here?"

"Kate." He heaved a sigh. Relief? "I've been trying to reach you."

She leaned against the door, keeping it partway closed. She'd expected to feel something if she saw him again. Longing, regret, anger. Something. The lack of emotion was a welcome surprise.

"I turned off my phone," she said. "But I guess you can understand why."

"I'm sorry I missed your call. So many reporters were trying to reach me that I turned mine off too. I just got your message when I got off the plane."

"What are you doing here?" Had he come thinking he could comfort her? Help her? Maybe he had a plan to make this disaster go away. He'd always been clever. And her own plan had failed.

"We need to talk," he said. "Can I come in?"

Kate looked across the street where two houses were visible from the front porch. It would be better than having Bryan seen on her doorstep. She opened the door wide and stepped back against the wall, giving him a wide berth.

Inside, she gestured him toward the sofa. She scanned the tiny, simple living room, seeing it through his eyes. It was a far cry from his contemporary city apartment. Bo appeared at his side, and Bryan inched away, but the dog only sniffed Bryan's shoe before following Kate to the recliner across the room.

"I'm sorry it got leaked." Bryan planted his elbows on his knees. "I'm sorry about the interview on TV. It must've been very uncomfortable for you."

Uncomfortable is hardly the word. "Your girlfriend must be having a field day."

"She's not my girlfriend. It was a big mistake. *She* was a big mistake."

Kate felt weary suddenly, like her bones might melt into the chair. "Let's not go through this again, Bryan. What's done is done. The main thing is that you can't talk to the press. You haven't, have you?"

"Of course not. I wouldn't do that to you."

He had some nerve acting as if he'd never hurt her. Kate stared him down until he looked away. "If anyone questions you, just say 'No comment,' okay?"

"Of course. I'll do whatever you want. I owe you that. I owe you so much more than that." His baby blue eyes shone under the lamplight. She'd once thought them beautiful, too pretty to be wasted on a man. Now they were a thin, cool sheet of ice, ready to crack under pressure.

"I know this is bad," Bryan said, "Our personal business all over the news, your career—jeopardized. I can't tell you how sorry I am, Kate."

His apology was sincere, his regret legitimate. Unfortunately it changed nothing.

But anger was futile. And even though he'd backed out of their wedding, it had been her decision to marry Lucas.

"What are you going to do now?" Bryan asked. "Can I help in any way?"

Kate shook her head. "I'm just going to hole up somewhere. My dad invited me to stay with him awhile, so I might do that. I need time for this to blow over, and time to rethink my career, if need be."

Two notches formed between Bryan's brows, and he shook his head as if to clear the cobwebs. "But what about—"

Kate realized her mistake too late. The public—and Bryan—didn't know the particulars of her and Lucas's arrangement. She'd never told Bryan the marriage wasn't a real one.

"Your marriage," he said. "It was just temporary? You're leaving him?" The hope in his voice was a warning siren.

A sick feeling worked its way into her middle, churning her stomach the way the wind churned the waves outside. "I'm going to visit my dad for a while, that's all."

His eyes narrowed. "It was temporary from the beginning, wasn't it? You never had feelings for him, never planned to stay married. It was just . . . a way out of the mess I put you in."

There was a certainty in his tone, and Kate knew she wasn't going to erase that. *He won't alert the media, so what harm is there if he knows?*

"Yes, it was temporary, all right?" she said. "But that's between you and me, and if you say one word to the press—"

Bryan extended his hands palm out. "I swear, I won't." He stood and crossed the rug, closing the space between them, dropping to his knees at her feet.

"Kate, do you know what this means to me?" He took her hands, pressing them between his own. The coolness of his palms, the shape of his fingers felt foreign against hers.

She pulled away. "It doesn't mean anything. It doesn't change anything."

"You need to get away. Come with me. We can stay at my place in Aspen. I'll take a leave of absence. You can figure out where to go from there."

Kate pressed her back into the cushion. "No, Bryan. It's over between us." She knew as the words left her mouth that she meant them now as she never had. There was nothing left, no feelings for him.

Because they've been replaced by feelings for Lucas. Kate shrugged the thought away.

"You don't mean that. Just think. We could move anywhere you want. You could open a counseling service like you did here. We could have a fresh start."

The thought of starting over was tempting compared to the months of uncertainty she faced, but she knew it was implausible. She was about to say so when the front door opened.

Somehow she'd missed the rattle of Lucas's truck arriving. He stopped on the threshold, his hand on the doorknob. His gaze darted between Kate and Bryan. She imagined the scene from Lucas's perspective and cringed.

∞

Lucas's heart stuttered at the sight of Kate and Bryan. He'd thought the unfamiliar car might belong to some nosy reporter and charged up the porch steps ready to confront the jerk who'd had the nerve to show up on their doorstep.

But it wasn't some reporter who knelt on the floor at his wife's feet. It was her ex-fiancé. The look of shock on Kate's face at his entry would have been comical if it weren't plain hurtful.

His hands balls into fists. "What are you doing here, Montgomery?"

Bryan stood slowly, blocking Lucas's view of Kate as if to guard her. What a joke. It was Bryan she needed protection from.

"Knock off the doting husband charade. I know the truth."

Kate stood, and Lucas's eyes went to hers. He saw guilt there. And something else, before her gaze dropped to the floor. It was enough to shake his confidence.

Lucas took a step closer to Bryan, wanting to beat the smug expression off his face. "Get out of my house."

"Not without Kate."

"Stop it, Bryan," Kate said. "You should go." She grabbed his arm, but Bryan didn't budge. Kate's hand trembled.

"You heard her," Lucas said. "Get lost."

Bryan turned to Kate and touched her arm. Lucas wanted to grab him by the collar and haul him out the door. He ground his teeth together instead. Did Kate want to go with Bryan? Is that why she regretted the night before? She'd apparently told Bryan their marriage was a sham. *Why would she have done that unless—*

"Come with me, Kate," Bryan said. He added something else, too softly for Lucas to hear.

Kate shook his hand loose. "No."

Bryan whispered something. He took Kate's face in his hands.

Something red and hot spread through Lucas. He surged forward. "Get your hands off my wife." He grabbed Bryan's fancy shirt and shoved him toward the door. Lucas had five inches and forty pounds on him, and Bryan knew it.

Bryan caught his balance in front of the doorway, smoothing his sleeves, regaining his composure. He nailed Lucas with a glare. "She's not your wife, *friend.* She's just playing house with you."

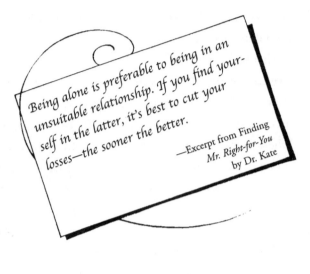

Being alone is preferable to being in an unsuitable relationship. If you find yourself in the latter, it's best to cut your losses—the sooner the better.

—Excerpt from Finding
Mr. Right-for-You
by Dr. Kate

Chapter Twenty-Seven

If Bryan hadn't left on his own, Kate would have shoved him out the door after the way he'd spoken to Lucas. She wanted to soothe the hurt from Lucas's face with a well-placed kiss, but the anger lining his stubborn jaw stopped the thought as it materialized.

Lucas exited the room, leaving her to wonder what he was thinking. She heard him open a cabinet, remove something. The cabinet door slammed shut. Then she heard the pouring of coffee and the sound of the pot clanking back into its cubby.

Kate didn't know whether to follow him or not. Clearly they had a lot to discuss. He must be wondering what Bryan was doing there. He must be wondering what she was going to do.

Kate checked her watch. They were due at his parents' in an hour. *How will I face them? How can I tell these people who've become my family that I'm leaving?*

How can I tell Lucas I'm leaving? But then, he must know there was nothing holding her here now.

Except what had happened the night before.

Kate peered out the living room window. The wind wrestled with the leaves. They were already beginning to turn. Fall had arrived, and changes were in progress. The warm summer days were gone, and the cooler autumn days would usher in the frigid winter.

She'd never enjoyed winter on the island. With the winds blowing in off the ocean, it was impossible to keep a warm house. She mentally put another check in the pro column for visiting her dad in Maryland. There were many checks in the column already. Increasingly, she felt the need to escape. And soon.

Lucas's sandals shuffled to a stop somewhere behind her. His presence pulled her shoulder muscles tight, pushed the air from her lungs.

"Did you ask him to come?" Lucas said.

Kate pivoted. "No." She hated that he thought it. Did he think last night meant nothing? She wouldn't have slept with him if she were in love with Bryan. *Surely he knows that.*

Lucas took a sip of his coffee from the oversized Nantucket mug. It looked small in his hands.

Kate had to tell him what she'd decided, but getting the words out was harder than she imagined. *Strange, when I planned to leave him all along.* When he'd planned for her to leave all along. It shouldn't come as any surprise now that there was no point in her staying.

Except for your feelings.

She brushed the thought away, zooming in on the logical reasons that had added checks to her pro column.

"We need to talk," she said. It was a start. A slow one, maybe, but easing into it seemed kinder.

"Go ahead." He held the mug in front of him, a fragile barrier between them. His feet were braced as if for a blow.

She hated that she would deliver it. "I'm leaving the island." She measured his reaction and came away with nothing. "Now that the word is out about . . . our marriage, there's no reason for me to stay."

Kate chest pounded with the force of her heartbeats, walloping her ribs like a prizefighter. She waited for his response—and got nothing but silence.

"I need to get away." She filled the gap. "I'm too accessible here, anyway, to the press. I think if I go away somewhere, this will die down more quickly."

It occurred to her that she was leaving Lucas to deal with the press, with all the locals and their questioning glances. She was sorry for that, but staying wouldn't make it easier. People would talk even if she stayed.

She wished she could interpret his expression, but the light from the kitchen silhouetted him. She kept talking. "If there's nothing left of my career when this is over, maybe I can open another counseling service." She tried to sound upbeat, but the words fell flat. She imagined driving away, leaving Lucas behind. Never seeing him again. Her throat closed off.

"Are you going back to him?"

It took Kate a moment to realize what Lucas was asking. "No." She shook her head emphatically. "Bryan is—It's over between us." Hadn't Lucas heard her telling Bryan to leave?

"He doesn't seem to think so."

"I don't have feelings for him anymore. I wouldn't have—" *Slept with you if I did.* If she finished the thought, it would raise the subject she wanted to avoid.

"Wouldn't have . . . ?"

Her mind went back to the night before, returning like a dehydrated woman to a spring of fresh water. Kate knew she'd never wipe the moments from the slate of her memory. She crossed her arms, hugging her waist.

"I'm going to stay with my dad awhile," she said, avoiding his question. "In Maryland. Hopefully the scandal will fade quickly."

He walked toward her, and she tensed with each step. But he stopped an arm's length away. She could see his face now, lit by the light seeping through the window behind her.

"You could stay here . . ."

Did he know how tempting it was, with him looking at her that way? His eyes burning a path straight to her heart? It was the first time either of them had hinted at making the marriage permanent. It took courage for him to verbalize the idea that had floated between them for days. The night before, they'd silently brought the idea to life, but now that he said it aloud, it had a pull stronger than a riptide.

Kate tore her eyes away. *Be strong. Think with your head, not your heart. Think of your parents. Think of what you've learned from all your experience.*

"You know it wouldn't work, Lucas," She said. "And even if you don't know it, I do." She felt him watching her and wanted to run now, far away.

"What was last night?"

The edge of hurt in his voice broke her. No matter what, no matter that she was leaving, no matter that it was over, she wouldn't leave him thinking it meant nothing. She wouldn't cheapen something so special.

She was touching his face before she knew what she was doing. "Oh, Lucas. Last night was—it meant so much." The words jammed her throat. Her eyes burned.

He turned away, leaving her hand to fall on empty space.

Lucas walked away, putting space between them. Kate's touch had too much power. He would be lost if she touched him again. How could she leave if she felt anywhere near what he did? The thought of being without her ripped him in half, worse in some ways than Emily's death. That loss had been no one's choice, something that just happened. If Kate left him, it would be of her own choosing.

But maybe she didn't feel the way he did. He knew she had feelings, but maybe the depth of his love was . . . unrequited. Such a proper term for such a painful feeling.

"Lucas?" His name on her lips reminded him of the night before. She'd said his name over and over. Would he ever forget the sound of it? The heady way it made him feel to have her as his own?

He needed to change her mind. *If she would only give me a chance.* He faced her again, and now that he saw her watery eyes, he wanted to be close to her again, holding her. But he couldn't think with her in his arms.

"Stay here, Kate. There's something between us; won't you stay long enough to figure out what it is?"

She wet her lips and swallowed. "I told you about my parents— about their differences and how miserable they were. What I didn't tell you was how it ripped my mom apart when they divorced."

She looked out the window, and the daylight lit half her face. "Even though it was her choice, she couldn't be without him. She started drinking." Kate gave a wry smile. "Of course, I didn't understand it at the time. But I know now she was using the alcohol to escape reality. And the reality was, she couldn't live with my dad and she couldn't live without him. She was miserable either way. What kind of hope is there in that?"

"We're not your parents, Kate."

"We're *just like* my parents. Opposites in every way. I don't think I could've found someone less compatible. I should've followed my own advice and distanced myself before there were—feelings."

She made it sound so rational. Like you could tuck unwanted emotions in a box and toss them. "That's crazy," Lucas said. "Love isn't some item on a checklist."

Her fingers clutched the curtain, and she wouldn't look at him. He'd expected an argument. He'd expected her to rationalize why her way was best. He would find a counterargument to everything she said.

"I'll make reservations on the ferry as soon as I can," she said. "Possibly today. I'll have to send for my things."

Lucas felt like she'd punched him in the gut. She wasn't going to defend her decision? Wasn't going to give him a chance to convince her? He couldn't believe it was happening so quickly. Not after the night before, when he'd felt like a surfer riding the crest of a dream wave. Now he'd crashed headfirst into the rocks.

She checked her watch. "I want to talk to your family before I go. I owe them an apology."

It was his heart she'd broken, not his family's. *Say something. Say something to stop her before her plans set in her mind.* "You're in the middle of a crisis. Wait until things settle down. Don't make a rash decision." It was something she would say, something she could relate to.

Her eyes darkened with her frown. "It's not rash, Lucas. I planned to leave from the beginning, remember?"

Chapter Twenty-Eight

Kate knocked on the Wrights' door, then clasped her shaking hands behind her back. Lucas had offered to accompany her, but she needed to face his family on her own. This was her fault, not his.

The door opened, and Susan's welcoming smile drooped. Kate watched the woman rise to her full height, watched her narrow chin notch upward. Regardless of how the woman responded, Kate was going to apologize to the family. Then she was going to have a heart-to-heart with Susan.

"Kate." Her name was a sour ball on the woman's tongue. "What are you doing here?"

"I came to talk to your family. Can I come in?"

Susan waffled in the doorway, clearly torn between opening the door wider and slamming it in Kate's face. Finally, she stepped back.

Kate followed Susan through the foyer and into the kitchen where Roy was putting a pan of dinner rolls into the oven. The smell of pot roast and garlic filled the air, and Kate's stomach growled in response. Jamie was on a stool at the kitchen island, a book propped open on the Formica counter. They both turned at her entry.

"Hi, Kate," Jamie said, a genuine smile on her face, and maybe a touch of pity in her eyes.

Roy shut the oven door and turned, offering her a nod and a reserved smile. Kate noticed his hands trembling for the first time and recognized it as a Parkinson's symptom. Guilt pricked her hard. As if the Wrights didn't have enough grief, she had made things worse.

"Is Brody around?" Kate asked. He was back from college for the weekend, and she hoped he hadn't left already.

"He went for a walk," Roy said. "Have a seat, Kate."

"No, thanks," Kate said. "I won't stay. I just wanted to tell you how sorry I am."

"I should think so," Susan said.

"Give her a chance." Roy pinned his wife with a look. "Go ahead, Kate."

Where should I start? There had been so much deception, and now the entire family was being publicly embarrassed. "I'm sure you're aware that my original fiancé backed out of the wedding on our wedding day. I can't begin to tell you how devastated I was. When Lucas offered to stand in, I thought it was crazy at first."

Kate tucked her hair behind her ears. "And then it began to seem like the only sane solution. With my book releasing the same day, I realized it would sink like an anchor if my wedding didn't go off as planned, and with all the media there to cover it—well, I guess I took the coward's way out."

Susan crossed her arms. Roy leaned his elbows on the island beside Jamie and studied Kate, the leathery lines around his eyes deepening.

"I never expected the truth to get leaked to the press. Lucas and I were going to divorce quietly after a year—we had it all planned. Obviously, everything's changed now."

Kate's throat was dry as desert sand. She wet her lips. "I take full responsibility, and I'm sorry for the embarrassment I've caused. I'm leaving the island this afternoon, but I wanted to let you know that you've become very special to me."

Jamie's eyes turned glassy and she blinked rapidly. Roy's face had softened, and Kate's own eyes burned. Even Susan seemed to lose some of her starch. That might change by the time Kate was finished.

Memories of the past few months flew through Kate's head at digital speed. The first time she'd met the Wrights, when she and Lucas had returned from their honeymoon. The time they'd come to watch her on *Dr. Phil.* All the walks with Susan. They were the family Kate never had, and she'd miss them. Even Susan.

Her throat thickened. "Thanks for opening your home to me. It was truly an honor to become part of your family, even if only for a little while."

Jamie jumped up and hugged her. "I'll miss you, Kate."

Kate returned the embrace. "Me too, Jamie. You're the sister I never had."

When they parted, Roy embraced her. "I wish you didn't have to go."

Kate wrapped her arms around his broad shoulders and spoke around her closed throat. "It's for the best. Thanks for all those home-cooked meals."

There was a moment of awkwardness as she faced Susan. "Can I have a word with you in private, Susan?" Kate asked.

Susan gave a short nod, her styled hair bouncing, and Kate followed her into the foyer. The woman turned to her and crossed her arms over her chest. The overhead light was harsh on the woman's face, making her appear older than her years.

Kate tempered her words with grace. "I wanted to talk to you about my mom."

Susan's jaw went slack; then she pressed her rosy lips together and looked away. "Lucas shouldn't have told you."

Kate shrugged. "I asked him why you didn't like me, and he felt he owed me an explanation."

"I don't want to talk about this with—"

"You don't have to say a word; just let me say my piece. Please." It was the last time Kate would see her anyway. The woman needed to hear the truth from someone, and if her own family wouldn't say it, Kate would.

"What my mom did was wrong. I don't know if she ever apologized, but it's too late for her to say it now, so I'll say it for her." Kate waited until Susan met her gaze. "I'm sorry. It was a terrible thing for a friend to do."

Kate wondered if it would help for Susan to know the misery her mom had gone on to endure. A failed marriage and a battle with alcoholism. Not to mention a premature death. Kate had dreamed of the kind of childhood Susan had provided her kids.

Kate could've sworn she saw a filmy glaze on Susan's eyes.

"I'm sure Roy regrets it as well," Kate continued. "And I hope somewhere along the way, he's found the words to tell you that."

"Saying you're sorry doesn't erase the pain," Susan choked out.

Boy, can I relate to that. How many times had Bryan apologized? "I know." She hoped Susan was remembering that Kate had her own heart broken not long ago. "But at some point you have to forgive the other person. It doesn't mean what he did was okay. It just means you're going to stop punishing him for it."

Susan stood to her full height, her jaws hollowing as she sucked in her pale cheeks.

Kate was treading where she was unwelcome, but the woman had held the mistake over her husband's head for over thirty years. Kate didn't know how Roy had endured it.

"Well, that's all I wanted to say," Kate said. She knew Susan hadn't wanted to hear it, especially not from her, but she hoped the woman took it to heart anyway.

Kate reached out and put her arms around Susan, feeling the stiffness of her shoulders, but embracing her regardless. "Thanks for all the walks, Susan. And for your hospitality."

She felt Susan's arms unfurl, felt her hands land on Kate's arms. It was enough.

Kate pulled back and smiled. "I'll try and catch Brody later. Will you let him know I'm looking for him?"

"Of course," Susan said.

Kate said good-bye one final time and left the house. Her feet took the uneven porch steps before she cut through the yard to the grassy knoll that separated their houses.

This is the last time you'll see them. You'll never sit down to a meal on that insanely high rooftop or listen to Jamie and Brody tease one another again. It's over.

Somehow, in a few short months, the Wrights had wiggled their way into her heart. And now she was leaving.

The crisp autumn air washed across her face, tugging at the short strands of her hair. She crossed her arms against the coolness and looked toward the ocean, the direction she'd soon go. A movement on the beach below caught her eye.

Brody threw something into the water, walking backwards, then turned toward his house. Kate changed directions, aiming her feet toward him.

When she reached the place where the long grass gave way to the sandy shore, Brody saw her. He stopped at the steps leading up from the beach, waiting for her approach. The wind pulled at his white T-shirt and tousled his blond curls.

"Hi," Kate said over the sound of the waves lapping the shoreline. "I was just at your house."

Brody nodded, his guarded smile reminding her of Roy's.

"I came to say I'm sorry," she said. "Sorry about deceiving your family. I never meant to hurt anyone, but I realize I have."

Brody dug his bare feet into the sand. "It wasn't right."

"I know," Kate said. "I'm not going to offer excuses." A seagull soared above the water and cried out—a lonely, high-pitched squeal. "I also came to tell your family good-bye."

Brody met her gaze, his eyes flinching for just a second. She watched the emotions dancing across his face. He'd never been good at hiding his feelings. "I didn't think you'd leave."

She shrugged, turning her face into the wind, letting her hair blow off her face. "Everyone knows the truth now. There's no reason for me to stay."

Brody studied her, his head cocked to the side. "Isn't there?"

His tone held a challenge, but she wouldn't take it. *There are things he doesn't know, doesn't understand. How can he?*

"How are things going this semester?" she said. "If you don't mind my asking."

The pause was so long, Kate thought he wasn't going to answer. When he finally did, she was relieved.

"You were right," he said. "About my being afraid to fail." He smiled and she saw a glimpse of the old Brody. "If you tell anyone that I'll have to come after you."

Kate held up her right hand, palm out. "I promise."

Brody sank onto the sandy wooden step, and Kate eased down beside him.

"Teaching is what I want to do," he said. "I think switching from major to major was a stall tactic because I was afraid I'd get out in the real world and fail. If you hadn't shown me that, I would have been a college student the rest of my life."

Kate breathed a laugh. "Nah, you would've figured it out."

"Yeah, when I was thirty and on my tenth major."

Kate was glad something positive had come from her time here, because everything else was a disaster.

Silence fell again. The seagull flapped its wings, flying away, growing smaller on the horizon.

"I'm still afraid," Brody said. "I guess that makes me a total wuss."

Kate traced a dry crevice in the step with her index finger. "It's fear that makes an act courageous, you know."

Brody drew in the sand with his big toe. "Huh. Never thought of it like that."

"You'll make a great teacher, Brody. I hope we can stay in contact." Kate huddled against the cool wind, tucking her knees close to her.

"Sure. There's always e-mail." He looked at Kate. "What about Lucas?"

Her heart wobbled at the mention of Lucas's name. "I suppose e-mail is out for him, huh? I guess we can keep in touch by phone."

"That's not what I mean."

He wasn't playing the part of Kate's brother-in-law now; he was a little brother watching out for big brother. She envied Lucas having a sibling that looked out for him.

"Lucas will be fine," Kate said. "It—it wasn't like that between us."

The words felt soiled coming out. It may have been true at one time, but not after the night before.

It hasn't been true for weeks.

"It's best that I leave." What would happen to her heart if she stayed? She'd already lost it to Lucas, and what hope did they have for a future together?

Brody nodded thoughtfully.

Kate let silence fill the space between them, let the sound of the surf rushing the shoreline fill the gap.

"Well," he said, "at least you won't have to fight your fear of heights anymore."

Kate smiled, remembering all the rooftop meals they'd shared. She elbowed Brody. "Fear of *falling*," she corrected.

Brody's expression changed, growing serious. "You know, a wise person once told me it's fear that makes an act courageous."

Kate's breath caught in her lungs as Brody held her captive with his pointed look. He knew. He knew she cared for Lucas. Thought she was a coward for running.

But sometimes, running was the courageous thing to do. At least, that's what she told herself.

Lucas was gone by the time Kate returned home. She realized he must've gone to his parents' house while she was on the beach with Brody. Kate made reservations on that evening's car ferry and packed her belongings. Everything would fit in the car except her treadmill. She'd have to send for it and her things from the apartment when she found a place in Maryland.

For tonight, she'd take the ferry to Hyannis then drive as far as Wareham or New Bedford, then find a hotel. She called her dad and told him she was coming.

By late afternoon, she was wondering if she was going to have to track Lucas down. She had to leave soon if she wanted to make the ferry, but she owed him a good-bye at least.

Kate was packing her laptop and cord when she heard Lucas return. He opened the door, and his eyes landed on her suitcases. He paused for a moment before shutting the door.

Kate wrapped the recharging cord around the battery pack and stowed it in her bag with the laptop, then zipped it shut.

Lucas pocketed his keys and leaned against the sofa back. Rather than focus on him, she looked at the sofa itself. How many nights had they sat on that couch, disagreeing about what program they should watch? Kate had learned it was easier to read in the evenings because they could never settle on a show.

"When do you leave?" he asked.

Bo nudged Lucas's leg, but when he got no response, he crossed the room and settled on the rug with a loud sigh.

Kate checked her watch. She had to leave soon or take the risk of missing the ferry. "Now."

He was wearing the black T-shirt that stretched across his broad shoulders, and the faded jeans that made his legs look long and solid. *I'll miss him.* Kate didn't want to consider how much. She just needed to get out of there. She could deal with the feelings of loss later, when she was a safe distance away.

Lucas watched Kate hitch the leather strap on her shoulder and turn to him. The moment seemed surreal. It was happening so fast. Last night they'd been closer than ever, and tonight she was leaving.

He wanted to beg her to stay. He swallowed his pride and opened his mouth to do just that. Maybe he could find the words that would change her mind.

But what good would it do to beg? She had to want to stay. She had to want him. He could love her all he wanted, but it had to be her choice.

He closed his mouth, clamping his lips over the words.

"I'm not sure how to say good-bye," Kate said.

Then don't. Stay. Stay with me forever.

Kate tucked her silky hair behind her ears. He would miss that simple action.

"Regardless of how this turned out," she said, "I'm grateful for what you did. I've never had anyone go to so much trouble to save my skin." She tried to smile, but it wobbled on her lips.

It was no trouble. It had been his pleasure. He wished he could save her now, save her career from spiraling out of control. Save their marriage from falling apart.

"I'm sorry I wasn't able to help your parents," Kate said. "I hope they'll work things out."

Tell her now. Tell her your parents are fine, that it was all a ruse to conceal the fact that you loved her from the beginning. Tell her you love her now and that if she stays, you'll spend every day proving it.

But he had shown his love every day for the past three months. And still she was leaving.

"Say something." Her brown eyes, warm as melted chocolate, pleaded.

He tried to imagine sleeping in an empty bed, waking to a quiet house, making coffee for one again. The thought hollowed his stomach.

"Is there anything I can say to change your mind?" He would say it, whatever it was. *Do you know how much I love you? I'd give anything to call you my own.*

Kate looked away, clutching her purse strap. "It's for the best, Lucas. You'll see. It's hard right now, but later . . . later we'll know it was the right thing."

"Are you trying to convince me or yourself?"

She checked the time. Her eyes seemed to catch on her fingers. He watched her touch the wedding band he'd bought her, watched her slide it down her finger with the engagement ring. She closed the distance between them, pocketing the engagement ring, and held out the wedding band.

"Keep it," he said.

She shook her head. "I can't."

When he refused to take it, she sighed softly and set the band on the end table. Lucas wanted to snatch it up and force it back on her finger. She was his wife, even if only for a short while longer.

But what good would it do? He couldn't force her to wear his ring any more than he could force her to stay. *Any more than I can force her to love me.*

"I have to go."

Lucas straightened. *Have it your way, Kate.* "I'll drive you."

"You won't have any way back."

He opened the door and picked up her bags. "I'll take a cab." He carried her suitcases to her car.

"There'll be too many people there," she said, her voice sounding like it was being pushed through a sieve.

Lucas loaded her bags in the backseat, then faced Kate. Her eyes glistened like the surface of the ocean on a sunny day. She didn't want to say good-bye in front of an audience.

Neither did he. "All right." He opened the driver's side door for her.

"I'll file papers for the . . . divorce. And cover all the costs." A breeze blew, and dead leaves scuttled past their feet. There was a nip in the air that warned of winter's approach. "And I'll send for my treadmill," she said. "I think I got everything else."

Including my heart. Did she think she could run from these feelings? Did she think mere miles would separate her from his love?

Lucas studied her face, memorizing the way her eyes looked when she squinted against sun, the way her brows puckered when she frowned. He reached out and smoothed the hair the wind had ruffled, wanting to remember the feel of it between his fingers.

She closed her eyes on a sigh. "I hate good-byes."

He thought of Emily and how sudden her death had been. He'd always regretted that he hadn't kissed her that morning when he left for work. He was running late and only called good-bye on his way out the door.

Lucas took Kate's face in his palm, waiting for her to look at him. If she was going to leave him, she was going to do it with her eyes wide open.

He closed the space between them, pressing a soft kiss to her lips. Her hair smelled of lilacs, and her lips tasted like honey. He wanted to remember everything about her. He wanted to close his eyes at night and be able to summon the feel of her lips on his, the sound of her voice.

Kate pulled away. "Good-bye."

She refused to meet his gaze as she lowered herself into the car and put her keys in the ignition. Refused to look at him as she put the car in Reverse and backed out of the drive. He watched until her car disappeared over the slope in the road, knowing that all that awaited him was a house that would feel empty without her.

His feet felt heavy as he entered the house. Bo, seeming to sense his sadness, nudged his leg, tried to shepherd Lucas toward the couch. But Lucas didn't want to sit and think. Think about Kate leaving—getting further away by the minute.

The room seemed big. Kate had decluttered every corner of the house, leaving it spick-and-span, but now it felt bare. The treadmill was the only token of her existence, and it stood in the corner like a memorial.

He walked to the bedroom and stopped in the doorway. The spaces where her alarm clock and jewelry box had been were empty. He saw something on her nightstand and went closer. A small blue-velvet box. He opened it and looked at the earrings he'd given her for their first-month anniversary. It was as if she'd wanted to leave everything behind, to have no reminder of her time with him.

A scrap of paper on the clean hardwood floor caught his eye, and he retrieved it. It was a list of things she'd done in her preparation to leave. A laugh caught in his throat. Kate and her lists. Someday she would learn that life is what happens when you're busy making plans.

He threw the paper in the wastebasket and left the room. It felt as if the walls of the house were closing in on him. He realized for the first time that the house smelled like Kate. He wanted to get away from this place, occupy his mind with something else. If it weren't so late, he'd go sailing.

Bo barked from the back of the house. Lucas followed the sound to where the dog sat by the back door. Bo craned his massive head around, looking at him with inquisitive brown eyes.

"Wanna go for a walk, boy?"

Bo wagged his tail.

At least it would get Lucas out of the house.

They walked westward down the beach, Lucas occasionally tossing a piece of driftwood for Bo to fetch. The sun lowered in the sky, casting a pinkish hue over the beach. Bo trotted beside him, sometimes wading into the incoming surf or chasing a seagull that landed nearby. The dog had just returned from such a chase when Lucas heard it: the haunting sound of the ferry's horn in the distance.

He stopped, a catch in his breath, a stutter in his heart. The sound was the period at the end of a sentence, the whisper of good-bye from a lover, the clock striking midnight for Cinderella.

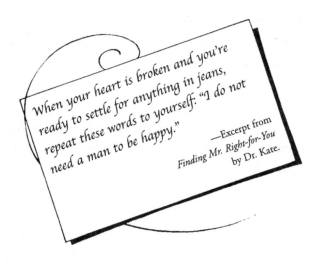

When your heart is broken and you're ready to settle for anything in jeans, repeat these words to yourself: "I do not need a man to be happy."

—Excerpt from *Finding Mr. Right-for-You* by Dr. Kate.

Chapter Twenty-Nine

Kate opened the *Columbia Flier* on the picnic table and perused the apartment rentals section. The savory smell of grilled sirloin wafted by on the breeze. Her dad, draped in a red canvas apron, checked the meat, then closed the grill lid.

Kate noticed a new apartment listing and marked the ad with a yellow highlighter.

"See anything interesting?" Her dad sat across from her and brushed a red leaf from the wooden table with the side of his hand.

"There are a couple new ones I'll check on tomorrow. I'm still considering the one on Green Meadow Drive." Kate didn't want to overstay her welcome. She'd planned on staying at a hotel, but her dad had insisted she take his spare room. And she had to admit it had been a relief to hide away the past three weeks.

"How much longer on the steaks?" she asked.

"Oh, seven or eight minutes," he said.

"I'll put the salad together." Kate entered the house through the sliding door, careful not to fingerprint the glass. She found the head of lettuce and chopped it, then sliced a ripe tomato and placed the knife in the dishwasher.

Her cell rang as she was getting the dressing. Every time it rang, her thoughts turned to mush. She hadn't heard from Lucas since she left, but Jamie had e-mailed her twice.

It's not Lucas, Kate. For heaven's sake. Get on with your life.

Bryan had called the day she arrived in Columbia. She'd told him not to call again, and so far, he'd respected her wishes.

She pulled her cell from her purse's side pocket and answered.

"Kate. How are you?" Her agent's voice greeted her.

Kate squelched the inevitable disappointment. "Hi, Ronald. I'm okay. Getting settled in, looking for an apartment, avoiding the media. You know, the usual." It had been easier than she'd hoped to avoid the press since only a few people knew her whereabouts.

"Yeah, I've noticed," Ronald said. "It looks like they've run out of things to say about you."

"That's what we were hoping." A flurry of papers had covered the story initially, and several tabloids had joined the fray, but the scandal seemed to have died down already.

"That part's working for us." The caution in his tone warned of a negative flip side.

"What's wrong? Have you heard from Chloe or Paul?" Her editor had been quiet. In fact, Kate hadn't heard from Chloe since their conference call over three weeks earlier.

"I called her this morning just to check in," Ronald said. "I'm afraid sales have dropped off quite dramatically. She mentioned the ugly 'R' word."

"Returns?" It was every author's worst fear—that the stores would be unable to sell their stock of books and would return them to the publisher, unsold.

Kate set the plastic tongs in the salad bowl and faced the sliding door. "I don't understand. I've done what they asked. I've avoided the spotlight, and everything has died down. I thought that's what they wanted."

"Yeah, I know. I called Pam after I talked to Chloe to get her take. The public is impossible to predict. They'd been hoping that with no new information, the story would die and the public would forget it."

"But that hasn't happened?"

"Pam said it's too early to say for sure. But the numbers aren't looking good."

Kate ran her hand through her hair. All this for nothing? The public apparently believed the reports and had decided she was a fraud. They were voting with their dollars, and she'd lost.

"Is it too late to fix it?"

"If you mean going to the press with your side of the story, Pam didn't recommend it. She thinks coming this late, it would feel phony. The public would be suspicious of all the time you were quiet."

Kate slapped the counter. "I was quiet because they told me to be."

"I know, kiddo, I know."

Kate dragged her hand down her hair and anchored the ends in her fist, pulling until her scalp stung.

"I'm afraid there's more bad news."

Kate braced herself. "My column?" If she lost her syndicated column, what would she have left?

"I'm afraid so," Ronald said. "I'm sorry."

Not my column. She'd already lost *Glamour*, but the column had been her baby forever. It was how she'd become Dr. Kate. She'd helped thousands of readers, and now it was gone. She remembered all the hours she'd spent reading letters and formulating answers. She remembered all the letters she'd answered privately because column space prevented her from answering all of them, and some of the letters seemed too desperate to ignore.

"We'll get through this, kiddo. Let's give it more time. Maybe your book sales will pick up again."

Kate grasped onto hope. "Is that what Pam said?"

If anyone would know, it would be Pam. Her publicity experience allowed her to read the public better than anyone.

"No, she didn't say that. But you're too good at giving advice to be holed up in some office. It's your calling, your gift, and we can't give up just yet."

It felt like it was over. She could write all the articles and books she wanted, but if readers didn't trust her anymore, what did it matter?

Kate hung up and put the salad on the table as her dad entered with a plate of sizzling steaks. They served themselves and began to eat. Kate hardly tasted the food.

They were halfway through the meal before her dad spoke. "You're quiet." He speared a chunk of meat and put it in his mouth.

Kate told him about Ronald's phone call and the apparent effect the scandal had on her career. "It's not looking good, Dad." That was an understatement.

He set his knife and fork down. "Look, Kate. I realize it must be devastating and maybe even humiliating for your wedding fiasco to be public knowledge. But your goal has always been to help troubled relationships. Ever since you were a little girl, you were helping people solve problems. You don't need fame or notoriety or even a book contract to achieve that."

Kate swallowed the bite of salad. He was right. She had enjoyed helping couples in counseling. However, it was more logical to prevent the impossible relationships than it was to fix them. And no one sought counseling until there was a problem. That's why writing relationship books made sense.

But lately, Kate wondered if she knew anything about relationships at all. Everything that made sense in theory was more complicated in real-life application. Case in point: Lucas.

Her stomach clamped down on the food she'd eaten, and she pushed her plate away, the sirloin half-eaten. A week ago, she'd realized her night with Lucas hadn't resulted in a pregnancy. She'd expected profound relief. Instead she'd gone to her room and closed the door before having a good cry. What was wrong with her?

"What's really wrong, Kate?" Her dad's brown eyes were an antique reflection of her own.

"My career is falling apart. Isn't that reason enough to be depressed?"

Her dad sliced the steak with the serrated knife and placed it beside his plate. "Is that why you don't eat? Why you stare off into space for minutes at a time? Why your eyes are so sad all the time?"

Kate's head throbbed. She'd had a constant headache since she'd left Nantucket. Like her body was having withdrawal from the island. *Or from Lucas.* She stifled the thought.

She stood and carried her plate to the sink. "I'd rather not talk about it." She didn't even want to think about it, but her mind never cooperated. She tried to put it behind her, but her thoughts returned to the island, to Lucas, like waves to a shoreline.

"It's that Lucas, isn't it?"

Kate gave him a warning look. He'd never been one to pry, and she hoped he didn't start now.

"Don't look at me like that. You've been moping around here for—"

"I am not moping."

"—three weeks, and I may be a man, but I know lovesick when I see it."

Kate gave a wry laugh. "Lovesick?" She pulled the sprayer from the sink and ran water over her plate. "It was an arrangement, Daddy, remember? You were there. You read the papers."

Her dad's chair scraped the ceramic tile as he stood. "And I saw the look in that boy's eyes on your wedding day." He held out his plate.

Kate pulled it from his hands. "That's ridiculous."

"Is it?"

She sprayed the salad dressing and A1 Sauce off the plate while her father cleared the table. Her father had imagined what he'd seen on Lucas's face.

"Anyway," Kate said. "It could never have worked. We were different as day and night."

"Opposites attract, you know." He leaned around her to wet a dishrag and went to wipe down the oak table.

"It's not like that. We have nothing in common, Daddy, and I'm not going to spend the rest my life arguing like—" She stopped, realizing she was crossing a line. Who was she to criticize her parents' marriage?

"Like your mom and me?" Her dad finished the thought.

Kate loaded the two plates back to back in the dishwasher and shut the door. The crestfallen look on her dad's face exacerbated her regret. "I'm sorry. I shouldn't have said that."

He nodded slowly. "No, that's fair." He leaned against the kitchen counter across from her, bracing his hands against the ledge, reminding her of the way Lucas had stood so many times.

"I've always wondered how much you remembered," he said.

She remembered more than the yelling. She remembered the time her dad had dumped sacks of her mom's new clothes out the front door. She could still see the new dresses, tags still attached, strewn across the spring green lawn. "When two people are so different, conflict is inevitable," Kate said.

Her dad shook his head. "Your mother and I weren't so different."

"Oh, come on, Daddy. She was a spender; you were a saver. She was messy and disorganized; you were a neat freak. She wanted to go places; you wanted to stay home."

"Is that what you think? That our marriage fell apart because we were too different?" Her dad drew in a deep breath, exhaled, then straightened and walked toward the living room. "Come sit, Kate."

She followed her dad into the room and sat on the center of the sofa, opposite his recliner.

"Your mother and I had a good marriage in the beginning," he said. "But soon, we began to disagree about a lot of things. At the time, I thought I was right about everything. I thought it was smart to control the money the way I did. I told myself I was looking out for our best interests. And I thought the house had to be kept a certain way. Your mom liked things neat too, but my standards were high. Unfeasibly high."

"Mom was a clutter bug."

"Not initially. The things I did drove her crazy. The way the labels on food packages had to be turned facing front, the way the towels had to be folded in thirds and hung in the center of the towel rack, the way our lives had to run by the clock, down to the second. It all became too much for her."

"You weren't the problem, Daddy. It was her. I remember. She was a spendaholic. She used to go out and shop and buy new furniture, new clothes, when we didn't have the money—"

Her dad tilted his head and gave a sad smile. "Your mom never liked to shop. She didn't care about new clothes or new furniture. She did it because she was angry with me."

"Why?" Kate shook her head, trying to make sense of it. "Why would she be angry with you?"

"You know what OCD is?"

"Of course. Obsessive-compulsive disorder. I've counseled a couple clients who—" Kate stopped, letting it soak in. *OCD.* "You, Daddy?"

"I didn't know it at the time. Your mom was after me for years to go and get checked. She insisted something was wrong, but I thought she was being critical. As the years went by, she got angrier and angrier. I wanted the house impossibly neat, so she made sure it wasn't. I wanted to control the money, so she spent it. I wanted to be punctual, so she dawdled."

Her dad pinched the crease in his pants, mechanically, following it down the thigh. "I didn't see any of it at the time. Of course, her actions made me furious, and we had terrible arguments. Unfortunately, you heard a lot of them. It was a vicious cycle that would've been broken if I'd just been able to see that I had a problem."

How could all of Kate's assumptions about her parents' marriage have been wrong? So much of what she advised stemmed from what she thought she'd learned from her childhood.

"One day, when you were eight or nine," he said. "I walked by your bedroom and heard you playing. I stopped and listened. Barbie was screaming at Ken, and Ken was yelling at Barbie. You were holding them face-to-face, and as you were talking in your angry little-girl voice, your mouth was all screwed up, your brows drawn together. I realized you thought that's the way families behaved. You thought that was normal."

Kate had spent a lot of time playing with her Barbies. When you were an only child, you learned to make believe. "I don't remember that."

Her dad folded his hands across his stomach. "It was then that I began to wonder if your mother and I would be better off apart."

Kate had thought it was her mom's decision. She'd been angry with her mom for months. But even though she'd blamed her mom—the woman was her caretaker, the one who fixed her French toast in the morning and made sure her favorite jeans were washed—Kate couldn't conceive of leaving her home. Even when her mom started drinking.

"When did you find out about the OCD?" Kate asked.

"Not until years later. You were nearly in college by then. None of the women I had dated could tolerate my behavior for long, and I finally opened my mind to the possibility that it was me."

Kate wasn't naive. She knew it took two people to nurture a relationship and two people to ruin it. But how had she gotten things so twisted around? Her mom had never set her straight, had never said a bad thing to Kate about her dad, even after they divorced. Instead, her mother drowned her sorrow in alcohol.

"I'm sorry about how I handled my marriage to your mom, Kate. I'm sorry you didn't have a better childhood."

Kate's eyes stung. "I appreciate that, Daddy. I know it's hard to make a marriage work under the best circumstances."

"I did love your mom. You know that."

"I know." *Does he know Mom went to her grave loving him? Mourning him?* Sometimes it was better not to know.

"I'm not very good at this stuff," he said. "But I love you, too, you know." He squeezed his hands together so tight, the tips of his fingers whitened.

Kate didn't remember ever hearing those words from her father. She'd known he loved her, but hearing them was a balm to her aching heart.

"I love you too, Daddy."

Sometimes there's nothing you can do but put one foot in front of the other.

—Excerpt from
Finding Mr. Right-for-You
by Dr. Kate

Chapter Thirty

Lucas dipped the tack cloth in mineral spirits and wiped the sawdust from the oak pie safe. One more coat of polyurethane and it would be ready for Sydney. He was eager to be done with that job. The day before she'd come into the shop to check on his work, even though he'd told her it wouldn't be ready for two more days. She'd closed the distance between them and caressed the unfinished piece with her slender fingers as if it were a man's arm instead of a hunk of wood.

"Very nice, Lucas. You have a certain touch." She smiled slowly.

He put space between them, wiping his hands on the rag. He'd done everything he could to make it clear he wasn't interested. He tried to show professional courtesy without stepping one inch past that line. For the life of him, he couldn't see why she continued to pursue him when there were probably a dozen men who'd be willing to buy whatever she was selling.

The phone rang, and Ethan called him. "If you'll excuse me . . ."

"Well," Sydney said, "I'll check back in a couple days then."

Now Lucas ran the cloth along the edges of the cabinet doors, taking care to remove every speck of dust so it wouldn't mar the finish. There was only one woman he couldn't get from his mind, and it wasn't Sydney.

Lucas glanced at the calendar hanging cockeyed from a prong on the pegboard. October 21. Today would have been their four-month anniversary. If Kate were here, he might've bought her a bouquet of daisies and taken her to Cioppino's for lobster. Afterward, they would've gone home, and he'd have put on her favorite classical CD and kissed her on the corner of her lip, right where—

Cut it out, Luc. You have got to move on. How many times had he relived moments of their time together? Especially the last night.

He'd tried to stay busy. He worked well into the night until he was too tired to do anything but shower and fall into bed. It was easier that way. He was tired of pitying glances from friends and neighbors. He could imagine what they were thinking. *Poor Lucas. First he lost Emily; now he's lost Kate. Tsk, tsk, tsk.* But no one brought up Kate, as if the very mention of her name would shatter him.

Everyone wondered where she was, though, including the media, some of whom had come to the island, hoping for an interview. Was it any wonder he spent his days holed up in his shop? Even here, he hadn't escaped the phone calls. Ethan intercepted them, and at least now the calls were coming farther apart.

The story had quieted down the past couple weeks—a blessing for Kate, he was sure. He supposed her career would rebound since the scandal died so quickly. She'd probably have her next book on the shelves next year sometime, and her life would continue as it had before he'd entered it.

But Lucas couldn't imagine his life returning to normal. Even though the story had fizzled out, he still found himself avoiding people. Even his family—a fact that hadn't gone unnoticed.

"We missed you at lunch Sunday," his mother had said when she dropped by the shop the previous week. Lucas noticed right away there was something different about her. She seemed less on edge. Happier, despite Lucas's withdrawal. Was his mom that happy to have Kate out of their lives?

Lucas didn't think she'd bought his excuse about being late on an order. His dad had come by later that week under the premise of borrowing his jigsaw, but Lucas had seen through that.

"You're putting in a lot of hours lately," his dad said.

"Business is good." He wasn't fooling anyone, and he knew it.

"You know, that Kate was something special."

Lucas clamped down hard on his jaw. Was his dad trying to rub it in? Didn't he know Lucas knew it better than anyone?

"She had a talk with your mom before she left," his dad said.

When had Kate had a chance to do that? Whatever she'd said must've worked a miracle. His dad said he was seeing a side of Susan he'd hadn't seen in years. She'd finally forgiven him for the mistake he'd made all those years ago. Lucas was happy for them.

Jamie visited him at the shop at least once a week and filled him in on her love life with Aaron. Brody kept bugging him to get an e-mail address so they could communicate more.

Lucas dipped the cloth in mineral spirits again and smoothed it over the drawer face a second time. He was nearly ready to apply the final coat of polyurethane when his shop door opened. Jamie entered, shutting the door. She turned and held up a copy of the *New York Times*.

"Did you see this?" Her chin jutted forward.

"See what?"

"The article about Kate." She extended the paper.

Lucas wiped the side panel of the pie safe, wiped the rim along the top, taking care to get into the crevices.

"Luc." Jamie approached, her flip-flops shuffling on the cement floor.

"I'm not interested."

The newspaper smacked against her jeans-encased leg. "You are, too, and you know it."

He moved around the pie case and wiped down the other panel.

"She lost her syndicated column," Jamie said.

Lucas's hand paused over the rim, then continued. Why had Kate lost her column? The story had died down just as her publisher hoped it would. Had the scandal done irreparable damage? *How could they cancel her column when she'd worked so hard? She's Dr. Kate, for pity's sake.*

"You have to do something, Luc."

He shook his head. "Maybe Kate decided to focus on books instead of the column."

"That's not what the article says."

Lucas looked at the paper, torn between grabbing it and reading every detail he could find about her life without him, and burning the paper so he could spare himself the agony.

"I'm sure she's fine. The story faded quickly enough."

"Her book sales are in the toilet."

Lucas arched his brow. "Did the article say that too?"

Jamie hitched her pointed little chin up a notch. "I've been keeping track of her numbers on Amazon."

"What's that?" He wished he hadn't asked. His sister was drawing him in, and he only wanted to put it behind him. He wiped the top of the pie case even though it was already clean.

"Amazon—where people buy books online?" Her look said, *Duh*. "She used to be ranked, like, below two hundred, and now her book is nearly at two hundred thousand!"

Lucas gave up on the pie case and threw his rag on the bench. He hoped it wasn't true. Kate was too good at what she did to let it all go to waste. "I take it that's a bad thing."

"Terrible. I'm telling you, her career is falling apart. You have to do something."

"Me . . . What am I supposed to do?"

Jamie dropped the paper on the bench and crossed her arms, eyeing him. She tapped her foot, her glittery pink toenails rising and falling.

"You didn't tell her, did you." It wasn't a question so much as an accusation.

"Tell her what?"

"That you love her."

Lucas turned and wrapped the cord around the sander, then hung it on a prong. His sister had gotten too good at reading his thoughts. Maybe it was all those romances she devoured.

"Well," Jamie said, "I guess that answers my question."

Lucas pocketed his hands. "That's between me and Kate, munchkin."

"How can it be between you and Kate if she doesn't even know?"

Little squirt. She was getting too smart for her own britches.

"It might've made a difference if she'd known," Jamie said. "I know it's none of my business . . . but I want you to be happy. Besides, if you hadn't helped me with Aaron, we probably never would've gotten together."

"How's that going, anyway?"

"We're still going out, but stop trying to change the subject. Are you going to help Kate or not?"

Later that night Lucas lay wide eyed in bed. Jamie's question rang through his head. *"Are you going to help Kate or not?"* But what could he do when she was gone? He couldn't turn back time or make that Stephanie chick rescind the story.

The headline that had appeared in *USA Today* snagged in his mind. *"Dr. Kate in Loveless Marriage."* Two of the tabloids he'd picked up had an article that focused on their loveless marriage arrangement.

When he'd read it, he'd almost laughed. Little did they know, there had been plenty of love in the marriage. Unfortunately it was all his.

Was it? Would she have given herself to me that last night if she didn't love me? His chest tightened, aching at the thought. Maybe it was only wishful thinking.

But what if it's true? What if Kate loves me? What if she only left because she's afraid?

He remembered the articles about their loveless marriage and wondered if it would accomplish anything if her readers knew he'd loved her. *Still love her*, he corrected himself. Would it somehow redeem her in the public's eyes?

Even if it did, there was no way he could trust the media. They were sharks, out for their scoop and willing to trample anything that stood between them and their prey. Even if Lucas could somehow convey his feelings to the media, they would twist it and warp it and use it to hurt Kate.

Maybe he should call that publicity woman Kate worked with—Pam? Maybe he could bounce the idea off her without letting Kate know. Maybe then, if he did everything in his power to help her, he'd finally have peace.

Love is always a risk.

—Excerpt from
Finding Mr. Right-for-You
by Dr. Kate

Chapter Thirty-One

"I'm going to the grocery, Dad." Kate shut the dishwasher, latched it closed, and pushed the button to start it. It whirred into action.

In the living room, her dad turned on the TV to a Taco Bell commercial. He reached for his wallet. "Here, let me pay this time."

Kate waved him off. "I got it." She picked up her purse. It was the least she could do when he was letting her stay there until she found a place. She had a nice nest egg in her savings account. "I might run by that apartment on—"

"Kate." Her dad turned up the TV's volume.

Kate followed his widened eyes to the screen. *Lucas.* Lucas was on TV. He wore a suit and tie. Her breath caught.

"—happened between Dr. Kate and her Mr. Right?"

The screen changed to show *NewsWire* correspondent Nancy Lopez. "Can you tell us how you came to be married to Dr. Kate?"

There was a quick clip of Lucas shrugging, a mischievous look on his face; then the camera cut to Nancy.

"Dr. Kate has been ridiculed for entering a marriage as if it were a business arrangement. Was it really a loveless marriage?"

The camera cut to Lucas. "Funny you should ask that." He gave his charming half grin.

The *NewsWire* logo appeared on the screen and a voiceover sounded. "Everyone wants to know why renowned columnist Dr. Kate married Mr. Wright, and *NewsWire* has the exclusive. Tune in tomorrow night at ten o'clock Eastern Standard Time."

Another commercial started and her dad turned down the volume. Kate sank onto the couch, numb. *I don't understand. Why did Lucas do it? Just when the scandal died down, he went and brought it to the surface again.*

"I can't believe it." She stood again and paced the room as anger fired through her veins, her heart beating double time. She was furious—and hurt. *Why is he doing this?*

"You should call him," her dad said. "Maybe there's a—"

Her cell rang. She pulled it from her purse, hoping it was Lucas, because she had a few things to say to him. Her hand shook as she answered.

"Kate, what's going on?" her friend Anna asked. "I just saw a promo for *NewsWire*—"

"I know. I saw it too."

"You didn't know about it?" She'd kept Anna up-to-date on everything through e-mail.

"No, I didn't know. I can't believe he's done this." Kate ran her hand through her hair.

"Just when everything was starting to die down," Anna said. "Why would he do it?"

"I don't know, but I'm going to find out. I'll call you back after I talk to him."

They hung up, and Kate looked at her dad. Her throat was tight, her head ached behind her eyes, and she wanted to hit something.

"Maybe there's an explanation," her dad said.

"Sure there is. About two hundred thousand of them." They'd probably paid him at least that for an exclusive. Did Lucas hope to expand his shop with the money? She'd never thought him ambitious, yet what other reason could he have?

She remembered how he'd turned down the opportunity to be interviewed on *Live with Lisa* alongside her. What had he said? *"Talking's not my thing. Words don't come easy to me, like they do you."* She remembered the sob story he'd told her about being paralyzed with fright in front of a school assembly. Apparently he could keep his composure if enough money was involved.

The betrayal hurt.

Kate dialed Lucas's number. He should be home by now, probably making a mess in the kitchen. *I hope he chokes on his dinner.*

"Maybe you should wait until you've calmed down." Her dad flipped off the TV.

The phone rang over to voice mail. The beep sounded. Kate tried to swallow the lump in her throat, but it was firmly lodged. "What are you doing, Lucas? I just saw the *NewsWire* promo. I can't believe—" Her voice wobbled, and she took a steadying breath. *I am not going to let him know he has me in tears.*

"I can't believe you'd do this. Call me." She disconnected the call.

She paced the room. She was a traveling earthquake, and Lucas was the epicenter.

"So, this is the guy you've been mooning over for weeks," her dad said. "He doesn't deserve you."

"He doesn't have me, Dad." Not now. Not after this. She couldn't stand the thought of him anymore.

Come on, Kate. Feelings don't evaporate simply because you've been betrayed. She knew it was true. All she had to do was remember Mrs. Hornsby and all the other victims of unfaithful spouses she'd counseled. But couldn't she just be mad without her internal therapist kicking in?

"Well, I suppose your career can't be damaged any more than it already was."

No, but Kate had hoped the public humiliation was over. She'd hoped to fade from the public eye and return to private counseling. The last thing she needed was to have the scandal revived. She'd thought if anyone would betray her to the media, it would've been Bryan.

She'd never thought for a minute Lucas would cave to the pressure.

Love is full of surprises.

—Excerpt from
Finding Mr. Right-for-You
by Dr. Kate

Chapter Thirty-Two

Kate tidied the kitchen, then straightened the seasonings on the wooden rack. Two more minutes. Each one passed like a turtle on Valium.

All day she'd tried to reach Lucas. When she called the shop, Ethan said he was out, yet he didn't answer at home. No one picked up at his parents' house, and her e-mails went unanswered. They were probably embarrassed by Lucas's betrayal. But maybe they'd been interviewed too. Maybe they were splitting the bounty and taking a trip to Europe to celebrate.

A dish towel fell to the floor and Kate kicked it, leaving it crumpled between the fridge and cabinet. No one from Rosewood had returned her calls either. She'd phoned Ronald first thing that morning, but he hadn't been able to reach Paul or Chloe. It seemed she had become persona non grata. They had to know about the exclusive. They were probably angry with her for letting it happen. *As if I had a choice.*

"Kate, it's coming on," her dad called from the living room.

Kate entered the room where her dad perched on the edge of the brown sofa, his elbows on his knees.

Kate sat beside him and hugged the chenille pillow to her stomach. A barrier for the coming sucker punch.

The *NewsWire* theme song played as the logo appeared. They showed previews of the upcoming segments, including the same preview she'd seen the night before. The first segment began, but it wasn't Lucas's.

When they cut to a commercial. Kate released her breath. "I hope it's not last."

Her dad crossed his legs at the knee. "It might be."

She'd waited all day, a nervous ball of energy. Why hadn't Lucas returned her calls? Why hadn't anyone returned them? Was he too ashamed to face her? *He should be.*

"Want some coffee?" Her dad asked. "I can put on a pot."

Kate shook her head. "I feel like I could run across water as it is."

When the show returned, they focused on the TV, but it was a segment about trans fats in restaurant food.

Kate wondered what questions they would ask Lucas. Would he tell them she'd cried herself to sleep on their honeymoon? Would he tell them his mom disliked her from the beginning because of whose daughter she was? Would he tell them about the special moments— the ones when they forgot their marriage was an arrangement?

Fear sucked the moisture from her mouth. Kate felt as if she stood on the gallows, with a thick rope at her neck, waiting for the floor to open. And there was nothing she could do but wait.

The segment ended and another commercial break ensued. It was half past the hour.

"Hang in there, Kate. Whatever comes, I'll be here for you." Her dad reached over and squeezed her cold hand.

"Thanks, Daddy." She couldn't sit anymore. She stood and walked to the patio door. Outside, darkness swallowed the yard and a sliver of moon peeked from behind a curtain of clouds. She kept remembering the last days with Lucas, the way he'd held her that night, pressing kisses to her forehead and chin, smoothing her hair from her face. She'd never felt more cared for, more cherished.

And now he's airing our dirty laundry on national TV. It doesn't make sense.

"It's back on," her dad said.

Kate returned to the living room, stopping behind the recliner. Evan Greggory began a segment about the sole survivor of a ferry accident overseas. They were saving Lucas's segment for last, which showed they viewed it as important. *They must've gotten some juicy material from Lucas.*

The ferry segment seemed to last forever. A long commercial break followed. Kate's heart rate tripled as she waited for the commercials to end. This was it. There was only twelve minutes remaining—only enough time for Lucas's story.

When the program returned, her dad cranked up the volume. The camera panned in on Nancy Lopez. "Welcome back to *NewsWire.*" She turned to a different camera. "She is the queen of relationships and the author of recent self-help book *Finding Mr. Right-for-You.*"

Nancy held up a copy of the book. "Dr. Kate's book was released with much media attention on her wedding day this summer, and it soared to the bestseller's list."

Kate nearly rolled her eyes. The book had barely made it to the bottom of the bestseller's list, achieving less than Rosewood had hoped.

Nancy continued. "But Dr. Kate's career recently turned upside down when it was revealed that her real fiancé, Bryan Montgomery, left her at the altar, and that Dr. Kate impulsively entered a loveless marriage arrangement with Nantucket native Lucas Wright as a last-ditch effort to save her book from certain death.

"Little is known about the terms of the arrangement or Dr. Kate's feelings on the matter, but *NewsWire* has gained an exclusive interview with the man who found himself at the altar with marriage expert Dr. Kate." Nancy smiled and turned as the camera cut to Lucas. "Welcome to the show, Mr. Wright."

Kate honed in on Lucas. He'd shaved, and his hair was combed neatly off his face as it had been at their wedding. He wore a dress shirt and tie she'd never seen. He thanked Nancy.

"Can you tell us how you knew Dr. Kate and for how long before the wedding?"

Lucas shifted subtly. He was uncomfortable. *Good.*

"Kate had been on the island for three years," Lucas began. "She was born there, but her family left when she was young. I didn't know her then. When she moved back, she wanted to open an office in town. She rented the space over my shop."

"Can you tell us what happened on the day of her wedding?"

He nodded slowly. "I was working in my shop that morning. Actually I was putting the finishing touches on the gazebo she'd asked me to make."

"For her wedding with Bryan Montgomery?"

"Yes. She'd hired me to build it months earlier. Kate came to the shop to check on it because I was supposed to have delivered it already. When she was there, she got a call from her fiancé."

"Mr. Montgomery?"

"Yes. I only heard her end of the conversation, but it was enough to tell me he wasn't going through with the wedding."

"What was Kate's state of mind after the phone call?"

Lucas tilted back, and he shook his head. "She was devastated. She was trembling." He gave a sad smile. "You'd have to know Kate to know how unlike herself she was after that phone call. She's the most calm, capable individual I've ever met. She's the kind of person you want during a crisis because she—She just takes care of things. But it was five hours before her wedding, and her groom just left her at the altar, and with the publicity surrounding the release of the book . . . who wouldn't panic?"

"How did you come to be part of the solution?" Nancy asked.

"It was my idea. I don't know where it came from. It was impulsive, and it seemed like the only solution at the time. She needed a groom, and I wanted to help her."

"That's some help. Why would you agree to step in and save her wedding?"

Lucas looked down at his lap and paused a moment. "The reason I gave Kate was that I needed her help on a personal project."

"But that wasn't the real reason, I take it," Nancy said.

"No."

"What?" Kate whispered, staring at the screen.

"We'll get back to that in a moment," Nancy continued. "What were the terms of the arrangement?"

Lucas's mouth tilted in a smile as if remembering the moment. "There had to be an escape clause. We agreed to remain married for a year."

"Was there a contract between you? Financial arrangements?"

"It wasn't like that. We knew each other well enough to trust one another. We kept our finances separate."

"And no money exchanged hands?"

A pink flushed climbed Lucas's neck. He looked like a bashful schoolboy. "She didn't pay me for the honor of being her husband, if that's what you mean."

Nancy's smile made it clear she was captivated by Lucas's charm.

"Can you define your relationship with Dr. Kate prior to the wedding? Were you lovers, friends . . ?"

Lucas ran his fingers between his neck and collar. "No, we weren't lovers. I guess you could say we were friends. We spent quite a bit of time together when I renovated her space into an office and apartment. She lived and worked above my shop, so we saw each other frequently." His smile tilted. "Kate probably would've said we were acquaintances. I think I got on her nerves a bit."

"You say that like you enjoyed it."

Lucas smiled. "Little bit."

Kate squeezed the cushion on the back of the recliner, unable to take her eyes off Lucas.

Nancy continued. "You've denied being paid to marry Dr. Kate, and you've hinted that the reason you gave her was false." The camera cut to Lucas's face while Nancy stated the question. "Why *did* you stand in as her groom?"

Lucas looked down at his lap, his smile faltering. He swallowed.

Kate wondered for a long moment if he was going to freeze as he had so long ago on a school gym stage. She found herself pulling for him, wanting to help him formulate an answer.

But then he spoke. "I wanted to help her. If you'd seen her after that phone call—she was panicked. Afraid. Hurt." Lucas shrugged. "I wanted to help."

"Why?" Nancy asked.

Kate leaned forward, her breath on hope's threshold.

He gave a sad little smile. As his head tilted down, his hair fell forward, partially covering his eyes. Then he looked back at Nancy. "I love her," he said in a throaty voice.

Kate sucked in her breath. She stared into his familiar face and felt an ache behind her eyes. *He loves me? He married me . . . because he loves me? But his parents' marriage—*

The camera stayed on Lucas even though he stopped talking. He was clearly uncomfortable, like he wanted to squirm right out of the starchy suit.

He filled the silence. "When I saw how upset she was, I wanted to fix it for her." He lifted one shoulder. "Maybe I was a little selfish too. Maybe I thought if she was mine for a year, she'd somehow fall in love with me too." He shifted, looking away. "I was trying to save her wedding. I guess it was wrong of me to take advantage. She was vulnerable. I came up with the idea and convinced her it was the only solution. If anyone's to blame, it's me."

He went blurry as Kate's eyes filled. She blinked, not wanting anything blocking her view of Lucas's face.

The camera cut to Nancy. "In reality, you were only married three months. What was it like?"

"Being married to Kate?" He smiled. "Great. Fun. Challenging."

"Challenging because . . . ?"

Lucas tugged at his suit coat. "Because I love her. Because I wanted the marriage to be real, and it wasn't." He paused, looking down again. "In three months she solved problems that have been in place for years. She's got this deep well of wisdom . . . I don't know where it comes from. If something's broken, she fixes it."

"Except your heart?"

The camera slowly closed in on Lucas's face. His jaw clenched, then loosened. "I'm not sure she knows she broke it."

Nancy smiled. "She does now. It's fairly common knowledge that Kate left the island shortly after the scandal erupted. Can you give us your thoughts on that?"

Lucas sucked in a breath and blew it out. He shifted.

Kate wanted to brush the hair out of his face, run her palm down his tense jawline and kiss away the frown on his lips.

"I didn't want her leave. I asked her to stay."

"But she didn't."

"No."

"Was she still in love with her former fiancé?" Nancy asked.

"I asked her that. She said she wasn't, and I believed her."

The camera cut to Nancy as she studied Lucas, a thoughtful expression on her face. "Why are you here today? What do you hope to accomplish?"

"I wanted to tell Kate's side of the story. I wanted to take responsibility for my part in it . . . ." Lucas pulled at his tie.

The camera cut to Nancy. "Anything else?"

Lucas looked down, then met Nancy's eyes again. "I wanted to tell her what I was afraid to say before she left."

He swallowed, then looked at the camera, his eyes burning into Kate's. She locked onto his face, feeling as if he were right in front of her, right now.

Lucas's chin came up.

Kate watched his lips, waiting.

"I want to tell her I love her," he said.

Kate put her hand against her chest, squeezed the stiff material of her shirt.

Nancy paused for a full three seconds, letting the words sink in. "On national TV?"

He gave his crooked smile. "I guess I'm laying it all on the line. I love her. I have for a long time, and I always will." He looked down again.

"That's a lot of pressure for a girl," Nancy said.

Lucas shook his head. "Hope not. That wasn't my intention. Kate's entitled to make her own choices, to choose her own life. I just want her to have all the facts before she does."

Nancy said something that tied the story into a neat bow, then signed off. Kate's dad flipped off the TV. Without the light and noise of the TV, the room fell into darkness and silence. Her mind whirled faster than a carnival ride.

"Well." Her dad flipped on the lamp.

Kate's legs felt wooden as she rounded the recliner and sank into it. She was shaking, her hands and legs trembling uncontrollably. *He loves me. He's loved me from the beginning.*

She felt a sudden, inexorable need to talk to him. To see him.

"Do you love him, Kate?" Her dad's voice broke through her thoughts.

Do I love him? She remembered the way he held her on the sailboat when she was sick. Remembered the way he held her when the scandal broke. Remembered how treasured she felt when he looked at her, touched her.

"Yes," she whispered.

But they were so different. It was why she'd left. She didn't want to wind up like—

My parents? Well, I've already discovered how wrong I was on that

284

one. It wasn't their differences that broke them apart but her dad's disorder.

But even with that understanding, her heart faltered in fear. *What am I afraid of? That I'm going to wind up alone and desperate like Mom?*

But I can't control the future. I can't even control the present. I just have to make reasonable decisions and hope for the best. Look how meticulously I planned my engagement and wedding. And still, it all fell apart.

Did her obsessive need to plan stem from a desperate desire for control?

Kate remembered the conversation she'd had with Brody that day on the widow's walk. *"I'm not afraid of heights so much as I'm afraid of falling,"* she'd said. Was that her problem? Why she'd nearly married a man she didn't love? Why she'd been in such a hurry to leave the man she did love? She was afraid of becoming her mom. Afraid of becoming like the hundreds of women she'd counseled.

Kate gave a wry laugh. Some psychotherapist she was. She was only now figuring out that she was avoiding love.

"You think you should call him?" her dad asked.

What should she do? She wanted to tell him she loved him. She wanted to say she was sorry for leaving. A shiver of fear snaked its way up her spine. What if it didn't work? What if he broke her heart?

It's already been broken. Let him heal it. Her advice to Brody came back to her: *"It's fear that makes an act courageous."* *Do I have the courage to love him back?*

Kate straightened. She did. She was ready to put it all on the line, like he had.

But she wanted to do it face-to-face. She wanted to touch him, feel the strength of his arms around her when she said the words.

"I have to go to him," she said firmly.

Her dad nodded.

She checked her watch. "I can be there by morning if I drive to Hyannis and take the ferry."

"And drive all night? Kate . . ."

"I have to see him." She had to tell him she loved him. She could take a flight, but then her car would be here. No, it was settled. She'd never be able to sleep anyway. She might as well spend the night closing the distance between them.

How much we trust others is often a reflection of how much we trust ourselves.

—Excerpt from
inding Mr. Right-for-You
by Dr. Kate

Chapter Thirty-Three

She didn't call.

It was impossible to soothe the ache in his gut. Lucas rolled over and stared out the window, where dawn stretched, spreading gray across the midnight canvas. He pulled Kate's pillow close, inhaling. The scent of her was nearly gone—that subtle lilac scent that perfumed her hair.

He'd been pleased with the interview, relieved that the words had come when he needed them, relieved that he'd survived the interview without cracking under the pressure. After the show aired the night before, he waited, pacing the floor until Bo tired of his excess energy and curled up at the foot of the sofa.

When the phone had rung, his feet made quick work of the

distance to the kitchen, and he answered breathlessly, not caring if Kate knew he was waiting for her call.

But it had been his mom. *"Honey, I'm so sorry. I knew you loved her, but I guess I just didn't realize how much."* She apologized for treating Kate badly and asked if he'd heard from her.

He didn't give up hope until after midnight. And even though he turned off the lights and lay in bed, he still couldn't sleep. His ears strained to hear the phone's ring. He slept restlessly, awake as much as he was asleep, and now that morning had arrived, his hopes washed away like a sand castle at high tide.

He forced himself from bed, showered, and put on a pot of coffee, draining the first cup like it was medicine for his wounded spirit. When Bo picked up his tennis ball and carried it to the back door, he stood.

"Go for a walk, boy?"

He followed the dog outside, past the gazebo—a constant reminder of Kate and their wedding day. He crossed the beach and turned eastward, tossed the tennis ball into the surf, and watched Bo lumber after it.

Had Kate even watched the show? He knew from her voice mail that she'd been angry when she'd seen the preview. What if she hadn't watched it?

Worse, what if she had? What if she heard his proclamation of love and didn't feel the same way? What if he'd accomplished nothing other than publicly humiliating himself?

I've done all I can. She knows how I feel now. The rest is up to her.

Bo returned the ball, dropping it in the wet sand at Lucas's feet. Lucas picked it up and heaved it into the waves before stuffing his hands into his pockets. His fingers wrapped around cool metal. Kate's wedding band. He ran his thumb around the smooth surface. Its presence comforted him, like he carried a piece of her with him.

Bo turned in a circle, the tennis ball between his teeth, his paws dancing in the foamy sand. The sun glittered off the surface of the water like a million diamonds. When Lucas reached Bo, he tugged the wet ball from his jaws and threw it as far as he could down the shoreline, then followed Bo's footprints.

❦

Kate stepped off the ferry, her overnight case clutched in her hand. She'd left her car in Hyannis since there was no room on the ferry. Now as the crowd dissipated on the concrete dock, she wondered if she'd be able to get a cab.

She tugged the baseball cap low on her head to avoid recognition and pulled her sweater tighter against the nip in the air. The trees had fully turned, washing Nantucket down in vibrant hues of yellow and red.

Her phone pealed, and she moved to the side of the dock as she pulled her cell from her bag and checked the caller ID. It was Pam. Kate didn't want to talk business; she wanted to get to Lucas. She was so close.

But her publicity gal wouldn't call on a Saturday for nothing. Kate answered. "Hi, Pam. How are you?"

"Good. Great. Have you seen the papers?"

Kate had seen nothing all night but the yellow lines on the road. And she'd given little thought to her career or what others would be saying. "No, why?" Kate was almost afraid to know, but Pam didn't sound dismayed.

"It worked! Listen to this. 'Dr. Kate's counterfeit groom broke his silence on TV newsmagazine show *NewsWire* when he proclaimed his love for the well-known author and syndicated relationship columnist.' Blah, blah, blah—backstory and quotes from the interview.

Ah, here we go. 'It seems, even in the case of unpredictable disasters, Dr. Kate's own brand of relationship magic works like a charm. Even for herself.'"

Kate sank to the cement ledge overlooking the harbor. Through the phone, she heard the rattling of newspaper pages. "There are a dozen more just like it. And I caught it on several cable news programs this morning too. They keep running the portion of the interview where Lucas says"—she lowered her voice—"'I guess I'm laying it all on the line. I love her. I have for a long time, and I always will.' Oh, man, he has every woman in America fanning her face, Kate. I'll bet your book is flying off the shelves as we speak."

I can't believe it. How have I gone from—

Something Pam had said earlier popped into her mind. *"It worked."* The words had been buried beneath the good news, but now they surfaced like a piece of driftwood through the sand, uncovered by the relentless wind.

Kate interrupted Pam. "Wait. You said 'It worked.' What did you mean?"

The rustling of paper stopped. A seagull swooped down and landed in the harbor, bobbing on the waves beside a fat buoy.

"You haven't called him?" Pam's tone revealed shock.

Dread filled Kate, numbing her to the fingertips. "What's going on, Pam?" Her thoughts spun. Terrible thoughts that tortured her. "Was this just a ploy to fix my book sales?" She could choke on the acid that rose in her throat. Had Lucas only been pretending?

"No, sweetie, it's not like that."

"Then what is it like?" Her voice quavered.

Pam sighed loudly. "You should hear this from Lucas. Why didn't you call him?"

Kate suddenly felt like a fool for driving all night like this was some 911 emergency. "I wanted to talk to him in person." Her answer was feeble. Kate swallowed the acid and her pride. "I'm here now, on Nantucket."

"Oh, I am such a dolt!" Kate imagined Pam smacking her own forehead. "I've ruined everything. Go. Go talk to him. I'm hanging up now."

"No, wait. Pam!" A click, then a dial tone buzzed in Kate's ear. She jabbed the Off button and gulped three breaths of air, laden with salt and exhaust fumes. What was going on? Had Pam called Lucas and devised some scheme to get her book sales back on track? What if Lucas hadn't meant any of it? But why would he have put himself through it if he didn't love her?

Uh, the money?

She felt like a sailboat, pushed at the whimsy of the wind, and she'd just suffered a gust from an unexpected direction.

But this was the new Kate. The one who didn't have to plan every action. She was going to go with the flow. And right now, she needed to find Lucas, find out if he meant what he said.

Kate stood, hitching the bag on her shoulder, and turned toward town.

When she reached Main Street, she hailed a cab and gave him the address. Though she hadn't slept, the phone call and nervous energy at seeing Lucas again kept her alert.

What will I say to him? Do I have the courage to face him? To put up my sails and let the wind take me where it may?

Her muscles tightened until they cramped. She relaxed her hold on the leather handle of the overnight bag as Lucas's words returned to her: *"Love isn't some item on a checklist."*

Maybe sometimes you had to loosen your grip. But it was scary. It required trust and faith. Two things she ran short on.

If there's anyone I can trust, it's Lucas. Kate allowed herself that.

Reminded herself it was true. He'd never given her any reason to distrust him.

"I love her. I have for a long time, and I always will." She'd played his words over and over on the drive, drinking them up, soothing her troubled spirit with the promise. But now she wondered if he meant them.

A picture of her mom flashed in her mind. She was hunched over the kitchen table in her terry bathrobe, a bottle of scotch in her bony hand. A photo album was open on the table in front of her, and her hand smoothed over the glossy page as if she stroked the face in the photo. How many times had she seen her mother like that, dying one memory at a time?

Kate shook the thought. She wasn't her mother. And Lucas wasn't her father. It was like he'd said all along. She needed to stop analyzing and let herself love him. Let herself be loved, if he was willing. She couldn't think of anyone more trustworthy.

When the cab pulled in the drive, Kate withdrew some cash and paid the driver, then gathered her bag and exited the car. Lucas's old truck was in the drive. He'd surely heard the cab on the gravel, yet even after it pulled away, the front door remained closed.

Kate walked toward the house and up the steps, hesitating on the porch. Lifting her hand, she rapped on the wooden door, anticipating Bo's loud, gruff bark. But the only reply was the sound of the wind swishing through the trees. The small window in the door revealed only darkness. She knocked again. Maybe he was in the shower. It was still early for a Saturday, though Lucas was normally out and about by now.

She bit her lip, wondering if she should enter. Before she could dissuade herself, she twisted the knob and stepped inside.

"Lucas?" The rich aroma of brewed coffee permeated the house.

The bedroom was empty, the blankets a tangled heap at the foot of the bed. The bathroom was dark, and several crumpled towels littered the floor. She smiled.

"Lucas?" In the kitchen, his empty Nantucket mug sat on the table. The coffeemaker was still plugged in. He must've taken Bo for a walk.

Kate exited through the back, passing the gazebo, tracing the numerous footprints down the sandy path. The beach was empty except for a few gulls, plucking through the wet sand. Kate looked down the shoreline toward the Wrights' house. The beach was deserted as far as she could see.

She looked the other direction, and her eyes paused on two figures: a man and a dog.

Lucas.

Her feet carried her down the shoreline, her heart pumping in rhythm with her quick steps. Halfway there, Bo spotted her and lumbered toward her, but Lucas stared out across the ocean, oblivious to her appearance. Bo reached her side and barreled into her leg, tail wagging.

"Hi, boy." At least Bo was happy to see her again. It was Lucas she was unsure of.

Kate looked at Lucas in time to see him turn. He stilled, watching her approach. She closed the distance between them with long, eager strides. As she neared, she tried to read his expression, but the sun glinted over his shoulder, making it impossible to decipher.

She stopped a car's length away, suddenly uncertain. Would he welcome her home after she'd left so suddenly? He'd asked her to stay, but would he forgive her for leaving?

Fear left her mouth dry, sucked the words from her lips. It clawed at her throat and churned her thoughts like sand in the surf.

Her limbs felt as stiff as a ship's mast. Tears glazed her eyes, and she told herself it was the biting wind.

Then he moved, walking toward her, stopping just a touch away. "You came back," he said.

His eyes were just the way she remembered, warm and soft. Welcoming.

"I had to see you," she said.

"Why?"

All the words she'd planned in the car scattered like startled gulls. Pam's call had changed everything. She was no longer sure of anything, least of all, Lucas's feelings.

"I saw the interview." *Was it all a ruse, or did you mean it?*

"I was hoping you'd watch." He tilted his head. "Are you angry?"

He was remembering the voice mail she'd left. Her anger had drained away with his proclamation of love. "No." The wind kicked up, and she pulled her sweater tighter. She had to settle this before her heart jumped through her rib cage. "Pam called."

He tucked his hands in his pockets. "She told you, then?"

Suddenly, Kate realized it didn't matter why Lucas had done the interview or what plan Pam had been talking about. She'd come to tell Lucas how she felt, and she was going to do it.

"She didn't tell me anything." Kate gathered her courage and drew a shaky breath. "I realized something last night while I watched you on TV." *"I love her. I have for a long time, and I always will."* His words were a pedestal for her courage.

"What's that?"

Kate swallowed the fear and took a step closer. The wind ruffled his hair, and she smoothed it from his face, then trailed her fingertips down the rough plane of his jaw. "I love you."

She ignored the burning in her eyes and plunged forward, a sailboat into the wind. "I don't know when it started or how it happened. I only know that you captured my heart, and I don't want it back. I want to stay here forever. I want to wake up to your stubbly, scratchy face and lie next to you in bed, even if you snore loudly enough to peel the paint off the walls. I want to—

Lucas broke off her words with his kiss. Kate felt his fingers sliding into her hair, knocking her cap to the ground. She relished the tenderness in his touch, and as he claimed her, she gave herself fully to him.

When she finally pulled away, it was only to look him in the eyes. "Did you really—love me from the beginning?" She had to know if it was true. Had to see him face-to-face when he said it.

One corner of his lip drew up. "Yeah."

She let it soak in. "And that's why you took me as your bride?"

He cupped her chin. "The only reason."

Kate released her pent-up breath. It was true, then. Everything he'd said, everything that mattered, was true.

Lucas reached into his pocket and withdrew something. He took her hand and opened his palm.

"My wedding band," Kate said.

He looked her in the eye, pausing with the ring at the tip of her finger. "I love you, Kate Wright. There aren't enough miles on the earth to separate you from it. I want you to be mine." He squeezed her hand. "Fully mine." He looked at her, looked into her.

"I want that too." Kate said.

Lucas slid it in place. It was right where it belonged.

I'm right where I belong.

He placed a kiss on her mouth and wrapped his strong arms around her. She felt safe in his arms. Loved. Cherished.

"Forever this time?" he asked.

She snuggled into his chest, inhaling the familiar scent of him, all musky and woodsy. *Man, I missed that.* "Forever." She smiled at the taste of the word on her tongue. No temporary arrangement this time. No twelve-month escape clause. She wanted in, and she never wanted out again.

She fingered the wedding band with her thumb. "My finger has felt naked since I took it off."

Lucas lifted her hand and kissed it. "Too bad I didn't accept the money for the interview. Could've bought you one heck of a diamond."

Kate squeezed his hand. "I could put the other one back on."

"Don't you dare." Lucas gave her a mock glare before pulling her back in his arms. "Did Pam tell you I called her?" He asked against her hair.

"You called *her*?" Kate couldn't imagine why he'd do that.

"I told her I loved you and asked what I could do to save your career and—" Lucas swept Kate off her feet, as a wave rushed under their feet. He set her down up shore on the dry sand. "Didn't think you'd want your shoes wet."

Bo bumped Lucas's thigh, a slobbery tennis ball in his jaws. Lucas tossed the ball a long ways down the beach.

"What did Pam say?" Kate slipped her hands into Lucas's, savoring the security of his warm grip.

"She said women love a fairy-tale romance."

Kate laughed, joy bubbling inside for the first time in a long time. "And you love being the knight in shining armor."

His shoulders rose in a shrug and he gave her his crooked grin. "If the armored boot fits . . ."

Kate elbowed Lucas then fell in step beside him as they walked toward home.

Home.

The word had a nice ring to it, and she felt a smile lift her lips. It wouldn't matter where she was or what she was doing, home would always be wherever Lucas was.

Acknowledgments

My deepest thanks go to all the people who had a hand in the making of this book. Thanks to my editor, Amanda Bostic, and the amazing team of creative, talented people in Thomas Nelson's fiction department. I'm truly honored and blessed to work with you. Thanks to Leslie Peterson for helping me polish the story. Thanks to my wonderful agent, Karen Solem, and my critique partner, Colleen Coble, who squeezed in my chapters while on her own tight deadline. Thanks to my writing buds, Kristin Billerbeck, Colleen Coble, and Diann Hunt: you bless my life in immeasurable ways!

A special thanks to my readers—you make it all worthwhile! I'd love to hear from you. E-mail me at denise@denisehunterbooks.com, or visit my Web site at www.DeniseHunterBooks.com.

Reading Group Guide

1. Lucas's love for Kate is an allegory for Christ's love for us. In what ways are the timing and qualities of Lucas's love symbolic of Christ's love?

2. What are some of the ways Lucas saved Kate in the story? What was Kate's reaction to his saving her? How has Christ saved you? Have you ever responded in some of the ways that Kate did?

3. One thing Kate was apt to do is fix things on her own. In our culture, that's a popular reaction. Do you respond to crises in a similar way? Is that the best way to deal with problems?

4. One of the hardest things to do when trouble comes is wait. Kate had difficulty waiting when her publisher was trying to find a solution to the problem. Is it hard for you to wait on God? Psalm 46:10 says, "Be still, and know that I am God." How can that be applied to trying times? Psalm 27:14 says, "Wait for the LORD; be strong and take heart and wait for the LORD." What can we learn about patience from this verse?

5. When Kate made the choice to leave Lucas, he knew it was a decision Kate had to make for herself. How has God been patient in waiting for you to come to Him?

6. When Kate left Lucas, he said that a thousand miles couldn't separate her from his love. How is Christ's love like that?

7. Lucas laid it all on the line when he faced his biggest fear and publicly proclaimed his love for Kate. How has Christ proclaimed His love for you?

8. Even though Kate broke Lucas's heart by leaving and by fighting her relationship with him, he gladly welcomed her back. Have you ever pushed Christ away or run from His love? What does it feel like to know that no matter what you do, He will always welcome you home?

About the Author

Denise Hunter is the award-winning and best-selling author of eight novels, including *Surrender Bay*, *The Convenient Groom*, and *Sweetwater Gap*. She and her husband are raising three boys.

the Wedding Machine

This book is dedicated
to my mother,

Betty Jelks,

and all of the remarkable ladies
who make up the wedding machine
in Greenville, South Carolina.

ALSO FROM BETH WEBB HART

Adelaide Piper

Grace at Low Tide

~ JUNE 7, 1969 ~

"You'll get this down to a science, sweet," Roberta said, hunching over the kitchen table in her beaded sea-foam cocktail dress and bedroom slippers. Her middle-aged hands were both dexterous and feminine, and they were almost always at work creating something exquisite. Ray studied them trancelike, hoping to learn their tricks. The well-worn platinum solitaire on Roberta's left hand caught the light as her long fingers curled into fists that funneled the white rice into a tiny tulle sack before cinching it tight with a thin satin ribbon.

"Now you try," Roberta said, passing the small plastic funnel to Ray.

The champagne from the rehearsal dinner was wearing off, and Ray felt like she was moving in slow motion. She took a good scoop of extra long grain rice and poured it into the plastic mouth where it spun down the funnel, filling the bottom of the gold-rimmed teacup.

"Good girl." Roberta smiled, looking around the kitchen at the plastic jugs of stephanotis, yellow roses, and daisies that would be formed into six nosegays and a cascading bridal bouquet by her small army of friends the next morning.

Roberta's army was composed of The Jasper Garden Club, The Colleton County Debutante Club, and the Wedding, Flower, and Altar Guild of All Saints Episcopal Church. As far as Ray could tell, these ladies were beacons of refinement and the force behind all that was civilized in Jasper, a small Lowcountry town between Charleston and Savannah tucked quietly behind Edisto Island and the ACE Basin.

Jasper would have been completely hidden if it weren't for Highway 17, the crumbling two-lane road that traced the coastline, splitting cypress swamps and tidal creeks edging right up to the 350,000-acre ACE Basin, where three rivers converged to form the largest, wildest estuarine preserve on the East Coast. Jasper bordered the northeast side of the basin where dolphins, gators, minks, otters, and every manner of waterfowl and shore bird prospered from the daily six-foot inflow and outflow of saltwater, freshwater, and brackish water that rose and fell on cue like the sun itself.

Ray had become best friends with Roberta's daughter, Kitty B., seven years earlier when they stole a watermelon together one August night just before the start of their sophomore year at William Bull High School. Ray had only been in town for two weeks when the pack invited her on a ride in the back of a pickup truck.

Now the laundry chute from Kitty B.'s bathroom down to the kitchen was open, and Ray grinned at the echoed chatter of her friends upstairs. She continued to prepare the rice sacks alongside Roberta. Though she wanted to be upstairs with the girls, Roberta was grooming Ray to lead the next generation of Jasper ladies in all facets of southern etiquette and entertaining—an unspoken understanding between them.

"Ouch, Hilda!" Kitty B. hollered from upstairs.

Hilda, the beauty queen of the pack, was hell-bent on trying a new curling technique on the bride that she'd read about in the beauty section of the Charleston paper. It involved wrapping an Ace bandage tightly around sponge curlers before securing it with a hairnet.

Ray went upstairs to get some satin ribbon for Roberta from the hall closet. Ribbon in hand, she peered into the bathroom to check on the gals.

"Ash this for me." Hilda held out her cigarette to Sis, the third and final bridesmaid and the fourth member of their pack. "And stop looking out that window. He'll be here soon enough, and you could learn a thing or two before your *own* big day."

"Oh, I wish mine were tomorrow," Sis whispered in Kitty B.'s ear. Sis and her fiancé, Fitz, had been a hot item since high school, and they never seemed to tire of making out for hours at a time in the back seat of his Chevrolet. It was the summer before their last year of college, and Sis had never dated a soul but Fitz.

Ray could hardly believe Kitty B. was getting married the very next day. Who would have ever thought she'd be the first to tie the knot?

Kitty B. readjusted herself on the lid of her rose-colored toilet in her pink tiled bathroom as she stroked Peaches, her mangy apricot poodle, who was licking her hands as she wrung them.

"Hold still," Hilda said while she and Sis wrapped the thick gauze tightly around the back of Kitty B.'s head.

"That hurts," Kitty B. said. "You're puncturing my scalp."

"Way-sa-minute," Sis said, as Peaches closed his gooey eyes and passed gas.

"Good gosh, that mutt stinks!" said Hilda, pinching her nose with a long metal hair pin. "I mean it, Kitty B. Put him down. Put him down or I'll gag."

"No!" Kitty B. cried so loud that Peaches stood up and started to bark.

Just as he was about to lose his balance, Kitty B. clutched him to her chest. "LeMar is allergic to dogs, and this is my last night with him." Then she raced into her bedroom, the loose end of the Ace bandage trailing down her back.

"Kitty B.!" Hilda threw her half-smoked cigarette into the pink toilet bowl. "We're not even finished!"

"Hush, Hilda," Sis said. "She's doesn't care about the hair."

Roberta came to the foot of the stairs and looked up at Ray.

"Throw me that ribbon and go see about the bride."

Ray nodded and ran into Kitty B.'s room to find her sobbing into her pink monogrammed pillow, while Peaches danced around her head with the Ace bandage in his yippy little mouth as the wide plastic curlers unraveled one by one.

Sis looked out the window, and Hilda sat at the vanity smoking a new Virginia Slim. She examined her mustache in the lamplight, making sure the peroxide had bleached every strand. "She's upset about the *dog*, Ray."

Ray lay down on the bed next to Kitty B.

"It's okay," she said into her friend's ear the same way her mama had comforted Mrs. Pringle when she learned that the cancer had spread to her bones. "Tomorrow you're marrying a tall, strapping opera singer from one of the finest families in the state."

"Who is allergic to my baby!" Kitty B. said, snorting into the sheets before wailing again.

"I know," Ray said, as she rubbed Kitty B.'s back.

When Kitty B. finally lifted her head, her chubby cheeks were red and her lips were contorted, and there was a spot on her pillow that was a mixture of tears and drool.

"You know I always thought I might end up as a dog trainer, Ray. And now I'm marrying a man who breaks out at the sight of one," she said.

"Isn't that what Old Stained Glass keeps telling us about marriage?" Ray said, looking to Sis and Hilda to give her a little support. They were all in premarital counseling with the local priest. "Compromise, remember?"

"LeMar can't help his allergies," Hilda said, pressing down a loose seam of the floral wallpaper by the window before reaching for another cigarette. "You shouldn't fault him for it."

"Hilda's right," Ray said. "You don't want to make LeMar miserable and uncomfortable with a pet, but there are other ways that he can make *you* happy." Kitty B. looked up at Ray, her plump cheeks shining in the thick air. She put her head on Ray's shoulder, and Ray stroked the clumps of curls that had come unraveled.

"You mean sex?" Sis whispered.

"Well, that's part of it, but I mean, he's going to vow to *love* her. And that means cherishing her and taking care of her always," Ray said.

"Oh, I can't wait!" Sis stood up and bobbed on the balls of her little feet, her petite frame casting a thin shadow on the wall beside the bed. "Let's give her the present."

Hilda set her cigarette in a porcelain bowl on the vanity and pulled a gift box out of her overnight bag. Kitty B. sat up straight and opened the box. It was a pale green silk negligee from Lots of Lace, a fancy boutique on Broad Street in Charleston.

Kitty B. grinned sheepishly, and they all started to laugh, and Sis pulled out a tube of K-Y Jelly that was hidden in the tissue paper behind the negligee. She handed it to Kitty B., who turned it round and round in her chubby hands as her cheeks began to redden. She looked up at Ray, her eyes glistening in the soft light of the bedside lamp.

Hilda took another drag and exhaled the smoke, which hovered around Sis's nodding head, and Peaches barked around the bed before nosing his way over to the window, where they spotted Fitz on all fours in his tan suit and penny loafers, shimmying across the roof toward them.

"Speaking of frisky," Hilda said. "Soldier boy's here."

They all turned to look at Fitz, who stood up at the window, loosened his tie, and licked his lips so that they caught the light from the upstairs piazza. He straightened out his slick gold hair for one of the last times before the army would shave it and ship him off to Vietnam. He winked at the pack of gals in their nightgowns.

"Go on," Kitty B. said, squeezing Sis's hand.

"Okay." Sis kissed Kitty B.'s forehead before climbing out of the window onto the roof.

"Get to bed, girls," Roberta called up the laundry chute.

"Yes, ma'am," Hilda said before turning back to Kitty B. The orange tip of her cigarette flared as she inhaled. Then her eyebrows rose as she exhaled deeply before adding, "Now tomorrow we'll just have to use the hot curlers. And we'll fix your face and let you soak in a warm bath for a half hour so the makeup will set deep down in your pores."

"All right," Kitty B. said, stroking the lace trim of her new nightie. Hilda walked over to the vanity, where she curled her own hair around the pink rollers before wrapping it in another Ace bandage.

Then the three gals piled into Kitty B.'s king-size bed for the last night they'd all be huddled together on the same stepping-stone— young, hopeful virgins promised to their small-town sweethearts.

At four in the morning, Ray awoke fully alert in bed. She lay perfectly still while Kitty B.'s dog walked across the bodies of her sleeping friends. He made his way from the foot of the bed, sauntering up to the headboard, then lifted his hind leg to pee on Hilda's bandaged curlers. Ray watched, detached, as a drowsy Hilda awakened, felt her wet curlers, put her fingers to her nose and shrieked.

Hilda was gagging when she got to the bathroom, turned on the bright light, and unrolled her curlers over the trash can. Kitty B. rubbed her eyes before propping herself up on her elbow. "What happened?"

"Peaches," Ray said with a quiet grin before calling, "Are you okay, Hilda?"

"No, Ray! No, I'm not *okay*! That filthy rodent *peed* on my *head!*"

Kitty B. giggled and scratched Peaches' scruff. Ray threw off the covers and walked into the bathroom and started hot water running in the pink tiled tub. "Come on, Hilda. Just wash it out."

Fitz and Sis peered through the open window.

"What's going on?" Sis asked.

"Peaches peed on Hilda's head," Kitty B. said.

Sis and Fitz chuckled, and Ray couldn't stop herself from chuckling, too, though she covered her lips with her hand. "Thanks a lot, y'all!" Hilda screamed. Then she pushed Ray out of the bathroom and slammed the door.

"Listen, Kitty B.," Fitz said through the window. "I'm real sorry I can't be there tomorrow."

"Don't worry," she said, swatting in his direction. "Just bring yourself back in one piece for me, okay?"

"He will." Sis pulled him next to her. Then Mayor Hathaway tapped at the closed bedroom door. "Get back to sleep, girls," he said.

"Yes, Daddy," Kitty B. said. "Now scoot," she whispered to Sis and Fitz. "I'll be back in a bit," Sis whispered into the window and let Fitz lead her onto the far edge of the roof.

By the time Hilda settled back in bed, Kitty B. was snoring lightly with Peaches beneath her forearm. From across the hall Mayor Hathaway blew a low and guttural sound through his nose that sounded like a cow's moo. Ray was wide-eyed beneath the covers as a light breeze rustled the trees. She could hear the scrape of one of the great live oak limbs as it brushed against the white reception tent behind the house. Peaches stirred for a moment before repositioning himself with his head in the nook of Kitty B.'s neck. Fitz and Sis's hushed whispers outside mixed with the soft snores and the crickets and the rustling of a raccoon or a water rat at the edge of Round-O Creek.

Ray had a secret. She kneaded her engagement ring—a tasteful solitaire set in platinum that Willy's mama had picked out from a fine jeweler in Savannah—around her finger with her thumb. This was her silent prayer: that who she was would stay tucked between her and the thick summer night.

Then Ray closed her eyes and fell, finally, into sleep as the pale gray of daybreak crept like a steadily rising tide into the Hathaway home on the Third Avenue of Jasper.

Mrs. Hilda Savage Prescott

and Doctor Angus Addison Prescott IV

request the honour of your presence

at the marriage of their daughter

Hilda Foster

to

Giuseppe Ricci Giornelli

On Saturday, the thirteenth of August

Two thousand and five

at twelve o'clock

All Saints Episcopal Church

Jasper, South Carolina

and afterwards at the reception

at Pink Point Gardens

ONE

Ray

~ 2005 ~

Ray sits in a hospital robe in the examination room of the Medical University of South Carolina's Women's Health Office thumbing through her wedding notes. *Durn Hilda*, she thinks. *I ought to be home right now getting ready for her daughter's Tea and See.*

It took three months for her to get an appointment with a gynecologist in Charleston, and the timing couldn't be worse. It's just days before Little Hilda's wedding, and Ray has one million things to attend to. Tonight she's meeting the gals to go over the final details, and tomorrow afternoon she will host the bridal tea and gift display at her home.

A nurse pops her head in and says, "Dr. Arhundati will be with you shortly."

"Thank you," Ray says as she wonders about the name Arhundati.

As someone taps sharply on the door, Ray braces herself.

A tall, young blonde enters the room, thrusts out her thin hand, and says, "I'm Melissa Arhundati."

"You look like you're my daughter's age," Ray says as she puts down her latest *Southern Living* issue. "In fact, you look like a girl from Priscilla's sorority. You didn't happen to go to UVA, did you?"

"No," the doctor says. "I went to the University of Chicago, and I was *not* in a sorority."

"Oh," Ray says. "It's just—I was expecting a man."

"Well," Dr. Arhundati says with a tight smile. "My husband is a physician, too, but I'm the only gynecologist in the family." The doctor examines the paperwork Ray filled out in the waiting room. "Mrs. Montgomery, correct?"

"Oh yes." Ray blushes and fans herself with her wedding notes. "I'm Ray. I apologize for not introducing myself."

The doctor claps her hands together and turns toward a chart on the wall. "Let's talk about the cessation of menses."

"I beg your pardon?"

"Menopause, Mrs. Montgomery," Dr. Arhundati says. "From the date of your last period and the symptoms you've checked off here, I think it's safe to assume you're experiencing the cessation of menses."

She points to a chart on the beige wall that lists the signs of menopause and reads them aloud. "Insomnia, osteoporosis, atherosclerosis, depression, mood swings, urinary incontinence, and vaginal atrophy."

"That can't be right," Ray murmurs as she straightens her shoulders and crosses her legs on the edge of the vinyl examining table in the flimsy gown with its thin, faded stripes. She feels like a bar code. Or a carton of eggs well beyond their expiration date. Who does this young woman think she is? Pointing to the word *atrophy* so matter-of-factly with her long, thin index finger.

Atrophy? Doesn't that mean wasting away? Shriveling up? Dying?

Dr. Arhundati adjusts the black square rims of her mod glasses as she flips through Ray's file. "Mmm. You left several sections of the medical history form blank, Mrs. Montgomery."

"Beg your pardon?" Ray says. "Angus Prescott of Jasper, South Carolina, has been my doctor for twenty-five years, and he's never asked me *any* of those questions."

The doctor furrows her brow and swings her long blond hair back behind her shoulder. She takes a step closer. "Well, it's important for us to know the medical history of your parents and grand-parents, especially any illness that applied to them, so that we can be vigilant in preventive treatment." She snaps the file closed and hands it back to Ray. "Why don't I give you a few minutes."

As the door clicks behind the doctor, Ray grabs the pen from her wedding notebook and makes up some names and standard illnesses to appease Dr. Arhundati: a little high blood pressure here, a little heart disease there, and even a thyroid disorder on her pater-nal grandmother's side so as not to appear too cliché.

But the truth is that the only person from her family tree that she has ever known was her mama, Carla Jones, and the woman somehow managed to keep everything a mystery. She hands Dr. Arhundati the forms when she returns; then she places her feet in the stirrups for her examination.

Now Ray races over the drawbridge between Charleston and Jasper. Dr. Arhundati sent her to the health food store in Charleston for some strange-sounding herbs, and she's way behind schedule. She's only got a few hours to make the final preparation for the Tea and See and get to Kitty B.'s for the last wedding meeting before Little Hilda's big day.

A reporter stands on the side of the bridge in a dry, bright orange raincoat. He's pointing at the salt marsh reeds, stone still in the August heat. Ray rolls her eyes. Eleanor is the third tropical storm this summer that they've said would hit the South Carolina Lowcountry, but Ray feels sure it will make the same northerly bump the others have and wind up somewhere along the North Carolina coast.

"Lord, protect Little Hilda's wedding day," she prays, then quickly pulls over at Pink's roadside vegetable stand and buys one of the last watermelons of the season to take to Kitty B.'s. Oh, and she just has to get an extra one for Willy. It's a special thing between them all—watermelons—and her husband particularly likes them. Ray loves to roll them over on their pale underbellies, where she thumps them softly with the pad of her thumb, then rubs her hand across the dark green seams.

Once Little Hilda's wedding is over, Ray will go right back to Angus's practice. He happens to be a wonderful physician and believes like they all do that her mama and Laura and Ray just appeared out of nowhere one late summer afternoon before their sophomore year of high school—one hot-to-trot Mary Poppins and her two shy daughters who descended out of the clouds with their three sets of big green eyes and their bright smiles.

~ AUGUST 16, 1963 ~

The second Friday after Ray moved to Jasper, the church youth group put a For Sale sign in her yard, which was the joke at the time. Ray didn't know whether to cry or laugh when she woke up that morning and walked out onto the dew-covered grass and pulled the muddy stake out of the ground. She leaned the sign against the side of the house, where it fell over and stayed for years, rusting behind the hydrangea bushes.

Then that night Kitty B. knocked on her kitchen door and said, "Wanna come out?" Ray was trying on a brand-new pair of linen pedal pushers that they had bought in Charleston just before the move. Her mama tore off the tag, pushed her out the door, and said, "Just go on, honey."

Ray looked up at the truckbed full of smiling faces. A boy she'd never seen before reached out his hand to pull Ray up and over the edge of the flatbed of Angus's truck. She took her place nervously between him and Kitty B. on the curve of the warm wheel well while Fitz held Sis on his lap opposite them. Hilda was in the passenger seat by Angus,

"Where are we going?" Ray said.

"To steal a watermelon." Kitty B. giggled.

Willy patted Ray's back. "It's the tradition. When someone new comes to town." He put his short, round hand out flat as if he wanted her to give him five. "I'm Willy, pretty girl."

Ray smiled and lightly slapped his hand. No one in Charleston had so much as noticed her existence. Her blossoming into a young woman. Except maybe Nigel Pringle, who was thankful to be rid of her.

But the Jasper teenagers had sought her out immediately. Probably her mama's doing, if she thought about it. Carla Jones was going to work for Willy's daddy, the state senator and small-town attorney, and she had bragged to everyone about how nice and bright her daughters were.

It was dark on the outskirts of town that night Ray first hung out with the pack. So black she could not even make out the figures of the strangers sitting next to her. The tunnel of live oaks dripping with Spanish moss outlined the pitch blackness until a porch light, usually a single uncovered bulb, lit up a patch of the land for a moment.

She might have been afraid except the thick summer air smelled so sweet and earthy that she couldn't breathe it in fast enough. It was like a warm and balmy laughing gas, and she let go into the intoxicating fragrance of salt air and withering corn husks and tomatoes so ripe she imagined them dropping off the vines around her.

When they reached complete darkness about ten miles out of town, Angus turned off the headlights and quietly pulled off the road and onto the edge of a field. There was the faintest light above the door of a shack where the woods met the field, and she could barely see the waxy tops of the watermelons lined up in tight rows in the open soil.

"Let's go," Fitz commanded in a loud whisper. He and Willy jumped right over the bed of the truck and lifted their arms up toward the girls.

Ray took both of their hands and let them lift her gently down. Fitz grabbed Sis by the hips and hoisted her down before spinning her around. He patted her on the backside, just once, before taking her hand and running out into the blackness. Ray had never seen such affection among folks her own age. She had been a scholarship student at an all-girls Catholic school in Charleston, and when she wasn't in school she was cooped up in the carriage house with Mama polishing silver and ironing linens for Mrs. Pringle.

As the pack laughed and ran into the blackness before Ray, she felt like she was at the edge of the world, and she stood stone still until someone took her hand. "It's all right." Willy led her gently out into the darkness as the soft, damp soil yielded beneath their feet.

"Grab the biggest one you can," Fitz instructed, and Ray could barely make out his outline as he bent down and rubbed the smooth, round melon tops. "It's a contest."

Of course, Ray had no idea about the water hoses lined up alongside the heaped rows, and as she felt from melon to melon, her foot became tangled in one, and she nearly tripped before Willy caught her in his short, husky arms.

Then a dog barked somewhere in the distance, and Angus whispered, "Grab one and get back to the truck!"

Ray knelt down and pulled the first one she could feel. It was heavy and wrapped in vines that were thin but tough, and Willy set his own down to tug hers loose.

"Big 'un." He chuckled as he ripped it from its cord. Then he balanced both of theirs on his hips as she scurried ahead of him back to the truck.

When the dog came closer, Fitz warned, "Look out!" and Willy dropped the fruit, then hoisted Ray up into Fitz's arms before hurling their melons into the flatbed. Just as Willy was about to climb over, the dog nipped his ankle and caught hold of the hem of his blue jeans. Fitz kicked the dog loose with the heel of his sneakers and pulled Willy in by his belt loops as Angus spun them away.

Fitz let out a whoop before planting a long, wet kiss on Sis. Kitty B. laughed as Willy scooted closer to Ray so that their hips touched. Then he rubbed his ankle and said, "That was a close one, y'all."

Kitty B. cradled her watermelon tight in her lap, and said, "Now y'all don't forget to give me the leftover rinds so I can pickle them."

They chuckled at her request; then they hooted and hollered in the blackness all the way to the church gym, where the high school was hosting its weekly summer dance.

When the pack wheeled into the church parking lot, Angus opened the back door of the pickup and lined up the melons. Ray's was the biggest. It was long and wide with deep green seams down its back. Angus inspected their yellow undersides and thumped the ripe edges. "The new girl's is the pick of the litter!"

Everyone cheered over Ray's melon, and Kitty B. hugged her, and little did Ray know it at the time, but she had officially become a lifelong member of the Jasper pack.

One knock on Willy's nubby knee, and Ray's watermelon split open down the center. Everyone grabbed a piece from the heart, sucked on it, and spat out the seeds and sucked some more as the juice ran down their forearms, even Hilda, who had been fretting about the soil on her white tennis shoes moments before.

Then they all ran into the darkened gym, the crevices between their fingers sticky and sweet, and they shagged until midnight when Coach Sanders shut off the music and flicked the lights on and off and on so that their muddy footprints and pink streaked arms were like photos snapped for an album or evidence of a small-town crime.

As Ray pulls back onto Highway 17, she gets stuck behind a tractor going ten miles an hour. Then she hears her cell phone buzzing in her pocketbook.

"Mama," Priscilla says from the other end of the line. "Where have you been?"

"At the doctor in Charleston," Ray says. "Then to the health food store where I had to buy some funny kind of herbs they want me to take—ginkgo biloba and don quai."

"Ooh," Priscilla says. "Herbs can work wonders. I took these rishi mushrooms last year when I had this awful chest cold, and they cleared me right up."

"Hormones can do wonders too." Ray comes upon an elderly man driving a tractor down the single lane highway. "When does your flight get in?"

"10:05, from LaGuardia."

"And you're coming alone?" Ray crosses her fingers.

"Yes, Mama," Priscilla says. "J.K. has a shoot, so he can't make it."

"Well, all right." Ray tries to hold back her enthusiasm. "I'll make sure your daddy is at the airport before ten."

Yes. Ray snaps her telephone shut. Priscilla's last two boyfriends have been so awful that Ray and Willy have named them Poop 1 and Poop 2. The current one, J.K. (Poop 2) is by far the worst. Priscilla was the valedictorian of William Bull High, but she took a wrong turn in college and wound up majoring in film and television production, of all the inane things. She met Poop 2 on the set of this reality TV show, *Knucklehead,* where the idiot pins raw T-bones to his clothes and roasts himself over a grill and calls it entertainment. Oh, Ray's got to get her away from him.

"No Poop 2 for the wedding weekend!" she calls to the heavy salt air. *This good news is almost enough to cancel out the fact that my private parts are withering on the vine.*

Ray claps her hands, presses the gas, and moves out into the two-lane highway to pass the tractor. A convertible sports car comes flying down the road opposite her, and she swerves back behind the tractor and barely misses the giant tires, their wide, mud-encrusted grooves spinning slowly forward.

TWO

Ray

Ray has set out a place setting of each of Little Hilda's crystal and china. She can hear her husband and nephew loading up their deer hunting gear at the top of the stairs, and she's not going to let them cross through the dining room and the gift display without her supervision.

Tomorrow Big Hilda, Little Hilda, and the other gals and their daughters will gather around her dining room for tea and a look at all of the beautiful wedding gifts: the three china patterns; the Chantilly silver; the crystal water, wine, and champagne glasses and the assortment of silver trays, vases, bowls, ice buckets, and fanciful knickknacks. It's the tradition for the mother of the bride to host the tea, but Big Hilda just wasn't up to having it in her home and Ray has all but taken over the wedding.

Yes, Little Hilda Prescott is getting married this very Saturday. Of course, Ray worries about her unconventional choice of mates, a first-generation Italian from New Jersey, a Democrat, no less. And Little Hilda has even decided to hyphenate her last name. Now how in the world should they monogram her silver and linens?

Ray and the pack are starting to resign themselves to the fact that their children will neither marry who they hope for nor behave in the way they think is most appropriate. The pack can hardly relate to their offspring, if you want to know the truth, and they were shocked that every last one of them hightailed it out of Jasper after college with no plans to return.

This could be the end of an era for the community that took Ray in more than forty years ago. As she watches the coral-colored condominiums go up along the edge of the Cumbahee River, she envisions the affluent retirees and transplants trickling out of the Kiawah and Hilton Head resorts in search of some little slice of small-town southern living. When she reads in the paper about the plans for the new Sally Swine shopping center with a Starbucks on the far side of town, she suspects that the come-yuhs are migrating her way, and she wonders what their kind will do to Jasper and the quiet way of life she has come to cherish.

Nonetheless, she and the gals must gear up for the good work the upstanding ladies of their community have been performing for many generations now—that is, to ensure that the daughters of Jasper are married in the proper manner.

~ APRIL 15, 1995 ~

"Weddings are of the utmost importance," Roberta said that day in the Jasper Nursing Home.

She had made it clear that Ray should take the helm of the Wedding Guild because it would not be long before the next generation would be tying the knot. The elderly woman had pulled out all of her files of wedding instructions—from determining the guest list and the way the invitation should read, to the gift arranging for the Tea and See and the acceptable combination of flowers for the church. She had compiled pages and pages of notes and photographs from the weddings she had coordinated, and she drew

arrows that pointed out the small but meaningful details, such as
the magnolia leaves in the fireplaces in the spring and summer or
the corsages for the hostesses and the bridal party to wear at the Tea
and See and the bridesmaids' luncheon. She had a photo of a silver
monogrammed tussy mussy with a lovely arrangement of ribbons
from the bridal shower for the bride to hold at the church rehearsal,
and she had samples of traditional handwritten envelopes that
should be referred to when addressing the invitations.

As Ray thumbed through the files, she was overwhelmed with
Roberta's trust in handing this honorable charge down to her.

Roberta lifted her arm and made a fist so that the pearl bracelet on
her wrist slid down to the edge of her lacy nightgown sleeve and continued, "You've already played a significant role in the rites of passage
for the younger generation of Jasper ladies, from their christenings to
their confirmations to their cotillions and their debutante seasons."

Ray nodded and blushed at Roberta's recognition of her leadership on these occasions. "But the wedding is the final and most crucial part of their crossing the threshold into adult society, and it is
up to you to carry on the tradition of honoring the young ladies of
Jasper in the proper manner."

The old lady turned to look out at the hummingbird feeder that
Ray had helped Kitty B. hang outside the nursing home window.
"Don't be tempted by this calligraphy fad. It's simply not how it
should be done."

"Oh, I know." Ray nodded emphatically. "I much prefer the
hand-addressed invitations in traditional cursive."

"And I'll roll over in my grave if you all ever type the invitations
or use those awful labels that folks with computers are using these
days!"

"Roberta," Ray said, "you know I would never let that happen."

"And return cards," Roberta said. "*No* return cards. One ought
to know that one must respond on their personal stationery when
receiving an invitation to a wedding."

"I couldn't agree more." Ray patted her mentor's arm.

"If you cave in, Ray," Roberta said, "if you go to return cards and provide these sorts of shortcuts, the other traditions that we've upheld for so long will eventually fade away."

"That won't happen on my watch," Ray said as she took Roberta's liver-spotted fist in her hand and rubbed her thumb gently across it. "It is an honor, Roberta, and you can trust me with this charge."

"I don't doubt it, child," Roberta said with that knowing glint in her weary eyes. "I know you understand the value of it."

"Careful!" Ray says as Willy and Justin lug their rifle cases through the dining room. The tip of Justin's case grazes a Blue Canton vase and a hideous red crystal decanter from that Texas come-yuh, Vangie Dreggs, which must have cost a small fortune.

"Please watch yourselves, boys!" Ray clutches her cheeks while the glass display shelves shudder between their brass hinges. Three silver trays rattle back and forth, and a green Herund hare figurine crouched as if in a thicket falls over on its nose.

"Think *Jeannie* lives in there, Aunt Ray?" Justin points to the decanter with a grin. Her fifteen-year-old nephew was described as s-l-o-w by the William Bull High guidance counselor before she sent him to the special needs school in Charleston. The look on his round face is so droll that she wants to kiss his forehead and rock him back and forth in her arms.

"Even Jeannie wouldn't be caught dead in that eyesore." Ray gently pats his shoulders from behind and guides him toward the kitchen door.

August 15 is the first day of deer hunting season in South Carolina, and it couldn't have come at a better time. Everything is set up for tomorrow's tea, and the longer Ray can keep the boys out of the house, the better.

"This is a big day, darlin'!" Willy beams at Ray while dancing toward the kitchen with the oblong case cocked on his shoulder. She watches her husband inching his way through the minefield of crystal and china.

Willy's a state senator just like his daddy was, although he doesn't look a thing like Ray thinks a state senator should look. He's stout with a stubby bald head and rough, nubby hands that look like they were made to pull watermelons off the vines instead of flipping through papers at the State House in Columbia. He's like family to most folks around Jasper, so everyone from the mayor to their housekeeper calls him Cousin Willy.

"How was the doctor, love?" Willy says.

"Awful." Ray rolls her eyes. "She's got me taking herbs, of all things. I'm going back to Angus as soon as I get the nerve to tell Hilda."

Cousin Willy squeezes Justin's shoulder and says, "What's the rule, son?"

"Just shoot bucks," Justin leans in to Ray. "Those are the ones with bones on their heads."

"Racks," Cousin Willy says.

Ray nods, though her mind reels with wedding concerns. She's got to pack her car with the birdseed and tulle for the meeting at Kitty B.'s. She hasn't had a chance to talk to Angus, either—to let him know he and his girlfriend can't sit on the same pew as Hilda, or she will simply lose it. She ought to double-check the forecast to make sure Eleanor doesn't have her eye on Jasper.

"The first deer rack of the season gets stuffed, right?" Justin says.

"That's right, son," Willy winks. "I've got a place picked out right over my desk for that buck's head."

"You mean right over *my* bed," Justin says, pushing Willy's forearm with his fist. Ray looks at them both and says, "Don't forget *my* rule, hear?"

Last year Willy and Justin had stopped by the house for a Co-Cola on their way from the deer hunt to the meat processor, and Ray pulled up from the grocery store to find a fat doe strapped to the top of the truck dripping blood through its open mouth onto her newly constructed slate driveway.

As she stopped beside the truck to examine the mess, she looked up and spotted a buzzard out of the corner of her eye circling her home. She knew it was nature's way, but she loathed the filthy creatures. They continually mar the pristine skyline with their large black wings and glossy eyes, scanning the salt marsh and the woods and roadside in search of the wounded and the dead.

"Ray," Cousin Willy called out to her. He was running toward her as the edges of her vision became fuzzy and her knees began to buckle. She let her groceries fall—eggs and all—and grabbed hold of the big metal mirror on the side of his truck as she fainted. He'd caught her and carried her into the house, where he laid her down on the couch, wet a cool dish rag, and rolled it up before placing it on her pale forehead.

"I do not want to see the poor creature until he's vacuum-sealed in loins and sausage links and neatly stacked in the freezer in the garage," Ray says to them both, looking back and forth into their eyes.

"Fair enough. We don't want you fainting again, sweet lady." Willy kisses her right on the lips before she has a chance to pucker.

Tuxedo, their black Labrador retriever, paces back and forth. He's seen the gun cases and knows that this means a trip to the country, where he'll chase rabbits and field mice around the cabin as the men file out into their stands.

As Justin calls Tuxedo into the flatbed, Cousin Willy adds, "Give my regards to the gals and LeMar."

"I will," Ray says to the back of his thick, round head.

In his camouflage and mud brown, knee-high snake boots, it

seems for sure that her worst suspicions are confirmed: she married a redneck who just happened to be born into an old and well-regarded Jasper family. Or maybe he was switched at the hospital.

Ray can't understand how the men can sit in those stands for hours at a time in this sauna while the no-see-ums nibble on their scalp and the mosquitoes suck their blood. Not to mention the chiggers and ticks that are always rooting for a way in.

"Willy," Ray says, scurrying out to the back porch, the humid August heat hitting her square on with its weight. "Are you worried about this storm?"

"Heck no, Ray." He turns back to her. "They're already predicting Myrtle Beach, and I'd be surprised if we saw a drop of rain from it."

"One more thing," she says, grabbing the banister to steady herself in the thick heat. "If you see Angus, will you tell him that we're going to seat him and his girlfriend or fiancée or whatever she is on the pew *behind* his former wife for his daughter's wedding?"

Cousin Willy swats Ray away. "Now you know it's a cardinal sin to talk about weddings among men at a deer hunt, gal."

"Do I have to handle everything?" She lets the screen door slam behind her as she retreats back into the cool air-conditioning, heading back to the dining room to make sure all of the gifts are intact. Despite the knot in her stomach that precedes every social function she hosts, she takes comfort in knowing her dining room is the picture of southern elegance. She loves how her mother-in-law's crystal chandelier dangles just above the silver cherub candelabra that once graced Mrs. Pringle's dining room on the Battery in Charleston where Ray grew up. When Mrs. Pringle was sleeping or playing bridge with her friends in the parlor, Ray used to run her finger along the fat rolls on the legs of the baby angel who held up the four candleholder. Her distorted reflection stared back at her from the glint of the silver bowl as her mother stood behind her polishing the chafing dish with one of Mr. Pringle's old undershirts and saying, "Pretty, isn't it?"

Tonight Ray will tape the drenched oasis inside of the silver bowl that sits on the top of the candelabra and fill it with the pale green hydrangeas, pink English garden roses, lilies of the valley, and extravagant lavender sweet peas that R.L., the local florist/antique dealer, delivered a few hours ago. The flowers are all soaking in their respective sugar water jugs in her kitchen—out of the direct sunlight, of course—as is the oasis which she'll mold into every bowl and vase in the house with a similar arrangement. She's even going to make an arrangement in a flat sweetgrass basket to hang on the front door and a round little pomander of pale green hydrangea with a sheer white ribbon for Little Hilda to hold as she greets the guests in the foyer.

Ray is tempted to snip the last blossoms of gardenias growing secretly behind Cousin Willy's shed. In her estimation they are the quintessential wedding flower, with their intoxicating fragrance and their delicate cream petals surrounded by those dark, waxy leaves. She bought the seedlings when R.L. and the gals weren't looking at the Southern Gardener's Convention in Atlanta four years ago, and no one has any idea she's been growing them. Sometimes she worries that the fragrance will give her away, but they bloom the same time as the confederate jasmine, which grows along the lattice work of the shed, and she can always blame the thick smell on them. It would take a truly trained nose to pick the gardenias out, and Ray possesses the trained nose of the bunch.

She tends the gardenias in the early morning when the rest of the town is asleep. She is saving these blooms for Priscilla's wedding, which she has been planning for decades now. It will truly be the most exquisite event Jasper has ever witnessed. A far cry from the meager reception that her mama pieced together in her backyard for Ray and Cousin Willy more than thirty years ago. Poor Mama had blown through Mrs. Pringle's money by then, and it was all she could do to offer a little punch and a lopsided wedding cake, which she baked layer by layer over a week's time in her small gas oven. It was an embarrassment in comparison to the elegant reception Roberta created for Kitty B.

Now as Ray repositions the crystal vases on the top gift shelf, she can't help but let her eye wander through the dining room window and across Third Street to Kitty B.'s old childhood home. The one where Peaches peed on Hilda's curled hair and Sis and Fitz spent the night in the shadows of the rooftop over thirty-six years ago.

~ JUNE 8, 1969 ~

Ray watched Roberta through the netting of her yellow bridesmaid's pillbox cap. She wanted to record her every gesture so she could one day imitate them. Roberta's white gloves were wrapped around the handle of the wide sweetgrass basket, and Ray marveled at how she could simultaneously pat her pale pink silk cap to keep her little extra boost of a hairpiece in place while offering the rice sacks to the wedding guests.

Then Roberta had them all line up along the brick pathway that led to the sidewalk and Third Street, where Mayor Hathaway's Lincoln Continental was parked, covered with shaving cream and a long string of Budweiser beer cans that stretched out for at least three yards. Angus and Willy's work, no doubt.

All of a sudden, Kitty B. appeared above their heads at the top of the piazza in a stunning going-away suit—a raw silk dress from Berlin's with a double-breasted overcoat to match. The suit had wide yellow and chartreuse stripes and a yellow straw hat. LeMar joined her in a seersucker suit with a yellow and blue striped bow tie, the first layer of his double chin already spilling over the lip of a starched oxford collar. After a few hoots and hollers up to the newlyweds, Kitty B. threw her bridal bouquet down. It landed right in Sis's outstretched hands—an old-fashioned cascade of white roses, stephanotis, and ivy cut from the vines that climbed the south side of the Hathaway home.

As Ray tore open her tulle sack that day and poured a little rice in Cousin Willy and Sis's cupped hands, Mr. and Mrs. Cecil LeMar Blalock trotted down the stairs and out into the green front lawn. The guests chased after them and threw rice at the tops of their heads. Mayor Hathaway's driver, Enoch, waited by the car door to carry the newlyweds to the Sea Island resort on the Georgia coast.

Ray tossed the rice and lifted her skirt to chase after the newly-weds, but she stopped after a few strides to take in their glorious exit as they scurried on the balls of their feet down the brick path. Kitty B. kissed her mama along the way, and then, all of a sudden, she slipped, and for a moment it looked as though she might not regain her balance from the white grains spinning beneath her char-treuse Pappagallo pumps. Then LeMar grabbed her gently by the elbow and steadied her just enough for her to regain her balance, and they ran for the car, where Enoch closed the door behind them.

Sis chased after the car screaming with delight as the car moved slowly down Third Street, the Budweiser cans rattling behind them. Angus pulled Hilda close, and Hilda stepped away for decorum's sake as her uptight father cleared his throat behind them. She cupped her blond curls, bouncing them in the palm of her mani-cured hands. Willy interlaced his stout fingers with Ray's as Mayor Hathaway and Roberta stood arm in arm, waving to the silver Lincoln, the sunlight glinting off the hubcaps and the metal rearview mirror before it crossed over the railroad tracks, turned right onto Main, and drove out of sight.

Before the salt marsh turned brown for the autumn that year and the first oysters of the season were harvested, Ray tied the knot with Willy, and Hilda did the same with Angus, and Sis wrote Fitz ten-der love letters addressed to his unit, though he'd stepped on a land mine in the Quang Tri Province by the time the first one arrived.

Fitz came home just before Thanksgiving in a pine box draped in an American flag, and they buried him in the Hungerford fam-ily plot in the All Saints churchyard. Sis still takes a bouquet or a plant over to his gravestone on the anniversary they had set for their wedding—May 6, 1970.

The front doorbell rings unexpectedly, and Ray is so caught off guard that she nearly loses her balance. Cousin Willy installed a new doorbell a few weeks ago that he bought on the cheap from one of those mega home stores in Columbia, and it rings from time to time on its own for no reason at all, which she finds quite disconcerting.

Of course, it's probably just R.L. with another shipment of flowers. She *knows* she ordered more lilies of the valley than he delivered. Or it could be Paley's Jewelers with a new wedding gift for the display. Then again, it might be her overactive imagination, and the chimes have not sounded except for in her mind, where she longs to see one of the faces of her past: Roberta, Mama, Fitz, or Laura, her younger sister, who she hasn't seen since she ran off two years ago with a fellow patient in her rehab clinic.

By the time Ray gets to the foyer, her heart pounds like the bass drum in the William Bull High School marching band, and she braces herself as she opens the large maple front door. No one is standing on the front steps of her house, and as she peers out into the yard, all is quiet and still. Something must have triggered the bell—a delivery truck moving down the street or a squirrel scurrying across the gutters. The thick air fills her lungs, and she looks down at the bits and pieces of slate laid out in a semicircle at the bottom of her steps. The arc connects with a path that leads to her new driveway which is meant to look *old*. The slate is part of a collection she bought from the demolished roof of a plantation kitchen house in Bluffton. Each slat is laid out haphazardly around her steps and across her yard where gray cement seals them together—remnants that once covered a cook's head two centuries ago.

As a hot flash starts in the pit of her arms, she realizes she would have nothing—no past, no history, no identity whatsoever—if she wasn't adept at taking hold of what scraps she could get her hands on and piecing them together in the guise of a whole. Not unlike a buzzard, she must admit, as she scans the skyline for the old opportunist. That one whose survival depends on the picking apart of a former life.

THREE

Ray

Ray loads the back of her Volvo station wagon for her trip to Kitty B.'s: four pounds of birdseed, five rolls of tulle, pink satin ribbons, and a pot of creamed corn for LeMar, whose migraines are back for the third time this year. He was diagnosed a decade ago with chronic fatigue syndrome after an awful bout with the flu, and he hasn't been back to work at Sally Swine since. He'll be headed straight for another evaluation at the Medical University in Charleston after he sings the "Ave Maria" at Little Hilda's wedding.

"This is Senator Montgomery's house." Ray hears the loud, raspy voice and turns to see Vangie Dreggs on a golf cart, of all things, toting a sporty looking middle-aged couple down Third Street. Ray watches as Vangie pulls onto her slate driveway. She's got that stout little Jack Russell in a basket on the backseat, and on the hood of her cart a magnetic advertisement reads, "Lone Star Lowcountry Realty" with a star-shaped photo of Vangie and her dog above her phone number and her Web site. *Tacky.*

"Let me introduce y'all to the first lady of Jasper," Vangie says to the couple. She turns back and gives Ray that big Texas smile, and Ray swears she's seen horse's teeth smaller than Vangie's. "Hi there,

Ray." Vangie's dog leaps out and starts sniffing around Ray's ankles. "Getting everything just right for the Prescott wedding?"

Ray takes off her sunglasses and walks toward them. "Hello, Vangie." She reaches out her hand to the strangers. "I'm Ray Montgomery."

Vangie stands up and straightens out her bright skirt and introduces the couple. "This is Tom and Janine Patterson from Toledo, Ohio." The little dog makes a dart into the side yard, where he sniffs around Tuxedo's pen.

"Pleased to meet y'all," Ray says as Tom Patterson squeezes her hand more tightly than necessary. Janine does the same and Vangie slaps Ray on the back and says, "Tom and Janine are in the market for a second home, and they're more interested in a small town than something along the beach—so here we are."

The print on Vangie's skirt sways with her wide hips. It's hot pink with monkeys climbing from limb to limb drinking out of martini glasses.

"Have you shown them those new condominiums on the Cumbahee?" Ray says.

"Why, yes I have." Vangie swats her glossy nails in their direction as the gold bangles on her wrist clamor together. "But they're more interested in old homes and a small-town flavor, so I'm taking them down to the end of Third Street to see the old Mims home."

"Sis's mama has put her house on the market?" Ray can't help but wince.

"Well, yes, Ray. She's been living at that Episcopal Retirement Community for two years now."

"Oh, I *know*, but I always thought—"

The dog runs back and scrapes his muddy paws on Mr. Patterson's khaki pants. "Down, Little Bit!" Vangie snaps. She picks him up and apologizes, and Ray decides not to finish her sentence. But what she always thought was that Mrs. Mims would leave the house to Sis, who would move out of her apartment on Main and be closer to her and Hilda, who lives just around the corner.

Mr. Patterson beats the dirt off his pants, and Mrs. Patterson smiles sincerely at Ray. "Jasper sure is quaint."

Before Ray forms a response, Vangie Dreggs collects Little Bit and her clients, pulls out of Ray's driveway, and turns toward Sis's childhood home down the block.

"See you later, First Lady," she says as Ray curls her slender fingers into tight fists. "By the way, we've got to meet about the Healing Prayer Revival Day before the next vestry meeting. The Reverend says he needs you to get behind it!" Vangie turns to the Pattersons and points to Ray. "She's the senior warden of that beautiful old Episcopal church on the corner. It's a little behind the times, but we're catching up, right, Ray?"

Ray shakes her head. Healing prayer? The Mims home going as a second residence to a couple from Toledo? Just the thought of it all makes another knot form in her gut, and she feels like she's been punched in the stomach by Vangie Dreggs in her hot pink drunken monkey skirt. As Ray slips into her car, she realizes Vangie is more than just a come-yuh or a Lone-Star nuisance. She doesn't think she's overreacting to say that Vangie poses a down-right threat to the protection and preservation of the town Ray loves, and she is not above planning a scheme to run her horse-toothed fanny out.

It's a twenty-five mile drive from Jasper to Kitty B.'s house at the tip of Cottage Island, where Ray will squeeze chronically infirm LeMar's hand and lead the final planning meeting for the wedding that will be here in four short days. She let Big Hilda, the mother of the bride, off the hook tonight since her contribution of addressing the invitations and altering the wedding gown are done, and they all know she'll be lucky to make it through the week without falling apart or retreating behind the wrought iron gates of her overgrown fortress where the thick vines of the Lady Banksia roses curl over her garden walls like the barbed wires at the top of the Beaufort County Detention Center.

Angus finally called it quits on Hilda three years ago on the grounds that she had become positively impossible to live with, much less love. She took it so bad that she didn't leave her house for nearly two years, and the gals had to sneak in on the heels of their mutual housekeeper, Richadene, after the first few months to make sure she was still alive.

~MARCH 4, 2004 ~

Hilda stood at her front door, gathering the nerve to step out and over her property line. It had been twenty months since Angus walked out.

"It's time," Ray said as she patted Hilda's back. "You've got to do this."

Hilda looked pale, but she was dressed to the nines in a creamy silk pantsuit she'd ordered over the telephone from Doncaster. Her frosted hair was molded into a shoulder-length bob with what appeared to be one enormous under curl that circled her neck like a brace.

Ray cleared her throat, and Hilda nodded once and reached out her thin arms. Kitty B. took hold of her left hand and Sis took hold of her right, and Ray swatted a broom at the spiderwebs at the front door and the voracious fig vines that were all but taking over across the threshold and around the porch columns.

When Hilda stepped out onto the sidewalk, the light of Third Street hitting her square on the face, she raised her bejeweled wrist to her forehead and said, "What I really want is an oyster po' boy from Opal Dowdy's."

And that's exactly where Ray drove them—four well-dressed ladies in their pearls and Ferragamos and decade-old Louis Vuitton purses. They didn't know if she'd want to go antiquing in Charleston or for tea in Savannah, so they had to be dressed for anything.

They crammed their middle-age hips into a plastic booth, sipping sweet tea and munching on oyster po' boys at Opal's. They weren't halfway through their lunch before Trudi Crenshaw, who Angus had just started dating at the time, walked right in with a sidewalk order for two. The poor gal turned white as a ghost when she spotted Hilda, who the town had deemed an official recluse by that time.

Opal's waitress called out, "Two chili cheeseburgers for you and the doc, Miss Trudi. That's four seventy-five." Ray noticed Hilda's back stiffen at the realization that the rumor was true—her husband was dating her hairdresser's sister. He *was* the only doctor in town.

Angus had always been fond of Trudi Crenshaw—the short and tubby manicurist with thick, smooth hands like catcher's mitts. Hilda used to make him an appointment with her once a month, and Cousin Willy teased him mercilessly about it.

Hilda stared Trudi down that day. Trudi's eyes widened with fear, and she threw a ten-dollar bill at Opal and raced out the door, her fleshy breasts heaving beneath her purple V-neck sweater dress and her cheap rhinestone sandals smacking the sidewalk. Hilda unfolded a napkin and laid it gently over her half-eaten po' boy and said to the gals, "Take me home, y'all."

Out of the corner of her eye, Ray sees R.L. waving from behind the glass of his "Flowers and Antiques" shop. She waves back before she crosses the railroad tracks and turns onto Highway 17.

Missy Meggett, the mail lady, honks behind the wheel of her mud-encrusted candy red Jeep, the one she had specially made with the steering wheel on the wrong side. Ray presses the brake and rolls down her window.

"Good afternoon, Mrs. Montgomery. I've got two packages for Little Hilda. I'll put them behind the azalea bush by your front door."

"Thank you, Missy. No one's home right now."

"I figured," she says. "Hope Justin gets a buck today!"

"I'd be happy just to get him back in one piece," Ray says before rolling up the window and pulling back on the old road.

Ray loves her town. Some days she does feel like the First Lady of Jasper, and like Cousin Willy says, they have more blessings than she can shake a stick at. So why is she prone to such fits of fretfulness as of late? Why does she feel so *undone*? The question itself makes her gut tighten as she heads down Highway 17, past Crenshaw's Beauty Salon, the Old Post Gas Station, Po' Pigs Bar-b-que, and the propane shop where the letters on the marquee read, "Ready for Eleanor?"

Maybe the fretfulness is over Little Hilda's wedding and all of the responsibility that comes with running Jasper's new generation of wedding directors. Roberta's last living comrades *do* have their eyes on Ray. Or maybe it's the fibroid tumors or the menopause in general. As her stomach continues to tighten, the avenue of live oaks on the road before her becomes fuzzy.

When Ray turns onto Route 172, the road becomes even more country looking. Garbage is heaped in the driveway of a mobile home set on cinderblocks, and a pile of wood is burning in front of a shack. The white, gnarled limbs of a dead oak tree are reaching up out of the salt marsh like a disfigured hand.

Christmas lights are strung around one of the mobile homes, and those cheap red bows that you buy at Wal-Mart are mashed flat along the metal railing of a tin porch. Ray wonders why some country folks keep them up all year long. Is it because they're too weary to take the ten minutes to take them down, or do they just not want to acknowledge the fact that Christmas has come and gone?

As Ray spots two men in camouflage climbing over a fence with rifles, she thinks of Cousin Willy and Justin who are somewhere back in these jungle-like woods. Angus has some land on Rantowles Creek where the guys hunt every evening that they can between now and the close of the season, December 31.

She pictures them now, up in the tall green tree stands, sweating in their camouflage and boots. They sit up there for hours without making a move, watching intently as the sun dips down in the trees and the creatures bedded down all day rouse themselves. It's dusk when the bucks come out to feed and move about. Willy says you can't hear them coming unless they're fighting over a doe, locking their racks together in their battle to mate. More often than not, they just appear as if out of nowhere sniffing through their black snouts before bending down to nibble on the millet and the corn. If the boys don't have a clear shot, they let them go. And if they shoot them, then someone must eat them. It's the hunter's creed around here. It's awfully noble, but Ray must admit there is only so much venison she can stomach.

When Ray arrives at Kitty B.'s, LeMar is rocking on the wraparound porch, listening to an opera. The living room window is open—no air-conditioning at Kitty B.'s since it was her parent's old island house and hasn't been the least bit updated. All Ray can say is thank heavens there is a breeze off the water.

The music pours out between the yellowed linen drapes as the powdery dirt from the road fills into her open-toe espadrilles, and she can feel its soft heat beneath the balls of her feet.

Kitty B. has set out their mascot at the bottom of her front porch steps—a garden statue of a bashful girl holding a basket of flowers. Roberta bought that for the gals the summer that Priscilla, Little Hilda, and Baby Roberta were born within a three-month span of one another, if you can believe that! She thought it would be fun to set the statue out at every rite of passage: their christenings, their confirmations, their cotillions, their graduations, their debutante balls, and now, their weddings.

Hilda has made bonnets and dresses for Miss C., the statue, to

wear all along, and today she's decked out in the most precious little
child-sized wedding dress and veil for the big weekend. Miss C. gets
her name from a Tuscaloosa girl who went to Converse with Kitty
B. and Sis. Her actual first name was "Miss Cotton"—no lie. It was
on her birth certificate and the passport she took on their trip to
Europe their junior year. Miss Cotton was a high maintenance,
plantation wielding princess like you might expect.

But in an unexpected turn of events which can most succinctly
be described as having the hots for her college philosophy professor,
Miss C. became all wrapped up in the feminist movement and the
general social revolution of the 1960s, and last the gals heard, she
had married a Native American sculptor from the mountains of
Western North Carolina and resides somewhere outside of Asheville
where she sells sun-dried vegetables. But her name was just so *southern,* and so were her parents and so was her debutante ball which
they all attended, pre-philosophy professor, that Miss C. just seemed
like the perfect name for a mascot. Anyhow, it is part of their ritual
to add something new to Miss C. each time someone hosts a wed-
ding-related event, and Kitty B. has added some of LeMar's pink
baby bud roses in Miss C.'s flower basket.

Now one of Kitty B.'s mutts, Otis, sniffs under Miss C.'s dress,
leaving smudges and black hair on the lace of the white eyelet train.
Honey, the yellow lab, who belongs to their "just going to live at
home and sponge off of my parents" daughter, Katie Rae, roots
around in LeMar's famous sweetheart rosebush that stretches as high
as the second story of their old home. Honey digs and digs until the
grass becomes soft dirt, then he pees right in the hole as Otis comes
over and pees on top of his puddle. Rhetta, the third in a string of
unkempt poodles since the days of Peaches, is rolling back and forth
over some leaves on the front lawn.

"Rolling in crap," LeMar says. "Well, that about sums it all up,
don't you think, Ray?"

Ray chuckles, then she spots Sis down by the dock with her sandals dangling from her fingertips. She's peering out over the Ashepoo River as the wake of a passing motorboat sends dark swells toward her. *Poor Sis*, Ray thinks. *She's never married, but she's way too youthful and cute to be considered an old maid.*

Ray sits down in the chair next to LeMar with the watermelon on her lap. She can smell chicken frying.

"What are we listening to?"

"*Salome*," he says. "Richard Strauss."

"Mmm," she says, though the music seems unexpectedly thorny and her gut begins to tighten again. *Salome*? Where has she heard that name before? The Bible, perhaps. Maybe the Old Testament? Or is that Samson she's thinking of, the man whose might was diminished after a haircut by his seductress, Delilah? Sometimes Ray thinks the Bible has more smut than a soap opera.

"How are you feeling, LeMar?" Ray pats the top of his hand.

He rolls his head slowly back and forth like he's warming up for an aerobics class. He's dressed in the tan garden suit he wears every afternoon while he fiddles with the rosebush and pokes at a few geraniums in the rusting window boxes.

The dogs chase Mr. Whiskers—a tail-less stray cat that Kitty B. has adopted—into the tree. LeMar nods in the direction of the kitchen and says, "My wife's killing me."

Ray's eyes widen as she thinks how to respond. Ever since Baby Roberta's death, there has been this wedge between LeMar and Kitty B., and it's a wonder their marriage hasn't gone the way of Hilda and Angus's.

"I don't think I would have this syndrome if it weren't for her," he adds, rubbing his right temple.

"Oh, come now, LeMar." Ray pats his hand. "That's not true, and you know it. Kitty B. loves you, and she would do *anything* to make you well."

He leans in toward her and says, "Listen. Salome is about to ask for John the Baptist's head on a platter."

Ray listens to the fitful music to humor him as the dogs bark up at the cat that is perched on the highest limb of the magnolia tree. A soprano sounds over the different sections of the orchestra, which seem to purposefully play apart from one another. The effect is confusion. The tone is fretful or worse. LeMar listens intently with his eyes closed and his lips pursed. He sniffs as if to ingest the notes.

"Hey there, Ray," Kitty B. says as she steps out onto the porch. Ray rises to kiss her old friend on the cheek as the dogs run up to greet their keeper. They lick the powdered sugar off Kitty B.'s soft fingertips as she takes a seat in a rocking chair. Then she kisses them on the mouths, their round pink tongues slapping her full, fleshy chin. Ray watches as Kitty B. wipes her sleeve on her untucked blouse. The tail-less cat tiptoes across the top of the porch rail and jumps onto Kitty B.'s lap. He turns toward the dogs and hisses, and they run off the porch and back into the yard, where they growl and bite at sticks and roll back and forth in the mud and leaves and crap.

LeMar shakes his head in something between disgust and resignation.

"Chicken's ready, sweetheart," Kitty B. says to him. "And I made you some deviled eggs and potato salad too."

"My wife thinks there's nothing Duke's Mayonnaise can't cure," LeMar says as he picks at a paint chip on the porch railing.

"And I brought creamed corn," Ray says. "And a watermelon."

"That's all I want," LeMar says, as he crumples the chalky chip between his thumb and forefinger. "Some of Ray's creamed corn and a slice of watermelon."

"Oh, nonsense." Kitty B. shakes her head and smiles earnestly at Ray. She scrubs the scruff of the feline who has settled in the depths of her lap. He begins to purr.

"See," LeMar says to Ray, "she thinks because the headaches are back I should eat and be merry, for tomorrow I will—"

"No, LeMar," Kitty B. says in a hushed tone. "It's a summer

night and my best friends are coming over for dinner and a meeting, and I wanted to make them a decent meal."

"You understand what I mean?" LeMar says to Ray while he eyes Kitty B. hard.

"Hi, Ray!" Sis calls, midway down the soft dirt path that leads to the water. She runs barefoot toward the house, a cloud of dust rising behind her, and Ray has never been more relieved to see her.

What astounds Ray most as Sis scurries toward them is how her dear friend appears to have hardly aged at all. Her soft black bob shows no sign of gray, and she's still got that terrific little figure—those thin ankles and that cinched waist and those perky well-proportioned breasts that seem immune to gravity itself. She must wear the same size she wore in high school! It's like time has stood still for Sis Mims. As if someone sealed her in the PVC pipe the town council used for a time capsule in their 250th anniversary of the founding of Jasper last fall, along with the church cookbook and the minutes of the town hall meeting and a photo of all of the children sitting on a joggling board in front of Mayor Whaley's house.

Sis's youthfulness strikes Ray as eerie sometimes. Granted, Sis is the only one among them to have had a hysterectomy thus far. But she bounced right back like nothing ever happened. Except for the blue pills that her gynecologist prescribed for her. She calls them her happy pills, and she shakes them like a maraca when Hilda rants about Trudi Crenshaw or Ray complains about her fibroid tumors or Poop 1 or Poop 2. "Ya'll really ought to try these anti-depressants," she says. "They have jump-started my *life!*"

Thing is, Ray cannot believe that Sis never married. Never had children. Never had sex, as far as she knows. Never had her offspring throw up or poop on her or grab for her breast in a feeding frenzy.

All she's really had is her music. The piano and the church organ and her students. They've set her up tens of times, with relatives and work associates and any single man they can get their hands on, but it never seems to work out. Ray hopes the new Episcopal priest,

the Reverend Capers Campbell IV, will be Sis's match. Honestly, it
was one of the reasons she voted that All Saints hire him. She wants
Sis to experience a little more of the companionship she's yearned
for since Fitz, and Rev. Capers couldn't do any better if he searched
the state over.

Kitty B.'s house is a wreck as usual. There are bills and magazines
and old newspapers scattered across the coffee table and black dog
hair on the upholstery and the corners of the room. No, she is not
blessed with any sense of domestic order, and Ray knows Roberta
would have a fit if she saw the way her daughter lived, with the
Hathaway family's old summer home rotting right before their eyes
and LeMar whining and picking paint chips on the sloping front
porch. Not to mention their youngest, Katie Rae, stroking her parrot up in her room with no college degree and no plan to ever leave
home or get a job.

But despite the chaos, Kitty B. is the best durn baker the town
has ever known. She bakes all of the cakes and sweets for the town's
social events, and she headed up the church cookbook publication,
Lowcountry Manna, a few years back. That book made so much
money for the parish that the vestry was able to put a new tin roof
on the sanctuary and the rectory. Kitty B. has won numerous pie
and cake contests across the southeast, and her lemon squares and
hummingbird cakes were featured in *Southern Living*'s special bak-
ing issue two years ago.

"Let's eat on trays in the living room," Kitty B. says, sliding the
newspaper across the couch and taking a seat.

As the gals load their plates with freshly fried chicken, LeMar
turns up *Salome*. He shuffles into the living room as they take their
first bites. "Now she's dancing with his head, girls."

"Turn that off, LeMar," Kitty B. says. "We're trying to *eat*."

LeMar nods and moves over to the stereo. He places his head on the speaker and says, "Next thing you know, Herod will have her killed too."

Richadene strides out of the kitchen and across the room and yanks the stereo plug out of the wall.

"Supper time," she says to LeMar.

"Poor John the Baptist," LeMar says to Ray as Richadene brings him a tray of fried chicken legs, a slice of watermelon, and a big helping of creamed corn. "He had his role to play in history, and then he was chopped right out of the picture at the whim of a seductress. It just doesn't seem fair."

Ray clears her throat and looks awkwardly around at the other gals. LeMar says a blessing and then excuses himself to eat on the porch, and they get to work sorting out the final wedding preparations. The Tea and See and the bridesmaid luncheon, the rehearsal dinner, and the wedding itself. It will take place at All Saints Episcopal Church, followed by a reception right across the street at Pink Point Gardens, a beautiful park on the water where colossal live oaks stretch their long moss-covered limbs out over the seawall. Little Hilda and Giuseppe will leave by boat—a fifty-foot yacht that Kitty B.'s brother, Jackson, has agreed to let them borrow for the occasion. It will be tied to the dock at the yacht club right next to the park, and the guests will line up on the seawall and throw birdseed on them as they race to the dock and sail away, standing on the upper deck of the grand vessel. Jackson will deliver them to the Sanctuary Resort on Kiawah Island, where they will spend one night before flying to Italy for their two-week honeymoon and tour of Giuseppe's homeland.

As the gals gnaw on the chicken bones, they strategize.

It's not the nitty-gritty details that concern them. Ray keeps the wedding box within arms' reach at all times, and she can handle any logistical emergency that could possibly come up among brides and bridesmaids. The wedding box consists of smelling salts, stain remover, buttons, needles and thread, safety pins, starch, a mini iron, breath mints, scissors, tape, bobby pins, tampons, Band-Aids, superglue, cover up, hairspray, baby wipes, Kleenex, and more. No button will pop, no heel will break that Ray can't handle; no stain or wrinkle will appear that can't be eradicated.

But there are other concerns with this particular wedding. There's the weather, of course, and the mosquitoes, not to mention the population explosion of various reptiles that have been a particular nuisance this summer, but more hazardous than that are the people and the tensions rising between them, so Ray refers to her notes and reels off the damage-control plan:

"If Hilda blows up at Angus's fiancée or whatever she is—Trudi Crenshaw—then Kitty B., you pull her outside and take her on a walk." Kitty B. nods and Ray continues.

"If Dennis Dannals shows up to take the pictures after having tipped the bottle as he is apt to do, Sis, you pump him with coffee and take the rolls of film out of his box so they don't get lost. And ask Capers to take over the camera. He took a photography course at the College of Charleston a few months back."

"Got it," Sis says.

"And if the good Reverend doesn't ask Sis to dance, let's force him to have a little champagne so that he will shrug off his inhibitions and spin her around in her spiffy blue dress with the big silk ecru sash and high-heeled sandals that Hilda picked out for her last May at the Copper Penny in Charleston."

"I can't believe how much I spent on that dress." Sis shakes her head. "I feel a little ridiculous about the whole thing."

"Oh, what else are you going to spend your money on?" Ray asks, hoping that Capers will finally notice the little knockout of an organist in his midst.

"I could have bought a whole new wardrobe with what that ensemble cost!" Sis says.

"Sis." Ray leans in toward her friend and nods once. "I'm going to put it to you plainly. None of us are getting any younger, and there comes a time when one must put all of one's eggs in a certain basket. You understand?"

"I guess," Sis says, her head shaking back and forth. "There aren't too many empty baskets coming through Jasper these days."

They all chuckle.

After they put aside their trays, they get out the tulle and the birdseed and the funnels and the satin ribbon and start making the sweet little sacks to hand to the guests before the bride and groom's departure.

"Well, anyway girls, we need to work out a damage-control scenario with one more issue," Kitty B. says.

"What could we have possibly left out?" Ray studies her notes one last time.

Kitty B. lifts up the newspaper she's been sitting on and points to the color image of Eleanor swirling across the Bahamas. "Oh, just a little tropical beast."

Ray swats her hand. She's tired of having to think about storms. "They've been predicting it'll hit Georgetown on a Thursday. Nothing to worry about."

"It almost always bumps north, and it's always at least two days delayed," Sis says.

"I know, I know, but every now and then it bumps south," Kitty B. says, "and you know how it slows down when it comes ashore, so there is a slight possibility we could be looking at a Friday sideswipe."

"I hope not." Sis pinches her chin.

Ray stands up and says in a firm tone, "I can't put much stock in worrying about storms. There are always storms looming in the tropics that could have our name on them, but in truth, it's been over a decade since our fair state has really felt the blow of one."

As the dogs begin to bark outside, Vangie Dreggs pokes her made-up face through the window between LeMar's speakers. "Just pray it away. I saw y'all's cars over here, and I just wanted to pop in and say hi."

Ray rolls her eyes. "So you just happened to be at the tip of Cottage Island?" she asks.

"Well, you know I'm looking at a piece of property out here."

"Really?" Ray says. "What in the world for?"

"For an investment . . . and a getaway. It's either this or Edisto Beach, and I just can't decide. Little Bit and I are testing the sunset at both places."

Vangie turns around toward the Ashepoo River and takes a mock picture with her fingers as her skirt billows up around her knees.

Why don't you just buy the whole durn county? Ray's tired of out-siders poking around Jasper in search of a little coastal living. Heck, Florida is already the north, and so are Hilton Head and Kiawah Island for that matter. Maybe the Texans should take over the rest of the southeastern coastline—buy it up and build their oversized houses and fancy chain stores around it. Is there no way to *stop* them?

A hot flash starts in Ray's chest and moves down her arms and up to the top of her head. She picks up the newspaper and starts fanning herself.

"Do come in," Kitty B. says to Vangie.

"Can't." Vangie winks. "Going to Charleston to hear Beth Moore speak at the Gaillard. Then out to dinner with some friends to the Peninsula Grill. Oh, I just love their coconut cake. It's eight layers, Kitty B.! I'll bring you a slice to the tea tomorrow."

"All right," Kitty B. says. "I'd love to try it."

"No, seriously, Ray," Vangie says as she lifts her palms up to the sky. "Just pray that storm away. The Lord won't let it ruin that sweet child's wedding day!"

Ray shakes her head, and Sis lets out a nervous giggle.

"Hope it's okay for me to bring my sister-in-law to the tea tomorrow?" Vangie says as she turns toward the porch. Ray bristles. "She's looking to buy a place in Charleston, and she wants to sam-ple a little of the outlying small-town life."

Flavor. Sample. It's as if Jasper County is one big spiral ham that

Vangie will slice off layer by layer until all that's left is the knobby bone.

"Why don't you give her a taste?" Ray says, but Vangie doesn't pick up the sarcasm.

Then the Lone Star Realtor of the Lowcountry bids the gals good evening, her heels clacking down the steps as she scurries out to her white Lexus SUV that looks like a slick horse pill that would be painful to swallow. They watch from the window as she pulls out, the silver Jesus fish on her bumper catching the afternoon light.

"Pray, pray, pray, pray, pray!" Ray says to the gals. "She thinks she's the Lone Star Coordinator of Divine Communications too. The gall! Do you know she's talked Capers into having some kind of 'prayer revival day' at All Saints? Now does that sound very Episcopalian to y'all? The Reverend Capers has lost his mind if he entertains all of this pray, pray, pray kookiness!"

"Pray for world peace!" Sis says.

"Or for a million more bucks!" Kitty B. adds.

"Or for God to snuff out my fibroid tumors!" Ray stands up and adjusts her skirt. "If she tells me to pray one more time, I just might slap her!"

"Or for Sis and the Reverend to fall hopelessly in love!" Kitty B. says, unable to stop the banter. "Or for LeMar's chronic fatigue to vanish!"

Kitty B. looks at a picture of Baby Roberta in her pink day gown the week before she lost her, and they all know what she really wants to pray for. She picks up the picture and plops down on the couch, and they come over and rub her back.

"Mama?" Katie Rae says from out of nowhere. She stands in the doorway with a nice-looking young man who has her parrot, Froot Loop, on his shoulder.

This must be one of the fellows she met from that online dating service. Kitty B. says she's been seeing the man who opened the new Serpentarium near the ACE Basin, a veterinarian, and his father is some kind of evangelical preacher. Ray looks down at her espadrilles. She hopes they haven't offended him with their banter.

"Oh, it's okay, sweetheart." Kitty B. pats her eyes with the backs of her palms and invites them into the filthy living room, where newspaper pages and birdseed are strewed amidst their trays of dirty plates and chicken bones and balled-up napkins. "These are my mom's gals," Katie Rae says to the young man.

He smiles and reaches out his hand in Ray's direction. "I've heard a lot about you all. It's a pleasure to meet you. I'm Marshall Bennington."

Sis stands up and pushes down the wrinkles in her pants and waits behind Ray to shake his hand. He looks each of them in the eye—and Ray has to admit, he's right polite and handsome, albeit slightly affected. Maybe she should get Priscilla onto one of those dating Web sites.

"What's that noise?" he says.

"Oh, that's LeMar snoring." Kitty B. shakes her head, and Ray looks out on the porch, where the sick man snoozes in his rocking chair as the sun makes its descent behind the trees across the water.

"So nice to meet you, Marshall," Ray says as she nudges Kitty B. "I better get going."

The gals quickly load Kitty B.'s silver chest, her china teacups and saucers and creams and sugars into Ray's backseat to add to the stash for the Tea and See. Next they load up Miss C. and the lemon squares and the petits fours, which Ray positions carefully in the way back. Sis drapes some towels around Miss C. so she won't knock into the sweets and flatten them.

"Don't forget the wedding presents," Kitty B. says as LeMar wakes up for a moment, smacks his lips, and drifts back into sleep on the rocking chair.

Ray doesn't see how she can fit any more into the Tea and See display, but Kitty B. went to Charleston last week on account of LeMar's doctor's appointment and so she stopped by Tirlants to pick up some wedding gifts. They're some of the most beautiful Little Hilda has received: four silver goblets, two teacups, six salad plates, a rice spoon, a place setting of silver, and a crystal ice bucket from Tiffany's.

"Well, y'all," Ray says as Kitty B. and Sis carefully stack the gifts in the passenger seat. "I'll just have to find a way to squeeze them into the display."

The summer day finally gives way to night as Ray pulls out of Kitty B.'s dirt driveway and heads home. As she bumps along the old road, she thinks of Eleanor chasing its tail over the Bahamas and Vangie Dreggs's foolish belief that her prayer could pop the storm like a pinprick in a balloon. Then she thinks back to Hurricane Hazel, the one that pummeled Charleston when Ray was ten and living in Mrs. Pringle's carriage house.

~ OCTOBER 14, 1959 ~

"You're crazy, Mama," Nigel had called to Mrs. Pringle from the bottom of the stairs as Ray and Laura sat huddled on the love seat in Mrs. Pringle's guest room. "You mean to tell me you'd rather be holed up with that whore and her two bastard daughters instead of with me on higher ground?"

It knocked the breath out of Ray when he said those words. She can remember literally gasping. *Bastard?* She didn't think she'd ever heard the word before, but, as if by instinct, she knew precisely what it meant. For the first time in her young life she was face-to-face with the harsh reality of what she was. The sharp and succinct title that defined her.

Her mama, with her persuasive way of softening the edges of life, had never made it sound like that. Ray's daddy was a soldier whom Carla loved, if briefly, before his deployment. A brave man who fought for their country and surely died in the line of duty, didn't he?

Bastard. Ray rubbed the pads of her fingers over that sharp word, and it pricked her as if it were the end of one of her mama's sewing needles.

Her mama ran out of Mrs. Pringle's bedroom to the top of the stairs and stood beside her employer. "Leave her alone!" she screamed down to Nigel. "She's eighty years old, and she's still got the right to make her own decision. She doesn't *want* to evacuate!"

Ray could hear Nigel scoff and punch at the crystals that dangled from the chandelier in the foyer as Laura curled up on the love seat and burrowed her head into Ray's chest.

"What did he mean?" Laura whispered.

"Mmm?" Ray asked, still trying to catch her breath.

"Mr. Pringle called us a name. Bastards. What does that mean?"

When that needle of a word pushed out of her little sister's mouth, Ray picked it up between her fingers, turned it from side to side, then pushed it into the pincushion of her heart, where it has been lodged ever since.

"Something bad, Laura," Ray said as the bile rose in the back of her throat. "Something awful."

Now as she drives down the gravelly island road with the sound of the goblets and the silver clinking together in the box, Ray knows she has no business running the Wedding Guild or posing as the first lady of Jasper. But, maybe that was part of her plan all along. To have her life so intertwined with the pack, have them so dependent on her that they couldn't throw her out if they wanted to. Even if they knew the truth.

Ray had married into Jasper society, after all, and borne two beautiful children who she thinks she raised well. Granted she spoiled them, but she and Willy provided them with everything, and they seemed to be making their way in the world.

Ray prides herself in how she rose to leadership under Roberta's tutelage with the ballet recitals and the Christmas pageants at church, then the debutante balls. Her role in coordinating the weddings of the next generation will seal her legacy and her place in Jasper society for good, despite the ugly truth of her origins.

Looking into the darkening woods with its tropical vines and scrub pines, Ray remembers her mama moving her daughters out of the carriage house and up to Mrs. Pringle's bedroom the night of the storm. They slept around the old woman's tall four-poster bed on the hardwood floor as the shutters slapped against the yellow clapboards and the water trickled from the edges of the panes and formed a puddle by their feet.

Now just as Ray turns on her headlights, a large brown figure leaps onto the road, then halts, its twelve white spears pointing up. He stands stone still. Like a wall. His nostrils flare, and his large black eyes glisten like moonlight on the smooth surface of Round-O Creek.

She brakes, but it's too late.

She barely registers the impact as the air bag bursts from its storage bin like gunfire itself and punches her in the face before enveloping her with its warm, ballooning latex as the smoke and dust spew out of its pores.

The steering wheel is hot and her face begins to burn. As she opens the window, she smells lemon squares and cake and looks in the rearview mirror to see icing dripping from the ceiling. Bits of cake have landed in her hair, and chunks of lemon squares are sliding down the windshield and the creases of the deflated air bag. With a cursory glance, Ray sees that Miss C. has landed in the backseat and has lost an arm, and she's sure that Kitty B.'s teacups and Little Hilda's crystal ice bucket and Christmas china are cracked beneath the tissue in their gift boxes.

On the hood of her Volvo is a twelve-point buck, and before she passes out she can hear Cousin Willy calling to her as he runs toward the car, but she's not sure if she's dreaming it.

"Ray? Are you okay?"

FOUR

Kitty B.

Kitty B. teeters at the top of the stairwell wondering what her middle daughter would be like or who she would marry if she had lived to be twenty-five like Little Hilda and Priscilla. They were all the same age, you know? Born within a four-month span of one another. The three watermelon seeds.

In Kitty B.'s daydreams Baby Roberta is a younger version of herself. How she looked and felt as a teenager, stealing melons with the pack or chasing after her older brothers down Third Street when they stole her hat or her report card or the notes carefully folded in her back pocket that she and Ray would slip back and forth during Mr. Unger's biology class.

It's strange that she misses the young woman her baby might have become. She wonders if when she is elderly and the gals' daughters become middle-aged, if she'll yearn for the midlife version of her child, if she'll imagine what particular way Baby Roberta would have taken her arm and led her out of the nursing home and into the noonday sun for a lunch at Opal Dowdy's or an appointment with Angus.

Suddenly aware of the wide crease forming between her hips,

Kitty B. turns to examine her turquoise linen dress suit in the hall mirror at the top of the stairs. She weighed in at one hundred and ninety pounds last month at the doctor's office, and she's not sure she can even sit down in the suit this year without it ripping open. She frowns at her wide hips and the gray in her long, stringy hair. She didn't have time to get the newfangled Spanx that both Hilda and Ray promised would suck it all in, and her girdle is so old that it is literally crumbling at the ends, leaving a trail of synthetic threads from her closet to the top of the stairs.

She suspects she won't be able to squeeze into her mama's sea-foam beaded gown that she'd planned to wear to Little Hilda's wedding, so she'll have to find a few hours to go to the plus-size shop outside of Charleston where the made-up fat ladies with their brightly painted nails come at her like a swarm of provoked wasps, piercing her skin with their questions, "Size sixteen, ma'am?"

She used to be a size eight, and she even went down to a six right after she had her firstborn, Cricket. But when she lost Baby Roberta at three months old, cooking was the only way to calm her nerves, and it was the one thing she seemed to have a knack for in the domestic realm. So she baked and sampled along the way and woke up one day to find a size sixteen staring back at her in the mirror.

One time when her youngest, Katie Rae, was in high school, she heard one of her school friends, Betsy Burnett, say, "I didn't know your mama was expecting."

"She's not," Katie Rae said.

Betsy Burnett blushed and covered her mouth. "Oh," she chuckled, nervously.

Now Kitty B. wobbles down the stairs, and there is a problem with one of her bone-colored Ferragamos too. One of the bows is cati-wompas, busted by Honey's paw one Sunday a few months back when she arrived home from church with the parish hall leftovers— a bowl of red rice and a Ziploc bag of poppy seed muffins. The Ferragamos are actually hand-me-downs from her mama. She inherited Roberta's whole closet, but it's too bad she can't squeeze herself into half of those beautiful clothes anymore. Heavens, her mama could dress! Roberta Hathaway was as regal as they came in Jasper, with her tailored suits and the fine Italian pumps she bought during her shopping trips down King Street in Charleston.

"I'm going," Kitty B. calls to LeMar, who is slumped under the covers in the room across the hall from hers. They haven't slept in the same room for over a decade now, and sometimes Kitty B. feels as though LeMar is more like a cantankerous older brother than a spouse. She hears the strain of the springs as he rolls over in the bed and yawns. "The coffeepot's on and there are some slices of toasted banana bread on top of the stove."

He moans and clears his throat, and from Kitty B.'s angle all she can see of his room is the eyelet curtains filling out like hoop skirts as the island breeze pushes through the window.

LeMar's room smells like medicine and metal and urine, and it takes all she can muster to go in there each day, pat his soft, wide back, and say, "Time to wake up."

Well, she's not even going to bother right now. She's been up all night making petits fours and lemon squares to replace the ones lost in Ray's collision, and if LeMar wants to lie in bed till noon and feel sorry for himself all day, so be it.

Thank God Ray is okay. Kitty B. just doesn't know if Little Hilda could get married without Ray at the helm of it all. If anything ever happens to her, the gals and everybody in their pack for that matter just might implode like an undercooked soufflé or a pound cake short of an egg.

In the kitchen Kitty B. stacks the five Tupperware containers of sweets as a large palmetto bug crawls out from behind her sugar jar and scoots across the countertop. She slips off the Ferragamo with the catiwompas bow and takes one swat at him, but he scurries toward the oven and escapes in a crack between the stove and the cabinet. She leans over and checks the rat trap beside the refrigerator. She catches a river rat in there every few weeks, but she doesn't dare tell the gals about that. They might not even eat her good food.

She's in a hurry to get these sweets in the air-conditioned car so they won't lose their shape in the midday August heat. With the containers stacked up to her chin, Kitty B. nearly trips over Katie Rae, who giggles uncharacteristically on the porch steps with the cordless phone stuck to her ear.

"Don't be late," Kitty B. whispers as the dogs run up and lick her knees, their wet noses leaving streaks of slobber across her snug linen skirt.

Katie Rae nods and waves her away. "Oh, I've got this *thing* later today," she says into the receiver. "It's where you go and gawk at all of the wedding gifts and ooh and ahhh over them. Rather obnoxious, if you ask me."

Before Kitty B. has to shoo away the dogs, they catch the scent of the next-door neighbor's goat that bleats at them through the rotting wooden gate. In a flash, the canines tear off to sniff through the white picket slats where the paint is peeling off the soft wood in jagged strips.

Oh well. Kitty B. looks back at her weathered home with its mold between the clapboards and its peeling paint and the muddy paw prints along the porch. There is a spot halfway down the screened door where Honey scratches and scratches until someone lets her in on cold nights, and there is a crack in the attic window where a magnolia limb fell onto the roof during a tropical storm *last* October.

As she pulls out of the driveway in the Lincoln Continental that used to belong to her mama, she looks up to LeMar's window to see Mr. Whiskers leap from the roof through the parting curtains.

"Scat!" LeMar's voice is so deep that she can hear him through the sealed car window and the blasting air conditioner that cools the melting makeup on her face. "Kitty B.! Get this cat out of here!"

Katie Rae puts a finger to her other ear and walks out to the dock to continue her conversation with the first real boyfriend they think she's ever had, and Kitty B. waves to no one as she turns the nose of the Lincoln toward the dirt road that leads to Jasper, leaving a swirl of dead oak leaves and one disgruntled husband in her wake.

"Thank God for you, Kitty B.!" Ray says, greeting her at the door before striking an Ava Gardner–like pose. "Now don't I look like death warmed over?"

Ray's deep purple eye, coated profusely in concealer and powder, can't be hidden. Kitty B. gawks at it. Beneath the eye, a stitched-up gash traces Ray's cheekbone in an awful blackish crimson.

"Are you all right?" Kitty B. bites her lip and cringes.

"It could have been a lot worse," Ray says. "That air bag saved my eye, the doctor said. And Willy just happened along the same road right behind me. I didn't wake up until I was in the Ravenel Hospital. They checked me out all over and sent me home around three in the morning."

"Oh, Ray." Kitty B. shakes her head in disbelief. "It could have been terrible."

"It *was*—for the buck," Richadene calls over her shoulder as she opens one of Kitty B.'s Tupperware lids and starts placing the iced petits fours on a tiered silver platter by the kitchen sink.

"How did it happen?"

"I can't really say," Ray says. "I was just driving home, daydreaming, I suppose, and the next thing I knew this enormous buck was striking a pose in front of me."

Cousin Willy pops his head in from the back garden. "Biggest one I've seen in years—over two hundred pounds. Bent the hood of the station wagon like an accordion." He walks over to Ray and pats her shoulder. "Now take it easy today." He examines her gash and gives her a kiss on the forehead.

"I will," Ray says. "Now go on. You know tea parties aren't your thing."

"Only you, Kitty B.," Sis says from the living room where she is pouring sugar into the china bowls at the tea stations, "could pull off making four dozen petits fours twelve hours before a tea."

Sis looks so fresh in her black linen pants and pink satin blouse with the mandarin neck. Kitty B. notices her newfangled sliders—what does Cricket call them? Mules? They have a sharp pointed toe, too narrow for an actual toe to fit, and a pencil-thin heel. Sis looks as though it could be her wedding gifts the gals will see while sipping tea, as if she has a whole exciting life ahead of her.

"Look at your shoe, Kitty B.!" Ray points at the dirt-smudged ribbon that dangles by a thread from the top of her foot.

Kitty B. looks down at the shoe and tugs at her skirt in hopes that they won't notice how tight it is, but the crease pops right back, and she walks toward the utility closet. "Got any superglue?"

"Oh, no, that will *ruin* the shoe." Ray firmly shakes her head. "You need to take it to Floride—she'll sew it on properly for you."

"Oh, Ray, I don't care about that."

"Me neither," Sis giggles. "I use a glue gun to put my buttons back on all the time, and do you see this spot right here?" She points to a moth hole in her black pants. "I just took a sharpie pen and dotted it so my skin looked black underneath right there."

"You shouldn't tell things like that, Sis," Ray says.

"Loosen up, Mom." Priscilla strolls through the kitchen in nothing but boxers and a black T-shirt that reads, "W" and in small letters below it, "IMPEACH THE PRESIDENT." Kitty B. wonders what in the world that means.

Priscilla's hair has these kind of thick, knotted ropes that remind Kitty B. of oversized cocoons or the tubular hornets' nests on the back of her house. Ray says they are dreadlocks, and she hates them to death.

"Hi, Priscilla," Sis says with her arms outstretched, and Kitty B. follows behind her to give her best friend's daughter a hug.

Priscilla smells like incense and body odor, like the hippie ladies that sell their crudely sewn dolls in the outdoor market in Charleston. When Kitty B. and Priscilla's necks lock, Kitty B. squeezes her tight, and she can feel her sharp little shoulder blades jutting out between her fingers like angel wings. Then Kitty B. wells up with her usual child-sickness, relieved that it is happening now before the bride arrives.

Sis pats Kitty B.'s back and Ray hands her a Kleenex. They know what this is about, and Kitty B. is thankful that they don't pay her much attention.

"Pris, have you showered yet?" Ray says.

Priscilla sniffs under her thin arms and crinkles her nose.

Ray presses at the black around her eye and winces. "The Hildas will be here in less than thirty minutes and the guests in less than an hour, honey."

Priscilla tugs at the back of her dreadlocks. She raises one eyebrow and says, "Tell me there's a halfway decent coffeehouse in Jasper by now."

"Coffee!" Ray's long, thin hands curl into two bony fists behind her back. "I've got coffee in the pot! Now grab a cup and get *ready!* You're the maid of honor, for heaven's sake!"

Priscilla wipes her nose on her T-shirt, and Kitty B. notices that she has some kind of small, silver hoop earring through her belly button. *Ouch! You'd have to hog-tie me to get that close to my belly with a needle.*

Priscilla walks over toward the coffeepot, which she lifts up and sniffs before pouring the contents out into the sink.

"Well, let's get to work, ladies." Ray turns back to the gals. "Sis, you put the final touches on the tea service, and Kitty B., can you pour the ginger ale in the fruit punch and stack the crystal cups around it?"

Priscilla scratches a blemish on her chin as she stares into the refrigerator, and Ray heads toward her and leans in close. Kitty B. can't make out what Ray says to her, but in a few moments, the young woman walks slowly up the stairs toward her room.

Ray points to the portrait in her dining room of Priscilla at five, in a pale peach smocked Easter dress carrying a bundle of daffodils from the backyard for the flowering of the cross at All Saints Episcopal Church. Kitty B. notices the dimples around the knuckles of the child's soft, round hands as Ray says, "Where did that sweet girl disappear to?"

Ray has outdone herself for the Tea and See. The floral centerpiece is so sweet and airy with the English garden roses and the pale green hydrangea, and there are similar arrangements in silver bowls and teapots and mint julep glasses in every little open space throughout the whole downstairs. The fireplaces are stuffed with fresh-cut magnolia limbs, and a large white bloom punctuates the center of each.

"Look at all the gifts!" Kitty B. says, clapping her hands together.

Little Hilda has received some gorgeous things. Probably on account of the fact that her father has been the doctor to everyone in the whole town for decades now. Angus has delivered every baby of Little Hilda's generation and beyond and set a countless number of child-sized broken arms for which he always writes a prescription for "ice cream on demand." He's helped each one of their parents through the aging and dying process. And now he's rescuing all the middle-aged women by dispensing hormones in record numbers as his gals endure *the big change.*

The gifts are elegantly displayed on glass shelves throughout the living and dining rooms. Complete place settings of all three of

Little Hilda's china patterns, plus her silver and crystal pieces, are arranged on an antique card table in the center of the side piazza. Below each plate is a white linen place mat that Ray bought with Willy during their trip to Ireland last April.

The food is presented on the finest compilation of their silver trays and bowls. It's as delicate as the floral arrangements and includes Kitty B.'s petits fours and lemon squares as well as Sis's shrimp salad and cucumber sandwiches and Ray's cheese straws, praline pecans, and fruit kabobs dipped in white and dark chocolate.

The tea stations at both ends of the dining room table are comprised of pots, creams, sugars as well as cups and saucers from the Mottahedeh china that they each received for their wedding presents, and the punch station has crystal cups that Ray bought at an estate auction in Walterboro. Kitty B.'s Mottahedeh pattern is "Duke of Gloucester," Ray's is "Blue Canton," and Hilda's is "Tobacco Leaf," on account of her mama's Virginia plantation ancestry.

Sis handles the mint julep and iced tea station, where the enormous collection of silver mint julep glasses and goblets that she inherited from her father's mother is set up on the antique sideboard along with lemons and fresh mint and delicate linen napkins with her grandmother's monogram.

"Don't you love how the silver goblets fog up when they're filled with ice?" Kitty B. asks no one in particular. She tugs at her skirt, glances toward the front door, and sees that Miss C. is back in business less than twenty-four hours after the wreck.

"Cousin Willy and Justin superglued Miss C.'s arm on sometime in the wee hours," Sis says.

Kitty B. walks over to the foyer to examine the statue closely. The sleeves on her pink dress cover the crack. A mini pomander of pale green hydrangea, a smaller version of the one made for the bride, dangles from Miss C.'s concrete wrist by a white satin ribbon.

"Martha Stewart doesn't have a *thing* on us!" Kitty B. says.

Ray winks at Kitty B. and beams with pride, despite the strain on her gash, as she hands Kitty B. a corsage that includes a rose, a piece of a hydrangea, and three sprigs of lavender sweet pea.

She hands her a stick pin. "Put it on."

"Me?" Kitty B. says.

"Of course," Ray says, pointing to Sis, who is pinning hers on in the hall mirror.

"One for every hostess."

"Mama would be so proud," Kitty B. says, and in her mind's eye she sees Roberta nudging God on the elbow and pointing down at the gals. "Now how's that for southern hospitality, Lord?"

When the doorbell rings, Kitty B. opens it to find the petite and beautiful Little Hilda standing in its center in a strapless pale pink and white seersucker dress. She's wearing the elegant strand of pearls they helped Hilda pick out at Croghan's in Charleston for her debutante ball four short years ago. Little Hilda is so lovely and delicate that she takes Kitty B.'s breath away.

"Hi, Miss Kitty B.," Little Hilda says as Kitty B. stares into her face, unable to utter a word.

"Don't you look lovely," Ray interjects, sliding the pomander of pale green hydrangea onto Little Hilda's minute wrist.

"Thank y'all so much," she says, looking to each of the gals. "Especially you, Miss Ray, for hosting this and for putting everything together." Then she tucks a loose strand of blond hair behind her ear and blushes. "Mama's running late."

Sis swats the air, "That's okay, honey. We know your mama very well, and we wouldn't expect it any other way."

Little Hilda grins before whispering, "Did y'all know that she still sits in a hot tub for an hour after putting on her makeup for it to 'soak in'?"

"No, not the Princess of Jasper?" Ray says cutting her eyes at Sis. "I can't imagine her spending more than, say, a *half hour* letting her makeup soak in."

They laugh at Hilda's expense.

"Well, there must be something to her lengthy grooming proce-dures," Kitty B. says, patting Little Hilda on the back, "because she's always the most gorgeous person in the room."

"Besides the bride," Sis says, hugging Little Hilda tight. "We're so happy for you, sweetheart."

Kitty B. tears up again, and Little Hilda reaches out to squeeze her hand. She's probably the most sensitive one out of all of their children, which surprises the socks off Kitty B., considering she was reared by the self-centered daughter of the dictator of Jasper.

"It's okay," Little Hilda says to Kitty B. as she dabs her eye with one of Sis's linen napkins. "I understand."

Next Cricket and Katie Rae arrive, and Kitty B. is delighted to see that Katie Rae found a skirt, not to mention a little lipstick. Those boys that she's meeting on the computer have got her primping for the first time ever. Kitty B. doesn't care what people say about the evils of the Internet, she's thanking the good Lord for online dating services!

"Hi girls," Kitty B. says. "Don't y'all look nice."

Truth is, Cricket is the only one in the Blalock clan to have got-ten her act together. She married one of the McFortson boys of the large and successful McFortson Funeral Home business that has locations up and down the South Carolina coastline. She even works there part-time while she and Tommy try to start a family. Cricket's dressed in a sleeveless, teal linen dress that looks like one of her tailored Talbots, size-four specials with a tasteful gold slider necklace that has an octagonal medallion charm with her mono-gram dangling just below the center of her neckline.

Cricket is in good shape and well-proportioned with a short hairdo that always looks freshly cut and in place, and sometimes she seems so together that she makes Kitty B. uncomfortable. Like maybe Cricket should be the mother and Kitty B. should be the daughter so that she could rear her up with the kind of order and organization that Kitty B. has never been able to muster.

"We came in a hearse, Mama," Katie Rae snickers, and Kitty B. notices a piece of pepper or spinach lodged in between her daughter's front teeth.

Katie Rae turns and points to the street, where sure enough there is a long black hearse parked in front of Kitty B.'s brother Jackson's house. "To carry the wedding gown."

"Of course," Kitty B. says. That is Cricket's role to play in the wedding—to pick up the wedding gown from the cleaners and carry it in the hearse, so it has plenty of room to lie flat, to the church dressing room.

Cricket clears her throat. "Check your teeth in the powder room," she whispers to Katie Rae, who covers her mouth and scurries into Ray's half bath beneath the stairwell.

"Good to see you, Mama," Cricket looks her mother up and down. "What happened to your Ferragamo?"

"Oh," Kitty B. says, patting her on the back as if to console her. "It broke on the way over. I'll get it fixed next week."

Cricket pulls a roll of double-sided tape out of her little square teal purse, then leads Kitty B. by the elbow to the corner of the dining room, where she kneels down and tapes the bow back on her mother's shoe.

"That'll hold it for now," Cricket says, standing up and shaking her head gently as her do settles back into place. She smiles at Kitty B. and pats her forearm. "You okay, Mama?"

"Yes." Kitty B. nods. "Now go over and greet the bride."

When Trudi Crenshaw, Angus's girlfriend who claims to be his fiancée, arrives *before* Hilda with her plump twelve-year-old daughter Dodi, the junior bridesmaid, in tow, they are all a little uneasy. Little Hilda greets them merrily, and Ray directs them to the fruit punch, and before you know it, half the women in town are making their way through the foyer. There's Mayor's wife, Tootsie Whaley, and Missy Meggett and the ladies who make up the garden club and Junior League of Jasper.

When Sis's mother and the rest of the older ladies arrive on a bus from the Episcopal retirement home on Seabrook Island, Ray runs out to greet them and help them down one by one, making sure their canes and walkers are on firm footing on her new slate walkway.

Some of them eye the hearse with concern, and Ray pats their hands and says, "It's for the wedding gown. Cricket's picking it up from the cleaners this afternoon."

Then Vangie Dreggs and her sister-in-law pull into the middle of the front yard in a golf cart as if they are on a putting green or in the small confines of an exclusive island resort. They come in with a bang, laughing and hooting and making their introductions.

Now Kitty B. notices Hilda's long white Mercedes as it creeps quietly up into the driveway. From the kitchen she sees Hilda check her makeup twice in the rearview mirror before slipping in through the back door in her cream silk pantsuit.

"Hi, gal," Kitty B. says, pinning the corsage on her and lying, "You haven't missed a thing."

"I'm sorry I'm late." Hilda fans herself with her hands.

"You look lovely," Kitty B. soothes as she rubs her friend's back.

"Thanks, darling." Hilda straightens her posture before she enters the dining room to greet everyone with a painted smile.

Kitty B. takes her place at one end of the dining room table, where she mans the Earl Grey tea station. Before she knows it, a line of tea drinkers forms, and she pours cup after cup of tea as the familiar buzz of feminine chatter swells up and falls away over and over like the waves on a choppy day at the mouth of the Edisto River.

The older ladies cluck over the gifts, and the young girls form a circle around Little Hilda, who blushes and shows her engagement ring, an antique-set princess cut that belonged to Giuseppe's great-grandmother who is buried in the Tuscan village of Trassilico that crowns one of the mountaintops they will visit on their honeymoon next week.

"How much do you want for the whole house, Ray, furniture

and all?" Kitty B. hears Vangie Dreggs say, half joking. She points to her sister-in-law, who's visiting from Houston. "Deanna says she'll give you a million-two for the whole kit and caboodle."

"Oh my," Ray says, straightening out her powder blue linen top. "Well, I appreciate your interest, I suppose"—she nods to Deanna—"but our home is not for sale."

"Of course it isn't." Vangie squints her faux emerald eyes. "I was just pulling your leg."

Ray laughs nervously and catches Kitty B.'s eye from across the room. *I told you so!*

Thing is, Kitty B. was the one who convinced the gals to invite Vangie to the Tea and See. Vangie has volunteered to do so much for the wedding that Kitty B. just felt they had to. After all, the "Lone Star" is putting up Giuseppe's entire family in her newest block of furnished apartments between here and Beaufort, and she managed to get a suite donated for Senator Warren, Giuseppe's boss, at the newfangled five-star Sanctuary on Kiawah as well as the honeymoon suite for Giuseppe and Little Hilda on their wedding night.

But the look on Ray's face tells Kitty B. that Ray thinks she was dead wrong in insisting.

~ JULY 7, 2005, ONE MONTH EARLIER ~

"You do have Vangie on the guest list for all of the Prescott parties, don't you?" Kitty B. asked Ray while they'd picked out the wedding tent from Thomason Rental.

"Don't be so naive," Ray said. "Can't you see that Vangie's just trying to buy her way into our town?"

"I don't think that's true." Kitty B. shook her head and turned to Ray. "She's gone out of her way to be helpful. You have to admit that."

Ray rolled her eyes.

Then Kitty B. blurted out, "You were new here once, too, remember?"

Ray's eyes narrowed as if Kitty B. had accused her of committing a crime. "That was thirty years ago."

Within seconds Ray pointed to the tent that she wanted for the wedding without so much as asking Kitty B.'s opinion and turned to face her.

"Let's go," she said.

Just as Kitty B. nods to Ray, who summons her to a talk in the kitchen, Little Hilda comes over with a frosted glass of mint julep and says in a hushed tone, "Miss Ray, have I told you about Giuseppe's friend Donovan?"

"No, honey," she says.

"Well," she says, her cheeks flushed from all of the excitement. "He's from New Jersey and he worked on Senator Warren's campaign a few years ago, and now he's a medical resident at Johns Hopkins in Baltimore. Anyway, he wants to be introduced to a nice southern girl, so I'm trying to persuade Priscilla to look after him this weekend!"

"Oh, that's a fine idea," Ray says and Kitty B. can see her tension over Vangie fading. Ray is no fool. A liberal Yankee is not ideal, but she would certainly take a nice doctor any day of the week over Poop 2.

With Ray diverted, Kitty B. ambles over to chat with Sis's mama and some of the other older ladies who were Roberta's friends. They all want a report on LeMar's health, and they are already organizing a time to bring over a casserole dinner next week. Just when she thinks her mama's gals are grinding to a halt on account of old age and death itself, Kitty B. learns that they still have a little more gas in the tank—what a pleasant surprise!

Then Sis comes over, pats Kitty B.'s elbow, and says, "Hilda's simply not acknowledging Trudi Crenshaw's presence whatsoever."

"What's Trudi doing?" Kitty B. asks.

"Well, go see for yourself and report back to me," she says. "I've been staring at both of them too much."

So Kitty B. grabs a cup of tea and checks out the situation. Trudi seems to be avoiding Hilda like the plague, making a point of scurrying into another room whenever Hilda changes places.

Now some of the guests are picking up the gifts and looking on the bottom of them to note the manufacturer or the pattern. This isn't the most mannerly thing to do, but one can understand since they are on display. Trudi follows their lead, noting to her daughter the names beneath the china and the crystal. But then, in a nervous frenzy, Trudi goes from picking up the gifts on display to picking up the knickknacks and doodads from the shelves and end tables all over Ray's home. Now, that's just not something you do.

Then Vangie Dreggs and her sister-in-law, curious as ever, are right behind Trudi, peering over her shoulder to see. Kitty B. knows that even the Lone Star pain in Ray's behind knows better than to do this, but, by golly, she's not going to miss the opportunity to snoop.

This goes on for about fifteen minutes—Trudi picking up antique plates and picture frames and books as Kitty B. watches in astonishment, sipping her tea and nibbling on a lemon square.

Suddenly, Hilda walks over to Trudi, who is studying the bottom of a small antique wooden box from Ray's great-aunt Nell Pringle, and says plainly, "The whole house is not on display."

Then Hilda grabs the box, turns it right side up, and continues, "Let's mind our manners," before she places it back on the bookshelf where it belongs.

"Oh my," Vangie says, with her hand over her thick painted lips. She turns back to her sister-in-law, who nods in acknowledgment, as though she is up to speed on all of the Jasper drama.

Kitty B. eyes Sis as the whole party seems to stop and stare. Then

Ray steps in. "Oh, don't give it a second thought, Trudi. I'm honored that you're admiring that piece. It belonged to a dear old aunt of mine from Charleston."

But Ray is too late. Trudi's eyes fill with tears before she scuttles out the front door, her hefty daughter Dodi chasing after her.

"Mama!" Little Hilda runs over. "That was awful!" The little bride slings the pomander off her arm and runs after Trudi. The ball of hydrangeas lands on the Oriental rug in Ray's living room, where it rolls beneath the coffee table, leaving a small trail of flowers.

Hilda looks up and around at everyone. A few throats clear before she says through clenched teeth, "Thank you so much, Ray and Kitty B. and Sis. This has been lovely." Then she walks through the kitchen and slams the back door.

The gals look around at one another, wondering why in the world she's mad at them, and the guests clear out faster than you can say, "Boo!"

FIVE

When they are all alone, Ray shakes her head and throws up her arms.

"Lord, I give up!" she says, patting her black eye and flinching at the pain. "We have worked ourselves to the bone for this wedding, and Big Hilda thinks she deserves every bit of it and more. As if we are on her daddy's payroll!"

She scoops up a handful of dirty silver forks and throws them into the sink before adding, "This is not the Jasper Mill monarchy! The mill is long gone. And so is Angus and so is Little Hilda. And we'll be gone, too, if she keeps this up."

"Let Sis and me clean up, Ray." Kitty B. says. "You need to rest."

"My eye hurts like the dickens." She pulls out some Advil from the cabinet above her and swallows three at a time. "But I'm too angry to rest."

Then Ray fills the sink with suds and scrubs the silver with a sponge. Kitty B. works with Sis to collect the dirty plates and cups and saucers and place them carefully at the sink. Then she picks up a hand towel and dries the forks and spoons before handing them to Sis, who places each one in its rightful silver box. Ray has a laminated sheet on each of the gals' silver boxes on which she has typed out the number of spoons, forks, knives, and serving pieces that belong in each box.

They all chose the same pattern—Chantilly by Gorham—at Roberta's suggestion so they could pool their silver resources for occasions such as this. Of course, they about died a few years ago when the book *A Southern Belle Primer: Or, Why Princess Margaret Will Never Be a Kappa Kappa Gamma* came out because it noted that ladies with the Chantilly pattern were "loose" in high school.

"I was a little loose," Sis had said when Ray pointed out the chapter one weekend as they sipped gin and tonics on Ray's screened porch at Edisto Beach.

"Yes, you were," Hilda said, ashing her cigarette in a pink conch Ray bought at the gift shop. "But at least you were monogamous."

Now the kitchen window is open, and Kitty B. hears Priscilla and Little Hilda, who have gathered on the porch with a few of their friends and a pitcher of mint juleps. They've slipped off their high-heeled sandals and relax with their legs over the arms of the wicker furniture where they murmur about the blowup and Little Hilda's frustration with her mother.

After everything is cleaned and put away, the gals retire to the other end of the piazza on the long porch swing that Cousin Willy installed last spring.

"Well, here's to that disaster," Sis says, handing Kitty B. and Ray mint juleps, which they sip heartily as they rock back and forth, consoling one another in the swampy air about the fact that the blowup wasn't their fault. It was just Hilda being Hilda.

Ray dips three napkins in an ice bucket and gives one to each of them to put across their foreheads.

"Hot flashes," she calls to the young girls, who are looking inquisitively at the older women. She puts the sopping linen around the back of her neck and adds, "Just wait."

Just wait is right, Kitty B. thinks. Menopause pales in comparison to the daily struggles of married life. She remembers the night before her wedding some thirty-five years ago. The curlers with the Ace bandage, the pep talk, the silk nightie. The gals had buoyed her with a sense of wonder and expectation about her life with LeMar, and she let them. How were they to know what was to come?

The girls giggle, their rosy cheeks filling with air as the gals wipe themselves down with the cool water. Then they settle back into their cushions as Little Hilda recounts the story of Giuseppe proposing to her on the steps of the Capitol last Fourth of July.

Kitty B. moans softly in the bittersweet gathering of her missing daughter's contemporaries. Her child ought to be right there with them. It's what she thought at their christening twenty-five years ago and at each of their birthday parties and their high school graduation and debutante balls, and it's what pains her each time she passes over their child-sized handprints sealed indelibly in the concrete on the corner of Third and Main Street. That someone who should be here is missing.

Suddenly, the sky turns gray from what could be an early band of Eleanor, and the wind kicks up, sending the dead oak leaves and the browning petals of the summer flowers spinning in circles.

Kitty B. lies back and so do Sis and Ray. They close their eyes and swing back and forth, enjoying the fresh wind on their face as the sweetest scent wafts over the piazza.

"Y'all, I swear I smell gardenias," Kitty B. says.

"Me too," Sis says, "I was trying to place it."

Ray keeps her eyes sealed shut as if she is asleep, as if she is soaking herself in this warm air and the sorely missed chatter of young girls on her piazza. She looks worn and fragile with her swelling eye and the black gash across her cheek. It makes Kitty B. uneasy to see her best friend wounded and suddenly looking every one of her fifty-five years.

"That's the confederate jasmine," Ray mumbles.

"No," Sis says, sniffing the air. "It smells just like those gardenias we carried in Kitty B.'s wedding."

Now Kitty B. pictures the small, fragrant bouquet her mama placed in her bedroom the morning of her wedding day. Roberta set the gardenias on the bedside table, then pulled opened the drapes to let the morning light in, and the gals squinted their eyes and moaned and burrowed beneath the sheets and pillows like earthworms, their arms and legs groping for cover.

"It's a glorious day," Roberta had said. "Y'all wake up."

If Kitty B. had known what lay ahead, she would not have risen and dressed and walked down the aisle that day.

SIX

Hilda

Big Hilda sees her daughter's reflection in her vanity mirror. The bride-to-be stands in the bathroom doorway the night before her wedding in the strapless raw silk cocktail dress they bought together at Saks in Charleston a few months ago.

"Hi, Mama," Little Hilda says.

Big Hilda thought the day Angus packed his bags and left for good was the most dreadful day of her life. But now she realizes that this wedding weekend will be the worst, watching her lovely daughter marry a foreigner while her husband sports his cheap and chubby girlfriend on his arm. She's heard that Trudi claims they are getting married, but she doesn't believe that for a minute. She hasn't seen a ring on her finger, and she can't imagine Angus marrying her or anyone for that matter.

"We have to be at the church for the rehearsal in twenty minutes," Little Hilda says, tilting her head gently to the side, the gold clasp on her pearl necklace catching the light. "You about ready?"

Angus has always said their daughter is a miniature version of Big Hilda. She's petite with a round doll-like face and wrists and ankles that you could easily fit your hands around. Sylvia Crenshaw, the town hair stylist, has fixed her golden hair for the wedding rehearsal and the dinner that will follow. It's up in a clean French twist with the faintest wisps curling around her forehead and her pearl drop earrings. Her little legs are balancing on a pair of super high silver heels like the models wear in the store windows in Charleston, and she's simply stunning.

Hilda couldn't be more proud of her or more shocked that she is no longer a child. She can feel the unfamiliar pinprick of tears below the surface, but they won't come.

"Almost, sweetheart," she says, turning slowly around on her vanity stool to face her daughter. Hilda looks toward her room to make sure that the door is closed. It's a funny thing, but no one has been in her bedroom since Angus left. She doesn't even let Richadene go in there to clean, and she keeps it locked when she's not home. She's spent some dark nights between those four walls, and for some reason it is important for her to seal it off from the rest of the world like a tomb.

"Mom, you're still in your bathrobe," Little Hilda says. "Giuseppe's going to be here in ten minutes. What can I do to help you?"

"Oh, you two can go on without me. I'll be right behind you." She swivels back around and unrolls the hot curlers in her hair.

Now Hilda feels her daughter's hands on her shoulders. She wants to turn back and pull Little Hilda into her lap and tell her how very much she loves her and how she wishes her all of the happiness in the world, but she doesn't. Instead she straightens up and starts rubbing her Clinique moisturizer on her face.

"Mama, I know this isn't easy," Little Hilda says, softly squeezing her mama's shoulders. "But I know you can get through this weekend. I really *need* you to make it through, okay?" Little Hilda takes a deep breath, and Hilda watches the pearls rise and fall across her collarbone. A crooked vein in the center of her daughter's glowing forehead has surfaced, and she knows it must be hard for her to tell her own mama to pull herself together and "deal"—as she would put it—at least for the next three days.

Hilda nods and looks down at her containers of makeup. She meant to allow time for a bath so she could soak the foundation into her pores, but she was distracted with painting her toenails. She has to do this herself now! Then she'd seen a little crease in her silk suit that needed ironing.

"Don't worry," Hilda says, as she watches herself in the mirror's reflection, reaching up to take hold of Little Hilda's hands. The liver spots across her knuckles surprise her, and she realizes that her hands are aging and looking more and more like her mother's each day, with dark brown splotches and prominent veins that snake across the surface like a topographic map. Well, at least she's not her mother on her own wedding weekend, that is to say, catatonic. Hilda's mother and father were still together, but he had her holed up on the mental ward at the Medical University of South Carolina, and it wouldn't be long before he signed off on her lobotomy. Sometimes Hilda suspects that her mother actually faked her craziness just to get away from him.

Like her mama, Hilda always has a lit cigarette nearby, its smoke ascending now from the crystal ashtray on the vanity. It rises, then curls before dissipating into the thick air like the minutes that ticked by as she counted down the long-awaited exit out of the sad, dark home of her childhood.

She can't help but wonder if Little Hilda prays the same way she once did—*God, get me out of this nut house and get me on with my life.* That's exactly how Hilda felt when she married Angus. Their union was her freedom. Her ticket out of hell.

~ SEPTEMBER 6, 1969 ~

Hilda tried to sprint down the aisle to the kind and handsome medical student beaming at the other end. Her high school sweetheart. But every time she lurched forward toward the altar, her father pulled her back.

"Take your time," he murmured; then he tilted his head toward one of the mill executives who was seated on the bride's side of the church and nodded. A whole group of the executives had flown down from New York for the wedding, and they had presented Hilda with the most extravagant gifts: a hand-cut crystal ice bucket from Austria, five place settings of her finest china, and four square sterling silver candelabras from Tiffany's that weighed more than the dumbbells Angus used to lift in the weight room of the high school gymnasium.

Angus was grinning from ear to ear that day as Hilda's father placed her hand in his, and when he felt the soft touch of her white gloved fingers, tears literally rolled down his full, flushed cheeks. She knew he was full of hope about their life together, so sure it would be as idyllic as his own parents' marriage.

Hilda's father cleared his throat as if to say, "Pull yourself together, boy," and she even squeezed her intended's hand and lifted her chin high behind her veil like a bothered nanny to let him know he'd need to collect himself to get through the vows.

Hilda guesses that describes her marriage in a nutshell—Angus gushing with emotion and her striking a stiff posture behind a veil. As she stares back at the reflection of her daughter standing behind her, she thinks of the time Angus saw an adolescent alligator skulking through their backyard and he called Cousin Willy. Those two went outside and wrestled it down and hung it on the tree until Marvin's Meats came by to pick it up for processing. It was one of the biggest fights she'd ever had with him, needling him about why they had to hang the creature in their yard instead of Ray and Willy's.

"For one thing, it came onto our property, Hilda," he said. "And for another, we only have *one* child to keep away from it, and they have *three*." Laura had run away for the first time by then, and Ray was looking after Justin too.

Thing is, Angus wanted more children, and he couldn't understand why Hilda didn't. It was the first real wedge between them.

"I want a family," he said many a night, cuddling up to her, stroking the back of her head. "I want brothers and sisters for Little Hilda. I want to fill up every bedroom in this big old house, and I want to wake up to the sound of several pairs of bare feet on the staircase. Don't you?"

It was all too easy to roll away from him and curl up into herself beneath the sheets like she did when she was a child. He would fall back on his pillow and sigh, but the next day he would greet her sweetly with a kiss in the kitchen and a pat on her satin shrouded elbow, and they would sit at the breakfast table admiring their daughter as his spoon knocked around the edges of the coffee mug so that the sugar dissolved in the blackness.

Looking back, Hilda sees that she was pretty good at giving him the cold shoulder. At shutting down whenever he reached out with the slightest suggestion of physical affection. Not to mention his plea for them to "go see someone." *I mean, really. How horrifying would that be?*

The truth is that she never would have had Hilda in the first place if he hadn't caught her in a weak moment with one too many glasses of champagne one New Year's Eve.

She was more than terrified of being a parent. Her mother had done a horrendous job, and she had no model to follow and no desire to bring an innocent life into this world where the nights are long and painful.

Sure, she wanted to relax like the rest of their pack and just get on with life, like Kitty B. and Ray, their own bellies swelling with watermelons alongside hers that year. But relaxing never seemed to happen for Hilda. She had the dearest, easiest husband imaginable, but she never could let go and enjoy him—not during sex, not during talks

late at night on the back piazza, not during walks along the seawall—
she just *couldn't*.

Of course, she's glad she had Little Hilda. She loves her more than
anything, and she's sorry that she's caused her distress over these last
few years. She knows Little Hilda worries about her. Ray and Kitty B.
and Sis tell her that Little Hilda calls one of them each week to check
on her. When Angus left, Little Hilda wrote her several times, telling
her that she loved her and that she wished Hilda would come stay
with her a while in Washington, but Hilda couldn't do that either. She
couldn't walk out of her house, not even into her yard, so how could
she get on an airplane and fly through the air to an unfamiliar city?

Hilda squeezes her daughter tight. "Give me ten minutes and I'll be
ready."

"Ten minutes, okay? I don't want you to go alone, and we really
shouldn't keep Father Campbell and the wedding party waiting."

Hilda makes up her face quickly and puts on this ivory silk suit
she'd bought over the phone from Neiman Marcus. Thank goodness for the sizeable inheritance her father left her.

The jacket is perfectly tailored with three-quarter sleeves and a
thin, flat bow belt, and the skirt is straight with the most delicate
flounced hem encircling her knees. She puts on her twisted strands
of small seeded pearls as a perfect final touch and slips on the open-
toe bronze heels that she and Sis picked out at Bob Ellis Shoes last
weekend.

As Hilda walks down her elegantly curved staircase, her daughter and her future husband smile up at her.

"You did it!" Little Hilda says, and she claps her hands lightly
together.

"Wow, Mrs. Prescott." Giuseppe grins, and even Hilda has to
admit he's a knockout. He's got dark hair, olive skin, and bright

pools of blue eyes with a dark blue ring encircling them. It's easy to see why Little Hilda crossed the hall on Capitol Hill to get a better look at him, despite his alien status as a Yankee, a first-generation immigrant, and most foreign of all, a *liberal.*

Well, he's sure embraced her despite their differences, and it's charming to see him decked out in full southern summer attire: a seersucker suit and a red bow tie printed with the South Carolina state flag.

Giuseppe narrows his eyes and reaches out to embrace his future mother-in-law, and she moves with precision to return his affection so as not to upset her hair or smear her champagne-colored lipstick.

"You look beautiful," he says while Little Hilda beams behind them, as if all is well, as if her wedding weekend will run smoothly after all.

Angus greets Hilda at the church door with a measured smile.

"You look nice," he says, then he puts his hand out as if his ex-wife is a wedding guest and he is honored to meet her. Hilda stares at the familiar pads of his fingers for a moment, then walks past him toward the altar, where Capers and Ray gesture for the wedding party to gather around for their instructions. Sis turns and waves to Hilda from her organ perch in the balcony above the church doors, and she nods back, thankful to see a friendly face.

Hilda hasn't stepped inside this church for over four years. She stopped coming after Angus left, though she knew he switched over to Trudi's Baptist church on the outskirts of town where there is no Tiffany stained glass window and no incense and no port wine poured into silver chalices for the sacrament. Talk about uncivilized!

Angus and Hilda were married at this very altar just over twenty-eight years ago beneath the ornate brass cross and the Ten Commandments chiseled in the marble panels behind it. And

Little Hilda was christened at the baptismal font on the left side of the altar along with Priscilla the winter after their birth. That was a bittersweet ceremony, since Kitty B. and LeMar had buried Baby Roberta two months earlier.

~ FEBRUARY 24, 1980 ~

Hilda peered out through the north side window during her daughter's baptism at the stone that marked Baby Roberta's grave—a small, rectangular outline with a fresh patch of grass in the center and a square frame at its head where an angel knelt above the name and the date of her very short life: *Roberta Ferguson Hathaway, October 14, 1980–December 20, 1980.*

The rectangular stones reminded Hilda of an empty bassinet, and her knees buckled at the thought of it as she stood before the baptismal font the morning of Little Hilda's christening.

It was Little Hilda's shrill cry after Old Stained Glass poured the cold water across her forehead that pulled Hilda's back to the ceremony. Baby Roberta was supposed to be christened with Hilda and Ray's daughters that day. They had decided upon a triple baptism, and Hilda quietly broke down the day the invitations arrived with Baby Roberta's name etched in the center of them. She immediately called the stationery store and asked them to reprint them. Then she asked Richadene to watch over her baby while she took the old invitations out to the backyard and burned them in a metal trash can, spearing them with the poker from her fireplace until every last piece of the embossed crosses and the names and the dates had turned to ash.

As Hilda takes her place in the mother-of-the bride pew, she hears the shuffle of feet on the slate aisle, and out of the corner of her eye she feels someone staring at her. When she turns, she sees it is Dodi, her ex-husband's girlfriend's daughter and the junior bridesmaid of the wedding party. Dodi bites the inside of her chubby cheek as she stares Hilda down. Hilda shakes her head in disapproval and turns to watch Giuseppe's relatives file in behind her, speaking in hushed Italian words.

When Dodi turns to talk to one of the acolytes, Hilda glances back and studies her. Her dull brown hair is curled in ringlets, and she's wearing a pale shade of lipstick and dangly, rhinestone earrings that are far too old for her. What is she, nine or ten? She's in an iridescent green full-length dress that looks like it was made for a 1980s prom, and she has these bushy black eyebrows that would put Brooke Shields to shame. Hilda looks around for Trudi, who ought to be appalled at how tacky her child is dressed, but she is nowhere to be seen. Hilda smirks at the possibility of having run her off from this gathering.

Now Ray, a patch over her black, swollen eye, directs everyone to the proper pews. She's decked out in a tailored pink linen suit with her mother-in-law's pearl hummingbird on her lapel. Hilda can't believe the stamina Ray has. If Hilda had hit a deer, she'd still be lying in bed with ice packs on her face.

"The south side is for the groom's family and the north side for the bride's," Ray calls. Vangie Dreggs stands like an unwanted shadow directly behind Ray. Naturally, she wants to join the Wedding Guild, and it is Ray's charge to show her the ropes.

Hilda turns back to greet her future in-laws, Anatole and Fiorella Giornelli. Now try saying that three times without getting your tongue tied!

"Hello," she says as Fiorella squeezes her hand and Anatole winks.

Hilda's not exactly fond of the pair after they put pressure on Little Hilda to convert to Catholicism before the wedding. It just annoys her to death how the Catholics think they're the only ones bound for heaven. How they don't even invite *her*, a descendant of a long line of landed-gentry Episcopalians, to their communion table because they think all non-Catholics are out-and-out doomed to hell! It really infuriates Hilda, and she is proud of Little Hilda for saying no, and of Giuseppe for standing behind her choice.

Just as Hilda tries to think of something else to say to the Giornellis, Capers shouts, "The Lord be with you," which means he is ready to get this show on the road.

God bless Sis. She's had to coordinate musical efforts with LeMar and two of the Giornellis' cousins, one who is a baritone and the other who is a trumpeter. The trumpeter's flight from New York to Charleston was cancelled this afternoon due to tropical storm Eleanor, and no one knows if he'll make it or not. The baritone, who has performed at the Met among other impressive venues, has a marriage partner of the same sex who is a dentist. Hilda was informed about this by Giuseppe and Little Hilda just a few weeks before they mailed the invitations, and the gals just about pulled their hair out trying to determine the etiquette of how to address his wedding invitation. Since Hilda is not only the seamstress of the bunch, but also the gal with the most elegant penmanship, they gathered at her house to go over the list, and Ray even checked out updated versions of *Emily Post's Etiquette* and *Crane's Blue Book of Stationery* from the library to see how they should address the invitation.

They didn't know if they should do *Dr. and Mr.* or *Mr. and Doctor* or *The Misters* or *Mr. such and such and Mr. such and such*. Quite a quandary, Hilda thought before settling on *Dr. __ and Mr. __*. Now why hasn't Emily Post addressed this yet?

As Hilda walks to the back of the church to take her place for the practice of the processional, she sees LeMar practicing his scales up in the balcony. He keeps squeezing his thick hands into fists, and Hilda can guess that he doesn't want to be completely upstaged in his own church by a pro who has performed at the Met. Sis has met with him several times over the last few weeks to practice his "Ave Maria" solo.

Hilda takes Cousin Willy's arm when she reaches the back of the church. He has agreed to walk her down the aisle for the seating of the mothers. Her husband has divorced her, her father is long dead, and she hasn't talked to her brother for decades, so she appreciates Ray's offering her husband's arm to escort her in and out. They haven't always had the smoothest of friendships, but Hilda is grateful to Ray for coordinating this wedding and looking out for her.

Sis starts to play "Jesu, Joy of Man's Desiring," and Ray waves Fiorella and Hilda on down the aisle. Willy pats Hilda's hand as they walk. He smells like Ivory soap and toothpaste, and his nose is as clean and shiny as the hood of his pickup truck on a Sunday afternoon after he washes and waxes it.

"Thank you," Hilda says to him as she keeps her eye on the familiar altar.

"My pleasure, gal," he says.

SEVEN

Hilda

After Ray walks the wedding party through the processional and Capers takes the couple through the vows, everyone steps out into the warm summer evening where a brisk wind means rain and likely a little nip from Eleanor.

Trudi Crenshaw waits in her bright yellow Volkswagen beneath a limb of an old live oak to take Angus and her daughter from the church to the dinner. Hilda watches them from the church steps as Angus opens the door and lifts back the seat to let the child in as the wind tousles a clump of Spanish moss that lands on the bright roof of the car.

Angus sits down gently next to his girlfriend and leans over to give her a kiss. She grins from ear to ear as if she couldn't be more pleased to be with him, the lifesaver of Jasper County. The man who binds up the broken arms and legs of accident-prone children and gives bags of free medicine samples to the poorest and the elderly who are burdened with all kinds of sickness and pain. She's one lucky duck is all Hilda can say. He is the catch of the town, no doubt about it.

The next stop for the wedding party is Alberto's, the new little Italian joint that sits in a strip mall at the lower end of Main Street.

It's quite an unconventional rehearsal dinner location, but this piece of the weekend is in the Giornellis' hands and, as Ray reminded her at one of their last wedding meetings, "One must go along with one's daughter's future family."

As soon as they arrive at Alberto's, Hilda slips into the bathroom to find Miss Cotton, with a little French soap in one hand and a linen hand towel hanging on her arm with Hilda's new initials, HPG, embroidered across the top. The gals have thought of *everything*, and for some reason the tears are there before Hilda has time to stop them, and she scurries into the stall as the foreign voices of what may be the wait staff or perhaps Giuseppe's family echo in the hall outside the bathroom.

This is so unlike me. Hilda dries her eyes and rubs at the mascara smudges. She can't help but be struck by what her friends have done, looking after her the last few years, and taking over this whole wedding. *Goodness knows I don't deserve their friendship.*

No, Hilda wouldn't have chosen a dark and narrow strip mall restaurant for a rehearsal dinner. Nor would she have chosen to have her daughter and her fiancé's name printed in red on everything from the napkins to the cigarettes to the bottles of Chianti. And the dyed green carnations, well, they're enough to give her the hives, but she doesn't say a word against them.

Thankfully, she is seated by Little Hilda and Giuseppe and his parents while Angus takes his place in the back of the restaurant with Trudi and Dodi. Sis is also at Hilda's table. She's single and easy to put in all sorts of places, but Hilda knows she's been purposefully placed here to support her tonight, and she appreciates Little Hilda's thinking of that. Suddenly the thought occurs to Hilda, *I am a single too.*

The food is quite good. The Giornellis have somehow talked the restaurant into serving Giuseppe's paternal grandmother's clam sauce over the pasta, and it is divine. After an ample serving of tiramisu and an offering of champagne, the toasts begin.

Giuseppe's father has done quite well in the knickknack business. He makes the plastic brides and grooms that go on tops of cakes. And a lot of the stuff you see in a place like Party City. He's a little rough around the edges, but it's obvious that he and Fiorella adore their eldest son.

They show a little slide show of their life in New Jersey and of Giuseppe at his graduation from Dartmouth and on the campaign trail with Senator Warren and on the steps of Capitol Hill where he took his first job. The last slide is a photo of their son and Little Hilda kissing in front of the Washington Monument on the night they were engaged. It was last year's Fourth of July celebration on the mall, and there are fireworks blossoming behind them in red and blue.

Angus's toast catches Big Hilda off guard. Just as she sips her cappuccino, her ex-husband ambles up to the microphone and reminisces about his daughter's childhood.

"There was the time she put on Big Hilda's lipstick at age four and grabbed her five-year-old cousin by the neck and kissed him until he cried and begged for release," he says to the gathering. "And another when Priscilla dared her to slide down the laundry chute and she landed head first on the ironing board and I had to rush home and stitch her forehead up. Then," he says, "in college during a brief Priscilla-induced tree hugger phase, they set out to walk the Appalachian trail one summer with a few other classmates and instead of me talking her out of it, she talked me into coming along, and I followed her and her crew for one month up and over the Blue Ridge Mountains until I got dysentery so bad that Cousin Willy had to come pick me up and bring me home, and still my little girl kept on going."

"Little Hilda looks fragile," he says, turning toward Giuseppe as he sums up his speech, "but she's no shrinking flower. The girl got shortchanged in the fear department, and she got a double dose of determination like her mama. She was determined to win your affection, Giuseppe, and she's never been happier. Now you just better hope and pray that she doesn't get her mind set on what kind of car she wants to drive, what kind of home she wants to own, or what kind of gift she'd like for her first anniversary, 'cause, Son, your goose is going to be cooked then. There's no getting this girl to back down."

He lifts his champagne glass and so does the rest of the crowd, and as Big Hilda takes a sip, a pain shoots through the side of her head, and she can hardly see for a moment. She can't tell if she's got a migraine forming or if she's just angry with Angus for taking a shot at her.

When she focuses again, Vangie Dreggs is up at the microphone giving a toast. The *nerve*! Not even Ray or Kitty B. are planning toasts. It's just not something the women do. But there is the Lone Star pain in their rear end making some crack about the Democratic Party and Senator Warren and New Jersey, and how even though she's a dyed-in-the-wool Texas Republican she'll even be nice to the senator because she thinks so much of Angus and his daughter and Hilda. She calls Hilda a dear friend and says that she and the gals have made all the difference in her life here in Jasper.

Sis rolls her eyes, and Hilda can hear Ray clearing her throat in disdain somewhere behind her. Then her head begins to throb. As the line of Giuseppe's extended relatives and friends form around the microphone with toasts to give, Hilda wonders if anyone will notice if she just lays her head down on the table. It's been several months since she's had a migraine, and this one is blinding—a hammer pounding the base of her head. Her new doctor says they're hormonal, and she expects them to subside once the menopause does.

"Sis," she leans over and whispers. "I need you to take me home."

Sis takes one look at Hilda's eye and nods, and Hilda tries to head toward the door without making a scene. She doesn't want to disturb Little Hilda, who is engrossed in a poem Giuseppe's cousins are reciting, but just as she's about to make it to the door, Little Hilda runs up to her. "You aren't leaving, are you, Mama?" she says. "The toasts aren't over, and Giuseppe has something special planned for the end."

"Darling, I have a migraine," she says clutching the back of her head.

"But you haven't even heard from half of Giuseppe's family, and I know you'll love hearing what they have to say. This is your chance to get to know them."

Amidst the crowd of murmurs, Hilda hears Angus let out a contrived cough and in it she hears, *Must you always let us down?*

Sis holds her by the elbow as her vision goes blurry. She can feel her knees buckle as the throbbing in her head grows stronger.

"I'm so sorry, darling, but I can't," she says. "I've got to get to my bed and wait this out."

Outside it is raining sideways because of the warm gusts from the Eleanor bands. It must not have been coming down for long, but now it flows like a river across the parking lot and into the drainage pipes. Hilda's bronze heels are drenched by the time she reaches Sis's car, a little Toyota, youthful and no-nonsense just like Sis. Oh, and of all things, soft seats that smell like mold. Hilda doesn't know why Sis doesn't spring for leather seats! What else does she have to spend her money on?

Just as she's about to thank Sis and close her front door, she sees stars in front of her eyes and then blackness, and before she knows it she is lying down in her foyer, her fingers grabbing at the wet fringes of the Oriental rug.

When she wakes up again, she is upstairs and Sis tries to open her locked bedroom door. "Go on home," Hilda says. Then she throws up her clam sauce right then and there all down her over-priced ivory suit.

The next thing she knows, Sis is wiping her mouth and asks her how to get into her bedroom so she can lay her down. Hilda doesn't answer, and Sis puts her in a chair by her vanity and picks the bedroom lock with a bobby pin. She turns on Hilda's bedside light and lets out a faint gasp when she sees what Hilda has done. How she's shoved three king-size pillows under the covers as if someone is sleeping next to her. As if the feel of her husband is still there.

Hilda, too embarrassed to look her in the eye, clutches her own head in an effort to ward off the pain. It's as fierce as ever. Sis lifts Hilda up and helps her out of her suit and slips on a nightgown from her closet. Then Sis brings her some Advil and a cool glass of water, and Hilda lies down on her pillow with lights like the fireworks in her child's engagement photo pounding around her head.

Hilda doesn't remember Sis turning out the lights or closing the sliding doors to her room. When she wakes up she is alone, and she rolls over and puts her arm around the mass of pillows. She envisions Angus getting into Trudi's car and kissing her. She doesn't think that Angus will marry her. They've been dating for two years now, and nothing has come of it.

If Hilda is honest with herself, she will admit that she holds out the thinnest strand of hope that Angus will come back to her. She tries not to think of it often, but in the middle of the night she often imagines how it might work. Angus suddenly on the front stoop of the piazza. Hilda welcoming him into the home they shared for three decades. "I want to come back," he would say to her. She would nod and smile and say, "Then come."

"Lord," she prays to the God she has distanced herself from since she was fourteen. She waves away the idea that He would listen to her and simply says to the darkness around her, to the air in her self-made tomb, "Don't let Angus end up with Trudi."

She lets out a sigh from somewhere deep in her chest. Then she embraces the wall of pillows, pulling them closely to her side, and drifts back into sleep.

EIGHT

Sis

Sis's phone rings early before the doves have made their first coo on the branch outside of her window. Her clock radio reads 5:07 a.m.

"We're sunk," Sis hears as she groggily presses the receiver to her ear.

"Ray?"

"Pink Point is under water, Sis! Go look outside."

It takes Sis two rolls to get across her bed as she groans, "The weather channel said we were in the clear last night except for a few outer bands."

"Well, the storm surge rippled back at high tide, and we're under a couple of inches of water right now. I just swept two flapping shrimp off of my porch steps, okay?"

"Can't you call the pump man?"

"I've tried him, but I can't get him to answer. Willy is banging on his door as I speak. That's how desperate we are."

Sis peers out of her blinds at the dark morning as the wet branches of her crepe myrtles bob back and forth, casting off their little white flowers like confetti. "All I can say is that I hope to God we've got power in the church so Ina can blow her pipes."

Ina's the name of the forty-stop organ that was sent back to London to be restored the year after the church hired Sis. A Mrs. Ina Louise Barrett Gardner, a descendant of the church's first priest, The Rev. T. Henry Barrett IV, who took his post here at the chapel of ease in 1794, paid for the organ's trip and restoration. They'd put a little brass plaque over the rows of keyboards with the woman's name on it.

Ina is like Sis's child in a way. For one thing it took nine months for her to be made over and until then Sis had to play Pee Wee, a whiny-sounding electric number that Fox Music House loaned her. She'd accompanied their former priest, Old Stained Glass, to greet Ina at the airport, where five strong men rolled her packaged body off a large metal ramp. Once she was hoisted up into the balcony, Sis wedged open the boxes of pipes with a wrench from the rectory and rubbed her hand across them as Stained Glass sprinkled holy water on each piece of Ina and dedicated her to the church's music ministry. Sis has spent more time with Ina than she has with most of the people in her life.

Now Sis sits in her car with one arm on the door handle trying to get up her nerve to make a break for the chapel in her new high heels. Little Hilda's wedding takes place in just two hours, and it's the darkest, most waterlogged wedding day Sis can remember. And that's saying something. She's played in 377 weddings over the last nineteen years as the organist and choirmaster at All Saints Episcopal Church. More than once, she's played three weddings on a Saturday, and it is typical to play two in a day now that The Lone Star of the Lowcountry and the like are parting the salt marsh grass on the quaint little chapel of ease and their whole town, for that matter. Seems like it won't be long before Jasper will be swallowed whole by the resorts and retirement communities that are spreading out like a disease from Charleston to Savannah.

Sis's daddy used to say time stands still in Jasper. From where she sits in the car she can see his gravestone rising to the left of the chapel, a long marble slat with his name and date in block letters and a quote from Psalm 31:15 that reads, "My times are in your hands."

There's a space right next to him where Sis's mama will go, and she has her choice of the one next to her mama or the one next to Fitz in the Hungerford family plot under the live oak tree toward the back of the crumbling brick wall. An ornate wrought iron gate surrounds the Hungerford plot. It's about the size of a bedroom, and Fitz's parents, grandparents, and great-grandparents lie in rest together there.

When Sis sits at the organ in the center balcony just opposite the stained glass portrait of the angel greeting the Marys in the empty tomb, she has a good view of Fitz's headstone between the black iron rods that enclose the family plot. It's awfully nice of his family to offer her a place there, even though they were never actually married. And you know, she thought for sure she'd find someone else somewhere along the way, but it just never seemed to happen.

Once she read that trees sense a hurricane before it hits. That they drop ten times more seeds than usual before one strikes—one of nature's remarkable attempts at self-preservation—and she wonders if the cabbage palmettos dropped their shiny black fruit around the graveyard yesterday.

Well, she hopes Little Hilda's not too upset about the weather. Ray says the backside of Eleanor must have scraped the ACE Basin at high tide, because half the town appears submerged in a few inches of the Atlantic Ocean. Sis can see Cousin Willy and Justin and Ray, black eye and all, in her rearview mirror. They're across the road at Pink Point Gardens in their rubber waders, pumping water out of the park by the seawall.

Out of the corner of her eye, Sis sees the rector, Capers Campbell, making a run for it from his car to the chapel. He has this funny habit when he runs of swinging his left arm fast and furious and keeping his right stationary and tight by his side.

He's never married, and the gals think it's about time he noticed Sis. Hilda helped Sis pick out this flowy little sky blue dress with a creamy silk sash for today. It reminds Sis of the one that Julie Andrews wore in the *Sound of Music* as she strolled around the moonlit grounds of the manor on the night of the ball, longing for the captain, who eventually met her there. And Hilda insisted she buy these fashionable beige sandals from Copper Penny. They have high heels and a thin strap that circles her ankles, and Sis really likes them.

Of course, she feels ridiculous wearing the heels and the dress on this gray and soaking wet morning, but she went ahead and put them on to avoid the chiding and to let Little Hilda know that despite the flooded town, they are going to pull off this grand event. At least right now she's wearing her choir robe over it so she doesn't feel quite so out of place.

But back to Capers. The gals have hosted him and Sis for dinner and for boat rides and even a trip to Edisto for the weekend, but he never seems to make a solid move in her direction. Maybe he's not interested. Sometimes they tell Sis to make some sort of advance. Life's too short and all of that. Pollinate before the hurricane. Drop your seeds, so to speak, but she feels kind of funny about cornering a man in a stiff white priest's collar and reaching out for his hand.

If you want to know the truth, when she gets right up close to him, he smells like her Uncle Bugby from Bamberg, kind of old mannish and mothballish. Kitty B. says she needs a nose pincher like the kind that swimmers wear, but Sis thinks you have to like the way someone smells. *What do they call that,* she thinks . . . *pheromones?*

Sis isn't sure she puts out any pheromones now, what with her female organs scraped out. After the hysterectomy last year she felt like a gutted watermelon. Nothing more than the knobby green strips of the rind that Kitty B. would take home and pickle.

Her hysterectomy hit her hard. There were no more watermelon seeds and no more anything, and she just sat down before Ina for several days and wept. There was this kind of darkness around the edges

of her vision, and she had weeks where she just sat on the couch and
stared into the blank space between her television and her kitchen as
CNN spat out the news while the days slid by like the ticker at the
bottom of the screen.

That's why the doctor at the Medical University prescribed the
Zoloft. Of course, Sis jokes and calls them her happy pills, but she
is a real believer in them because they stood her up and got her moving again. She takes one every morning with her cereal and coffee,
and just before she pops one in the center of her tongue she says,
"Thank you, Lord!"

*Well, I probably don't have pheromones anymore. But maybe I put
out happy vibes, which is worth something, right?*

~ MAY 24, 1978 ~

"Put out a good vibe," Roger Rosenthal, the cellist, said at their first
Spoleto Chamber Music rehearsal at the Dock Street Theater. He
was a virtuoso and a hippie from New Hampshire, and Sis fell in
love with him in a matter of days.

She was living in Charleston at the time and had been invited to
serve as a stand-in pianist for the chamber music series featuring
Roger's up-and-coming string quartet.

Sis dated him for the summer, and she loved the way he smelled,
sort of like sweat and marijuana and candle wax. They listened to
the Shostakovich cello concertos. They attended the opera and the
modern dance performances and the end-of-festival concert on the
rim of the butterfly ponds at Middleton Plantation.

Once, after a few glasses of wine in the carriage house apartment
where the festival was housing him, he unbuttoned her blouse and
tenderly kissed her chest until she had to pull away.

"What's wrong?" he said.

Sis's heart was pounding in her throat and as much as she wanted to say, *Nothing, nothing is wrong,* and pull him close, she couldn't ignore the war between her mind and her body, and all she'd been taught about love and sex and marriage and God.

"Look, I didn't even have sex with my fiancé until the night before he went to Paris Island, Roger," she said. "I can't just whoop it up with some guy who breezes into Charleston for the summer."

Then he took her shoulders in his hands and looked at her head-on. "You're a grown-up, Sis, my sweet southern belle. Isn't it time?"

Just behind him she eyed his cello in its case decorated with stickers from the wide array of countries to which he'd carried it. Roger'd been letting go and enjoying all over the world, and she had to admit she envied him. Next week he was off to Buenos Aires and Montevideo for a concert series, and in September he was headed to Vienna to teach a semester of master classes.

"Sure, I *want* to," she said as she pulled at a strand of his long wavy hair. "But love needs to be part of it, I think. And maybe even commitment too. That's what I've grown up believing."

She felt shame as the words came out of her mouth. She felt unsophisticated and unenlightened, and yet she couldn't let the notion go any more than she could have cursed God or her parents or the brutal war that snatched away her fiancé's life and her very future.

Roger smiled and nuzzled her cheek with his unshaven chin before closing her shirt back up and taking her in his arms like a child. "You're a dear," he said. "And I hope you find what you're looking for."

At the next lull in the rainfall, she dashes out of her car. As she's bolting toward the church steps, out of the corner of her eye she sees a limb fall on what looks like her daddy's grave. In the split second she takes to pause and see where it landed, her new, expensive and extremely high heels sink down into the thick grass, and the muddy water pours into their arches.

Squealing, she steps from side to side hoping to get a foot free, but she sinks deeper until she's almost up to her ankles in mud and she can feel the suction of the soft ground pulling her in. Just as she's about to fall forward in her choir robe, Giuseppe's cousin Rupert and some other tall, olive skinned man, who she's assuming is Mr. Dentist, grab her by the elbow and pull her out. They hoist her up in their arms and carry her toward the church porch, her choir robe brushing across the wet and muddy ground.

"Thank you, Doctor and Mr. Rupert," she says, flustered as she takes off her shoes and bangs them against a church column to get the pluff mud out.

Rupert laughs and rubs his hands together, "You're welcome, Elizabeth." He can't quite get with the southern nicknames.

"This is not the dentist. This is my brother, Salvatore, the trumpeter, mmm?"

"Oh yes, of course." She'd practically forgotten about the Giornelli family trumpeter. He was supposed to arrive yesterday evening, but his flight was cancelled due to the storm. "It is a pleasure to meet you." He is kind of this older version of Giuseppe with a curly thatch of salt and pepper hair and deeply set blue eyes.

"How in the world did you get here?" she asks as she turns to knock on the door in hopes that Capers or LeMar will hear them and let them in.

"Hertz rent-a-car." He grins as she turns back around. "I drove right through Eleanor all night and lived to tell about it, Elizabeth."

"Well, I know Giuseppe and Hilda will be so pleased. Now, let's hope the sheet music hasn't turned to mush." She picks up the garden hose on the side of the steps and sprays out the last bit of mud from her heels.

Her choir gown is drenched, and she slips it off and drapes it over her bag. When she looks up, she sees the trumpeter marveling at her wet silk dress in a way that Rupert and the Mr. Dentist wouldn't, and she can feel her face redden. Before she knows it Capers is standing at the doorway watching her and in the background she can hear LeMar practicing his scales.

"Y'all okay?" Capers says, and he seems to be admiring Sis too. *Heck, I should have poured some water over my clothes long before this if I'd known it would get his attention.*

"Yes," she says, patting her rosy cheeks, "these nice Italian boys rescued me from being sucked into an early grave."

Capers chuckles and shakes his head. "All I can say is thank the good Lord for generators because the power's been out since late last night."

Sis races up the back stairs to see about Ina and the sheet music for the wedding. She thinks she put them all in the drawer beside the organ, but she might have left them out on the stand, and she can guess the leaky spot in the ceiling to the right of her is brown with water drip, drip, dripping down on the "Ave Maria" and the "Laudate Dominum."

Ina and her two hundred and fifty pipes are located in the west gallery at the rear of the nave. She's pretty intimidating with the three manuals—keyboards—and the pedals to play the lower notes. Talk about multitasking. You can't see all of the pipes from the outside, but they're packed in behind the wooden case built by a British company in 1795.

All Saints was merely a chapel of ease between Charleston and Savannah three hundred years ago. In 1714 it became the second church outside the city limits of Charleston, but one of the great revolutionary generals became so fond of worshiping here that he paid for the creation of the organ himself in 1762.

The organist before Sis, Mr. Enoch Kershaw, was a serious and well-respected musician who seemed to take command of Ina and much of the church for that matter. He was tall and broad around the middle and even Old Stained Glass yielded to him when pushed. When he retired, Sis was shocked to death that they asked her to take over the position.

An organist is supposed to have confidence and chutzpah, so why does she shudder when it comes time to take her post? Most days she feels like she's still a kid. Like something might happen today that will forever change the course of her life. She feels most like a kid right here in front of Ina in the balcony where she sits every Sunday morning and where she will sit today for Little Hilda's wedding.

Sis's mama rides thirty minutes every Sunday in her retirement community's bus to worship in her church and listen to her daughter play. She's always in the group of five or six who stay until the church is emptied and Sis finally finishes the last note of the postlude. Sis can see them gathering as she peers into the round, rearview mirror she hooked onto Ina's right side. It's usually Ray and Cousin Willy and the last remnants of her mama's friends who haven't passed on. They applaud like mad for a few seconds, and Sis turns around and waves like a child at a piano recital.

Truth is, Sis always feels small and unworthy when she sits down at the grand instrument. But pretty soon the church fills with people, and Capers looks at her and she straightens the music sheets, nods to the choir, and there is nothing left to do but play the keys and work the pedals with the balls of her feet so that Ina can blow her pipes. And once Ina blows, once the air pushes through the brass cylinders and the fan flushes the sound up and out into the very air around the altar and the pews where the colorful hats and balding heads bobble above the open hymnals, a kind of calm strength envelops Sis, and she thinks, *All things come from you, O Lord, and of Thine own have I given Thee.*

Today is no exception and now that the sheet music is intact at the top of the music rack, she gathers the musical men around Ina and they rehearse their parts. As usual, she stumbles here and there as she directs them.

Halfway through the rehearsal she sees Cricket and Kitty B. roll up in the McFortson hearse with the wedding dress. Cricket sports a strapless floral dress, and Kitty B. has poured herself into her mama's beautiful beaded satin gown. Sis hopes to heaven it won't pop open when she sits down. They both have on their knee-high rubber boots.

Ray runs over and helps them as they slowly lift the wedding dress out of the hearse. It is covered in layers of plastic from Lafayette Cleaners, and they hold it high above their heads as they head toward the parish hall.

Kitty B. comes back to get the boxes of shrimp salad sandwiches and grapes and Co-Colas that Ray insists the wedding party partake of before they get dressed. Once when a bride fainted at a wedding, Ray said, "These girls need a little pick-me-up before the ceremony. Otherwise their blood sugar will drop and their nerves will get the best of them."

It seems like no time at all before the groomsmen arrive in their white dinner jackets, a white orchid boutonniere on each of their left lapels. They wait at the church doors at Ray's direction, take each guest by their left arm and lead them to their seats. Bride's guests on the left, the groom's on the right.

Through the balcony window Sis spots Hilda in the graveyard with the bridesmaids, getting her photo taken with her daughter. *Poor thing.* She seemed so unbearably pitiful last night crawling into bed next to that wall of pillows as if Angus had never left, and it broke Sis's heart to catch a glimpse of her secret despair. Sis won't tell the other gals. It was not something she was supposed to see, and she'll just try to forget about it. But she has half a mind to drop some happy pills off at Hilda's with a little note that says, "Just give them a try."

Well, Hilda looks gorgeous today as usual. She's in this ornate lace top with capped sleeves and a straight full-length cream skirt with an ivory sash at her waist. She's fancier than the bride in her simple silk strapless dress, but Little Hilda is radiant beyond words, and no gown in the world could dim that glow. She's wearing the handmade veil that Giuseppe's mother purchased from a dressmaker in Florence thirty years ago for her own wedding. Its scalloped edges frame her head like petals, and she has a girlish shine on the tops of her smooth cheeks as she leans toward her mother and flashes her soft smile.

Both Senator Warren and Senator Hollingsworth are here. One on the groom's side and the other on the bride's. They each have an aide accompanying them. Little Hilda has the funniest stories about working as Senator Hollingsworth's scheduler. She has to water the tree outside of his Georgetown townhouse and scout out the meetings and engagements he attends outside of Capitol Hill. He's so bad about finding his way into unfamiliar buildings that he makes her write in-depth descriptions about what doors to open and what elevators to take and what turns to make at what point down the hall to make it to the correct meeting destination.

Ray is at the back with Kitty B. and Vangie, lining up the groomsmen one by one for their entrance. She must have run home in a hurry to change, and Sis can see through the window across the road that she left R.L. and his florist crew in charge of putting the final touches on the tables beneath the tent.

LeMar sings the final notes of the "Ave Maria," and Hilda kisses Little Hilda as they move into the narthex. Hilda gives Angus the cold shoulder as Cousin Willy holds out his arm, and Ray directs the mother of the bride to the back of the aisle and Sis begins to play "Jesu, Joy of Man's Desiring" by Bach.

Hilda looks stiff as a board as she walks in on the arm of Cousin Willy. *I'm kind of relieved that her parents aren't here to walk in before her*, Sis thinks. Hilda's father always gave Sis the creeps—so upright and uptight like he might just be a machine himself, as efficient as the ones in his mill that crushed the pine tree trunks and smashed the wood into a mushy pulp. Her mama was so glamorous but somehow in another world. She had a nervous breakdown before they graduated from college, and Sis wishes she could have gotten her hands on some happy pills before they committed her for good.

Sis looks back to Ray in her eye patch and teal silk dress. Ray straightens one of the groomsmen's boutonnieres and picks a fleck of lint from another's white dinner jacket. The best man, Giuseppe's father, must be nervous because he's gnawing on a piece of gum. Ray opens her beaded purse and holds out a napkin. He looks at her curiously then spits the gum inside of it. She pats his back and sends him to the front of the line, where he will lead his son's friends down the aisle after the seating of the mothers.

Ray discreetly points out the young man Little Hilda wants to set up with Priscilla. He's handsome as can be with his broad shoulders and blond hair and wide grin. He's got teeth as straight and white as Vangie Dreggs. He ought to be on a toothpaste commercial.

Then Giuseppe comes out from the sacristy with Capers and takes his place at the altar. He bites his lip, concealing the grin he eventually lets spread across his face as the groomsmen walk in one by one and take their place beside him while Sis accompanies his uncle, who gives a glorious trumpet performance of the "Te Deum" by Charpentier.

The bridesmaids are lovely in their pink Kentucky eyelet dresses from Lilly Pulitzer that Ray and Hilda picked out, since Little Hilda was too busy with work to take the time. There are two girls from Sweet Briar College where she attended and two from Capitol Hill and of course, Priscilla, her childhood companion, is her maid of honor—dreadlocks and all. Ray pats her own daughter's shoulder, gives her a kiss, and instructs her down the aisle.

Now Sis vamps for a few minutes because she can see from her side mirror that the bride is not in place for the procession. She's done the fanfare three times now, and she replays portions of the "Prince of Denmark's March."

She watches as Little Hilda converses with her father to the side of the sanctuary threshold. He must be giving her some parting words and he wipes his eyes as he speaks, sweet Angus Prescott. It's the same thing he did at his own wedding to Hilda, where Sis stood beside her at the altar three decades ago. As Sis sees Little Hilda's gown alight on the threshold along with Angus's shiny black shoes, Ray gives her the thumbs-up and she plays the heck out of Wagner's "Entry of the Guests" from *Tannhauser* as Salvatore plays the trumpet with a passionate virtuosity, and the guests stand and watch the bride enter on the arm of her father.

"The Celebration and Blessing of a Marriage" begins on page 423 of the Book of Common Prayer, and though Sis has heard it hundreds of times, she still shudders when Capers says to Giuseppe and Little Hilda, "Now I charge you both in the presence of God that if you know of any reason why you may not be united in marriage lawfully and in accordance with God's Word, you do now request it."

Neither of them utters a word, and when Capers asks the couple to turn toward each other for the vows, the whole congregation seems to exhale.

Hilda and Giuseppe beam at each other as Capers reads the Gospel and gives a heartfelt homily about servanthood in marriage. Sis is so enamored with his sentiment that she's sure she can overlook the way he smells if he asks her to dance tonight. She hopes he asks her, this dear unwed man of the cloth. Why didn't he ever marry?

Now she can't help but let her emotions get the best of her, and before she knows it, she's as soggy as the ground outside as she witnesses Little Hilda and Giuseppe recite their vows. When they exchange the rings, Salvatore hands Sis a linen handkerchief out of his pocket, and she presses it to her eyes as she turns around on her bench to watch Giuseppe at the center of the altar say, "Hilda, I give you this ring as a symbol of my vow, and with all that I am, and all that I have, I honor you in the Name of the Father, and of the Son, and of the Holy Spirit."

And Sis believes that it is true. That this young man does honor her, and she's so thankful that the daughter of her dear friend has found someone to partner with her in life, to adore her and look after her.

Capers closes with a glorious prayer from the red prayer book that says, *"Let their love for each other be a seal upon their hearts, a mantle about their shoulders, and a crown upon their foreheads. Bless them in their life and in their death. Finally, in your mercy, bring them to that table where your saints feast for ever in your heavenly home; through Jesus Christ our Lord, who with you and the Holy Spirit lives and reigns, one God for ever and ever. Amen."*

"Amen!" Sis can't help but shout as Giuseppe embraces Hilda. Then LeMar pats Sis on the shoulder to remind her that it's time to begin the recessional.

NINE

Sis

Sis walks her mama, the only parent alive out of all of their friends, from the church to the wedding tent at Pink Point Gardens, where Miss C. greets them at the park entrance. The statue is adorned with a white lace gown that belonged to Priscilla's old Madame Alexander doll, and in her arms is a little arrangement of white and yellow orchids. She's wearing a leftover piece of the trimming from the veil that Hilda made for Cricket's wedding, and this is attached by a headband made out of white and yellow orchids. Ray has put a little white umbrella above her head and a small pair of rubber boots by her feet. As the breeze lifts her dress, Sis sees beneath her slip a blue lace garter around her thigh, decorated with white silk roses and little pearls inside each of them.

Sis's mama leans toward her. "There's not a piece of concrete in all of the state that gets as much attention as Miss C."

Next to Miss C., twenty pairs of rubber boots are lined up in a row, and there are two urns filled with white umbrellas in case the sky opens up again. The sun is out now, and it slowly dries up the soggy ground as the Lowcountry fauna make their way out of the nooks and burrows where they hunkered down for the storm—birds, squirrels, pelicans, terns, hawks, even palmetto, bugs which are enormous flying cockroaches that are everywhere in the summer. It is the season for love bugs, too, and they're mating in midair around the guests, joined at the rear and flapping at odds with one another.

"Aren't the orchids gorgeous?" Sis turns to admire the exotic flowers shooting out in all directions above the tables with their soft white and brown spotted yellows and bright pinks. She spent all yesterday afternoon with Ray wrapping the satin ribbon around the bouquets and molding the oasis into the enormous silver vases and moss covered urns.

"Not as gorgeous as the priest walking your way," her mama says. "Hold your shoulders back, dear." Mrs. Mims quickly hobbles under the tent with her elegant cane to give Sis some space.

"Hi, Sis," Capers says. He gently touches her elbow. "The music was glorious as usual."

Sis corrects her posture and smiles up at him. "Thank you. I thought your homily was the best I've heard."

Capers pulls a handkerchief out of his back pocket and pats his forehead. The air is swampy. Sis can practically feel her makeup melting.

"Let me get you a Bellini," Capers says, motioning toward one of the servers passing by. "I heard the Giornellis brought their own family recipe."

He reaches out and grabs two glasses off the tray.

"Thank you." She smiles and tucks a loose strand of hair behind her ear. "I've never tried one."

Just as he lifts his glass for a toast, Vangie Dreggs comes up behind Capers and pats him on the back. "Are those Bellinis?"

"Yes, I believe they are." He notices Vangie staring at his glass, and he says, "Want to try one?"

"Why, thank you," she says, and she grabs the drink out of his hands. "Reverend, I need to talk to you for a few minutes if I could. Do you mind, Sis?"

Sis steps back and blushes. "Oh, of course not."

"I'll catch up with you in a little while," Capers calls to Sis.

"All right." Sis scoots under the tent and finds her mother talking to Cousin Willy.

"Come see what Kitty B. has cooked up, gal," Willy says to her. He has a heaping plate of pickled shrimp and sausage balls. "I've got to eat fast before Ray puts me back to work."

"*Where's* the priest?" Mrs. Mims whispers.

"Oh, Mama." Sis rolls her eyes and leads the elderly lady over to the S-shaped tables crammed with silver trays of ham biscuits, pickled shrimp, stuffed mushrooms, venison pâté, fruit and cheese in ornately carved-out watermelons, smoked salmon with all the trimmings, sausage balls, and pimento cheese garnished with little cocktail pickles.

Sis's mama gets a nibble of shrimp and a ham biscuit and points to another corner of the tent where Richadene's brother, Melvin, is carving a beef tenderloin and serving it on rolls with horseradish and mayonnaise. Next to Melvin, R.L.'s chef friend from Savannah is serving up shrimp and grits in large martini glasses.

Kitty B. scurries over. "Aren't those martini glasses fun! Y'all need to get over there and try some shrimp and grits."

"Kitty B.," Sis's mama says as she grabs a champagne glass from one of the servers. "You have done a beautiful job with the food. Your mama would be awfully proud."

"Thank you." Kitty B.'s cheeks redden.

A server whispers in Kitty B.'s ear and she says, "Excuse me. It's nearly time to cut the cake. I do hope you'll try a piece." She points toward the center of the tent and hurries toward the cake, displayed in all of its glory with the bridesmaids' bouquets all around it.

It's Kitty B.'s specialty: a lemon sour cream pound cake with a little hint of Grand Marnier liqueur. Each tier is iced with an ivory-colored buttercream and decorated with pearl drops and an elegant piped pearl border. A cascade of real white orchids starts at the top tier and curls its way down the side to the bottom, encircling the base with delicate white petals and dark pink centers.

Sis helps her mama to a seat and surveys the room. The beach music band, the Embers, are performing the hits that she and Fitz used to shag to on the boardwalk at Myrtle Beach, and Priscilla is already dancing with the doctor friend of Giuseppe's. His name is Donovan or something grand like that, and he's a medical resident at Johns Hopkins. Priscilla's pale brown dreadlocks are flapping in the warm breeze like limp snakes. The young man appears clean-cut and handsome, and wouldn't Ray be thrilled over the possibility of someone usurping the place of Poop 2? Sis shudders at the thought of that smelly stunt fool from the absurd reality cable show.

Ray comes over and leans in close to Sis and her mama. "She let me do her makeup," Ray whispers, and they all admire Priscilla and her partner on the dance floor. "She even let me cover up her tattoo with my concealer." Ray pats her own eye in excitement and then bites her lip from the pain.

"I noticed," Sis says. "Now sit down and take a break, gal. You are going to wear yourself out."

"Can't."

"Ray," says Sis's mama. "You've done a splendid job with this wedding." She pats the seat next to hers. "Let me tell you how impressed I am with your talents."

Sis smiles as Ray takes a seat and leans in toward her mother. The Embers are singing, *"It's a beautiful morning . . . I think I'll go outside for a while and just smi-i-ile,"* and Donovan must have some southern roots because he spins Priscilla around like he's a card-carrying member of the Sandfiddler's Shag Club. Bless Ray's heart—she's had fantasies about Priscilla's wedding for decades now. She's tried to set her up with many a fine young man from the Lowcountry, but it always backfires on her. Priscilla is bright as a button, but she couldn't be any more opposite from Ray.

Maybe it's an act of rebellion or just that she's different, but she has no interest in the society life her mother adores. Maybe she's got the Laura or the Carla Jones gene, or perhaps she's just a purebred member of this new generation of young people who seem to want to flee their roots as fast as possible and chase after the kind of free-spirited life that Roger the cellist pursued back in the '60s.

Sis wonders who will carry on the social traditions of Jasper after she and the gals are gone—but it's not something that upsets her the way it does Ray. It is simply something that she is curious about. The town is changing, Ray is right about that. But then again, maybe it's time for a change.

Much of the staff from Senator Warren's office is here to support their chief-of-staff, Giuseppe. The Senator herself arrived at the church in a limousine, and she stands just outside of the tent now, whispering to an aide, her brown heels sinking into the thick mud. Behind her Sis notices an osprey diving into the water. It comes back up with a four-inch-long mullet, its wet tail flapping back and forth in an effort to break free. The osprey takes flight above the seawall, and the fish's tail drips water over several of the guests outside of the tent. The bird nearly loses hold of the mullet right over Senator Warren's head, and just when Sis thinks the fish is going to flap right into her martini glass of shrimp and grits, the bird strengthens its grip, recovers the mullet, and soars to the top of one of the live oak trees for his own celebratory feast. Whew!

Well, that's the way it is with weddings and life in general as far as Sis can tell, one near disaster after another and a whole lot of igno-rant bliss.

Senator Warren clinks Senator Hollingsworth's glass of cham-pagne, and they laugh in a nice moment of bipartisanship. Rupert and his dentist dance in an embrace, and all of the guests seem swept up in the joy of the celebration as they dance and toast and hug one another. Salvatore, the Italian uncle, plays his trumpet beside the band as the bride and groom dance. The mosquitoes bite despite the two zappers Cousin Willy set up along the edges of the gardens, and from time to time someone slaps at their neck or their arm.

The couple must have cut the cake somewhere along the way because Kitty B. passes out thick pieces on the china plates they pooled together from their own collections.

"Would you look at that?" Sis's mama says as they watch Katie Rae kissing her date intensely at a table in the corner. He is supposed to be very religious. His daddy is the pastor of one of the hand-raising nondenominational churches outside of Charleston where Vangie Dreggs goes to hear speakers. She gave them all a book she bought there called *The Purpose-Driven Life*, and she wants to start a Bible study in her home and teach them how to say prayers to heal people, of all things.

"The purpose of her life is to drive us crazy," Ray declared after the vestry meeting a few weeks ago in which Sis had to make a presentation about the music offerings for the fall.

When Sis looks over to the dance floor she sees Capers shagging with Vangie as the Embers play "Sweet Carolina Girls."

"As if," Ray comes over to say. "*As if* she is a sweet Carolina girl."

"Yes." Hilda slides over in her one moment of composure. "How about pushy cowgirl with a butt the size of the state from whence she came!"

"Hilda!" Sis says, covering her mama's ears.

"Well, come on," Hilda says. "She could give Kitty B. a run for her money. Sis, you want me to go pour a glass of red wine on her dress?"

"Ladies." Cousin Willy shuffles over with his index finger raised to his lips. They giggle as if they are sixteen and in the watermelon field again as he scratches his bald head, which glows in the mid-afternoon, post-storm humidity.

"Where've you been?" Ray says. "I haven't seen you in an hour."

He lifts up his duck boots to reveal the mud caked up to his shins.

"You don't wanna know," he says.

"Oh yes, we do," she says.

"Getting rid of a copperhead."

"What?" Hilda says.

"The storm must have flushed one out of the swamp because just before the church let out, I found the rascal over by Miss C. Justin and I trapped him with a shovel and put him in a pillowcase."

"Good heavens!" Ray squeals and even Hilda laughs out loud. "What size?"

"'Bout four feet," he says.

Ray rolls her eyes. "What would the senators have thought of us then? With a copperhead snaking around the tent!"

Now Sis watches Angus walk over and pat Hilda on the back, to which she bristles. "Well, our daughter looks happy," he says. "Quite a pair, don't you think?" He pats her back once more and puts his hand back to his side.

Hilda does not respond. She stands up and steps to the side of the tent to greet an old suitemate of hers from Converse College.

Angus pulls a handkerchief out of his jacket and pats his brow and looks around the tent at the wedding he hosts. He nods to Sis and her mama and then to a couple that go dancing by. Before long, old Mr. Jameson hobbles up to him, pointing to a dark spot on the top of his right hand. Angus turns to the side, puts on his glasses, and examines the man's hand with care.

"Are they like in the mafia?" Sis hears Priscilla ask Cousin Willy and Ray with a naughty intrigue in her eye.

"No," Ray says. "What makes you say that?"

"Well, what's with the bag o' cash?" Priscilla points.

Sis had heard about the money bag Hilda was sewing, but she'd forgotten about it in all of the hoopla.

Now she sees it dangling from Little Hilda's wrist—a white satin bag with a silk rope tie—and one by one Giuseppe's friends and family saunter up to the dancing couple and slip an envelope inside of it.

Will Capers *ever* ask Sis to dance? After all, she spent a fortune on this dress trying to get him to notice her, but now he nibbles on shrimp and grits with Vangie on a live oak tree limb that touches the ground outside of the tent.

"I'm tired." Sis hears her mama's voice, turns toward her, and nods.

"I'll take you back to my apartment."

As Sis watches her mama stride on her high heels through the parking lot of the apartment building, she wonders if her mama worries about her, that she has no husband, and no daughter for whom to plan a wedding. Her mama rarely brings it up, but Sis senses it upsets her from time to time. Sis knows her mama wonders who will look after her when her mama is gone.

Well, of course it's been tough being the old maid of the town, but in some ways it's probably not as bad as poor Hilda, whose husband left her. It breaks Sis's heart to think of Hilda's dark room and the pillows in the space next to her in bed. Maybe she should tell the other gals about it. They don't usually talk about that sort of thing. That is, some subjects, usually the most painful ones, are just off limits in their friendship foursome, but it might be time to change that too.

After Sis gets her mama in the apartment, her cell phone rings.

"Hey, Sis. It's Capers."

"Hey there."

"Listen, I was hoping to get a chance to dance with you," he says. "Want to meet me at the seawall at sunset?"

"Yeah," she says. "Just let me get Mama settled and see if the gals need me to help shut things down."

"All right," he says. "I've got my own Embers CD in the car, and we can dance all night if you want."

Dance all night? Now that certainly doesn't sound like something Father Mothball would say, but then again, she thinks he's partaken of a few glasses of champagne and maybe his guard is down, which could be a very good thing.

"Sounds like fun," Sis says. "See you in a little bit."

When she turns her back her mama is already on her way to the guest room. "Don't you worry about me," she says. "You just get on back to that priest." She grins at Sis.

"Oh, Mama," Sis says.

"Don't 'Mama' me," she says. "It's never too late, sweetheart."

By the time Sis gets back to the reception, the sun is setting and Kitty B., Ray, and Cousin Willy are breaking everything down. They tell her to go on and find her dancing partner at the seawall. So she takes off her heels and scurries past the tents and the gathering of Giornelli men who are toasting and taking shots of ouzo beneath the live oak trees and over to Capers, who is sleeping on the seawall a few steps from his car, music spilling from his windows, a half empty bottle of champagne and two glasses beside him.

"Capers," she says, leaning in to him. There is a little pool of drool spilling out of his mouth, and when she nudges him all she can smell is her Uncle Bugby. He's deep into his champagne-induced slumber, and Sis guesses she'll have to load him up and get Cousin Willy to help her take him over to the rectory.

Well, she doesn't want to walk over to the gals and disappoint them with her perpetual lack of romantic activity, and she's still in the mood to dance, so she just stands on the seawall by herself and sways back and forth to the Embers and the sound of Salvatore playing his trumpet in the oak trees behind her. As she dances, she watches Giuseppe and Little Hilda, who are touring the waterway on Kitty B.'s brother's fifty-foot yacht. What an exit for them!

They are dancing too, on the deck, stepping back and forth as the wind gusts blow Little Hilda's lace veil up and around her. *They have their whole lives ahead of them,* Sis thinks. A trip to the Italian Riviera and a tour of Tuscany, where Giuseppe's family is from, then back to a nice little condo in Alexandria, Virginia, that sits right by a subway stop that will carry them to Capitol Hill each day.

As Sis sways, she thinks about the seeds the trees drop before a hurricane, and wonders why humans don't have this kind of eminent drive. At least she never did. She should have gotten busier trying to pollinate before her doctor sent her to be carved out. It didn't hit her until recently that she has no linkage. No next generation. No mark on the world. Nothing to outlive her.

The gals say this is not true, that she has her music and her piano students, but she suspects she's missed something. Everything else in her life trotted at the same pace with rest of the pack. She grew up, went through puberty, fell in love, got a degree, and a job—but it stopped right there, and she can't help but think she's been in a holding pattern ever since. That her midlife is just a shadow of her friends' experiences. That her legacy is nothing more than a little winged fruit from a live oak tree that lands in the surf only to be swallowed up by the Atlantic Ocean that licks the shore incessantly with its forceful tongue.

Now she watches the river rats furrowing in and out of the rocks along the seawall and she imagines the alligators and the herons and the snakes on the banks of the ACE Basin warming themselves in the last minutes of daylight.

Before long, Ray and Kitty B. come over with a slice of cake and a bottle of champagne. They have worked themselves to the bone, and they finally got rid of Vangie, who is more of a nuisance than a help with her constant need for instructions and approval. Ray takes one look at Capers passed out on the seawall. "Well, take a look at Romeo!"

Kitty B. giggles and Sis joins them as they take their place on the water's edge, letting their feet dangle over the seawall. They talk about how beautiful it all was and how Senator Warren ought to have been impressed and how happy Giuseppe and Hilda looked and how thankful they were that Hilda made it through the event without breaking down and how Priscilla took a real liking to Giuseppe's friend and how strange the money bag was and how Angus had to get Mason Kidd to open the bank on a Saturday afternoon so he could safely store the cash in the lockbox and how obvious it is that Capers Campbell likes Sis if he invited her to come out and dance on the seawall with him.

As the horizon turns from a pale gray to a fiery pink, the gals laugh and toast and watch Little Hilda and Giuseppe's yacht make its way beneath the bridge and around the bend as the herons and pelicans and terns flap their wings back to their damp and damaged homes to roost.

TEN

Hilda

Hilda didn't want to come out to the beach this weekend, what with all the memories of her and Angus on Edisto. But the gals just insisted that she come, and she owes them all such a debt of gratitude. Especially Ray, who practically put her daughter's wedding together single-handedly and pushed on through the weekend, car wreck, wounds, and all. And Hilda knows how badly Ray wants to show off the work she's done on the Montgomery beach house in the last year. Plus, it's Ray's birthday next week, and Cousin Willy is having a big barbeque to celebrate, and Hilda's already sent her regrets since she's avoiding Angus and Trudi. Maybe he'll notice her missing and come to his senses.

Hilda grew up vacationing at the house two doors down from the Montgomerys'. The yellow one right in front of the washout where the beach curves toward the bay and the ocean peters out and becomes the sound. Her older brother, Davy, used to shoot off Roman candles at the end of the boardwalk, and her mama would smile her hundred-watt smile and wave to them from the screened porch. Her mama always wore a wide straw hat at the beach and white rimmed sunglasses with black lenses, and she didn't think Hilda could see her sleeping or weeping behind them.

When her daddy came home, Hilda's mama took to the bed, where she watched Ed Sullivan and smoked NOW cigarettes with an empty conch shell for an ashtray on her lap.

"What are you thinking about, Hilda?" Sis says. They are sitting on the freshly painted white wicker furniture at the end of Ray's porch sipping a strong pink drink that Vangie Dreggs whipped up in a blender.

"What are we drinking?" Hilda says, ignoring Sis. Maybe if she downs a couple of cocktails she can excuse herself to her room for the night.

Ray leans in to say "Cos-mo-pol-i-tan," as Vangie bends Kitty B.'s ear about the properties she's considering for her second home.

"Tell me that's not the most ironic thing in the world," Ray adds, shaking her head. The swelling has gone down around her eye and her stitches have dissolved, but Hilda can't help but cringe at the fresh red scar above her friend's right cheekbone.

"Ray," Sis says in a hushed tone.

Ray lifts her eyebrows. Hilda takes another sip in hopes that the icy drink will calm her nerves. She's just not used to being out like this, though she has to admit the sea air smells awfully good.

"I'm not over it," Ray says as she leans in toward the wicker coffee table to pick up the bowl of stone crab claws to pass around.

Hilda rolls her eyes. Now who is Ray talking to? She isn't exactly sure what transpired, but somehow Vangie Dreggs invited herself to the weekend, and Ray had no way of telling her no. Frankly, Hilda is thankful. It gets everyone's focus off her.

"Why, thank you, Ray," Vangie says, dunking her claw into the creamy curry dip. "I think South Carolinians are simply the most hospitable in all the country."

Kitty B. says, "Well, that's nice of you to say." She sees no rattle on Vangie's tail.

Ray bites the inside of her cheek and hands out her new square linen napkins. They have a pinkish-orange crab embroidered on them, and they match the white and salmon-colored striped cushions on the wicker furniture. Ray is one of those people who likes for everything to match in a cutesy kind of way at her beach house, and for some reason this annoys Hilda. The beach is one of the few places that can and should be rustic and random with a hodge-podge of furniture and decor.

"I just read the other day that Charleston was voted the friend-liest city in this big national survey," Sis adds.

"Maybe that's why the Yankees are flocking down here like there's no tomorrow," Ray says.

"Mmm. Mmm," Vangie says as she slurps her drink. "That's true, but I'll tell you those Yankees are going to bring a lot of money into this area, and we'll all be better for it."

Ray clears her throat and shakes her head.

"You're from Charleston, aren't you, Ray?" Vangie asks. "Tell me who your family is there."

Ray sits up on the edge of the rocking chair, pushes back her shoulders, focuses on a patch in the screen just beyond Vangie, and says, "The Pringles."

"Oh my, the Pringles," Vangie says. "You know my sister says they are one of the oldest families in the city. In fact she pointed out one of their old houses to me—the pale yellow one on the high battery with the triple-story piazzas. My word, those ceilings must be fourteen feet tall!"

"Yes," Ray says. "I spent a lot of time there."

Sis lets out a nervous giggle, and Hilda feels like causing some trouble.

"Ray grew up in that yellow house," Hilda says. "At least that's what we've come to assume. I don't know why she's so guarded about the whole thing."

Ray shoots a look in Hilda's direction. "I'm not *guarded*."

"Sure you are." Hilda rubs the knobby outline of the pink crab on the linen napkin she's draped across her knee. "In all the years we've known you, you've never once told us a story about your childhood."

"Oh, tell me a story!" Vangie says. She puts her cocktail down and spreads out her fingers like she's in a jazz dance number. "You know I'm writing a book! About Texas and the healing ministry and my small group and South Carolina and real estate and all of the amazing things that have happened to me since I came to the Lord, and I want to include all of you in it!"

Ray shoots Hilda a look, then says to Sis, "Can you go stir the Creole for me?"

"Okay," Sis says, "but don't start the story without me."

Kitty B. grabs the acrylic pitcher of cosmopolitans to refill the glasses, and all eyes are on Ray when she sits down in her large wicker rocking chair. The rocker's back is tall and round and it fans out around her like a throne, and Hilda has to admit, she's enjoying this. Ray, with her clandestine past and her whole life so maddeningly together. She's bugged Hilda ever since the night she won the watermelon-stealing contest back in high school, all dressed up in her linen pedal pushers and her white eyelet shirt.

Instead of sitting back and rocking, Ray moves to the edge of her pink and white striped cushion and begins. "We lived with my great-aunt, Lindy Pringle. It was my sister and Mama and me. My father died in the war."

As Ray's face reddens, she pats it with her napkin and continues. "Anyhow, I remember when we bought our first television. It was the day before Queen Elizabeth's coronation, and Mama had sewn Laura and me matching dresses to wear because Great-Aunt Lindy had invited all of her friends over to see the ceremony on the new television. It was a lovely affair—very formal and very Charleston with 'Oh Be Joyful' punch and cheese biscuits and cucumber sandwiches and candied pecans. Most everyone in Charleston is an Anglophile, you know?"

Ray looks down and brushes some sand off the side of her leg. Then she rubs her fingers back and forth across the woven arms of the wicker chair at least four times before they realize that this is the end of the story.

"Ah, well, that's nice, Ray," Vangie says. "I can picture it! Do you have any photos?"

"Well, not *here*." Ray scratches around her fresh scar. "I've got some at home. How did that Creole look, Sis? Think we're about ready to drop the shrimp in?"

"Yeah," Sis says, sipping her drink.

"Say, Ray," Hilda adds, "that's not much of a *story*."

Ray's back bristles, and Hilda can't imagine why she's enjoying herself so much.

"You know, I have to agree," Kitty B. giggles. "I've got a much better story about that coronation."

"Let's hear it!" Vangie says, her emerald eyes glistening in the porch light. "I'm all ears."

Then Kitty B. tells a story about how her daddy, Mayor Hathaway, invited the whole community of Jasper to the Town Hall to watch the coronation on their new television. Shortly after a large group gathered, her brother Jackson tripped over the cord when her other brother, Buzz, was chasing him, and the television fell over and crashed. Then the whole town raced out of the building because kooky old Mr. Sandeman shouted, "There are fumes from inside that machine that can poison you!"

The gals all hoot and holler and laugh about how Kitty B.'s daddy and Old Stained Glass and the town doctor before Angus, Virgil McDougal, went ever so cautiously back into Town Hall wearing operating masks to survey the damage.

After they catch their breath, Sis says, "Look at that sunset," and they turn to watch the fiery orange ball make its way behind the Pines of Otter Island in just a few short minutes.

When they sit down to dinner, Vangie Dreggs tells some crazy stories about her childhood on a cattle ranch in Grand Saline, Texas, that involved her spirited grandmother and a pack of angry dwarf goats.

"Now that's a story!" Sis laughs as she passes the biscuits a second time.

Kitty B. takes two. "I'll say."

Hilda looks at Ray. "You could take a lesson in storytelling from Vangie Dreggs, Ray."

Ray's face reddens, and she stands up and picks up her plate and Sis's.

"Hilda, I wouldn't have invited you to come along if I thought you were going to be critiquing me every second."

The table gets quiet as Ray takes the plates over to the sink and comes back for more. "There's key lime pie on the counter for dessert," she says, "and decaf brewing in the pot. I think I'm going to turn in for the night." She picks up Hilda's plate.

"Oh, Ray, c'mon," Hilda says, lighting a cigarette. "We were just pulling your leg a little. I mean, you're so durn tight-lipped about your childhood and all."

"Forget about that," Kitty B. says, clapping her hands and reaching for a deck of cards on the table. "We're just getting started having some fun, y'all. I was hoping we could play a game of hearts or 'oh hell' after this! Like we always do, Ray. And then we can start scheming again about how to get Sis and Capers Campbell together."

"Oh, my." Vangie blushes and chuckles nervously as Little Bit scampers over and hops onto her lap. "They would make a nice pair."

"No thanks," Ray says, staring Hilda down. "That accident's catching up with me, and I'm plumb *worn out* from the wedding. It's no wonder is it, Hilda?"

Hilda sees where this is going, and she narrows her eyes, "Ray . . ."

"Don't 'Ray' me. Your friends here spent a whole lot of time, energy, and money getting your daughter married while you, Miss *Princess* of Jasper, stayed holed up in your home like a hermit crab and graced us with your presence for a few moments during the weekend."

Hilda puts out her half-smoked cigarette, stands up, and stares Ray down. "That's enough, Ray. After all I've been through . . ."

"After all *you've* been through? As if you didn't bring it on yourself," Ray says. "It's no wonder Angus threw up his hands. He's only human, you know?"

Vangie Dreggs is speechless. She bites her lip and looks down at the remnants of a half-eaten biscuit as Sis and Kitty B. turn to comfort Hilda, but it is too late.

Hilda storms out the porch door, running down the boardwalk and into the balmy night, the salt air lifting her hair and separating it into stringy strands. She is barefoot and she doesn't care how hard the shells feel beneath her heels as she hits the beach. She runs toward the surf, crying and hoping to God she doesn't see anyone she knows out here. When she gets to the water, she half thinks she's going to jump in and swim out into the warm, dark depths until she can't take another stroke. But she doesn't.

Instead, she turns and heads toward the pier, letting the saltwater lick her knees. She walks for more than an hour along the beach with the water up to her thighs, wetting her khaki Bermuda shorts as the wind carries her tears toward her hairline, leaving thin sandy streaks across her cheeks.

"To hell with you, Ray Montgomery," she says. "You think you know how it is, but you don't. You have no clue, you finicky Charleston witch. It was you who tried to edge your way into the Jasper pack just like Vangie is doing now. You have no idea what my life has been like. Not the beginning of a clue."

After Hilda passes the pier and the Edisto Motel, she realizes she can't just walk to Jasper in this blackness, so slowly she makes her way back to Ray's house. She tiptoes up the stairs and takes a seat on the little deck at the end of the boardwalk, where she lights a cigarette and hopes none of them will notice she's returned. The lights are on in the upstairs bedrooms, and she supposes that everyone has retired to their own space to read their beach book instead of cackling on the screened porch in a game of hearts. She wishes she could just get in her car and leave, but of course, Sis gave her a ride and she's stuck here in the first lady of Jasper's made-over house with salmon and aqua-colored nautical knickknacks every which way you turn.

As she hugs her knobby knees to her chest, she watches two children come out of the yellow house where her family used to stay. They are carrying buckets, and the father jogs closely behind them with a flashlight.

"Slow down," he calls. "Wait for me."

~ JULY 19, 1956 ~

"Where the heck have you two been?" Hilda could hear her father calling to her and her brother, Davy, when they were hunting for ghost crabs one summer night.

Davy was twelve and Hilda was nine, and they had met up with a girl from Davy's class named Marcia Tarleton who Hilda could tell had an awful crush on Davy. Marcia's little sister, Bonnie, was a year younger than Hilda, and the four of them had so much fun chasing the crabs out to the surf that Davy asked the girls if they'd meet them back in a few minutes after they went up and checked on their mama, who fell asleep every now and then with a lit cigarette in her lap.

"Your mother has nearly worried herself to death," her daddy hollered from the doorway of the screened porch, his hands on his hips and his lips pursed. The bright storm light at the top of the stairs illuminated his gray suit and the dark tie he had loosened at the neck.

Mama? Hilda thought. She had been snoozing in front of the television in her bedroom with an empty gin and tonic in a bright plastic cup, and Daddy hadn't come home yet from one of his business dinners with the mill executives who flew in from New York from time to time to brief him about the union's plans to infiltrate the company. The executives told him about Norma Jean, who had stood on her loom at the textile mill in North Carolina, and that he'd have to be prepared to pull folks down from the pulp machines if they pulled a stunt like that around here. Hilda's daddy usually stayed in town when he had one of those meetings, and they weren't expecting him to come out to Edisto that night.

"We were just on the beach hunting crabs," Davy said, sprinting up the stairs to the porch doorway. When he met their daddy, he placed the bucket on the rail and spread his palms out wide to show they had nothing to hide.

"Well, I hope you had one rip-roaring good time, Son, because neither of you are going out of this house at night for the rest of the week."

"Dad, c'mon," Davy said. "This is our vacation. We aren't doing anything wrong."

Their daddy stuck out two fingers as if to make the peace sign and poked Davy right in the collarbone, where he lost his footing and scuffled down two steps.

Then Davy's outstretched hands turned into fists, and he grabbed the bucket on the rail and threw it down at his father's wingtip shoes, where two ghost crabs and a heap of wet sand spilled out across the wooden planks.

Her daddy grabbed Davy by the collar and shoved him down what was at least ten stairs, where he landed at Hilda's feet with a thud.

"I hate you," Davy said under his breath as he picked himself up and reached out for Hilda's hand.

Before he could stand back up, their father was down the stairs, grabbing him by the collar and taking him out on the end of the boardwalk, where he pulled down Davy's pants, grabbed a cast net by the fishing rods and swatted Davy over and over on his hips and backside, the little metal weights at the end of the net making welts on his bare skin.

Hilda stood stone still, watching her brother yelp and shout for mercy as Marcia and Bonnie's flashlight made its way up the beach to meet them. When their beam shone on Davy's welts and his daddy's arm coming down with the blows of the swinging cast net, Marcia shrieked and dropped her glowing light, and Hilda tried to make out their shadowy outlines as they ran back down the beach toward their home on the other side of the pier.

Through the bedroom window that opened onto the screened porch, Hilda heard her mama stirring in the bed, but she never emerged from her room, and Hilda was the one who brought an ice pack to her brother as he lay belly down on the hammock beneath the house, vowing to run away as soon as he had the money.

The Princess of Jasper. Hilda shakes her head as she watches through the sea oats while the children's flashlights scan the beach for ghost crabs. *Maybe I did think of myself that way when I was young.*

Hilda's father, David Savage, opened the Jasper Paper Mill that resuscitated the dwindling businesses in town in the 1950s. Over three hundred people came to Jasper to work at the mill, and the Savage family lived on boss man's row in an antebellum house at the edge of the mill village drive. The village was made up of shotgun houses on cinderblocks with no running water and big, brown barrels for bathing, but Hilda's house was grand with its tall white columns, and her family had a cook and a housekeeper and running water and a television set, and as a child she really did think they were like royalty in a crude little kingdom where trucks carrying limbless pine trunks barreled by their home each evening.

When her mama would give her a dime and send her down to Condon's department store to buy a new pair of shoes or a milkshake at the lunch counter, the black men in Jasper as well as the poor men would literally move off the sidewalk to let her pass.

"Morning, Miss Hilda," the men would say, tipping their hats or nodding their heads before stepping off the curb.

Maybe Ray is right. I assumed I ruled the town—back then, anyway. Her mama didn't help matters much. When she was coherent, she would sit at Hilda's vanity and brush her hair for a half hour at a time, lifting it up to the morning sunlight pouring through her bedroom window. Her mama drove to Charleston and bought fine fabrics for the local seamstress, Mrs. Chalmers, to make smocked dresses and slips and pantaloons for Hilda with little lace borders and thin satin ribbons. She would send Hilda down the mill village row with the fabrics and over to a little apartment above the sweetshop on Main Street, where Hilda would sit for hours and watch Mrs. Chalmers cut the fabric according to the patterns and sew her exquisite wardrobe together. One day when Mrs. Chalmers's arthritis was acting up, she called Hilda over to her sewing table and said, "Why don't you help me with this, child."

Hilda's mama never cared when she and Davy went down to the beach at night. She would put on her lipstick and a long bed gown and sit on the sofa doing the crossword puzzle before pouring herself a second cocktail.

Looking back on it, Hilda figures that her mama was just miserably homesick and depressed with her small-town life. She was from Richmond, Virginia, and claimed to have bluer blood than anyone from South Carolina. David Savage had met her at a Virginia Military Institute game where her father served as the president of the college.

Hilda's parents had two versions of the "how we met" story. Her daddy's was that at the end of the game when the cadets threw up their hats in a victory gesture, Hilda's mama ran across the stands, knocking over drinks and tripping over legs, to catch his hat, and she carried it over to him and said, "Hi, I'm Martha Louise Staunton."

Her mama's version was practically the opposite. That she was sitting there, cheering on the team for the final touchdown when her daddy took off his hat and threw it like a Frisbee into her lap.

At any rate, her parents met at the game. David was from a poor tobacco farming town on the Tennessee border, but he was handsome and driven, and Martha Louise fell for him and followed him up and down the East Coast as he made his way up in the paper mill industry. Hilda was seven when they landed in Jasper, and her mama took one look at their beautiful new home and said, "This is it. We're not moving again." Her mama liked being in the Lowcountry at first, but the heat and the bugs and the reptiles weren't nearly as romantic as she'd imagined, and she didn't have a friend in the world except for her afternoon toddy.

Hilda's daddy was almost always mad and ranting. He was trying to keep the unions out. He was fighting off the employees' demands. And he was fending off the KKK, who put a burning cross in their yard after her daddy promoted a black man to manage the pulp production.

Hilda's brother did try to protect her from her daddy's wrath. Once when their father was shouting in a harsh tone for Hilda to get in the house and look after her mama, Davy tackled her and hid her beneath the camellia bushes, her smocked dress picking up the leaves and dirt and the stains from the dark pink petals.

"He's in a rage," he whispered. "If you go in now, you'll get it good."

"But I can't stay out here all night," she mouthed, picking the petals from her dress.

"He'll storm out when he sees how bad off Mama is tonight," Davy whispered. "When he gets in his car to drive around, you can sneak in and go straight to bed."

Hilda nodded and Davy walked toward the porch to tell Daddy that she must be out with her friends.

~ SEPTEMBER 18, 1962 ~

Shortly after her fourteenth birthday Hilda woke up in the middle of the night with her daddy in bed next to her.

It had been six months since Davy ran away. He hopped on a train headed west with some money his grandparents had sent him for his sixteenth birthday, and they had not heard a word from him.

Hilda was not entirely surprised to feel her father's touch beneath the covers. Old Stained Glass had preached the Sunday before that depravity knows no class boundaries, and she knew David Savage was an angry, desperate man.

For the first several times, she pretended like she was asleep, but as the months went by and she entered high school, she would turn over to him, her body drawn to the warmth of his groping hands in her half-sleep haze. It was strange and awful and sad.

Of course she knew she couldn't fight her daddy off, but the worst part was that her body responded to the power of his touch. She will never discard the shame of this, nor will she forgive the body she inhabits or the God who created it to respond to such a thing.

Angus never knew. No one knew, except for her daddy, what went on those two years. And once just after her sweet sixteen, her mama called to her daddy from one of her rare, lucid moments in the night.

"David?" she said from their room shortly after he had slipped under Hilda's covers. He stood up, wiped his brow, and went back to the bed he and his wife shared, and he never came back after that.

Now as Hilda watches the father chasing ghost crabs with his two children up and down the beach, she listens intently to their laughter. One of them is shouting, "Daddy, over here! Look at this one!" The other is shrieking with both fear and delight, "Get him! Get him!"

Before long, the mother comes down with a baby on her hips,

and she watches her children and her husband chase the translucent little crustaceans that dart in and out of the holes along the surf. When they call, "Did you see that, Mama?" she hollers "Yes!" with wonder and encouragement.

"Hey, gal," Sis and Kitty B. call as Hilda looks up to find them shuffling down the boardwalk toward her with an extra cosmopolitan in their hands and a bowl of boiled peanuts.

"You okay?" Kitty B. says as she and Sis sit down on either side of Hilda and pat her bony shoulders.

"Yeah," Hilda takes a gulp of the fruity drink before reaching for a peanut.

"Here you go." Sis lifts the bowl. "A little Carolina caviar for you, Your Highness."

They laugh a deep laugh as Hilda splits the seam of the shell with her thumbnail and nibbles on the soft, salty meat cradled inside.

"You know Ray didn't mean it." Kitty B. pulls Hilda close.

"She did so," Hilda says as the salt air blows their hair in all directions. "But you know, she's right. It's no wonder he left."

"Hilda." Sis squeezes her bony shoulder. "Don't say that."

Hilda throws the damp shell into the dunes. "I was a terrible companion."

Kitty B. and Sis look to each other like they want to say something to make her feel better. Hilda senses neither one of them can find the words.

"And now I might just spend the rest of my life alone." Hilda rubs her hands together. "I might die alone. Do y'all realize that?"

Sis bites her lip, and Kitty B. pokes at the boiled peanuts with the tip of her index finger.

"I was a horrible companion, but I never dreamed Angus would *leave*."

"We know," Kitty B. says as she puts the bowl of peanuts down and wipes her finger on her Bermuda shorts.

"Sometimes I imagine he'll come back," Hilda says. "Come right through the door with that old leather suitcase he bought when we were in Greece on our honeymoon. Do you think it's crazy for me to think that way?"

Just then Ray hollers from the screened porch, "Kitty B.! Katie Rae is on the phone, and she says it's an *emergency*!"

LeMar, they are all thinking, and they run toward the porch door, where Ray hands Kitty B. the cordless as they stand like a wall around her. Hilda too.

"What?" Kitty B. shouts in disbelief. "You've only known him for six weeks, darlin'!"

"Heavens to Betsy! Do you think Katie Rae's engaged?" Ray murmurs as Vangie and Little Bit step out onto the porch to see what's going on.

"She can't be," Sis says as Kitty B. listens and says, "Mmm. Hmm. My, that sounds nice," into the receiver.

"Do you think she swallowed a watermelon seed?" Sis whispers nervously.

"I bet she did," Hilda says almost before she can stop herself.

"A watermelon seed?" Vangie asks as Little Bit yips around their legs until he pushes through their wall of bare legs and reaches up for Kitty B., who has already shown him some attention.

"Sounds like Katie Rae is engaged," Sis whispers. "And since she's only known the boy for a short while, we wonder if she's expecting."

"Well, that would explain it," Ray says to Hilda. There is a softness in her eyes, and Hilda knows that what transpired between them earlier is over and Ray is sorry.

"No, I can't!" Kitty B. continues, "Why in the world do you want to get married so soon? Have you talked to your daddy?"

When she hangs up, the gals lead her over to the couch and bring her a thick slice of key lime pie.

She takes a big bite, sits back, and says, "Well, y'all, Katie Rae's engaged to that religious reptile man, and she wants to be married by Christmas."

"Do you think she's swallowed a watermelon seed?" Vangie asks. Hilda swallows a secret grin—Vangie is clueless. This is *not* something you just come right out and ask the mother of the bride.

Four distinct worry lines form across Kitty B.'s forehead. "Maybe," she says. "She's only known this boy since June."

"She met him on the computer," Ray informs Vangie.

"Oh, yes, my cousin met a man that way," Vangie says, scratching Little Bit beneath the chin. "And I might do the same if I can't win the affection of a local."

Kitty B. shakes her head in disbelief. "Of course I have no idea how LeMar will react, and goodness knows we have no money to put on a wedding. He's been out of work for years now, and y'all know we've about run through my inheritance."

"Don't you worry about that," Vangie says. "We'll all pull together in this, won't we, ladies?"

Ray rolls her eyes at Vangie. "Of course we will. We have for decades and decades, haven't we, gals?"

Sis and Hilda nod, and Kitty B. gets a faraway look in her eye and then smiles. "Well, I have to say, as crazy as it sounds, I'm kind of happy for her. I never thought she'd find anyone, and she sounds more excited than I can ever remember."

Ray pats Kitty B.'s knee. "Good."

"Tell us more," Sis says. "How did he propose?"

"On a picnic at the Columbia Zoo," Kitty B. says. "Right in front of the orangutan exhibit—Katie Rae's favorite."

"Aww." Sis cocks her head to the side.

"Odd, but sweet," Hilda adds.

"They're both animal lovers," Kitty B. says. "He has more pets at his house than she does, and she says he's always rescuing some dog or cat from the shelter. Of course he runs that reptile place over on the ACE."

"Sounds like they'll have one lively home life," Sis adds as Ray pulls out a pad and a pen, turns on the porch light and says, "Let's start brainstorming."

Vangie claps her hands in glee, and Little Bit jumps off the salmon-colored couch and barks around her ankles.

"I've already got some ideas." Ray clicks the top of her pen and starts writing.

Hilda fights back a yawn. "Let's hear them."

"Yes!" Kitty B. shouts as she sits up and pats her brow with a linen napkin. "I can't wait to hear them all!"

ELEVEN

"What in the world?" LeMar says from his rocking chair the next afternoon as Katie Rae and her fiancé stand on the front porch of the Cottage Hill house and show him the solitaire on her left hand. Gounod's *Romeo et Juliette* plays in the background. Kitty B. went to see the opera with LeMar a few months ago at the Spoleto Festival. It was set in a contemporary New Jersey community where the Capulet family ran a funeral home. LeMar listens to Act Five, in which the lovers die praying for divine forgiveness, at least once a week. *He's so melodramatic*, Kitty B. thinks.

"You two hardly know each other, Katie Rae," he says, a knowing look in his eye.

Then he turns to Dr. Marshall Bennington. "Son, when you came to ask for her hand last week, I thought I made it clear that this needs to happen at least six months down the *road.*"

Marshall clears his throat over the tragic music. He pulls at his starched oxford collar before smoothing out the pleats in his khaki shorts. "Sir, I'm thirty-five years old. I've been asking God for a wife for nine years now, and I know that Katie Rae is the answer to that prayer."

An out-and-out smile, teeth and all, spreads across Katie Rae's face. She looks frumpy compared to Marshall in her untucked T-shirt and cutoff jeans, but at least she bothered to put on some small silver hoop earrings and a little lipstick too.

"Might be," LeMar says as he pinches his nostrils. "But I don't think you've been with her long enough to know."

"Marshall's a good man, Daddy," Katie Rae says, furrowing her wide brow. Her chubby cheeks begin to flush as she adds, "A better man than I ever dreamed of meeting."

"You're only twenty-two, child." LeMar tries to meet her eyes. "You haven't finished college and you've never held down a legitimate job or a long-term relationship, and you think you can make a decision like this after knowing someone for two months?"

Katie Rae's cheeks fill with air and her eyes narrow. She grabs her head with both hands, and her solitaire catches the crisp light of the September afternoon. Then she dashes out toward the dock with Marshall fast on her heels. The dogs think this is a game of chase, and they follow raucously behind, nipping and barking at Marshall's ankles.

LeMar holds the palm of his hand up to Kitty B. as Romeo drinks a vial of poison in the Capulet crypt before seeing Juliet rouse.

"Don't utter a word, Kitty B.," he says. "I know what's going on."

"Oh, you do?" She grinds her teeth. "Please tell me what you know, LeMar. Tell me why you've gone and mortally insulted our daughter in front of what might be the only man that is ever going to love her."

LeMar shakes his head back and forth, then he grabs at the back of his neck.

"Y'all are speeding this up on account of my headaches," he says, sitting down in the rocking chair. "You want me to be there before whatever shows up on that MRI eats me up. You've all but bought my headstone, haven't you?"

He bites his lip and conducts the orchestra for a moment with

his thick hands. His fingers remind Kitty B. of the link sausages she
buys at Marvin's Meats.

Of course. She gets it now. *Somehow this has got to be about you
and your make-believe illness!*

Out of the corner of her eye, she sees Marshall and Katie Rae
climb into the johnboat. Katie Rae cranks the motor and steers
them out into the river.

The two labs stand like statues on the edge of the dock and
Rhetta, the poodle, barks and yips for them to take her too.

"You know, LeMar," Kitty B. says. "This has nothing to do with
you."

He leans back in the rocking chair and closes his eyes. She stands
there staring at him for a whole minute, and she knows he just hopes
she'll disappear.

"Stop tuning me out." Somehow Kitty B. gets the nerve to stand
right in front of him and lean down on the arms of his rocking
chair so that he is forced to sit upright.

When he opens his eyes she says, "First, you are *not* going to die
and you know it. Angus says it's probably just another CFS symptom. No one here has written you off, except maybe *you*. And as for
Katie Rae, did you ever stop to think that she is one year older than
I was when we got married?"

He closes his eyes again and shakes his large head gently back
and forth. "Oh, and we've had a marriage made in heaven," he says.

Kitty B. stands up straight, her knees trembling, and wonders
what to say next. How in the world did they come to this? How did
they go from adoring one another the way Marshall and Katie Rae
do to hardly having a relationship at all? They live two separate lives
under their crumbling roof, and as far as Kitty B. can tell, the only
feeling LeMar has toward her is contempt.

She goes and cuts the CD player off and walks back out to the
porch with her back to him, watching the black ripples from Katie
Rae's wake slap the edge of the mud banks. The salt marsh is start-

ing to turn from green to brown, and by December they'll be such a pale, ashen gray that she will have a hard time believing they will ever regain their color.

"Well, I don't know what we can do about the mess *we're* in, LeMar," she says. "But I do know that we shouldn't drag Katie Rae down with us."

He closes his eyes again, and she turns to face him.

"This nice man loves her," she says. "He respects her and sees what very few people have seen in her, and if we forbid her from taking hold of that, then we may very well ruin her chance at happiness."

LeMar plays dead.

"Now I'm going to wait down at the dock for them," she says. "And I'm going to tell them that they have my blessing to get married and they should proceed with or without you. You hear me?"

He pinches his face, and short dark marks run across his lips like a crudely drawn time line. She turns and walks toward the dock as Honey and Otis run up to greet her. Rhetta remains at the water's edge, barking into the air.

As Kitty B. takes her seat on the dock, she pats the dogs who are vying for her attention. Their muddy paws leave streaks across her apron. It's the hot pink apron that the gals bought her when she finished the church cookbook, and it has "Editor-in-Chief, *Lowcountry Manna*" embroidered on the front with the publication date.

The gals seem excited about Katie Rae's engagement. Kitty B. doesn't know why LeMar can't be. It's been a fast courtship, but goodness knows they never thought Katie Rae was ever going to move out of their house, much less meet a man and marry him. It's a practical miracle as far as Kitty B. can tell, and as happy as Marshall is, it seems *they* should be thanking the good Lord for His grace.

Now the goats bleat across the fence as the sun makes its way down toward the water's edge. When it rises again Kitty B. will drive LeMar down to the Medical University in Charleston for his third MRI of the year. The old paranoid curmudgeon.

He's been sick and aching more often than not since she's known him, and some days it seems like he takes great satisfaction in his sufferings the way a tongue can't help but work its way over a sore tooth.

The doctors will look at him. Look at the inner workings of his body and wonder why he is such a head case. Why he wants to believe that he has some fatal disease. *Then they'll look at me.* She shakes her head. *They'll look at me and wonder, "Why does this fellow want to die so badly? He must have an astoundingly horrible home life."*

Some days she'd like to leave him at the hospital for the nurses and doctors to deal with for a few weeks. Isn't it terrible to think like that? She knows it's not right, but *good grief,* she can't help herself.

Tomorrow she'd like to hand him over to the nurse and then make like she's going to the waiting room to snip recipes from her cooking magazines, and the next thing you know she'd be halfway down I-26 to her cousin's house in Roanoke, Virginia. Or maybe she could go to one of those weight loss spas in Arizona or drive to the airport and catch a plane to New York City, where she'd make her way to Rockefeller Center and stand outside the *Today* show studio, holding up a sign that reads, "Get well soon, LeMar!" before stepping back into the folds of the crowd.

Just as she pictures the look on LeMar's face while he reads the *Today* show sign on the screen in front of his hospital bed, Katie Rae and Marshall come around the mouth of the Ashepoo River and toward the dock. The wind pulls back her daughter's thin dark hair so that it dances behind her like the streamers in a wind sock. Her intended's arm rests on her back as she turns the boat around and eases up to the marsh bank.

When Marshall scurries to the bow of the boat to grab the line, Kitty B. reaches out her hand, and he throws it to her. She tugs them toward the edge of the dock and ties the line tight as the dogs bark in delight.

"Where's Daddy?" Katie Rae says, looking toward the porch.

Kitty B. looks back to see the rocking chair empty in the shadows of the autumn dusk.

"Who knows?" she says, reaching out to help them out of the bobbing boat. "Maybe he's run away." *Maybe he beat me to it.*

"No ma'am," says Marshall pointing up toward the house, where LeMar teeters on the threshold with four of her mama's old crystal flutes and a bottle of champagne.

He nods his head in an invitation, and they walk across the yard toward him as Honey and Otis sniff each other and Rhetta bolts past them toward the porch, yipping at a high pitch as if she understands that the time has come to celebrate.

Katie Rae follows suit and Marshall even breaks into a little jog on the way toward the sloping porch.

Looks like we're going to have a wedding. Kitty B. hopes to high heaven that Katie Rae doesn't have her heart set on having it out here. This is a beautiful spot, but it would cost them a fortune to get the place in shape. The house needs a paint job something awful, and their yard is nothing more than holes of black dirt where the dogs dig and sniff and do their business.

Now Otis and Honey chase each other around Kitty B.'s legs as if to round her up as LeMar embraces his baby girl and his future son-in-law in the center of the sloping porch. Kitty B. hears the cork pop, and she watches as it ricochets off the porch roof and lands in the browning azalea bushes by the steps.

"Hurry up, Mama!" Katie Rae calls. "It's time for a toast."

Mr. and Mrs. Cecil LeMar Blalock

REQUEST THE HONOUR OF YOUR PRESENCE

AT THE MARRIAGE OF THEIR DAUGHTER

Katherine Rae

TO

Doctor Roscoe Marshall Bennington, Junior

ON FRIDAY, THE THIRTIETH OF DECEMBER

TWO THOUSAND AND FIVE

AT SIX O'CLOCK

CHRIST ON THE COAST CATHEDRAL

CHARLESTON, SOUTH CAROLINA

AND AFTERWARDS THE RECEPTION

AT THE HOME OF THE BRIDE

TWELVE

Ray

A barbeque in Jasper County does not mean hamburgers and chicken breasts on a fancy gas grill. Yankees call anything you cook outside "barbeque." The word *barbeque* in Ray's neck of the woods is a *noun*, not a verb, and it means a whole hog tied to a spit with chicken wire and rope and roasted in an outdoor oven, usually in someone's backyard or some parking lot. And the fixin's that must accompany it are baked beans, collard greens, white rolls, cole slaw, and rice topped with a sweet gravy made from the drippings and other unmentionables that the pack calls hash. Jasper folks sort of take the "don't ask, don't tell" approach with the hash. *We don't want to know what's in it,* Ray thinks, *but it sure tastes good.*

Cousin Willy hosts a barbeque in honor of Ray's birthday every few years in their backyard, and it's always the same thing: a fifty-pound hog he buys from Marvin's Meats that he cooks slowly on the charcoal pit by the dock. He's been rotating the beast every hour since sunrise, and Ray has never seen him so excited.

"Whatcha got up your sleeve?" she asked him as he and Justin shooed her out of the shed this morning.

"You'll find out," he says, trying to conceal a grin. "Now go on and get ready for your shopping spree."

He's even consulted with the gals on this party, and they've brought over red and white checked tablecloths for the tables he hauled over from his office. Hilda is out there right now putting out Miss C. and the cutest little old-fashioned ceramic piggy banks on the tables which R.L. has stuffed with sweet little arrangements of bright orange zinnias and black-eyed Susans and forget-me-nots. This is the one party that Ray stays out of, but she is thankful that the gals guide Cousin Willy with the decor, invitations, and the guest list.

"I've only got one request," she said to him a few weeks ago when he started making the birthday plans.

"Name it," he said as he scribbled down the menu on a legal pad.

"Just don't invite that Texas transplant, and I'll be happy as a clam."

Cousin Willy scanned the guest list and found Vangie Dreggs's name and address.

"Kitty B. put her on here," he said, and he squinted with concern.

Ray's stomach tightened, and she could feel the heat rising up and around her neck.

"That's because Kitty B. doesn't see what I see."

"And what's that?" he said. "You know Vangie's gotten real involved with the civic life around here and the ACE Basin preservation, and it might just hurt her feelings, Ray."

"You mean *you* are letting her buy her way in too?" Ray picked up an old copy of the church bulletin in the mail pile and fanned her face. "I've told you before, the woman is bad news, and I've been around her enough now to *know*. She's bringing strange ideas into the church and she's selling old family properties to people from way off. Before long we'll be surrounded by strangers and dark houses that serve as second homes that the owners will use once or twice a year. What kind of civic life will that yield, Cousin?"

"C'mon now, Ray," he said, his eyes turning soft on her. "It does a place good to freshen up the gene pool from time to time. You can't deny that can you, sweet?"

As she started to throw the bulletin at him, she saw Vangie Dreggs's name at the top of the page of announcements. The Lone Star had joined the flower guild and the altar guild, and Capers had appointed her as the new head of the evangelism committee too. Under her committee title she had written a bold and capitalized blurb that said, "HEALING PRAYER REVIVAL DAY—JANUARY 5TH. MARK YOUR CALENDARS!"

Oh brother. Ray threw the whole thing at Willy. It fell apart in midair and landed at his feet.

"I'm not talking about gene pools," she said. "I'm talking about my fifty-fifth birthday, and I do not want that woman spoiling the evening with her booming voice and her fake eyeballs and her less than appropriate talk of real estate and healing prayer, all right?"

Willy picked up the bulletin and read the blurb, then chuckled. "It's your party," he said. Then he stood up and put his arm around her, which would have been nice had she not been so durn *hot.*

"Thank you," she said smiling at him as she thought, *If this doesn't send her a message then nothing will.*

Cousin Willy pulled Ray close to his thick chest and said, "I want you to enjoy yourself."

That is the truth. He does want me to enjoy myself, Ray thinks. Today the marquee in front of the Jasper Motor Lodge reads, "Happy Birthday, Ray," and so does the digital sign at the National Bank of South Carolina, and she knows it's all his doing.

And so is the fact that their son, William, came into town from

Atlanta with Carson, his chic and urbane wife. They drive up around lunchtime in this sporty little convertible BMW with the top down. During their driveway conversation, Ray looks at her reflection in the mirrored sunglasses covering her son and daughter-in-law's eyes—a short round version of herself like the one she stares at in the wavy mirror at the county fair.

"I see myself in your glasses, Will," Justin says as he rides up on his bicycle with a roll of wrapping paper in a Family Dollar bag.

"Oh, yeah," William says. He pulls off his glasses and lets them drop around his neck on the nylon strap that holds them together in the back.

Carson rubs her painted lips together. They are so glossy that Ray expects to see her reflection in them too. Then Carson pulls off her sunglasses and snaps them into a bright red case with Armani written across the top of it.

Carson is from a wealthy Atlanta family, and she and William are both lawyers at the same labor law firm. Truth be told, Ray has always resented her a little for wooing William away from his home. Of course Jasper could never compete with Hotlanta, but Ray kind of thought William would eventually settle back down here and get interested in state politics. He's shown zero interest in that since Carson entered the picture.

"I'm traveling all the time, Daddy," he says to Cousin Willy as Ray gets them a Co-Cola and serves up some pickled shrimp that Willy and Justin caught in their sweet spot the other day. The sweet spot is some bend in a creek off the Edisto River, but those two will never divulge the exact location, not even to Ray.

Carson puts her hand on the back of Ray's tall and handsome son as he puffs up his chest and continues, "Just last week I was in San Francisco and Seattle, and then another associate and I stopped by Las Vegas for two nights on our way home. Our wives flew out to meet us, and I won twelve hundred bucks over the weekend. Can you believe it?"

"Sounds like you're livin' mighty high on the hog, Son," Willy says.

"It's not too bad." William punches his dad on the shoulder before silencing the beep coming from his cell phone. His eyes narrow as he studies the number, then slips the phone into the back pocket of his corduroy pants.

"You get work calls on a Saturday?" Ray asks.

Carson chuckles and nods. "Yeah," she says. "We do."

Now I tell you one thing, Ray thinks, *I never would have said "yeah" to my mother-in-law. Mama didn't teach me all I needed to know about etiquette, but I certainly knew enough to include my "ma'am" and "sir" with my "yes" and "no," and I answered my elders that way until they met the grave. Carson is from a nice family and ought to know better.*

Just then they all hear a large *thwomp* from the edge of Round-O Creek, and Tuxedo runs onto the dock and barks at the swirling water.

"Get back here, boy!" Willy hollers harshly down at him.

"Look at the size of that thing," William says, pointing to the water, where two bulbous eyes and a large, square snout surface.

"Uh!" Carson says, grabbing William by the arm. "What is that?"

As the pointed knobs of the back and the tail surface, she shrieks and covers her mouth.

"It's just a gator, honey," he says patting her.

Justin and Willy laugh as Tuxedo runs up onto the back deck and growls.

"An *alligator*?" she says.

"Heck, yeah," Justin says. "You mean you haven't ever seen one?"

He looks into her dark green eyes as if she were quite a mystery.

"Um, *no*," she says. She shakes her head in what seems to be a cross between disgust and disbelief.

"They don't have those in Buckhead, Justin," Cousin Willy says, "except in the handbag section of the department stores."

"What's he *doing* here?" Carson says.

"Oh, they come in and out of here from time to time," Willy says. "There's an overpopulation of them right now, and they're looking for food."

"He probably smells the hog," Ray says.

"Yep," Willy says. "He wants an invite to Ray's party, but he's not going to get one."

"What are you going to do about him?" Carson says.

"Eh, we'll give him a few days to get out of here." He flashes a smile. "If he doesn't, then we'll go in after him."

"Tell William about last week's hunt," Justin says as he bounces on the balls of his feet.

"Yeah," William says. "You said you had a story for me."

"Well." Willy glances back at Ray, and she nods because she thinks Carson can handle the wildlife story.

"I shot a beautiful buck last week from twelve," Willy says.

"What's twelve?" Carson asks. She's not taking her eye off the gator, who remains motionless in the center between their dock and the salt marsh on the other side of the creek.

A blue heron lands for a moment on the edge of the water, but it quickly takes flight when the gator turns ever so slightly in its direction.

"That's one of the deer stands on Dr. Prescott's hunting property," William says, as he puts his wide hands around the back of her neck and gives her a little massage.

"It's the one built in a tree overlooking a tidal creek that feeds into the Edisto River."

"That's right," Willy says, and Ray can tell he's proud that William remembers, even though he hasn't been hunting with his daddy in close to three years now.

"Anyhow it was the start of the rut season, and I spotted a nice-sized doe walking out at dusk, and she was followed by a beautiful buck with a nice-sized rack."

Willy spreads out his arms wide to indicate the size.

"A ten point," Justin adds. "At least 150 pounds."

"Man," William says. "So is the rack at the taxidermist?"

"Ooh," Carson says, squinting her carefully plucked eyebrows.

"Nope," Justin knocks William on the elbow. "*Listen.*"

"Okay, so I had a nice clean shot at his broad side, and I hit him smack in the shoulder, as far as I could tell."

Carson puts her face into William's chest, but Willy is too excited to stop now.

"Anyhow, the doe took off into the woods, and the buck had enough in him to dart across the creek to the other side of the bank, where he collapsed on an oyster bank."

"So what did you do?" William asks.

"Well, I put on my waders and took one step into the creek to retrieve her when a gator—must of been about a nine-footer—skulked up onto the bank and grabbed the buck's hind legs and dragged him down into the water."

"No way!" William says, his eyes lighting up.

Carson covers up her ears and frowns.

"Yep," Justin nods right behind Willy.

"It was unbelievable," Willy says. "Darnedest thing I'd ever seen."

"I'm sure glad he didn't cross that river," Ray says. "If that gator was big enough to take that deer, who knows what he could have done to your father?"

"Eh." Willy waves Ray away. He's taken care of a few nuisance alligators in his time, and he doesn't seem to fear them.

"We could go wrestle that one down right now, Uncle," Justin says, rubbing his hands together, "before he gets Aunt Ray's hog."

Willy makes a side-angled glance at William and winks.

"Want to, Son?"

"What?" Carson uncovers her ears. "You mean go into the creek and get that huge reptile?"

"Sure," Cousin Willy says.

Carson pinches William's back and says to her father-in-law, "Are you insane?"

"Carson," William says, as he tugs on a strand of her smooth, golden hair. "Daddy's been catching alligators most of his life."

She whispers something in his ear; then William shakes his head. "Better not, Daddy."

"I agree," Ray says, patting Carson on her back. "I want y'all in one piece for my party, and that gator wouldn't think of rankling a yard full of people for a bite of barbeque."

"C'mon, Uncle," Justin says. "I'm ready to get my rope and go."

"The girls are right," Willy says. "We'll get him next week if he doesn't move on."

Then Willy turns to his son and his nephew. "Let's check the pig," he says, and they follow him out to the charcoal pit, where he lifts the lid and turns the hog over so it's upside down.

"Good grief," Carson says, looking at the spectacle. "This is too much for me, Mrs. Montgomery. Let's go shopping for your birthday."

"Okay, darlin'," Ray says, a little perplexed by the woman's fear and a little concerned about her hold over William.

Hunting used to be her son's out-and-out passion. He used to drive for hours from college to hunt down here, but ever since they sent him off to that expensive law school in Atlanta, he doesn't do that anymore. Ray has always been thankful that Justin has Cousin Willy for his father figure, but now she's glad that Cousin Willy has Justin. She can't imagine Justin ever leaving town, and they'll likely have a good time together fishing and hunting for years to come.

An hour later Ray and Carson are at a new store on King Street where Annie's Boutique used to be. A stylish but bohemian-looking lady Ray's age practically coerces her into trying on a brown and orange cotton pants outfit with small splotches of turquoise tie-dye designs all around it and a large necklace made up of rectangular turquoise stones. Ray feels a little strange in it, but she takes Carson's lead since she's the gift giver.

"C'mon, Mrs. Montgomery," she says. "Don't you want something that doesn't scream 'Talbots' for a change?"

What's wrong with Talbots? Ray wonders.

She turns back to the three-way mirror. She suspects that she looks a little like a gypsy past her prime, but she hopes that there is some style to this getup that she can't quite discern. Some message that says "a young and vibrant fifty-five." *That's the problem when you're my age—when you try something trendy, it's hard to gauge if you look absurd or admiringly fresh.*

As Ray picks up the price tag, she nearly falls over. The skirt alone is $260.00, and the top is $145.00. Who knows what the necklace costs?

"Don't look at that," Carson says, gently pulling the tag out of Ray's hand. "It's great on you. And William and I want to get you something nice."

So Ray has nothing to do but trust her daughter-in-law's chic sensibilities, and before she's buttoned her jacket Carson has charged the whole thing to her platinum card. The sales lady hangs the get-up and drapes it with a silver plastic bag that shimmers in the sunlight as they walk across King Street to the parking garage.

Then they head back to Jasper and over to Sylvia Crenshaw's beauty salon to get Ray's hair done. Ray doesn't care what Hilda says—she is *not* paying a hundred dollars in Charleston every time she needs a new do just to avoid Trudi Crenshaw. And as soon as she gets the nerve, she's calling to cancel her next appointment with Dr. Arhundati and head back to Angus for her menopausal medical needs. *Hormone replacement therapy, here I come!* she thinks. *Oh, I can't wait!*

"Wanna get a manicure?" Ray says to Carson, who turns her nose up at the outdated *Ladies' Home Journal* magazines on Sylvia's coffee table. Trudi waves at Ray and motions Carson over.

"Okay," Carson sighs. "Do you do French?" she asks Trudi.

"Yes ma'am." Trudi repositions her hips in the pink round seat.

Ray nods and waves a thank-you to her, and she smiles back as if to say, "This town is too small to be enemies."

Ray is relieved to be back in the care of someone who understands her hair and knows how to make it do. "I've missed you, Sylvia."

"Me too." Sylvia fusses with Ray's bangs. "Fill me in on everything. I hear Priscilla has a new man who's a friend of Little Hilda's."

"That's right." Ray is thankful to be able to gush about how Priscilla and Donovan have been seeing each other quite regularly these last few months since Little Hilda's wedding. "I can't help but keep my fingers crossed about it."

Then she thinks of her last conversation with Pris a few days ago. Poop 2—that daredevil, J.K. Neely—has not liked her relationship with Donovan one bit, and he keeps calling her and writing her these mournful love letters that describe in graphic detail how strongly his heart aches for her.

"Don't respond, Pris," Ray said to her the other day when she called to read her one.

"I won't, Mama," she said. "But you have to admit, his letters are sort of sweet in a bizarre kind of way."

"Bizarre is not what you want for a lifetime," Ray said to her.

"I know," she said. "Well, Donovan is picking me up for a pops concert on the Mall, so I better get ready."

"Have fun!" Ray said, trying to keep a lid on her excitement.

"Oh, I hope this one works out, Sylvia," she says as Sylvia pumps her foot at the base of the chair and lifts Ray up.

"Sounds like it will," she says. "And if it does, you know I want an invite to the best wedding Jasper will ever feast their eyes on."

It will be grand, Ray thinks as she stares back at herself in the mirror while Sylvia works her hair with a comb. She can almost smell the gardenias in Priscilla's bouquet and pinned across the lapel of Donovan's white jacket. If she has her way, it will be a May wedding. *Lord, let it be,* she says as her heart pounds around her chest like a trapped bird. *Please, oh please, let this one turn out the way I want it to.*

"So what would you like for your birthday?" Sylvia asks Ray as she takes a hunk of hair from the back of her head and clamps it with a hot pink clip. She picks at the strands beneath it and adds, "Other than Priscilla to marry that nice young buck?"

"Oh, I don't need a thing," Ray says.

Then Sylvia leans in with a concerned look and whispers in Ray's ear, "Honey, you've got a few spots back here. Did you know about that?"

Ray's eyes open wide and she examines herself in the mirror. "What do you mean?"

"A few bald spots." Sylvia discreetly holds up a hand mirror and shows Ray the two bare places in the back of her head. Her scalp looks as pale as can be with all of that black hair around it.

Ray shakes her head in disbelief. "Put that away," she says to Sylvia, who puts it down immediately and begins resuming the cut.

Ray feels the familiar flash of heat coming on. This one starts in the top of her head where Sylvia is tugging and clipping, and it works its way down to the pit of her stomach. How could she have missed this?

"Need some water?" Sylvia says.

Ray nods her head.

Sylvia pulls a water bottle out of the fridge near her station and when she hands it to Ray she whispers, "It's perfectly normal at our age." Then she nods toward the manicure station and says, "My sister Trudi has them, and so did our daddy. It tends to run in the family. Was your daddy bald?"

"Oh," Ray says. "He died when I was very young, so I don't know."

"Well," Sylvia says as she teases a large clump of hair on top and says, "It's easy to cover up for now with the rest of your hair and a little hairspray, but I can find out what Trudi does about hers. She takes some kind of women's Rogaine or something. I'll let you know next week."

"Thank you, Sylvia," Ray says. She puts her fingers up to the back of her head and feels her scalp. Sylvia pulls Ray's hand gently away and says, "Don't give it another thought. I'll cover it up good for tonight."

This menopause is a nightmare, Ray thinks. She's got hair popping up in places she doesn't want it to, and she's losing it in places she desperately needs it. It's like her body is against her. Snuffing out her womanhood before she has time to blink.

With a new hairdo and a fresh manicure, Ray and Carson race home. Ray changes into her new outfit, comes down the stairs, and vamps for her boys. "Here it is."

The outfit is so unlike her, but Cousin Willy never seems to have an opinion about clothes and he says in earnest, "It's nice. Real nice."

"And different," Justin adds. "All that brown and orange reminds me of camouflage."

Ray smiles and shakes her head. "Camouflage? Is hunting all you ever think about?"

"Nope," he says as Cousin Willy hands him a stick of summer sausage to slice. "I think about fishing too."

She flaps her hands at them.

"You've got to come fishing with us sometime, Ray," Cousin Willy says. "We'll blindfold you on the way, of course."

Justin laughs. Ray doesn't know if Willy is kidding or not, and she can tell by the funny way Justin is tilting his head that he doesn't know either.

Miss C. is in the backyard greeting everyone with a cone-shaped birthday hat and several birthday blowers in her concrete basket. She looks like a beauty pageant contestant with a red sash tied across one shoulder and down to the opposite hip that reads, "Ray's Big Day!"

"Hey, hey!" Kitty B. says as she and LeMar come through the back deck and set the birthday cake on the counter. She's made Ray's favorite—her seven-layer coconut cake—and she's also made a peanut butter pie and a bowl of banana pudding.

"Good gracious, Kitty B.," Cousin Willy says. "That all looks so good!"

LeMar nods and pats his head with a handkerchief.

"How are you feeling?" Ray asks him.

"Not too bad," he says as he shakes Willy's and Justin's hands.

Kitty B. whispers to Ray, "The MRI was clear again. Surprise, surprise."

Then Sis comes right through the kitchen door with her seven-layer dip and chips. "Great outfit, Ray."

Ray spins around for the gals. "Can I can pull it off?"

"Uh-huh," Kitty B. says. "Where did you get it?"

"Carson got it for me today in Charleston," she says, and just then her son and daughter-in-law come down the stairs and into the kitchen looking like the most handsome couple you ever saw.

William sports olive pants and a white oxford shirt with his initials on the chest pocket, and Carson is in fancy blue jeans and a silky brown poncho with lots of tassels. She's got on these pointed high heels that will sink right into the soft ground as soon as she steps foot in the backyard. Now Ray envisions Carson with her heel stuck in the mud in the barbeque buffet line. She hopes she won't sprain her ankle, but she doesn't feel like it's her place to tell her to change shoes.

"Well, who do we have here?" Kitty B. says as she runs to embrace them.

"Don't y'all look wonderful," Sis says, following behind her.

"Indeed," LeMar says, putting his hanky back in his pocket and shaking William's hand.

Cousin Willy leads everyone through the deck and into the backyard to the beverage table, where he's got cans of beer in barrels and cups of iced tea so sweet it will curl your hair.

When the pack is outside chatting, Rev. Capers shows up with a nice bottle of wine. Willy has hired his favorite bluegrass band, Three-Legged Pig, from Columbia and they've set up on a little stage he built by the edge of the creek. Kitty B. has brought her dogs, and Justin lets Tuxedo out, and they sniff around the yard together. Then Trudi and Angus show up, and Sylvia and her boyfriend Bubber, and R.L. and Mayor Whaley and Opal Dowdy and Cricket and Tommy and the rest of the friends and family on the list.

When everyone's gathered together and they're just finishing the blessing, Cousin Willy squeezes her hand. "Will you looky here, Ray?" He nods in the direction of the driveway, where Priscilla and Donovan smile at her behind the white picket fence.

Priscilla waves both arms over her head. "Hi, Mama!"

"Oh, what a surprise!" Ray grabs her cheeks and runs toward them. "When did you get here, sweetheart?"

Priscilla kisses Ray on the cheek, grabs the tips of her elbows. "We just flew in."

Ray squeezes her daughter tightly and then pats Donovan on the back. "Well, come on in, come on in and get yourself a beer."

"Mama, you look fabulous," Priscilla says as Cousin Willy comes over and hugs her tight before giving Donovan a firm handshake.

"Happy birthday, Mrs. Montgomery," Donovan says. His cheeks are rosy and he's just adorable. He's so tailored and clean-cut that it's hard for Ray to imagine he's a Democrat. Anyway, he is just precious in his barn jacket and khaki pants and penny loafers. He's got this short hair parted on the side and these big green eyes with long dark lashes and furry eyebrows.

"Howdy, Sis," William says with Carson standing right behind him.

"One afternoon back in Jasper, and he's already talking like a country boy," Carson jokes. "Better look out, Donovan."

William gives his sister a tight squeeze and says, "Let's dance," and Ray watches as he leads her out to the dance floor and spins her around to the twang of the banjo.

Maybe this trip back home will rekindle William's love for the place where he grew up. Where the air is clear and the light is bright. Where southern hospitality thrives and folks pour all they've got into their social occasions, even such an inconsequential one as her turning fifty-five. It will be such a shame if neither of her children ever moves back home. Makes her wonder if she ever should have sent them off to those fancy, overpriced out-of-state colleges in the first place.

After everyone eats, LeMar takes the microphone from the band and sings "Happy Birthday" to Ray. Then Kitty B. brings out the coconut cake with sparkler candles. After Ray opens what she assumes is the last present, Willy brings out a huge box wrapped in coral and pink stripes with a big white bow.

The band stops and everyone gathers around as Ray gently tears open the paper. At the edge of the box she sees the gray and pointed tip of an antler, and she shrieks and jumps into Justin's arms. Willy opens it the rest of the way, and Ray sees it is the enormous head of a buck mounted on a white-striped wooden panel with a little plaque below his head.

First Deer of the Season
Ray Jones Montgomery
August 15, 2005

Ray doesn't know whether to scowl or weep, though everyone around her claps and cheers.

"Thought we could put it up at the beach house," Willy says.

"Mmm," Ray says. "We'll see about that."

"You won it fair and square, Aunt Ray," Justin says. "You got the first one of the season with the grill of your pretty green car."

Ray laughs as the band starts back up and the guests begin to dance again.

Now no outdoor party is complete—at least in the men's eyes—without some sort of fire that everyone sits around. So Willy and Justin light a small bonfire that they built earlier in the day. Ray and the gals sit around it in the lawn furniture and start telling old stories about the watermelons and the dances and jumping off the old Macon Bridge into the Edisto River.

Capers sits by Sis and chats awhile with her, and just when Kitty B. offers to give her a lift home, he says, "I'll walk you home, Sis."

Sis's eyes glisten in the fire. "Okay," she says.

"All right." Kitty B. tries to keep her cool as Rhetta nips at her ankle. "That's a fine idea!"

As the folks Ray's age begin to say their good-byes, Carson and William amble out on the dock with Donovan and Priscilla, where Justin has set up the Chiminea and started their own fire. Cricket and Tommy join them, and so do Marshall and Katie Rae.

Like grade school children, they move their flashlights around the creek in search of the alligator. The boys chuckle and the girls shriek with fear and delight as the light hits an old stump on the edge of the marsh. Ray loves the sound of their banter as it wafts over the creek and back toward the house.

That night as Ray turns on the television and waits for Cousin Willy to give her a turn in the bathroom, she comes across J.K. Neely on the television as she flips through the channels.

"Look!" she calls to Willy. "It's Poop 2!"

Willy peers around the corner with the toothbrush in his mouth.

"Same old imbecile," he says, and they both watch Poop 2 climb up in some kind of enormous slingshot where he will be pulled back and launched over some muddy lake in Tennessee.

They gawk at him as his cohorts snap the sling and his body is hurled out over the water. He flails his arms and legs in midair for several seconds until he does a belly flop into the lake. Ray is thankful, oh so thankful, that he is launched out of Priscilla's life for good.

Now she pictures the gardenias whose buds are just beginning to form secretly behind the shed as she peers out of the bedroom window and listens to her children chuckling around the bonfires with their significant others. She thinks of Capers walking Sis on home, and she hopes Vangie Dreggs tootled by in her golf cart earlier in the evening as the sound of the bluegrass band and the rising voices surely sent her the message.

There's not a thing in this world that could ruin this moment for Ray. Not a hot flash, not a trip to Dr. Arhundati, not even the fact that her hair is falling out in clumps or that her children live too far away with no plans to return. Sometimes she worries that time is passing by faster than she ever thought it would. Other times she fears she'll wake up one day only to realize she is older and weaker than she ever imagined. Or that her friends will finally see her for the farce she is—a bastard girl, the daughter of a housekeeper, who has no right to be the First Lady of Jasper. But she shoves all of that to the side for tonight. It's a celebration, after all. It's her moment to revel, and she knows she would be a fool not to savor it.

Ray tiptoes to the bathroom and puts her arms around Willy's hips as he swooshes mouthwash around in his puffed cheeks.

"Thank you," she says as she squeezes him tight. "Thank you for a wonderful birthday."

She rests her chin on his soft, bare shoulder and gives him that knowing look in the bathroom mirror. He wipes his mouth and turns to face her, and she leads him to the bed where she turns off the lights, and they quietly make love as the moonlight glistens on Round-O Creek and their grown children talk and laugh around the fire on the dock in their backyard.

The next day, after Ray feeds the kids a hearty breakfast and gets them headed on their way back home, she goes over her notes for a wedding session with the gals that Sis will host in her apartment this afternoon. Time is ticking on Katie Rae and Marshall's wedding, and there is a lot that needs to be pulled together in the next week—namely the ordering of the invitations and the guest list—if they are ever going to make it.

When the doorbell rings, she thinks it's probably no one as usual. These days the testy thing is activated by almost any large truck barreling down the road. Willy has got to fix it! It rings twice more before she realizes someone must really be at the door.

"Hi, Ray," Vangie Dreggs says. She stands there all polished and painted in a white fur vest and cream wool pants, her big white horse teeth grinning. Little Bit is sniffing around Ray's topiary, and Vangie shakes a big box wrapped in shiny silver paper that says "Happy Birthday" across it.

"Hello, Vangie." Ray is shocked at the sight of her.

"Well, I just wanted to drop a little something off for you."

"Thank you," Ray says. She doesn't want to ask her in, but Vangie just stands there, smiling and shifting her weight from side to side, and Ray doesn't see how she can avoid it.

"Can't you come in for a cup of coffee on the piazza?" she says.

"I'd love to," Vangie says. "I hope the party was a grand success." She picks Little Bit up and follows Ray through the dining room to the kitchen. "I'll just put him in the backyard."

"Good," Ray says, and she pours her a cup of coffee.

Little Bit barks all around the yard nipping at Tuxedo's tail in an effort to rouse him as Vangie sits on the porch sipping coffee and asking Ray in detail about the party: who was there, what were the presents, how were the kids, wasn't she surprised. *How does she know so much?* The gall! This woman is a scandal. She can somehow break every rule in the etiquette book and continue on in life. It's obscene.

Ray studies Vangie, her painted lips and her perfectly fixed white hair.

"Now, look, Ray, I want to ask your help with something."

"Oh," Ray says. "What is it?"

"I want you to help me coordinate the Healing Prayer Revival Day. It's going to bless the socks off the community the way it did for me in Houston when I first attended one. It literally changed my whole outlook on life." Vangie claps her hand gently. "Now you are one of the most influential people in town, First Lady, and I think that if you participate, others will follow suit."

What a piece of work. Bringing me a guilt-ridden birthday gift and then goading me into her wacky revival day. Well, Ray's not going to be painted into this corner.

As she opens her mouth to refuse the request, she hears a splash and a yelp and a *thwomp*.

"Little Bit!" Vangie races to the edge of the deck where she sees that a good-sized alligator has her Jack Russell's hindquarter between his jaws. As the gator starts to spin, Vangie runs out into the yard and down into the marsh where she sinks into the pluff mud.

"No!" she cries. "No!"

Cousin Willy comes running around from the driveway. He must have just gotten back from the airport. He bolts in the water and swims toward the gator as Little Bit makes one more yelp before the gator dunks him under. Justin runs out of the shed with a rope that he throws to Willy, who knots it and leaps toward the bubbles coming up from the center of the creek.

A few yards away Ray spots the gator's tail swishing fast on the way toward the other side of the bank. He's gotten away with Little

Bit in his jowls, and he doesn't resurface until an hour later when his eyes pop up near the marsh on the opposite bank as Ray and Willy console Vangie Dreggs, who weeps hysterically on the edge of the creek, pulling at her helmet of hair and rocking her head back and forth in disbelief.

"I'm so sorry," Willy says as he pats her back with his wet hands.

"We really are," Ray hears herself say.

Vangie turns to Ray and looks at her inquisitively; then she throws herself into Ray's arms and hugs her tighter than she's ever been hugged before, her large head resting in the crook of Ray's neck as the new turquoise necklace from Carson digs into her collar bone. "I know y'all are, Ray," she says. "I know y'all are."

THIRTEEN

Hilda

When Hilda peeks out the window by her sewing table, her throat tightens. Angus is parallel parking his car on the street just in front of the wrought iron gates. He hasn't stepped foot in their home in over a year, and she doesn't move a muscle as she watches him carefully unlatch the gate and stride toward the front door.

She quickly drops her cigarette in her teacup and races to the hall mirror to inspect herself. She hasn't put on a drop of makeup today, and she's still in her nightgown and the long, brown silk house robe she put on this morning when she came downstairs to work on a new set of curtains for the breakfast room.

She grabs a tube of old lipstick that she keeps in the antique desk in the foyer and quickly applies it before opening the door.

"Good afternoon, Hilda," Angus says. He's still in his church suit—a gray houndstooth with a green and white striped bow tie.

"Well, hello," she says, stepping to the side to let him by. "Come on in, Doctor."

Her cheeks redden as she feels her heart pound intensely. For a moment she wonders if Angus can actually hear it; then she shakes her head and pulls the sash on her robe tight. She can't believe how worked up she is, but she knows there is a part of her that has imagined, no—more than that—*hoped*, he would come walking back through the door of their home in an effort to make amends.

Yes, she's been chilly to him in public, but surely he knows the reason why. She was devastated when he left, and she desperately misses the life they shared. Even the most mundane details like the sound of his calm voice on the phone with his patients, the smell of his aftershave and the sight of those little bits of Kleenex he tears and puts on his face when he cuts his chin shaving. Most of all, she misses his kindness. He was always looking after her, bandaging her finger when she pricked it with a sewing pin and rubbing her temples gently when her migraines came on.

"May I sit?" he says as they walk into the den that looks out over the back piazza and the salt marsh. The yard man cancelled on her last week, and the pittosporum bushes need a pruning something awful. Shaggy and thick, they cast a gray shadow over the white wrought iron bench in the garden.

"Please." She nods at him. "Would you like some coffee?"

"No, thank you," he says, looking up at her. He motions toward the sofa and takes a seat on the far end. "We need to talk."

Hilda smoothes out her silk robe and takes a seat next to him. Her bony knees knock together beneath the shimmery fabric, and she squeezes them tight in an effort to still them.

"Listen, Hilda," Angus says. "I don't know any other way to say this except to come right out with it."

She nods and tries to smile. She hopes her bare cheeks aren't too shiny, and she wishes she had taken the time to fix her face this morning. Nonetheless, this is the moment she's been waiting for, and she straightens her shoulders and lets her lips relax into a faint grin.

He nods and looks around the den of his old home. He stops for a moment, and she watches his eyes settle on the portrait of Hilda and Little Hilda above the fireplace. In the painting Hilda sits on the white bench in the garden, and Little Hilda stands beside her,

her arm resting on her mother's shoulder. She gave the portrait to Angus for Christmas the year before Little Hilda graduated from high school. She can remember Little Hilda pulling off the sheet above the fireplace and Angus's eyes brimming with tears.

Now Angus looks back at her. "Trudi and I have set a date. We're getting married."

Hilda clears her throat as a wave of heat rushes over her. It starts at the top of her head and works its way down into her neck. Her chest burns as if she has just leaned against the old radiator in the house by the paper mill. She thinks of that radiator from her childhood and how it rattled for two days when her father turned it on after the first freeze of the season. She swallows hard, and she can't find any words.

What a fool she is. What a fool to think this visit was about anything other than his final step away from her. She adjusts her posture, fans herself with her hands. "All right." She nods emphatically. "Thank you for telling me." Then she stands and motions toward the foyer. "Let me see you to the door."

He follows her lead as she escorts him to the foyer. She feels a drop of perspiration roll down her cheek, and she bites the bottom of her painted lips.

"Hilda," he says. "Trudi and are going to do this fast. We've been together for a while, you know."

"Yes," she says, narrowing her eyes. "You must be very ready."

She swings open the door, but he stops it midway and closes it gently back.

"We're getting married in a few weeks—Thanksgiving night, in fact. I want you to know so you won't be shocked when you hear it from the gals."

"Aren't you considerate, Angus," she says. She bites her lip again and closes her eyes in an effort hold back her tears. She's so hot she thinks she might faint.

"There's more," he says. He reaches out and lightly touches her shoulder with his fingertips as if to steady her from a great distance. "Trudi and I have bought a little place on deep water on the north side of Edisto Island, so we won't be living in town anymore. I'm going to retire in a few years, and I thought it was wise to go ahead and settle on a retirement spot."

One blow after another. Several years ago Hilda and Angus chose a plot of land on the south side of Edisto as a spot where they might one day retire. They bought it just before Little Hilda graduated from high school, and they even built a crab dock out over the marsh. The three of them would travel out there on a pretty Sunday afternoon and feast on a picnic at the end of the dock. As Angus and Little Hilda set the crab traps and waited for supper, Hilda would flip through her *Southern Living* magazines and point to the house plans that might work for their spot. She even had the whole thing drawn up by an architect in Charleston—a white clapboard two-story wedge-style plantation house with double piazzas and a red tin roof.

Angus received the lot in the settlement. Hilda got the house in town.

She takes a deep breath and refuses to look Angus in the eye. She can't believe he has no inkling of what she's longed for these last two years and no desire to reconcile with her. She's been holding out for him to come back around. She has prayed to the God she fears— *begged* Him in the black hours of the night. She knew she needed a miracle; it was the only way she could return to the life she loved, their life together. She could not help herself from clinging to the hope of it.

Hilda shakes her head in disbelief. The pinprick of tears burns her eyes, but she wipes them away quickly with the heels of her hand.

"Angus," she says, removing his hand from her shoulder. "You're an idiot to go through with this. To marry that tubby, tacky beauty shop manicurist. It's ridiculous! It's embarrassing! It's—"

"It's right for me," he says. His eyes narrow and he takes her by the elbow this time. She can feel his firm grasp beneath the thin sleeves of her gown, and she flinches before taking a step back.

"Hilda, she's a good woman." She turns and walks toward the den. "She's warm and loving, do you hear me? She's not locked up in some strange world of pain or numbness or whatever it is. And if she ever got that way, I'll bet my right arm she would *do* something about it."

"Get out of my house," Hilda turns around to say. She walks briskly back to the front door and firmly shoves Angus out onto the piazza before slamming the door behind him. She can hear him pacing on the front stoop as she locks the knob and the dead bolt.

"Hilda!" he shouts to the closed door. "There's more I want to say to you."

Her head pounds now. A migraine coming on. She pulls at her hair as the pain creeps across the sides of her skull. The back of her nightgown is soaking wet, and she unfastens her robe as he continues, "This conversation is not over."

Then, as if by instinct, she runs to the dining room and grabs two of the four large square sterling candlesticks that one of the mill executives gave her as a wedding gift decades ago. They are solid and feel heavy in her hands, like dumbbells.

She can hear him clearing his throat and tapping his fingers on the door, and she unlocks it, opens it fast and hurls one of the candlesticks as hard as she can at his shoulder.

"What are you doing?" he says, grabbing the top of his right arm. "That hurt!"

Before he has a chance to step back, she throws the other one. It hits him right above his left eye, and a small gash forms just above his brow.

"What the heck?" He pats his forehead and examines the blood on his hand as she runs back in the dining room and grabs the last two candlesticks.

When he sees her coming, he turns and trots toward his car, holding his hand against his brow.

Now Hilda runs into the front garden, her bare feet slapping the cool, mossy bricks of her walkway. She watches Angus slam his car door and examine his wound in the rearview mirror. He pulls a handkerchief out of his back pocket and presses it against his right eye as Hilda swings open the wrought iron gate and steps directly in front of his car. She bangs on the hood of his sedan with the candlesticks, first the one in her right hand, then the one in the left.

"Hilda!" he screams.

A young family, the Maybanks, happen upon this scene on their walk home from church. Mr. Maybank quickly grabs both of his daughters by the elbow and herds them over to the opposite side of the street as his wife follows closely behind, her sling-back heels clapping against the road.

Hilda continues to bang on the hood of Angus's car with the square silver candlesticks. Her robe falls open and her long white nightgown is damp and clinging to her sides as she delivers one blow after another, leaving deep dents across the smooth, blue surface of his Lincoln sedan.

Angus honks his horn as if to send a warning, then reverses quickly, holding the bloodied handkerchief over his eye. He turns the car around as she lurches forward and makes like she might chase him down the road in her bare feet.

She tries not to look across the street, where the Maybank girls in their pale blue smocked dresses can't help but stop and stare at the drama unfolding on the corner of Third and Rantowles. In fact, two other cars have stopped and pulled over to the opposite side of the road as if this were a show. *The most privileged gal in Jasper coming apart at the seams.*

She can feel them all watching her as she drops the candlesticks in the street, ties her robe tight and walks back through the wrought iron gate and beneath the Lady Banksia rose vines, her chest rising and falling quickly in an effort to catch her breath.

When she gets in the house, she locks and bolts the door, then looks at her sweaty, haggard reflection in the gold gilded mirror in the foyer.

Someone knocks on her door. A male voice says, "Mrs. Prescott? Mrs. Prescott, you all right in there?"

She turns and heads up the stairs as the man continues to knock, and the chatter of the onlookers rises and swells on the street in front of her gate. She locks herself in her bedroom and falls into her unmade bed.

It is true. She stares at the crack in the ceiling above her bed. *I will die alone. I will waste away in this house by myself.* Then she turns and pounds the pillows in the place next to her, before kicking them off her bed.

FOURTEEN

Ray

Ray checks her watch. She's in an after-church meeting about the Healing Prayer Revival Day that Vangie organized, but she would prefer to be having her teeth filed.

She just couldn't say no to Vangie this time, what with a gator on her property devouring Vangie's dog right before her very eyes. It will just be a few months of this nonsense, and then the revival day will be over and done, and perhaps by that point Vangie will have set her sights on another Lowcountry town to sell off or evangelize.

"Now, here's a sample schedule of how we held this day at my old church in Houston," Vangie says as she licks her finger and passes out the stacks of papers to the vestry members.

"First we started with teaching and preaching, then moved to the laying on of hands for those who wanted prayer, and we concluded with the Generational Healing Eucharist."

"The laying on of hands?" Gus Dowdy, the town pharmacist, asks. "What do you mean by that?"

"Well," says Vangie, blinking her big, round eyelids and clapping her hands together once. "That's where we invite folks to come forward for prayer and two or three of us will gather around them, put our hands on them, and pray for whatever their need might be."

Gus nods his head. "They don't start acting funny, do they? Like the folks on TV?"

"Well," says Capers, "I've been to a few of these kinds of things before and the Holy Spirit can manifest itself in a number of ways. It is possible that someone might weep or feel a burning sensation or even rest in the Spirit."

Ray rolls her eyes. She can't understand why Capers would support such outlandish notions. He's from a nice Charleston family, but somewhere along the way she thinks a screw came loose. Rumor has it he was swept up in this whole church *renewal* movement, and now he talks about the Holy Spirit all the time. Sometimes he even claps his hands, closes his eyes, and sways to the hymns in church. And just last Sunday she saw him lifting his hands up to the sky during the "Doxology." It's doggone irreverent. What would Queen Elizabeth I think of all of this?

"Yes!" Vangie reaches across the table to squeeze Capers's hand. "It's true about the resting. That's why I'm going to bring some of my smaller Oriental rugs to put around the front of the church. We don't want anyone to fall down on a hard surface."

"Oh my," says the elderly Mrs. Henrietta Graydon. "I've never seen a thing like that in the Episcopal church."

"Me neither," says Gus. "Sounds kind of Pentecostal to me. You aren't going to have any snakes around, are you?"

Ray can't help but laugh. She loves watching these older folks set Capers and Vangie straight.

Just as Capers opens his Bible to defend the practice of the laying on of hands, Justin comes riding up to the window on his bicycle.

"Aunt Ray," he says, as he cups his hands around his eyes and peers inside. "Come on out. Mrs. Prescott's in trouble."

"Excuse me, y'all," Ray says, and she hurries outside of the parish hall where she meets Justin in the parking lot.

"What happened, son?"

"It's Mrs. Prescott, Aunt Ray. Henry Hamrick says she flipped her lid. She was banging on the Doc's car with some kind of ginormous candlesticks."

"Oh, no." Ray covers her mouth.

"And there was blood too," Justin says. "Drops of it all across the sidewalk."

Ray runs into the sanctuary where Sis is reorganizing the music for the choir. She calls up to the balcony, "Something's happened to Hilda! Come on!"

Sis runs down in her choir robe, and they dash next door to the parish hall kitchen where Kitty B. is packaging up a leftover tray of ladyfingers from the after-church coffee hour. She drops her tray in the sink and follows them.

"I wonder what in the world happened," Kitty B. says as they race down Church Street toward Third.

"Well, we won't know until we ask," Ray says. "Let's get on over there and talk to her."

When they get to Hilda's house there is a handful of onlookers, mostly teenagers, milling about the sidewalk.

"Y'all go on." Ray shoos them away with one flap of the back of her hand. The gals scuttle through the garden toward the door where they take turns banging for twenty minutes. They don't hear a peep out of Hilda.

"I'll be right back." Ray makes two fists and heads through the gates.

She runs home and gets the megaphone that Cousin Willy uses from time to time on the campaign trail. She marches back into Hilda's front garden and yells into the mouthpiece, "Hilda, if you don't come down here right now, I'm going to call the police and have them tear down this front door. Do you hear me?"

For a moment Ray thinks she spots some movement behind the curtains upstairs in Hilda's bedroom, and they wait for several minutes on the front piazza for the door to open.

When it doesn't, Kitty B. plops down on the porch, takes off her heels, and rubs at her swollen feet. Sis takes off her choir robe and joins Kitty B. as Ray paces back and forth, considering their next move.

"Y'all think I should call up again?"

"No," Sis says. "Let's give her a little while."

"Wonder what happened," Kitty B. says, trying to hold back a walrus-sized yawn. "Should we call Angus?"

Just then Ray's cell phone rings, and Cousin Willy is on the other end. She pops off her clip-on pearls and pulls the phone close to her ear. "Where are you?"

"Well, I'm sitting here with Angus in the emergency room in Ravenel. He drove out to the deer stand with a gash the size of my thumb across his forehead and asked me if I would tote him over here."

"Well, what did he say happened?" She looks at the girls, and she can feel the worry lines forming across her forehead.

"He and Trudi have a set a date to get married," Willy says. "He went over to tell Hilda, and she went berserk. Threw a bunch of silver at him and beat on his car."

"Oh, my word," Ray says. "Is he all right?"

"Nothing a few stitches won't take care of."

Ray snaps her phone shut and gives the gals the news in a hushed tone. Sis grabs her mouth and her eyes start to water.

"Poor Hilda," Kitty B. says, shaking her head back and forth so that her gray strings of hair sway this way and that. She leans forward and says in a hushed tone, "I think she always thought he would come back."

Ray shakes her head and studies the black Vaneli pumps she bought at Belk's the last time she was in Charleston. They're scuffed up now from her dash back to the house for the megaphone.

She sits down on the arm of the bench. "I'm worried about her in there. Do y'all think I should get someone over here to get this door open?"

Just as the words come out of her mouth, a piece of Hilda's fine Crane's monogrammed stationery slips out of the mail slot in the front door and lands on the brick floor of the piazza.

Sis jumps up and grabs it. Then she reads it to the others:

"Don't you dare call the police, Ray Montgomery. I'm not dead, and I'm not planning on doing anything else destructive today. However, I will not come out of this house. I won't come out today, I won't come out this year, and I might not come out this *decade*. If you try to get in here by force, you'll regret it. It will be over my dead body. Do you understand?" Sis looks up. "And it's signed H."

Ray shakes her head in frustration as Sis folds the note back. Just who does Hilda thinks she is, threatening her like that? And anyway, how in the world is she going to survive in there?

"Anybody have a pen?" Sis asks.

"What in the world for?" Ray says.

"I'm going to write her back."

"Oh, good." Kitty B. offers a sticky pen she's scrounged up from the bottom of her large, lumpy pocketbook. "I think you should."

"Don't be ridiculous," Ray says, grabbing the pen out of Kitty B.'s hand. She throws the pen on the bricks and runs over to the door and starts banging on it.

"Hilda, open this door right now! I know you're downstairs, and we want to lay our eyes on you."

Ray runs over to the window and peers inside, but Hilda is nowhere to be seen. The inside of the house looks perfectly intact except for the dining room where four long white candles lie haphazardly around the Oriental rug beneath the table.

Ray picks up the megaphone and starts to holler to the upstairs. "Now just what are you going to do? Stay in there forever? How do you plan on surviving? Barbour's Grocery only delivers on Tuesdays now!"

"Wednesdays," Sis whispers.

"Oh, whatever," Ray shouts. "Now stop this foolishness and let us in!"

Sis, who pulled the pen out of the bricks just after Ray threw it down, shows Kitty B. what she wrote on the back side of the note, then she slips it through the mail slot.

"Don't play her stupid game, Sis!" Ray calls through the megaphone. "She's got to grow up and come out. She can't spend another year cooped up in here."

"Ray," Kitty B. says gently. "I think you need to settle down, honey."

"Me too," Sis says, turning to face Ray. "Hilda's had what may be the worst day of her life, and the last thing she needs is for us to shout at her through some megaphone. She needs some time, and if we're her friends, we should give it to her."

Ray rolls her eyes at them both. Then she puts the apparatus back to her mouth. "I'm coming back tomorrow, Hilda. And I expect you to open this durn door!"

"Ray," Sis calmly pulls the megaphone out of her clutches. "Stop that."

Kitty B. nods and neither of them look away when Ray stares them both down.

Ray grabs her forehead. "I don't see how y'all can put up with this dramatic nonsense. I can hardly stand it anymore."

Sis and Kitty B. take Ray lightly by the arms and lead her out of the garden and through the iron gate. As they walk back toward the church, Sis says, "Why don't we call her tonight? She did answer the phone when she went into hiding before. And we can take turns dropping by over the next few days. I think she'll let us in eventually."

"All right," Kitty B. says. "I'll drop by tomorrow on my way to the cookbook meeting. I can drop off something for her to eat too. We can take turns with that. Maybe bring her a little of whatever we're having for supper for the next few days."

Ray doesn't say a word, but she faintly nods in agreement. Hilda is the most selfish, stubborn woman she has ever known, and she can't believe she didn't come down and let them in. They are her best friends.

As they round the corner into the church parking lot, she takes a deep breath and says, "I guess I'll call Little Hilda and tell her what's going on. The Princess of Jasper has locked herself up in her house again, and this time she's not even talking from behind her door."

As Sis and Kitty B. walk to their cars, Ray puts her fist on her hip and says, "Sis?"

"Yes?"

"What did you write on that note to Hilda?"

Sis stops just before she opens the door of her little Toyota and says, "I just wrote, 'We understand.'"

Ray raises her eyebrows as Sis nods and hops into her car.

"Well," she hollers as Sis starts her engine. "Well, I *don't* understand!"

FIFTEEN

Ray

It's been ten days since Hilda locked herself in the house, and no one has heard a peep from her since. Little Hilda and the gals have tried to call her every day, but she has yet to respond. The only note she has written is to Little Hilda and all it said was:

Please understand, sweetheart. I need some time alone. Love, Mama

The day after Hilda went into hiding, Kitty B. made up a schedule and for the next several days, the gals took turns every evening knocking on the door and dropping off a little portion of whatever they were having for dinner. She has yet to answer the door, but she does clean the casserole dishes from the dropped-off meals. They are always waiting in a shopping bag on the bench on the piazza at the crack of dawn the next morning—the only evidence that she's still alive in there.

Today Ray happens to have a doctor's appointment scheduled with Angus.

It's her first time back to see him since her two-year detour to Dr. Arhundati's. His office looks a little different than she remembers. He has new wallpaper—kind of a bright and gaudy tropical print, and there are faux tropical flower arrangements on every table in the waiting room. The worst part is the smell. Some kind of sweet pineapple air fresheners are plugged in a few of the electric sockets, and the stench is thick and nearly unbearable. Ray's got a headache by the time she's finished the first sentence in an old *Time* magazine she unearthed from a pile of *People* and *Us* stacked on the waiting room coffee tables. Where are the *Southern Living*s anyway? Must be Trudi's influence. Hilda would just die if she saw this.

When the nurse shows Ray to the examining room, she is relieved. It's just as she remembers—a simple white and green striped wallpaper, an old burgundy pleather examining table, and a counter lined with various medical instruments as well as jars of tongue depressors, bandages, and lollipops.

Ray remembers taking William here when he jumped off the second-story piazza and broke his arm. That was one awful break. Oh, and then there was the time she accidentally put the ringworm medicine on Priscilla's eczema, and she feared her beautiful daughter might be scarred for life. The small dark splotches didn't leave her arms for months.

There is a quiet tap on the door, and in walks Angus with a large bandage above his eyebrow.

"Hi there, Ray," he says.

Ray sucks her teeth and motions toward his eye. "She got you good, didn't she?"

Angus nods and rubs his forehead. "Yep," he says. "Real good." He leans his elbow on the counter. "Have you heard from her?"

"No. Not a peep. She's gone into hiding again, and I don't know when she'll come out. Won't even answer the phone this time."

He takes out a handkerchief from his back pocket and pats at his forehead.

"I feel for her, Ray," he says. "I tried for years to get through to her, you know?" Ray nods sympathetically as he continues, "But she never made one move toward getting help. And now I've got to get on with my life."

"I know," Ray says. "I understand. She's the most difficult woman I've ever known."

Angus nods and taps his chin with the back of his pen. He stares at some place on the wall behind Ray.

She studies the bandage on his forehead and continues. "I'm trying my best to come up with some way to get her back out of that house. I worry about what will happen to her if she stays in there."

"I do too, Ray," he says, furrowing his brow. "But keep trying. You gals might be the only ones who can force some sense into her. I certainly never could."

He scans the jars neatly arranged on his counter and turns back to her.

"What can I do for you?"

"You can prescribe me some of those heavenly hormones," Ray says. "So I won't lose my mind or melt away with these hot flashes. And yes, I've read about the risks and I don't think they are significant enough to bother me. The benefit outweighs them, my friend."

"All right." He chuckles. "I hear you. And how about those fibroid tumors, are you still suffering?"

"From time to time," she says. "Oh, and my hair is falling out too. Isn't that lovely?" Then she points to the scar on her cheekbone. "And this awful thing doesn't seem like it's going away. Do you think I should see a plastic surgeon about it?"

Angus looks at her scar in the light. "Let's give it another six months, and then we'll see."

He steps back, folds his arms, and smiles at her. "As for the hair, I'll give you the name of the dermatologist in Charleston who can help you. It's not that uncommon. However, if you continue to suffer from the tumors after you're on the HRT for a few months, you may want to consider a hysterectomy."

Ray nods and says, "I will consider it. Maybe after we get through the next wedding season."

Angus shakes his head in agreement, then gives her a quick exam and the little white slip of paper with his signature and sends her on her way.

"Oh, yes!" she murmurs as she drives over to Myrtle's Pharmacy. "Sanity, here I come!"

As Ray exits the pharmacy, Vangie comes scooting up on her golf cart with a client in tow. She's got a picture of Little Bit in an ornate silver frame superglued to her dashboard, and at the bottom of the frame is an inscription:

Little Bit Dreggs
April 20, 1999–October 8, 2005
All creatures great and small. The Lord God made them all.

"Ray," she says, waving her hands. "I've got to fill you in on the meeting. We've got another one this Sunday too."

"Meeting?" Ray thinks. She is surprised Mrs. Graydon and Gus didn't nip that whole revival day in the bud.

"Okay," she says. "I'll try and make it."

As she opens her car door, Vangie speeds up next to her. "How's Hilda?" she says.

Ray looks at the stranger sitting next to Vangie. It's a woman about her age dressed in a white tennis skirt and an orange knit shirt. She's wearing a visor and two diamond stud earrings the size of the raspberries Ray bought at the farmer's market on Edisto last weekend.

Vangie turns to the woman and says, "Just a little small-town drama." She nods toward Ray. "Nothing this gal can't handle."

"I'm Ray Montgomery." She gently extends her hand toward the stranger.

"Well, I'm sorry," Vangie says. "This is Donna Zimmerman. A client from New Jersey."

"Nice to meet you," Ray says.

"In fact," Vangie says, "our next stop is the Allston house across the street from you. A developer has bought that property, and he's going to subdivide the main house into several condominiums and add a second set in the backyard."

Ray feels her jaw drop open. "Condominiums?" she says. "Across the street from me?"

"The demand is high," Vangie says as she inches toward the road. She turns back and calls, "Let me know what happens with Hilda, okay?"

And why is it any of your business? Ray wants to call back, but she wouldn't dare. Not in front of a stranger anyway.

"All right," she says, clutching her brown bag. Then she starts her engine and zooms off before Vangie can say another word.

When she gets home, she pops the little green pills of estrogen and progesterone, and Willy comes bobbing into the kitchen.

"You look good," she says, noting the spring in his step. Just as she is about to tell him the dreadful news about the Allston house across the street, he says, "I'm not as good as you're going to be."

"What happened?" she asks. "Did Hilda come out?"

"Nah," he says. He pulls a can of Co-Cola from the fridge and pops it open before leaning toward her and whispering, "But Priscilla's beau called me at my office today."

Ray's eyes grow wide and she runs over and grabs Willy's shoulders. "He did?"

"Yes ma'am," he says. "Donovan's flying down here next Thursday to meet with me. Wants to *talk* to me about something."

"You don't think—"

"I do," he says. "He also wanted to know if you might be able to do a little shopping with him that afternoon."

"Ring shopping?" she says as she bounces on the balls of her feet.

"We won't know until he gets here," Cousin Willy says. "But I can't imagine another reason he might be calling."

SIXTEEN

Kitty B.

The gals say it's only proper for the groom's family to contact the bride's family after the engagement, but when three weeks go by without so much as a peep from the Benningtons, Kitty B. asks Ray for advice.

"Just pick up the phone and call," Ray says.

Two days later Kitty B. and the gals, minus Hilda, are traveling up Highway 17 to meet Pastor and Mrs. Roscoe Bennington at Christ on the Coast on Sam Rittenburg Boulevard. They're all tastefully dressed in their favorite pantsuits and pearls. Of course Kitty B.'s bow is still taped to her left Ferragamo, and she checks on it every few minutes to make sure it's still intact.

Ray drives, as usual. She can't stand to have anyone else at the wheel. She doesn't even offer the front seat to either of them. She bought a gorgeous yellow orchid for Kitty B. to give to the Benningtons, and she thinks the front passenger seat is the safest place for it.

Kitty B. is irritated to no end. LeMar ought to be with them making this visit—he is the father of the bride, after all—but he claims to have woken up with a rash all over his chest, though he won't even let her see it.

"Of all days, LeMar," she said to him. "I suppose you just want to stay home then?"

"Yes," he said, "I do." Then he closed his bedroom door in her face.

Kitty B. was so mad she didn't even make him his breakfast or a fresh pot of coffee. Instead she dropped three dog bones outside of his bedroom, waddled down the steps, and opened the front door wide to let the dogs in.

"There," she said as she drove down the dirt road and over to Ray's. "Those rascals will keep him busy."

"Do you think this church is in a strip mall?" Ray asks ever so tentatively, as they squint through the window and across the parking lots trying to make out the addresses on the glass doors of the flat-topped shopping complexes.

"Well, I don't see how it can't be." Sis looks back and forth down the four lane road as they pass Skatell's and TJ Maxx.

"Now what did they say it was across from?" Ray glances over her shoulder at Kitty B.

"The Chuck E. Cheese," Kitty B. says as she inspects her chicken scratch on a crumpled recipe card. "It's across from the Chuck E. Cheese and just to the left of the Pet Superstore."

Kitty B. makes a face at Sis, who can't help but let out a giggle. "I know." Kitty B. shakes her head. "How awful do you suppose it's going to be?"

"Let's just hope they don't insist on hosting the wedding," Ray says as she reapplies her dark pink lipstick in the rearview mirror at a traffic light.

"It *has* come up." Kitty B. checks her own lipstick in her compact mirror. "Marshall said he'd love to have the ceremony at his daddy's church, and Katie Rae hasn't suggested otherwise."

Sis pats Kitty B.'s round knee. "Don't fret." Kitty B. puts her hand on top of Sis's and squeezes it tight. Her knuckles whiten and her wedding rings catch the light. She can see clumps of cookie batter caught between the prongs that hold her solitaire in place.

As much as she likes Marshall, sometimes she wonders why all of their children can't find nice All Saints parishioners from Jasper to settle down with. Oh, she's not as bugged about it as Ray is. But she likes the fact that the gals all married men they either grew up with or knew of from a close distance. There was always something to anchor and connect them—either their parents were friends, or they attended the same college, or they were card-carrying members of some other upstanding Episcopal church in the diocese. The more she thinks about how Katie Rae and Marshall met over the Internet, the more uneasy she becomes. *It's peculiar,* she thinks. *If the Internet had been around in my time, the gals might be strewn across the country by now, married to men with different accents and unusual customs. We might be dealing with snowstorms and terrorists and mass transportation and who knows what else? Think of it!*

Right after the Taco Bell, Kitty B. sees the church sign out of the corner of her eye. "There it is," Ray says, turning the car toward a parking lot.

On the left end of the strip mall a brightly lit sign reads, "Christ on the Coast Cathedral." The font reminds Kitty B. of the bubble letters Cricket used to write on her schoolbooks and her backpack and her plastic picture frames. The letters are in lavender, and beside them is an image of a rip curl wave with a bright orange cross rising out of the clouds above it.

Sis squeezes Kitty B.'s hand, and before you know it Ray waves her fingers in front of their wide eyes and rouses the gals out of the car. She leads the way toward the entrance, lifting her pointed chin and looking over her shoulder, reminding Kitty B. of Ray's mantra, "Let's rise above it all, gals."

Shawna Bennington meets them at the entrance, which is an

automatic door like the kind they have at K-Mart and Sally Swine. She steps on the metal foot pad and the door goes flying open.

"Come on in, ladies," she says.

The reception area has two-toned walls that are a shade of grayish lavender and a dark violet. Faux ficus trees with waxy leaves flank a purple pleather sofa, and a faux fern in a plastic gold planter sits on the coffee table. There are glossy black-and-white posters in plastic frames hanging above the sofa and behind the vacant receptionist's desk. One says in bold block letters: "I'm free to choose life or death." The other has an image of a large Band-Aid with a quote in the center: "It was good for me to be afflicted so that I might learn your decrees."

Shawna Bennington's hair is blonde, wiry, and frayed on the ends like she's used the curling iron one too many times. She's wearing snug white pants and a white angora sweater with little gold sequins sewn into star shapes across the neckline. Her middle-aged paunch has gotten the better of her, and in her tight white getup you can see a muffin top that the Colony Bakery would be proud of. She's teetering on the clear acrylic heels of off-white leather boots.

She gives everyone big hugs and offers them all a piece of Doublemint gum while she leans over the purple receptionist counter and pages her husband, who answers his phone, "Pastor here."

"I'm Katie Rae's mama, Shawna," Kitty B. says, reaching out to squeeze her hand. "My husband is not feeling well today, so I thought I'd bring my friends. They're all helping me with the wedding."

"Oh, I'm sorry to hear that," she says as she crumples a stick of Doublemint between her teeth. "I mean the part about your husband."

"Don't be," Kitty B. says. "My husband never feels well." Kitty B.'s feeling a little nervous, and she hopes she doesn't spit out *every* thought that flashes across her mind. She's relieved when Sis comes over and pats her shoulder gently.

Ray looks at Kitty B. like she's got a screw loose, and then Sis interjects. "He's got that awful chronic fatigue syndrome. Are you familiar with it?"

"I am," Shawna says. Her thin glossy lips form a shimmery "O" of concern as she chews her gum. "Marshall has told us all about it, and we've got him on the prayer list here."

"Tell Dwight I need to meet with him about the revival music," a voice booms down the hall.

"Here comes Pastor," Shawna Bennington says, and the gals turn toward the hallway expecting to see a large man that will match his voice and the physique of his handsome son.

Well, wouldn't you know Pastor Bennington is as short as Sis, which is saying something. In fact, if they went back to back, she might have him beat by half an inch.

At first Kitty B. thinks he's talking to himself like a crazy man, but then she sees this metal contraption wound around his left ear, and she realizes it must be some kind of telephone.

"Gotta go," he says, and though he seems to have ended his conversation, he keeps the piece around his ear. How odd.

"Hi there." He puts his hand out to meet Ray, who is the tallest of the three.

Ray steps back and nods in Kitty B.'s direction, and the preacher says to Sis, "You must be Kitty B."

Kitty B.'s still staring at the contraption wrapped around his ear. It reminds her of a *Star Trek* episode Katie Rae made her watch one time. Before she has a chance to correct him, he pulls Sis into a side embrace, kisses her cheek, and says, "We sure love Katie Rae."

Sis pulls back fast and looks over to Kitty B., but Roscoe keeps holding her tight.

Kitty B. walks up so close that she can smell his smell—like Listerine, pencil lead, and aftershave. Beneath his cheeks are small, deep craters where he must have suffered some kind of awful acne as a teenager.

Sis tries to pull away, but he won't loosen his grip. Finally, Kitty B.

reaches out her hand. "I'm Kitty B., Pastor Bennington. And you can sure bet we feel the same way about Marshall."

Roscoe lets go of Sis. "Pardon me," he says. Then he turns to Kitty B. "So you're the wonderful woman who gave birth to the love of my son's life!"

Shawna claps her hands together and smiles Kitty B.'s way, the small, gray piece of chewing gum peeking out from between her molars. Then she nods to her husband, who says, "Sorry for all the confusion, ladies. Let me show y'all around the cathedral since we're going to need a church in a few months."

The Benningtons lead the gals down an officelike hall and then around a corner where four large faux wooden doors with metal handles open into a large amphitheater. A bright purple carpet lines the aisle. The walls are lavender, and the altar is this kind of awful plum mauvish with an acrylic podium and a big baptismal pool where Katie Rae told Kitty B. that folks get dunked quite often. There is a large overhead screen that has the "Christ on the Coast Cathedral" logo lit up in its center and there is the faintest music playing in the background. Kitty B. stops and listens until she identifies the tune. It's that "Shout to the North and the South" song Capers made them sing on their All Saints mountain retreat last year. It's one of the songs that camp folks like to flash pictures of mountaintops and rainbows on a screen alongside the words.

Once Sis told Kitty B. that as a musician she is relatively uninspired by these songs, as they can often be broken down into chords that resemble some old rock or Motown tune. "I much prefer the hymnal," she confided.

To the left of the podium is a smaller stage where it looks like a rock band is set up. There are electric guitars, amplifiers, drums, a keyboard, and more microphones and wires than you can shake a stick at.

"You know we told Marshall and Katie Rae that we'd love to have the wedding here," Pastor Bennington says, opening his stout arms and puffing up his chest as if he's offering them St. Peter's Basilica.

"I heard some mention of that," Kitty B. says, trying to catch her breath. Her mama would be absolutely horrified if she thought Katie Rae might get married in a place like this. Kitty B. can't help but move her eyes back toward Ray, who bristles her back as if she's just stepped barefoot on a pinecone. She walks over to Kitty B., squeezes her wrist in assurance, and says to Roscoe and Shawna in her strongest voice, "Well, we have a lovely and historic Episcopal chapel of ease in Jasper—"

Roscoe clears his throat and Shawna speaks up, "It's just that Roscoe *has* to marry them. He's been looking forward to this day for many years now."

"Mmm hmm," he says as he nods his head and pats the base of his acrylic podium. "We adopted Marshall more than thirty-four years ago this year, and we're more thankful for him than you can ever know."

There is an awkward silence where Kitty B. can't help but hear her own breathing. Her ears are burning as though she's about to lose her balance, and she knows she's obliged to respond.

"I didn't know that," she says. Of course, now it makes all the sense in the world. Marshall doesn't look a thing like Shawna and Roscoe. And his brain for science. He must have come by that from his biological parents.

"Oh, yeah," Roscoe says. "He was born to a young gal in Bald Knob, Arkansas, and her kin attended our old church in Pyatt, and they knew about our troubles conceiving."

"Well, that's a wonderful story," Ray says, smiling her proper albeit slightly frozen smile.

"Indeed." Kitty B. nods her head fast and furiously. She knows it's not all that important where they hold the wedding, but something is rather depressing about having it in an old K-Mart on the side of Highway 17. It lacks some sort of beauty or sacredness. She can't quite put her finger on it, but it just doesn't feel right.

Roscoe examines the tops of his black loafers and says, "There's more to see, ladies. Let's show them the meeting hall, Shawn."

"All right." Shawna rubs Kitty B.'s back. "We think it's perfect for the rehearsal dinner."

The meeting hall is a big blank box next to the sanctuary. It's like a fourth-rate conference room with a black carpet, gray walls, and stains in the ceiling from where the air conditioner must have leaked. There is a small gathering of people in the corner who hold their hands together and bow their heads in prayer.

"Overeaters Anonymous," Shawna whispers, the pop of her gray gum resounding in Kitty B.'s ear. "They meet here on Thursday mornings."

Ray comes over and says to Shawna, "We certainly don't want to disturb them. I think we have the idea, don't you, Kitty B.?"

"Indeed," Kitty B. says.

When they go out into the hall, Roscoe and Shawna invite them over to El Dorado for the Mexican buffet lunch, but Kitty B. declines, citing the need to get home and check on LeMar.

As they say their good-byes, Sis says, "One more question. Do you all happen to have an organ?"

Roscoe winks at Sis. "Naw," he says. "Our services are contemporary. The organ went out with the typewriter, don'tcha think?"

"No, she doesn't, Pastor Bennington," Ray jumps in to say. "Sis is the organist and choirmaster at our historic chapel of ease. In fact, she's played for hundreds of ceremonies. She's quite gifted."

"Oh, my apologies," Roscoe says. He comes over and squeezes Sis's elbow. "We keep forgetting that the whole world hasn't gone contemporary."

"I'll tell you what we do have, though." Shawna points to a little booth that overlooks the sanctuary. "We have our own videographer on staff, and he's agreed to do the whole event—ceremony, reception and all! Isn't that wonderful?"

Kitty B.'s simply too shocked to comment. She and the gals have always talked about the fact that they think the ceremony should *never*, under *any* circumstances be recorded. It's a Holy Sacrament, not some birthday or retirement party. Years ago the All Saints Vestry approved the Wedding Guild's request for a "no video camera" policy during weddings or any other church service.

All she can do is nod and wave good-bye. Shawna tilts her head to study Kitty B. as if she's some kind of a riddle; then she grabs Ray's arm and asks in earnest, "Is Kitty B. hard of hearing?"

When the gals get back in Ray's car, Kitty B. just breaks down. "It's the tackiest place I've ever seen."

"Hold yourself together until we get out of the parking lot," Ray warns, but Kitty B. just can't help it. She plunges right into Sis's lap and weeps like there is no tomorrow as Ray nods to the Benningtons who stand on the threshold of the automatic door and wave.

By the time she sits back up again, Ray pulls into the Krispy Kreme shop and Kitty B. spots the glow of the "Hot Doughnuts Now" sign in the front window. There's not a Krispy Kreme in Jasper, and the gals know that the fresh glazed doughnuts are Kitty B.'s favorite. They order a couple dozen and take their seats by the window as they watch the newly fried rings of dough sizzle in the hot grease before sliding down the conveyer belt into the shower of icing.

"It could be worse," Ray says. "It can always be worse."

"That's true," Sis says. "Remember when Cricket and Tommy were getting married and his daddy wanted to have the rehearsal dinner at the funeral home?"

They all laugh and Ray says, "Yeah, Tommy McFortson kept pointing across the cemetery to the marsh and saying, 'There's not a better view in town.'"

"Well." Kitty B. wipes her bleary eyes. "At least his mama had the sense to talk him out of that, and they had a beautiful dinner at the Country Club of Charleston."

"That's true." Ray nods. "Somehow I don't think the Benningtons are going to be persuaded so easily."

"Me neither." Sis's face softens and she turns to Kitty B. "But let's think about the big picture for a minute, gal. I mean, at least the Benningtons are good people. Decent and well-meaning, don't y'all think?"

They all nod, and Kitty B. takes another bite of her warm, sweet doughnut.

"All right." Ray pulls out her notebook. "We've just got to figure this thing out." She dabs her icing-encrusted fingertips on the paper napkin and says, "Kitty B., you've got to talk to Katie Rae and tell her all of her options. Then she and Marshall will just have to decide. This is their day, and it's really up to them."

Kitty B. shakes her head and says, "I'll try." She hopes Katie Rae has the sense to insist on All Saints.

"Okay, worst-case scenario." Ray leans in toward the center of the table as if the Benningtons are right behind them. "We have the ceremony in the Flying Purple People Eater Church." She spreads her hands out wide and rests them on the table. "Still, the reception at Kitty B.'s will be glorious. We can do the trellis of poinsettias like we wanted. And those twinkling lights on the limbs of all of the live oak trees. Oh, and a big tent with a chandelier or those wrought iron lanterns that R.L. bought last year at that auction in Atlanta. We can have a beautiful pomander of mistletoe dangling from each lantern.

"I tell you, Kitty B., by the time folks drive out to Cottage Island, that awful *cathedral* will be a distant memory, and they'll leave with an image of a crisp and beautiful winter evening under the stars."

"My place is a wreck, though, y'all," Kitty B. says, reaching for a second doughnut. "You have to admit that. The house is sagging, the yard is awful, and with LeMar's medical bills, it will be all we can do to pay for the reception. I'm never going to get the place together in time."

"Hush, Kitty B.," Ray says. "We're going to find a way to make this work. We'll pitch in and get this thing done, won't we, Sis?"

"Yes, we will," Sis squeezes Kitty B.'s hand. "It always comes together."

When they pile back in the car, Ray points to the orchid she meant for Kitty B. to give to the Benningtons.

"Don't worry about it," Kitty B. says. "It's my turn to take something to Hilda's tonight, and she needs it more than they do."

As they drive down Highway 17, Kitty B. can't imagine how the wedding is going to come together in the next six weeks. She dreads telling LeMar about the purple church with all of its guitars and microphones and speakers. In fact, she wishes she didn't even have to go home and face him.

Out of the corner of her eye she spots a sign in one of the strip malls with a profile of a poodle. It reads, "Lowcountry Canine Training School" above the poodle and then in small cursive letters beneath his paws, "Sign up to be a dog trainer today."

Kitty B. sighs. Some days she feels like she slipped off track some time ago. That maybe she ought to be somewhere else doing something else, but she suspects there is no way to get back to that place now.

She hears Ray cluck as they pass by the outlet mall going up outside of Ravenel.

"You see that?" Ray says. "That's only twenty miles away from us. I tell you gals, change is creeping down this highway, and it scares me to death."

"Don't they have a Liz Claiborne in there?" Sis says.

"Sis!" Ray says as she eyes her in the rearview mirror. "Yes, they do. And that's the whole problem, don't you see?"

Sis giggles and slaps the air with her little hand. "Not all change is bad, Ray."

Sis looks to Kitty B. "Don't you agree?"

When they all get back to Ray's, Kitty B. gets her own car and drives on around to Hilda's house and walks the orchid up to the door and knocks.

She stands at the door for several minutes before calling, "I've got one of your favorites for you, Hilda. An orchid. One of those yellow ones with the chocolate spots. And some ham biscuits that keep well in the freezer."

She rests her ear against the door, but she doesn't hear a sound. The last thing in the world she wants to do is get in her car and drive home to LeMar, who will be sitting in his bed waiting for her to fix him supper and fill him in on all the details of the Benningtons and their church.

I don't blame you, Hilda. She peers into the peephole. *Right now I wish I could hide out in there too.*

SEVENTEEN

Sis

Two days ago the Reverend Capers Campbell walked right over to Sis while she was practicing on Ina and said, "May I take you to dinner on Saturday?"

"Why yes," she said, surprised. She could feel her cheeks turn pink, and he smiled and said, "I'll try to get a reservation at Suzanne's."

"Great!"

I'm nervous, Sis writes to Hilda this afternoon when she picks up her casserole dish and drops off a few blueberry muffins and a carton of milk. *I have a date with Capers tonight.*

Just as she walks back to her car, she hears the faintest footfalls behind the door, and she wonders if Hilda came down the stairs to get her note. She waits for a while for the door to open, but it doesn't. Sis imagines Hilda just beyond the door, reading her note. She walks back onto the piazza and says. "I'll let you know how it goes, Hilda. I'll write you as soon as I get back." Then she turns and heads toward the gate, checking back every few seconds to see if the door opens.

An hour later Ray and Kitty B. meet at Sis's house to go over the guest list for Katie Rae's wedding for the umpteenth time, but in truth Sis knows they're here to give her advice and help her pick out an outfit.

"So did he really ask you out in the sanctuary?" Kitty B. asks.

"Hush, Kitty B.," Ray squints her eyes as if the sun is in them. "Don't highlight that part."

"Why not?" Sis looks up from over her new stylish black bifocals and winks.

"Yeah," Kitty B. says, reaching for one of the miniature pecan tarts she's brought for a wedding taste test. "That's my favorite part. It makes it all seem *forbidden* or something." She bites down on the tart, and it takes her several chews to get her teeth loose. Then she points to the list and says, "Now what am I going to do, y'all? The Benningtons have added forty-five additional people to the groom's list."

"What?" Ray says. "They are already way over their limit with the one hundred and fifteen names they submitted last week! I'm sorry, but they're just out of control. Katie Rae needs to instruct Marshall to call them down on this."

"I know." Kitty B. uncovers another tray of potential sweets: mint-covered pecans, lemon squares, and chocolate-dipped macaroons. "It's just that he feels obligated to include certain members of his congregation."

"If you ask me"—Ray straightens her shoulders—"I think the Benningtons are taking advantage of the situation. They must think just because y'all live on the water and own a few antiques that this will be no skin off your back."

"Well." Kitty B. wipes the powdered sugar from her fingertips on the sides of her Lowcountry Manna apron. "LeMar told me he thinks we should just let it go."

"Really?" Sis cocks her head and raises her eyebrows. "LeMar's not concerned?"

"He's not this week," Kitty B. says. "In fact, ever since Vangie sent her painters and the landscape folk over to the house to fix things up, he's gotten a new spring in his step. He's gone out to his old baby bud rosebush and started pruning it, and he's even been meeting with a composer at the College of Charleston who is writing an original piece for him to sing at the wedding."

"That's wonderful!" Sis bobs her chin up and down. "Maybe this is just what he needed to jumpstart himself."

"I sure hope so, Sis," Kitty B. says, folding over the new additions to the groom's list. "Either that or he's become a full-blown schizophrenic."

The gals chuckle and Kitty B. declares, "Let's forget about the guest list for now. I'd rather focus on Sis and getting her ready for her date."

"Gals." Sis can't help but shake her head at them. "Y'all act like we're still in high school."

"Don't be critical." Ray pulls up the Saks shopping bag at her feet. "Let's have some fun and pick out what you're going to wear."

"You practically look like you could be in high school, Sis," Kitty B. says. "It's true. Isn't it, Ray?"

Ray nods and Kitty B. continues, "You look like you're in your early thirties at the most, Sis. I don't see how you do it."

Sis waves them off. "Hush." But they pull her up from the chair and walk her into the closet, where they sort through her options.

"I do wish Hilda were here," Ray says. "She's the one who really knows how to put things together, but I brought this in case you might want to try it." Ray pulls out the turquoise necklace that Carson bought her for her birthday. Sis feels the weight of it in her hand and says, "I'm afraid I'll look like a crooked-neck egret in this. I don't think I have the strength to hold my head up with it on."

Ray nods. "I'm not sure I like it either, but my daughter-in-law said it was very stylish."

"Of course, anything I have would look like a tent on you." Kitty B. points to her wide hips. "And everything I own is at least twenty years old. But I did pull out this red blouse from Katie Rae's drawer. I thought the color would look great on you."

"Y'all are sweet," Sis says. She knows they can't help but get excited about a romantic prospect. It's just the way they are. "But I think I'd better wear something I'm comfortable in." She tries on a few of her outfits and finally, they settle on a brown silk blouse Sis bought from Ann Taylor last year with a little lace around the trim and a pair of camel-colored wool pants and some dark suede flats with little square buckles on top.

"Are you going over to Sylvia's?" Ray whispers after they approve Sis's choice.

"No need to whisper," Kitty B. says. "Hilda is way out of earshot now."

"No, I'm not going to get my hair done." Sis looks at the clock ticking above her stove. "And it's not because I'm boycotting Sylvia." She looks in the mirror and back to Ray, "I think my hair looks fine the way it is. I'm just going to give it a little washing and go."

"That's a fine idea." Kitty B. turns to Ray. "Part of Sis's charm is how natural she appears. Now let's get out of here and give her some time to get ready."

"Table for two at Suzanne's," Capers says with a side-angled grin as he closes Sis into the car of his Mercury sedan.

Suzanne's is a wonderful little restaurant on the marsh between Jasper and Cottage Island. The chef used to be a sailor and his ship, *Suzanne*, broke down off the coast. He decided to cast his anchor in the Ashepoo River while he attended Johnson and Wales's cooking school where he learned how to create the most scrumptious "season-inspired" lowcountry cuisine. The restaurant was featured in *Southern Living* a few years ago, and since then folks from Savannah and Charleston drive the full hour to dine there. It's difficult to get a reservation without a few weeks' notice.

"How'd you manage that?" Sis cups her hands together, but he has already closed the door and he can't hear her as he makes his way around the front of the car to the driver's side.

Funny how when you are on a date for the first time in a long time, your senses are as heightened like when you were a child. The car smells like air freshener and mint and something a little musty too. Sis tries to place it as Capers pulls out of the parking lot and onto Main Street. She can feel the tug of the engine switching gears as they head out of town and toward the island.

When they arrive, Sis and Capers learn that it will be a thirty-minute wait until their table is ready, so they get two glasses of the house red wine and sit out on the dock behind the restaurant where Capers spots two osprey and one bald eagle making its way toward its roost. When he points at the eagle he lets his right arm fall down across Sis's shoulder, but his arm feels stiff. He doesn't pull her close, so she won't let herself soften and lean in. They sit in this awkward, uptight position for at least ten minutes until the host calls to them from the porch with two menus in his hand.

Though the sun hasn't completely set, it is very dark inside the restaurant. The walls are made of a deep brown wood, and the tables are draped in a burgundy cloth. The only light is the green legal lamp above the host's station and the small candles burning in a miniature fishbowl on each table.

"So, Sis," Capers says after he orders an appetizer of smoked wahoo and beer-battered fried shrimp with a Tabasco dipping sauce. He stops to straighten out the bread basket and the salt and pepper shaker, and then he leans in toward her. The candlelight dances on his chin, and Sis worries that he might suddenly feel the heat of it.

"I'm sorry about finking out on you at the Prescott wedding a few months back." He looks down at the fishbowl and becomes mesmerized by the candlelight for a moment.

Sis smiles and feels herself blush, but it's too dark in the restaurant for him to notice. "That's all right," she says. "That champagne can sneak up on you."

"Really," he says. "I don't take a drink too often, and when I do it goes straight to my head."

"I understand." She leans over and pats his hand.

"Well, I've been here at All Saints for a little over a year now," he says, "and I'm finally starting to get my bearings and understand the church community."

"It's a nice fit." She gives a reassuring nod. "You seem to really know who you're preaching to. And I think you challenge people in a good way."

"It's a good place." He shrugs his shoulders and says, "With Ray Montgomery as the senior warden, I have the sense that I don't have to worry with any of the logistical details."

"Oh, that's right," Sis says. "She's got you covered. She could run All Saints with her eyes closed."

"Yeah," he nods. "And then there's Vangie with all her big ideas. I know she rubs folks a little the wrong way, but I think her heart is in the right place."

"Oh, me too." Sis smoothes out a wrinkle in the center of the tablecloth. "She'll learn to tone it down."

"Anyhow, all that help frees me up to focus on the ministry," he says. "And the preaching."

"Good," she says as his soft, green eyes search hers.

"You know what else I'm thankful for?" He leans in again so that she's sure the flame is going to burn his skin.

"Tell me." She nudges the fishbowl with the candle to the side.

"How you make that organ come to life." He leans back and rubs his chin, and she feels her cheeks redden again.

Then the appetizer arrives, and the waiter fills up their wine glasses. After they sample the shrimp and wahoo, Sis says, "Well, I'm guessing you know my story."

"Yes, I do." He reaches out and pats her hand quickly and somewhat mechanically. "I'm so sorry about your loss."

"It was a *long* time ago," she says. "Over thirty years. Ancient history, I suppose."

"Loss is loss," he says. "I've been in this line of work long enough to know that time doesn't heal all wounds. In fact, it often makes them worse."

"It was awful." Sis looks up at him. The light catches the edges of his straight, square teeth as he winces with concern.

"I sure loved Fitz, but I think it was kind of a young love, and I don't know what it would have been like over time. I'm sure I romanticize it in my mind. Anyway, I always thought I would find someone else."

"And?"

"Well, much to my surprise and disappointment, it just never seemed to happen."

"I'm sorry."

Sis takes a gulp of her wine and waves his sympathy away. "Enough about my old story. I'm sure everyone and their brother has told you about me. What about your story? Why didn't you ever marry?"

"I've never been real good at that kind of relationship," he says, drumming his thumbs on the side of the table. "I blame that mostly on my home life when I was a child."

"Yeah, that'll do it to you," she says. "I think that's what did it to Hilda, but I'll never know for sure."

"I've tried to call on Hilda, but I can't seem to get a response." Capers scratches his ear.

"No one can," Sis says. "You know she didn't leave her house for twenty months when Angus first left, and now that he's getting married, I'm not sure she'll ever come out again."

"Please tell me what I can do for her," he says.

"I honestly don't know," Sis says. "But I'll tell you if something comes to mind."

Then Sis reaches over and squeezes Capers's elbow. She wants to know more about his past, so she pushes. "Weren't you ever in love?"

"I did manage to have a girlfriend, once." He scrapes the crumbs off the table with his other hand. "It was that time when college was about to end and the girls were on the hunt to find a mate. I stumbled into this lovely girl from Savannah. Was engaged to her," he says. "Jane Anne Blakely, my late-college sweetheart. We'd made plans for me to attend MBA school at UNC so I could get enough education to help run her father's shipping business."

"What happened?"

"I got the call to ministry," he says, as he wipes his damp brow with the dark napkin.

"How did it come?" A kind of obsessive curiosity comes over Sis that she can't quite conceal. She's been going to church all her life, but she's never tired of stories about how one receives a call to ministry. It's such a mysterious and thrilling thing to have happen. To have God single you out and set your life aside for full-time service.

"I was helping with the youth group at the church I attended in college. I was taking them up to the mountains on a retreat weekend. It was a literal mountaintop experience at the Kanuga Retreat Center. I was looking at the cross at the foot of the lake early one morning, and the mist was rising up from the water in such a way that I just knew what I had to do."

"Wow," Sis says as the waiter delivers their entrées. The scallops and grits with a mousseline sauce for her, and the roasted quail with a Madeira gravy for Capers. "I love those stories."

Capers bows his head and says a short but lovely prayer and then nods warmly in her direction.

"So I'm guessing your college sweetheart wasn't too keen on the idea?"

He takes a bite of quail, relishes it for a moment, then says, "I prayed and prayed she'd go along with it, and she seemed to at first. She always seemed intrigued by the fact that I went to church and helped out with the youth group, but eventually she pulled away."

"Oh," Sis says, narrowing her eyes. "That's awful."

"I mean, I certainly think her father influenced her. And then the bishop selected Nashotah House for my seminary."

"That one up in Nebraska?"

"Wisconsin," he says shaking his head. "I think it was the idea of three years in that part of the country that really put her over the edge. She hated cold weather. Anyhow, one Sunday morning when I was walking home from church, she pulled up beside me in her little Chevrolet convertible, handed me the ring back, and that was that."

"I'm so sorry, Capers." Sis can't help but shake her head with sympathy.

He takes another generous sip of wine and looks down at his plate. "I'm not, Sis. I'm right where I'm supposed to be, and in the end I think the good Lord was protecting me from a relationship that would have always been pulling me away from what I was called to do."

When they get back in the car, Capers puts on an old Catalinas CD and says, "Wanna try shagging at the seawall again?"

"Okay," she says. He reaches his arm across the seat and puts his hand on top of hers. It feels slightly cool and damp and for some reason her hand wants to wriggle out from under it.

When they pull up to the seawall, Capers turns up his CD player too loud, and it cracks for a moment and then has a kind of fuzzy sound for the rest of the evening. He puts his hand on her back and then takes it away again. She can't help but think of Fitz and the way he set his hand firmly on the small of her back with such certainty.

Is this what time does to men? Makes them uncertain? She tries to picture her life with Fitz as it might have been. Would he still have his hand firmly above her hips? Would she still be fending him off in the car as he became frisky?

She usually tries to stop herself from this fantasy. It's like reopening a scar and seeing that there are places beneath the top layers that still haven't sealed over. They would have been married for thirty-four years by now. Her guess is that they would have had more children than anyone. "I want four at least," Fitz said once when he'd come over to help Sis babysit the McMillan clan. He would wrestle Dan and Betty down to the ground and tickle them until they begged for mercy. "Me too," she said as she held the baby, Lucy, on her lap. Sis was an only child, and she didn't want to wish that loneliness on anyone.

She recalls all of this as Capers takes her hand and leads her hesitantly in the right-two-three, left-two-three, rock-back while they shag along the seawall. Despite the step-togethers and the spins and the wrist turns, he seems as distant and perfunctory as the buoy that bobs beyond water's edge, marking the path to the Intracoastal Waterway. *Mmm. Why can't I warm to him?*

When Capers walks Sis to her door, she notices for the first time in months the dead bugs that have piled up in the plastic cover of her porch light. There is an abandoned spiderweb on the top outer corner of the door with decaying pockets of eggs that are wound tight in its center. She turns and smiles at him in the dull light of the doorway as a moth thumps his wings against the porch light and crickets call to one another in the marsh across the street.

Capers takes a deep breath as though he is psyching himself up for a bungee jump and leans down and gives Sis a quick peck on the cheek. He stands upright, touches her shoulders, and smiles. "I'll see you in the church house tomorrow."

"See you there." She gently nods.

"Enjoyed it, Sis," he says as he turns and walks toward his sedan. She lets herself in and watches him through her window as he meanders to the car. When he drives off she touches her cheek and tries to identify a pungent smell that she can't quite pin down until, as his headlights hit the road, she realizes once again that it is the unmistakable scent of mothballs.

She wishes she enjoyed Capers. How can she be so uninterested in such a godly man with a tender heart and heartbreaking story of rejection? She doesn't know. Maybe she's too critical of potential suitors. Perhaps that's been her problem all along. Maybe she lacks enthusiasm about dating altogether now that she's middle-aged and everything but her breasts have been removed. But there is that mothball smell and those clammy hands, and she doesn't see how she can get past them.

She sighs and goes to work shutting down her little place for the night—the routine of cutting off the lights, checking the stove, brushing her teeth. Ray is on the answering machine, and so is Kitty B., but she won't call them back. There's so little to report, and she feels terribly lukewarm about the whole thing.

She climbs in bed with a novel she doesn't want to read. It's about a girl who thinks she inadvertently contributed to the murder of an old friend, but her husband is determined to prove to her and the world that she is innocent. It's not such a bad read, but the fact is that Sis is tired of hearing about people living, loving, and dying on the thin yellowed pages of books while she remains trapped in this pattern of sameness like a caged lab rat that has been force-fed some age-defying pill. She's weary of her mundane sleep-and-wake life. Her coffee-and-curl-her-hair-in-the-morning existence that repeats itself over and over like the formula in a romance novel.

She knows she shouldn't let her mind wander back to Fitz. But right now all she wants is to imagine the night they stole the watermelons to celebrate Ray's arrival. She can hear the tomatoes plunking off the vines, and she can smell the open soil and the rinds of the melons already beginning to soften. They are out in the dark field, and Fitz rips the watermelon off the thin, tough vine as she looks up every so often at the black night before them.

Then she thinks of the countless nights they drove back down that same road for years to come, in search of a secluded place to park. She can see the live oaks, the arc of their outstretched limbs, and the tunnel they formed around that sweet darkness that promised the quiet and seclusion they so desperately craved.

"Should we pull over here? Or here?" he would say. This must be what married couples have in the privacy of their own homes when everyone is bedded down and the air is still and black. Fitz and Sis sought it as often as they could on that country road. They were hungry for it, groping and grasping at one another in a kind of sweet desperation. Then a light from a passing pickup truck would come by, and they felt exposed. Sis would lie still in the backseat as Fitz sat up and stared down the headlights, willing the car to pass without any trouble. Truth is, there was nowhere to go and be alone. And yet they pursued the promise of the patch of darkness before them as they drove down the country road—that black, gaping hole on the horizon that they never could reach.

And now Sis can't help but weep into her pillow. Something she swore off years ago. Something she thought the happy pills had taken away, but she supposes she can't expect them to solve everything. She weeps and weeps and prays that Mrs. Johnson in the upstairs apartment doesn't hear her and phone her mama or, worse than that, Ray.

Tomorrow Sis will have to face the gals again, and they'll want to know how it went, but she won't have the heart to tell them that she's hopeless.

Suddenly she thinks of Hilda and her promise to write her about the date. She picks up a piece of notebook paper and scratches out what she hasn't been able to say to her mama or any of the gals in all of these thirty years.

I'm trapped in a time warp, Hilda. Trapped in the back of Fitz's car, wanting only him and knowing that I'll never have him—not on this earth, anyway. Why can't I find my way out?

She seals the letter in an envelope and even though it's midnight, she puts on her jacket and walks the two blocks down to Third Street where she drops the letter through Hilda's slot.

Sis sees the light come on in the upstairs bedroom. Then she nods and walks home along the dark sidewalks of the quiet town. *There, I've said it.* The brown leaves from the live oak trees swirl around the street corner. *And I've said it to someone who just might understand.*

EIGHTEEN

Sis

Katie Rae has gone on the Special K diet. She's eating two bowls a day and then a salad for supper at night, and the pounds are dropping off.

"Don't lose anymore," Ray says. "We won't have time to take in the dress if you do."

It's a month before the wedding, and they're meeting over at Ray's while Katie Rae gets her final fitting. Vangie Dreggs is there too. She's arranged for a seamstress from Hilton Head to fill in for Hilda and take up the dress.

Ray seems excited about something. So excited that she doesn't seem annoyed by the seamstress or Vangie, who asks her to bring down the full-length mirror from her bedroom.

She's pacing back and forth with such a spring in her step that Sis calls Kitty B. into the bathroom. "What's Ray got up her sleeve?"

"I don't know," Kitty B. says. "She's so blown up I think she's going to pop."

"Hmm," Sis rubs her lips with her index finger. "We don't have Hilda to poke and prod her, so you and I are going to have to give it a try."

Kitty B. nods her head and says, "All right. You go first."

After the fitting, Vangie pins each of them down about volunteering at the upcoming revival healing day—Sis will do the music and Kitty B. will coordinate the luncheon. Then she excuses herself for a real estate closing down the street.

Next Cricket comes by in the hearse to pick up Katie Rae and the seamstress and the dress and take them on over to the cleaners. And once the three gals are alone, Sis turns to Ray.

"You're more puffed up than a peacock, Ray," Sis says, patting the sofa firmly. "Now sit down and tell us what is going on."

Ray spins around twice, plops down in the center of her Sheraton love seat, and adjusts her posture. Then she leans forward. "Donovan flew down to meet with Cousin Willy last week, and then I took him to Croghan's in Charleston where we picked out the most gorgeous ring for Priscilla you ever saw."

"No!" Kitty B. says. "I can't believe it!"

Ray bounces up and down on her sofa like a child who is about to be fed a large slice of cake. She nods her head and her face burns with color. A thin lightning bolt-shaped vein on the side of her head surfaces. Sis and Kitty B. gather around and embrace her.

"Can you believe it?" Ray says, squeezing her hands into tight fists. "Priscilla is going to get married to a wonderful doctor from Connecticut!"

She looks them both in the eye and her pupils seem awfully dilated. Then she looks beyond them toward the portrait of Priscilla in her debutante gown above the hearth and says, "We've got to pick a date and select the invitations and find a gown!"

"I think she should wear my gown," Sis blurts out and Ray turns to her with a look that is some disconcerting mixture of sweetness and sympathy.

"Why not?" Sis opens her hands wide. "It's so stylish and delicate and Priscilla will think it's retro by now. Sort of a Jackie-O look. She's into that vintage style, isn't she?"

Well, why shouldn't she offer it? The gorgeous gown is still hanging in her childhood closet at her mama's house wrapped in the cocoon of some old yellowed bed sheets. She bought it the month after Fitz left for Vietnam.

~ SEPTEMBER 17, 1969 ~

Sis never had a feeling that something would happen to Fitz until the day she and her mama drove to Atlanta to try on the dress. She was an only child, so her mama wanted to go all out for her wedding. They had reserved Magnolia Plantation for the reception because it would take place during the peak of the azalea blossoms. Her mama had hired a caterer from Charleston and a florist from Atlanta, and Roberta and their generation of the wedding machine were handling the rest. Fitz's mama was a wonderful baker, and she invited Sis over several times to taste test a variety of flavors for the wedding cake.

They had ordered the invitations—Crane's, no less—and Sis's mama had sent off to get the Mims family crest, which is a handsome coat of arms with a knight's helmet and a shield with three stars and a lion standing up on his hind legs. The dye is what the stationery lady in Charleston called it, and it would be imprinted in the center at the top of the wedding invitation. It cost an absolute fortune, but her mama wanted everything to be just so.

Sis is not one that worries. She inherited that disposition from her mama. Sis's daddy, on the other hand, always worried about everything. He worked for Hilda's father as the personnel manager at the mill, and he was constantly worried that the union would get in when his back was turned.

He worried about accidents too. Once he stepped on one of the kittens from their house cat's umpteenth litter. Sis will never forget her poor daddy picking up that limp kitten and cradling it in the palm of his hands. He literally wept for hours. Then he wouldn't even go into the den where the litter was. He made his way to the stairwell from the kitchen and went to bed without smoking his pipe—like he enjoyed doing in the den each evening—until all the kittens had been given away.

Well, when Sis's daddy heard that Fitz was enlisting, she could see by the sagging jowls on his long face that he was concerned. He would watch the evening news reports of the war with a great intensity, and turn it off whenever she came through the room.

Sis and her mama were in Atlanta, and she was trying on a wedding gown. The dress was glorious. It had an elegant off-the-shoulder bodice with lace and beading and a silk A-line skirt with beading all along the edge and the train. Sis was always a little person, and it didn't overpower her. It was just right.

Then her mama brought out the lace veil with scalloped edges Sis had bought in Italy the summer between her sophomore and junior years of college. She leaned forward and, as soon as the sales lady helped her mama fasten the veil with bobby pins, they turned Sis around to face the three-way mirror, and she looked herself in the eye and thought: *He's not coming home.*

Eight days later they got the call. Sis and her parents were taking a break from going over the guest list. They were sipping Co-Colas on the back porch when Mr. Hungerford's Chevrolet pulled up in their driveway. It was the one that Fitz and Sis had spent countless hours in the backseat of throughout high school and college. She knew its leathery smell and every curve of the upholstery from the humid nights spent making out on the edge of town.

Sis's mama looked at her. Her daddy grabbed the glass out of Sis's hand and nodded for her to greet Mr. Hungerford. She walked down the steps and met him as he stepped out of the car. His lips were gray and pursed, and she noticed the loose skin beneath his chin wriggle like a gizzard's as he said, "Sis, honey." And that was all he could say.

Yes, Sis thought. *Yes, of course he's gone,* but she said, "No." And she grabbed Mr. Hungerford's arms and tugged at them hard as she fell down on her knees. The poor man shook his head briskly back and forth and knelt down beside her and let her fall into his tall, thin chest as Sis's mama came up behind her and rubbed her back with her gentle, little hands as if she'd failed a math test or fallen off her bike. Her daddy seemed paralyzed in his porch seat with his large hands around his head. She could hear him weeping into his soft, white handkerchief. Later Sis would learn that Fitz had stepped on a land mine less than a mile from his base.

The dress arrived a month later. Sis's mama had cancelled the reservations, the caterer, the florist, and the invitations, but she had completely forgotten about the dress. Sis was walking a piano student to his bicycle when the postman arrived with the package. Her mama was driving up from a trip to the grocery at the same time, and she tried to intercept it. Mrs. Mims left her car door open and waved at the postman to get his attention as she ran toward him, but she was too late.

Sis grabbed the package and ran up to her room and tore it open. She just had to try it on. It was glorious. The bodice was snug in all the right spots, and the beading on the silk skirt was exquisite. She had a little trouble fastening the silk covered buttons, but she contorted her arms in all sorts of ways to get the center ones fastened as her mama knocked and knocked on the door. She could hear her daddy weeping once again as she put on her makeup and her white kid gloves and positioned the veil just so.

Then Sis phoned Kitty B. and Ray and Hilda from the closet in her bedroom, and they raced over at once to see her in it. Kitty B. was already pregnant with Cricket by that time, and she could hardly get up the stairs.

"This is not a good idea, girls," Sis's mama said as Ray and Hilda pushed Kitty B. up toward Sis's room. "This is only going to make it worse."

"Oh, just let her show it to us, Mrs. Mims," Hilda said. She pushed through Sis's mama and banged on her door, "We're here, gal."

Sis unlocked the door and Hilda opened it and her mama and daddy gasped as she turned to face them. Kitty B. burst into tears and Hilda smiled and Ray shook her head and said, "It's magnificent, Sis. You're the most stunning bride I've ever seen."

Now Sis looks up at her two friends who are staring at her from the couch. She doesn't know how long she's faded out, but Kitty B. stands and pats her back and Ray musters up a response to the offer.

Sis can see the wheels turning in Ray's head, and she has no idea what she is going to say. She probably thinks it's bad luck or something, to wear her wedding gown.

"That might be an idea, Sis," Ray finally says. Then she furrows her brow. "Of course, Priscilla is a little taller than you, and she's a little bustier too. It might not fit, you know?"

"That's true," Sis says. She wants to give her an out because maybe the dress is bad luck or at least Ray might worry that it is, and Ray ought to enjoy her daughter's wedding after all she's done for everyone else.

"Never mind," Sis says. "It probably won't work, and I'm sure Priscilla would like to pick out something new." She quickly excuses herself. The gals assume she's going to the church for her daily organ practice.

"Say hi to Capers," Kitty B. says.

"I've told you, Kitty B.," Sis turns back to say. "There is nothing between us." But what Sis hasn't told either of them is that Capers asked her out twice more in the last month, and she turned him down both times. The second time they were standing over the copy machine in the church office, and she took him by the arm and said, "Capers, I'm sorry. I don't know what's wrong with me, but this just doesn't feel right."

He stared for a moment at the reams and reams of paper stacked beside the copier and said, "Thank you for being honest with me."

"You're welcome," she said.

Then he looked up and met her eyes. "God does have a plan for each of us."

She bit her lip and nodded. "I hope so."

Now as Sis walks out into the crisp December afternoon, some of the last leaves from Ray's maple tree swirl down onto the brown grass. Instead of going to church she walks the few houses down to her mama's old home and goes up to her room. The wedding dress hangs at the far end of her closet, and she stops to breathe in the stale air for a moment before she pulls it down and carries it out to her car where she shoves it in the trunk.

"Where are you going with that dress, Sis?" Kitty B. calls from her car window.

Sis looks up, guilty. *She thinks I've gone and lost it for sure now.* She straightens up. "Goodwill."

"Oh, now Sis, don't do that." Kitty B. parks her car and opens the door toward Sis.

Next Ray comes running out of the front door and along the brick path toward the opening of her garden gate that leads to the street.

"Now, look what we've done!" Kitty B. says to Ray as they move in on Sis.

"Don't come any closer," Sis says, holding up her hand to stop them.

"Sis Mims," Ray says. "Hand me that dress right now."

"No," Sis says, turning to her. "I will not."

Kitty B. looks over to Ray in disbelief.

"It really might work for Pris," Ray says. "Here, let me see it."

"No it *won't,* Ray," Sis says as Kitty B., her eyes brimming with tears, inches closer toward the dress.

"It's okay, Kitty B." Sis holds up a hand to stop her.

"It's something I need to do. Somebody might like a dress like this. It's not bad luck or anything. But more than that, I've just got to get rid of it, you know? If I have to face it when I'm cleaning out that house after Mama dies, I might lose my mind for good. This dress has been hanging in my closet for thirty-four years now, and I need to get rid of it. Can't you understand?"

Kitty B. nods and pats her eyes with the tips of her fingers. Sis waves her away and says, "C'mon now. This is old. This is history. And I've got to find a way to put it behind me."

Sis doesn't look back to Kitty B. or to Ray. She can't. Instead, she just slams down the trunk and doesn't even worry about the fact that a little bit of the sheet and the tip of the beaded train are hanging out of the back. She just hopes a bird doesn't crap on them.

"'Bye, gals," she says as she gets in her car without giving them another look. The faster she does this, the better she will feel. She just knows it. She just knows it. And she tells this to herself over and over as she races down Third Street onto Main and crosses over the railroad tracks toward Ravenel where the Goodwill sits right between a K-Mart and a Buck's Pizza.

Whew! She hits the open road of Highway 17. *I feel better already.*

NINETEEN

Ray

"I'm going out," Ray calls to Willy on her way down the street. "I've left some cinnamon rolls on top of the oven for everyone, and there's a fresh pot of coffee on."

"All right," he says. "I'll let folks know."

It's been eight weeks since Hilda closed her door to the world, and Ray thinks it's time the woman showed her face. She's been spying on the delivery boy from Barbour's Grocery who drops a package off at the back of Hilda's house every Wednesday morning, and today she's got about an hour where she can duck down in the pittosporum bushes and wait for Hilda to open the back door. She's just got to lay eyes on her and see what kind of condition she's in, and if she can get a word in, she knows she can convince her to open her door for Little Hilda, who's in town for Thanksgiving weekend and Angus's wedding.

Just like clockwork, the young man walks through the wrought iron gates and around the back of the house with two bags full of groceries. She can see a half carton of milk peeking out of the top of one of those bags, and she knows Hilda won't let that sit outside for long.

When the boy leaves, Ray shimmies through a doorway in the

brick wall that runs alongside the house and she crouches behind one of the larger bushes. She waits for fifteen whole minutes without blinking an eye, but she doesn't see any movement on the back porch.

It's the day before Thanksgiving, and the children have descended for the holiday and the wedding. Except for Priscilla. She's on the way to Ridgefield, Connecticut, to meet Donovan's parents. If Ray weren't so worried about Hilda, she'd be on top of the world, thanks to the hormone replacement therapy and her daughter's imminent engagement.

She skipped yesterday's vestry meeting to pick up Priscilla's ring from Croghan's. Then she took it to the Charleston airport where a special courier will deliver it to Donovan in Baltimore tomorrow.

Vangie's voice was on her answering machine when she got home last night. "Ray," she said. "We need to talk. The revival healing day is only six weeks away, and I need you to help me with the sign-up sheets."

Ray rolled her eyes. *Too busy for that nonsense.* Then she pushed the delete button on the machine and started polishing the silver for her Thanksgiving feast.

She's offered Priscilla's room to Little Hilda and Giuseppe, and they arrived last night looking so grown-up. It was awfully strange for Ray to show them to Priscilla's peach and white eyelet room where Little Hilda spent many a night during her childhood. It gave Ray a funny feeling—the realization that her daughter's best friend is officially allowed to spend the night in the same bed with a grown man. But the way Giuseppe picked up Little Hilda's bag and carried it up the stairs made Ray well up with a kind of hope and excitement about their union. And Priscilla's future one. Hilda would be so proud. It's time for her to come out of her shell and see her daughter, and Ray is not afraid to wait her out.

The bushes poke at Ray's ribs as she pushes back into them. Maybe she should have worn some of Willy's camouflage. She rubs her neck and stares at Hilda's back door. It's awfully hot for November, and she should have brought some of that bottled water Justin brought home the other day from that Costco in Charleston.

Suddenly, she feels something creeping up her neck. It's some kind of bug or spider, she is sure, and now it's crawling down her back.

"Ahh," she shrieks as she feels it bite her skin.

Before she knows it she has to strip off her sweater and her blouse and swat at her back until it's gone.

By the time she gets her blouse back on, she looks over at the back piazza, and the groceries are gone. Well, doggone it.

"Hilda!" she screams.

She comes running out from behind the bushes with her sweater buttoned wrong and her hair sticking out in all directions and bangs on the glass door of the back piazza.

"Hilda Prescott, open this door! I need to talk to you!"

She peers through the window, but all she can make out is the sofa in the den and the corner of a grocery bag on the kitchen counter.

"Your child is in town, and she's staying at my house!" Ray hollers. "Don't you want to come out to see her?"

The house seems more still than ever. Like it's holding its breath. Ray can't detect the slightest sound or movement, and she wonders where in the world Hilda is hiding—in the linen closet or the kitchen cupboard or maybe behind the sofa.

"Come on out now," Ray says. "I just want to lay eyes on you."

Her forehead is up against the glass. "I really might call the fire department this time. Or maybe I'll get Willy and Justin to climb up to the top piazza and open the door. I know that one has never had a working lock."

She paces the moss covered bricks, but the house doesn't even creak. There is no sign of Hilda. That stubborn old mule. How long does she expect to pull this off? Ray will find a way to get her out of there. But how?

"Fine," Ray hollers at the door and takes a step back. "You're going to miss your daughter and your son-in-law and a whole lot of other things unless you get your nerve up and step out here. Do you hear me, Hilda?"

Now Ray sees her reflection in the glass, and she quickly rebuttons her sweater. Then she licks her palms and tries to flatten her hair. She's got to call Sylvia Crenshaw for an emergency appointment. She can't have Thanksgiving dinner or attend Angus's wedding with this bedraggled do.

Of course, Sylvia won't be available the day before her sister's wedding, but Ray's going to drive over there right now and beg her to do it. Sylvia's got a soft spot, and she won't be able to turn Ray away.

TWENTY

Kitty B.

Kitty B. spends Thanksgiving morning in the kitchen basting the turkey and making the dressing and gravy. Marshall and his parents are coming over for dinner, and Katie Rae went into Charleston to take part in their Thanksgiving service. Tommy and Cricket are coming over, too, but the funeral home is short staffed for the holiday weekend, and they have to attend to the family of a teenage boy who crashed his car into a live oak tree in the wee hours of Tuesday morning on his way home from a party in a cornfield on the outskirts of town.

Kitty B.'s felt a lump in her throat ever since she heard about that accident. When someone young dies, it hits her hard, and it takes her back to the time when she lost Baby Roberta. Next week will be the twenty-seventh anniversary of that awful night, and she's trying not to think about it too much. If she lets her mind go there, she'll be screaming at God by the end of it all, and that only seems to make it worse.

She tries to shake off the thought of it for the sake of the holiday. Her family hasn't had a full-blown Thanksgiving dinner since LeMar fell ill a few years ago, so she's making all of the old favorites:

rice and gravy, oyster pie, cranberry sauce, green bean casserole, and pickled artichokes. And of course, her mama's homemade biscuits that just melt in your mouth.

She's even dusted off the old cornucopia basket she used to put out when the girls were little, and she's created a table centerpiece that Ray would be proud of with dried corn, pumpkin gourds, plums, apples, and tangerines. Kitty B. wants things to be nice for Marshall and Katie Rae and the Benningtons. This should be a joyful time, and if she can pull this dinner off, she hopes it will be the beginning of many holidays spent around the table together.

As Kitty B. pulls out the silver butter tray Hilda gave her for a wedding gift over thirty-five years ago, she prays, "Lord, carry her in your arms today." Tonight Angus will tie the knot with Trudi, and she knows Hilda's heart is just shattered. She's on duty at Hilda's this evening since Ray and Sis have been called on to help with the wedding. After dinner breaks up here, she'll make a nice basket of leftovers and take them into town. She figures she'll sit in Hilda's garden all evening just to let her know she's not alone.

"LeMar," she calls up the stairs. "It's ten o'clock, and I could sure use a hand. Time to get up now."

"Can't," he shouts from behind the door in his room. "Come up here, Kitty B. I need to talk to you."

Oh, Lord, she prays. *Give me patience.*

When she rounds the stairwell and knocks on his door, she can hear Wagner's *Parsifal* playing on the CD player by his bed.

"C'mon in," he says as he turns down the music.

"What's wrong?" She pushes at the old, swollen door until it opens. LeMar's propped himself up on four pillows and he's still in his nightshirt and boxers. Both of his hands grasp his throat.

"My neck aches," he says. "I think it's swollen."

He turns over and points to the base of his head. "Take a look at it for me."

Kitty B. peers over and takes a gander at his neck. Aside from a little pinkness, it doesn't look any different than it looked yesterday or the day before that.

"Looks all right to me," she says. "Now you told me you were going to help me with this dinner. The guests are going to be here in a few hours, and there is no way I can get everything together without you."

"Doggone it, Kitty B.!" LeMar shouts. He hurls the glass of water by his bed down on the ground and it shatters. "I don't feel good, and all you can do is shout orders at me."

Kitty B. shakes her head. She walks stiffly over, stoops down, and picks up the shards of glass. The thought half-crosses her mind to leave a sharp piece down there for the next time he gets out of bed, but that would only provoke more whining and maybe even another exasperating trip to the Medical University.

"I'm sure you just slept on it the wrong way," she says. "You've been feeling so much better, remember? Now you've got to help me welcome the Benningtons into our home."

"Not today, I can't," he says. "Call them and tell them I'm under the weather."

Kitty B. carefully holds the pieces of glass in her wide hands. "No," she says. "You were too ill to meet them a few weeks ago, and I'm not going to tell them that again."

"What are you saying?" he asks. "Are you saying I'm making this up?"

Then he reaches for the back of his neck and rubs it. "I need some ibuprofen or I'm going to pass out from the pain."

Kitty B. walks toward the doorway. She's not going to wait on him hand and foot today. "I'm sure there's some in your medicine cabinet. Now I'm going down to check on the turkey."

As she sets the fine china and silver on the table, she hears him grumbling.

"We're all out," he finally hollers and she wants to say, *I'm not leaving to go get some now. You can go.*

But she knows he won't go on his own. LeMar rarely drives. He was never very good at it, and since he's been home the last few years, he asks her to chauffeur him everywhere.

So she calls their neighbor, Mr. Tidemann, the ones who raises the goats, and he meets her on the dirt road between their homes with an unlabeled bottle of aspirin that looks like it could be twenty years old.

Before long the Benningtons arrive in their minivan with Katie Rae and Marshall in tow. Shawna has made some kind of greenish marshmallow concoction that she calls Watergate salad, and she's also made some macaroni and cheese with crushed potato chips sprinkled on top.

"Where's Daddy?" Katie Rae says as Kitty B. greets them on the porch. She's set up a little drink station against the porch railing with a little iced tea and her father's famous Bloody Marys that he made every year for Thanksgiving dinner.

"He's under the weather," Kitty B. says. "Again." She hopes they can't detect the sarcasm. "I'm so sorry."

"That's too bad," Roscoe says. "We were really looking forward to finally meeting him."

"Yeah," Shawna says as she squints her eyelids. They're painted a shade of bright green, and they sparkle in the midday sunlight.

Marshall leans into Katie Rae. "Should you go up and see him?"

Katie Rae looks to Kitty B. "Yeah," she says. "Mama, I'm going to see if I can talk him into coming out."

"Go ahead, honey." Kitty B. snags a strip of peeling paint that dangles from the porch railing. "You might have better luck than me."

The Benningtons all prefer iced tea over Bloody Marys, and Kitty B. wonders if their denomination is somehow connected to the Baptists. They sit on the porch and nibble on her pickled shrimp appetizer and these wonderful new spinach and pine nut tarts that she pulled from last month's *Southern Living*.

Lowcountry autumns are glorious and today is no exception. The sky is a clear blue and the water reflects the sun as the ripples of the incoming tide pour in, filling the surrounding marsh banks. Thankfully, the dogs are too lazy to play chase, and they nap together beneath the rosebush after sniffing thoroughly around the Benningtons' minivan. Mr. Whiskers, the cat, is nowhere to be seen, and Kitty B. hopes to heaven that he's not in the kitchen nipping at the turkey.

On the porch, they can all hear the dull roar of *Parsifal* as it pounds against the window panes in LeMar's room above them. Kitty B. recalls bits of the production LeMar took her to see at the Newberry Opera House several years ago. There was this tall spear— the one that was used to pierce Christ—that Parsifal had to recover in order to heal the king of an order of knights who guard the Holy Grail. Kitty B. kept worrying that the lead was going to trip and stab himself with it. *Opera*, she thinks. *What melodrama.*

Within minutes Katie Rae returns. She holds her hands palms up and says. "He says he needs to stay in bed and rest his neck."

"Oh, dear," Roscoe says. "Think I could go up and pray for him?"

Marshall clears his throat dramatically in an attempt to put the brakes on his dad. Kitty B. guesses that Marshall knows enough about their family to know when to let LeMar be.

Roscoe sits back and nods. "Well, y'all just tell me if you'd like me to."

Kitty B. nods and helps herself to a tart. "He'll live," she says, trying to strike a cordial tone. In truth, she is not convinced that all of LeMar's ailments aren't in his head, but she's not about to voice her suspicions to the Benningtons. Who knows what they would think of her—a wife who doesn't believe her husband. Surely that's a big-time sin.

"What a nice place," Shawna says as they watch a row of pelicans cross low over the river. "Marshall tells us it belonged to *your* family."

"Yes," Kitty B. says. "I grew up spending every summer here, tubing down the river or curled up in the tire swing reading a book."

"Nice," Shawna says.

Kitty B. pictures herself barefoot in a smocked dress, climbing up the oak tree just in front of the river. "'Course my parents had live-in help back then," she says to the Benningtons, "and there was always somebody to chase after my brothers and me and make sure we didn't get into too much trouble. There was a lovely lady, Lucy, who was our housekeeper, and she would bring me in the kitchen every afternoon and let me help her cook dinner. She's the one who really taught me how."

"What a gift she gave you," Roscoe says.

Kitty B. can see Lucy coming out on the front porch and hollering up at her. "Get down from there, child. It's time to pickle the watermelon."

"Yes," Shawna says. "Katie Rae gave me the *Lowcountry Manna* cookbook for my birthday last week, and I'm going to make something from it for our next covered dish supper."

Just as Kitty B. is about to set the turkey on the table, Tommy and Cricket arrive, dressed for business. Tommy in a navy suit and tie and Cricket in a straight, black and white houndstooth dress from Talbots that hits her at the knee. They are as polite as can be to the Benningtons, but Kitty B. can tell they're out of sorts.

Tommy makes himself a giant Bloody Mary, and just as he is about to sit down on the sofa, Cricket nudges him and says, "Daddy's not around. You better go carve the turkey."

"Girls," Kitty B. says to her daughters as she walks toward the kitchen. "Why don't y'all give me a hand?"

When Cricket walks through the kitchen door, a roach the size of a stick of Juicy Fruit gum scurries across the kitchen counter toward the green bean casserole, his antenna waving wildly in the air.

"Disgusting," she says. "Mama, *why* don't you get somebody out here to spray. Those palmetto bugs don't exactly give me a good feeling about eating this meal."

Kitty B. turns to Cricket. "Honey," she says. "We live on the edge of the river with bugs and water rats and raccoons galore, and there's not enough spray in the world that could keep them out."

"Hush," Cricket says. "Don't let the guests hear that, Mama. It's disgusting. Normal people *don't* live this way."

Then Katie Rae walks in and closes the door behind her. "Did you say there was a rat in here? I can hear y'all in the living room, you know?"

"No," Kitty B. says as she takes off her shoe and prepares to smash the roach as it inches its way over to the coffeemaker. "Just a palmetto bug." She takes one good swipe at him, but he swiftly makes his way behind the oven.

"I bet you have droppings in your cabinets, Mama." Cricket opens up the silverware drawer and starts inspecting.

"Katie Rae." Kitty B. dusts off a tray and hands it to her. "Make your daddy a plate and take it up to him for me, okay?"

Katie Rae nods and dips her finger in the gravy bowl. "Mmm." She says.

Kitty B. dips her own finger in for a sample. "Think it has enough salt?"

Cricket shakes her head as she rubs a paper napkin around the inside corners of the drawers. "Mama, please wash your hands before you touch any more of the food. It's uncouth."

"Do you see anything?" Katie Rae says as she peers over Cricket's shoulder.

"Yes, I do." Cricket takes a napkin and presses it down into the drawer.

"See," she says as she opens the napkin to reveal the tiniest black speck.

Kitty B.'s face reddens. She called her daughter in to help, not for a kitchen inspection. Who in the world could keep palmetto bugs out of a house on the river?

"Put that away," she says to Cricket. "Now let's have a nice dinner, okay?"

Dinner runs smoothly except for Cricket pushing her food around her plate. One little insect, and she can't enjoy the meal it took Kitty B. two days to prepare. Honestly.

The Benningtons compliment Kitty B. on the food, and she is delighted when they go back for second helpings. After she serves the pecan pie, everyone clears out pretty quickly and Kitty B. is left to do the dishes by herself. Her daughters are so used to her running the kitchen that they don't seem to give the sink full of dishes a second thought, and she's not about to say anything to them. She'd just as soon do them herself than have Cricket grading her washing technique or the insides of her china cabinet.

Just as she clears the pecan pie plates, LeMar stumbles down the stairs in his boxers and his T-shirt.

"Kitty B.," he calls. "I'm telling you I need some ibuprofen. Not some of this decrepit aspirin from Tidemann."

"Well, why don't you go and get some, LeMar? I've got an entire holiday dinner to clean up after and then I've got to go see about Hilda."

He walks into the dining room clutching his neck. She looks up from the pile of teacups she's stacking to see his eyes squinting at her.

"You are going to be the death of me," he says. Then he turns and storms back up the stairs.

Kitty B. lets out a deep sigh. She drops the china on the table, grabs her keys, and drives the twenty miles into town to buy some packets of ibuprofen from the only place open on Thanksgiving

Day—the Exxon station. Then she drives back home, walks up the stairs, and puts them on his bedside table with a glass of water.

"I'm going to Hilda's," she says. "Maybe you'll feel better with me out of the house, since I am the one responsible for all of your misery."

She packs up some leftovers and heads toward town. She's so mad at LeMar she can't see straight. As she speeds down the dirt road, the small brown oak leaves swirling behind her, she must admit that she's been mad at him for over twenty-five years now.

~ DECEMBER 21, 1979 ~

LeMar and Kitty B. waltzed to the big band at the Sally Swine Christmas party at the Azalea Club outside of Bluffton. Kitty B. had just stopped nursing Baby Roberta—no one nursed babies past a couple of months back then—but her breasts still ached, especially at night, and they pounded when LeMar pulled her close before he dipped her. A teenage girl from the other side of the island was watching Cricket and the baby, and Kitty B. was anxious to get home to see about them. However, LeMar had recently been promoted to regional manager of several stores in the Lowcountry, and they needed to stay a good while at the party and visit with the executives and their wives.

"Sing for us, LeMar," Mr. Bouton asked. He was the president of the Sally Swine Company, and LeMar wouldn't dare turn him down. Not that LeMar ever minded having a turn in the spotlight. He went over and whispered to the pianist, and then he launched into a solo of "O Holy Night."

They didn't pull into Cottage Hill until around midnight that evening. The babysitter was snoring on the couch in front of the television, and Cricket was asleep, curled up in a ball in the center of her bed with all of the covers kicked off.

When Kitty B. rounded the corner into the baby's room, she thought Baby Roberta was sleeping soundly on her belly, and she didn't want to disturb her. She leaned in close and gently touched her diaper to see if it needed changing.

As she patted the infant's backside she noticed that her chest was not rising and falling. Then she felt her plump little legs and they were cool to the touch. She quickly turned her over and pulled her to her chest. She patted her baby's back over and over as LeMar stood in the doorway and cocked his head to the side.

"Something's wrong," Kitty B. screamed. "The baby's cold! I can't tell if she's breathing."

LeMar grabbed the infant out of her hands. "What? My word, Kitty B.! What did you do?"

She ran downstairs to the telephone and called the hospital and then Angus and when she went back up, LeMar had barricaded the door. She could hear his wails from inside.

"An ambulance is on the way!" she yelled as she pounded on the door. "Let me in, LeMar! Let me in!"

"No!" he wailed from behind the thick door. "I will not!"

Kitty B. fell to her knees, grabbed her aching chest, and prayed, "Lord, help us!" just as a sleepy-eyed, six-year-old Cricket stumbled out of her room.

The weeks and months that followed were a blur. Cricket couldn't understand what had happened to her baby sister, and Kitty B. couldn't bring herself to voice the lies the elderly ladies in the church had told her. "One of God's sweet angels took her in the night."

No, she thought. *It was something awful that stole her away. Something darker than the pitch-black fields on the country road.*

LeMar wept silently for weeks on end as Kitty B. tried to comfort Cricket and warmed up the stacks of casseroles that the ladies of Jasper kept bringing over.

He wouldn't look at Baby Roberta's room. He couldn't even walk by it. And when the gals came over to help her pack up the clothes and the baby blankets, he drove away from the house and didn't return for two weeks.

Mr. Bouton from Sally Swine called and his parents called and Cricket asked, "Where's Daddy?"

"On a trip," Kitty B. said. "He'll be back soon."

"Has an angel taken him away?" Cricket asked.

It was Cousin Willy and Angus who brought LeMar back. They went to New York and found him sitting out in front of the Metropolitan Opera House in the same clothes he left in.

When he came back, Kitty B. tried everything she could to make him feel better and keep her family intact. She cooked his favorite foods and rubbed his back as he stared into space and listened to *Wozzeck* by Berg over and over.

Her parents gave them the house at Cottage Hill, and they sent them money each month until LeMar could get himself together.

When Katie Rae was born a few years later, he did seem better, and he even went back to work for several years. He wept quite often during Katie Rae's infancy, and he checked on her several times during the night. Then somewhere along the way his tears turned into rants, and they were always directed at Kitty B.

He blamed her. He blamed her for Baby Roberta's death, but she can't for the life of her understand why.

Kitty B. pulls up to Hilda's. She has some index cards so she can write her friend a sweet note. Something like, "Thinking of you on Thanksgiving."

However, when her pen hits the card, she can't help but write down the thoughts that have been bubbling up inside of her for decades now.

Sometimes I look around and wonder how my life got to be this way, Hilda. I married a difficult man. I live in my parents' old summer cottage and eke by on their inheritance. I'm overweight. I drive a crappy car. I have children who don't pay me a lick of respect.

But that's not even the worst part. The worst part is how life just seems to happen to me, you know? It's like I have no control over it. I couldn't stop the tragedy twenty-seven years ago, and I can't stop the misery today. All I seem to know how to do is just stand here stunned as life thrusts itself on me.

Take it. That's all I've ever done. And I'm sick of taking it.

Love, Kitty B.

She puts the letter through the mail slot and rings the doorbell. "I've got a nice Thanksgiving dinner for you, Hilda. I'm going to run back home to my Aunt Ruby's for a few minutes so you'll have plenty of time to come out here and pick it up and enjoy it. Be back in an hour. I'm not going to leave you alone tonight."

Kitty B. drives around town several times to give Hilda a chance to discreetly get the food. Aunt Ruby moved out to the retirement home on Seabrook a few weeks ago, but Hilda doesn't know that. As she passes the Baptist church, she sees all of the wedding guests filing out of their cars and into the sanctuary. Ray and Sylvia are on the church steps manning the guest book, and Cousin Willy stands by Angus, who is pacing in the parking lot. This is the second time Willy will serve as his best man.

Oh, Hilda, Kitty B. thinks. *You do know what I mean. You have to take this union, and you don't want to. I don't blame you for putting up a fight. In fact, I kind of respect you for it. It's more than I ever would have had the guts to do.*

She thinks about the letter she wrote, and she wonders if Hilda is reading it right now. She can't help herself from driving back out of town and toward Cottage Island, thinking of LeMar all the way.

When she pulls up in front of the house, LeMar is sitting on the rocking chair with a heaping plate of leftovers and a Co-Cola.

"Back already?" he says as he stares beyond her at his rosebush.

"No," she says. "I'm not back, but I have something to say to you."

He winces and grabs his neck, but he does not look her in the eye.

She takes the plate out of his hands and dumps the food over the porch railing and into the azalea bushes where the dogs come running up to sample it. She leans against the rail right in front of him and stares him down until he is forced to look up.

"LeMar," she says. "Maybe you will never go back to work. And I don't expect you to touch me or hug me or share a bed with me. I don't even expect you to ever feel good again. To ever wake up and say, 'I'm feeling good today.' That's a decision you've made. To feel awful all the time. And I don't expect that to change."

She looks down at the wagging tails in the azalea bushes and catches her breath. "But I do expect you to treat me with decency. To treat me like a human being. Not your cook or the face you yell at when you're frustrated or the Grim Reaper who has come to destroy you.

"You *can* treat me decently, and it's not too much to ask. And I'm here to tell you this today: If you can't, then I'm leaving. I'll move in with Sis or Ray, and you can take care of your own self. You can fix your own food and listen to your own whining and change your own bed sheets. You hear me?"

He grabs his Co-Cola and takes a sip. Then he cocks his head and stares back at her.

"I'm not bluffing," she says. "You try me." Then she turns back toward the car.

When Kitty B. arrives back at Hilda's, she sees that the food is gone. She walks up to the piazza and rings the doorbell. "I'm just going to sit here on the piazza and study some cake recipes," she calls.

She sits down on the bench and just as she's arranging her cooking magazines, the light flips on above her.

"Thanks, Hilda," she says with a smile. "Glad to see you're still moving around up there."

Kitty B. can't remember when she's felt so at peace. She's not scared and she's not anxious and she's not even hungry like she usually is after a confrontation. She *means* what she said to LeMar, and it's up to him whether or not to heed her words. Now she breathes the soft air in and out again before letting out a satisfied sigh. She stays this way on Hilda's porch until midnight, studying the cake recipes and clipping her favorites to try for Katie Rae's wedding.

TWENTY-ONE

Sis

"Well, your baby girl's wedding is upon us." Sis holds up a piece of wire and Kitty B. snaps it with the pliers. It's the Saturday after Christmas, and the gals are decorating the flying-purple-people-eater cathedral.

"I know," Kitty B. says.

Ray paces back and forth, examining the poinsettia arrangements, then goes to her pocketbook and writes something in her notebook.

Sis looks at Kitty B. and rolls her eyes. Then she whispers, "Ray can't seem to *focus.*"

"I know," Kitty B. whispers back. "I wish Hilda were here. She'd keep her on task."

"It was twelve weeks last Sunday." Sis shakes her head in disbelief. "I can't believe she hasn't let us in to see her for that long."

"Or at least called us so we could hear her voice." Kitty B. holds up the pliers and snips another piece to go around a magnolia leaf Christmas wreath.

Sis can see that Ray's mind is on Priscilla's big day. She keeps writing in that blasted "ideas" notebook as if she's critiquing Katie Rae's wedding before it even happens.

Hilda told Sis that Ray is secretly growing gardenias behind the screen of bamboo in her backyard, and Sis has half a mind to sneak over there and see for herself. Who knows what other special touches she's been concealing?

~ APRIL 5, 2004 ~

Sis and Hilda dropped by Ray's one afternoon to see if they could borrow a few more wine glasses for Little Hilda's engagement party. Ray was at Sylvia's getting her hair done, so Justin led them to the shed next to the garage and said, "Try in here."

There were boxes and boxes of china plates and wine glasses and fluted champagne glasses stacked to the ceiling that read, "Pris" on them, and they knew she must have purchased them somewhere along the way and was saving them for her daughter's wedding.

"Think you should ask Ray if we could use some of those?" Sis asked. They were low on champagne glasses too. It was going to cost a fortune to rent them from the party store in Charleston, and Ray knew it.

"*No.*" Hilda crossed her thin arms and crinkled her nose. "She would have offered if she'd wanted to. That crafty little hoarder."

On the walk back, Hilda lit a Virginia Slim and said, "Ever since Ray moved to Jasper, she's been looking for an angle to trump everyone else, and I can't say I'm all that surprised she's been withholding that stuff."

"Really?" Sis's eyes grew wide. "I am. She's the one who pulls us all together to make these things happen."

"No doubt." Hilda exhaled and walked through the cloud of smoke before her. "Ray does roll up her sleeves on behalf of all of us. That's true, Sis. But she's always holding a little something back for herself."

Sis considered the notion. Ray seemed like a tireless worker to her. Just the day before she was ironing all of the linens for the engagement party. "I don't know if I believe that, Hilda."

"I'm not saying she doesn't work hard. I've never seen someone polish silver the way she does or iron a linen tablecloth." Then Hilda leaned in and said quietly as they rounded the corner of Third and Rantowles, "It makes me wonder just what she did growing up. That kind of thing comes from experience, you know?"

"What do you mean?" Sis asked.

"I just mean it's important to Ray to trump everyone else—in the etiquette department, in the happy marriage department and most importantly, in the offspring wedding department. She's got something to prove. Think about it."

Sis has thought about it. She knows Ray grew up in the Pringle home on South Battery, but they all kind of have the feeling that she actually worked there instead of residing there as a member of the family.

Of course after the beach house scene last September, she's not going to dare bring it up. But what she wants to say to Ray is, "Do you think that matters to us? 'Cause it doesn't."

Now Ray marches down the purple carpet in the center aisle and checks the placement of the four trees of vibrant red poinsettias that all but cover the bandstand and the acrylic altar. "All I can say is, thank the good Lord this is a Christmas wedding. A whole lot of poinsettias and greenery can upgrade even the tackiest of places."

"Hush, Ray," Sis says. She looks around to make sure the Benningtons haven't entered the sanctuary.

"Oh come on." Ray swats her hand at Sis. "It's the truth." She walks over to one of the magnolia leaf wreaths they made last night at her house and readjusts its thick red velvet bow. "Let's go to the conference room to see how the decor for the rehearsal dinner is coming, gals."

"No," Kitty B. holds her hands up. "You know the rehearsal dinner is out of our hands, Ray. Let's just let it go."

"But I hear they have M&M's that say 'Katie Ray and Marshall' on them." Ray chuckles. "Don't you think we should drop those in the sink and say it was an accident?"

"What's got into you, Ray?" Sis puts her hand on her hip. "Lack of taste is not a character flaw. Even you should know that."

"You're right." Ray picks up an extra velvet bow and ties floral wire around it. "I'm just so wound up about Priscilla and Donovan." She attaches the bow to the center of Roscoe's podium. "Donovan was going to propose today during a cruise along the Annapolis harbor, and they'll fly into Charleston tomorrow morning just in time to make the wedding."

"We're very excited for you," Kitty B. says.

Sis nods and adds, "But we need to fry one fish at a time, and the fish of the day is Katie Rae."

Ray checks her cell phone for messages and excuses herself for a moment. When she returns, she outlines the altar with a fresh garland she made out of pine needles and says to Kitty B., "Shawna invited me in to see the rehearsal dinner set-up when I went to the bathroom."

Sis scoffs. "Ray! Have you not heard one word I've said this afternoon?"

Kitty B. walks over and says. "How bad?"

"It's worse than dyed green carnations."

"Now how can that be?" Kitty B. whispers.

"Artificial." Ray nods her chin, leans over a little closer and adds, "White artificial roses with dewdrops."

The microphone must be on because her voice echoes throughout the sanctuary, and all they can hear is the disapproving tone of the words "dewdrops, dewdrops."

"Shh," Sis says. "Y'all are terrible." She imagines that the sound system pipes into every room in the entire facility, including the conference room where poor Shawna Bennington is frantically setting up. Heck, for all Sis knows the videographer could be catching Ray on tape!

Ray just swats Sis away. She doesn't even seem to care. She's on such a high about Priscilla's engagement that she's not even thinking straight. Sis has *never* seen her unconcerned about how she appears, even to folks like the Benningtons.

"Get ahold of yourself, Ray," Sis blurts out. "If Hilda were here she'd tell you to come down off of your high horse and focus on Katie Rae."

"*My* high horse," Ray says. She sticks a twig of popcorn vine in her hair and rolls her eyes. Then she busies herself readjusting the poinsettias at the altar and picking out any stray or unsightly leaf. "Now if Hilda had the nerve to say that to me, I'd say, 'Isn't that the pot calling the kettle black?'"

"Oh, all right," Kitty B. says, walking up the stairs and patting Ray on the shoulder. "If you're so upset about it, then why don't you just go in the conference room and offer to do the flowers." Kitty B. turns Ray around and points her toward the door.

"You two are awfully feisty today," she says to them. "What's gotten into you?"

Just then Marshall and Roscoe Bennington walk in.

"Look at the well-oiled Jasper machine in motion, Daddy," Marshall says.

"You were right about them," Roscoe says, looking up at his tall, thin son.

Then he looks at the gals and says, "This place has never looked better, ladies, and I mean that. Y'all are something else!"

Sis nudges Ray forward as if to say, "Here's your chance, high horse."

Thank heavens the stalwart composure that Ray's perfected over the years kicks into gear as if by default, and she straightens up and smiles. "Why, thank you, Pastor Bennington. I'm so glad y'all are pleased with it."

Then Sis watches Ray point to where the video camera sits on a tripod as she says, "Do you think I could put some greenery on top of the, uh, camera?"

After the gals deck the halls, they race home to change and get right back for the rehearsal. Sis directs the music, and she's hired dear old Mr. Corley from the Charleston Symphony to play the trumpet, and of course LeMar is the soloist. He commissioned a composer at the College of Charleston to set an Archibald Rutledge poem to music. It's titled "Love's Meeting," and Sis can't wait for everyone to hear it. She rented an electric organ from the Charleston Music House, and it doesn't sound half bad. The gals are all counting on the music and the flowers to be the two focal points of the ceremony.

LeMar sounds glorious singing the sweet love poem. He's got a little glint in his eye, and Sis thinks he looks healthy and strong for the first time in years. He's on top of the world as he puffs up his chest and brings the words of the bygone South Carolina poet laureate to life. Then Mr. Corley bursts into his solo for the wedding march, and before the bride is halfway down the aisle, Sis hears a thud behind her.

She turns to find Mr. Corley on the floor next to the organ. He's tugging at the top of his left arm with his right hand.

The wedding party looks back to see what all of the commotion is about, and Sis screams, "Help! The trumpeter's collapsed!"

Roscoe and Marshall run up the aisle and over to Mr. Corley. Marshall starts administering CPR as Roscoe prays and speaks in some kind of foreign language. Sis calls 9-1-1 on her cell phone.

The whole room holds its breath as they hear the sirens coming toward the building. Sis recalls Mr. Corley mentioning that he was going to have a stent put in the week after the wedding. This was the last event he could commit to before the procedure.

The paramedics race in and pick Mr. Corley up and carry him out on a stretcher as Katie Rae paces back and forth and rings her hands and says, "Oh my. I hope he's okay. This is terrible."

Sis watches Kitty B. walk over to comfort her daughter. "I think he'll be okay," she says.

"Me too," says Marshall as he runs back over to Katie Rae and pulls her toward him.

"He's conscious," Marshall says to them both. "He's in good hands now."

The rehearsal and the dinner are solemn affairs. Roscoe leads the wedding party in a group prayer for Mr. Corley, and then there is nothing left to do but walk the wedding party through the ceremony. The crowd shuffles toward the conference hall for the rehearsal dinner, and no one seems to bat an eye at the imitation flowers or the personalized M&M's.

Sis feels Ray's firm arm on her elbow as she walks toward the conference room. "What are we going to do about the music?" Ray says. Kitty B. grabs her other elbow and says, "I don't know."

Now Giuseppe is on their heels. He taps Sis's shoulder and says, "My Uncle Salvatore is teaching a master class at the Brooklyn School of Music right now. He's been looking for an excuse to get back down here. How about if I call him? He might be able to catch the nine p.m. flight out of La Guardia."

Ray whispers to Sis, "That's not a bad idea."

"Would you?" Kitty B. turns to Giuseppe to say. Then she adds in a hushed tone, "I think my husband will out-and-out flip if we don't have a trumpet. He thought the music would really make the ceremony."

"Fine by me," Sis says.

Ten minutes later, Giuseppe returns and says, "Salvatore will be here by midmorning. He says he can rehearse with you tomorrow afternoon, Sis."

"Great," Sis says. "Tell him to meet me at All Saints at eight a.m."

By the end of the crab cake appetizer Sis gets word that Mr. Corley is stable. He's going to spend the night in the hospital and get his stent put in tomorrow.

"Meanwhile," Roscoe says, "a trumpeter is en route from New York to fill his place, and it is time to honor the engaged couple."

Then Roscoe and Shawna give a slide show with sentimental music of Marshall growing up, and there is not a dry eye in the house. There are photos of him in church and with his wide array of pets including a ferret, a cottonmouth snake, and an iguana. When he was in high school, he volunteered at the animal shelter, and there is a photo of him rescuing three cats and four dogs that were stranded during Hurricane Hugo. The shots end with a few of him and Katie Rae at the Serpentarium feeding the alligators and conducting a show with the snakes. Sis swears she's never been so smitten by reptiles in her life.

Then Cricket gets up to give the cutest toast. They are not drinking champagne, just iced tea and a little sparkling grape juice with the dessert. These nondenominational folk have more rules than Sis would ever have guessed. Anyway, Cricket recites a poem about her sister, the animal lover, and how she always knew God had someone in store for her.

Sis wishes that Hilda were here to see it all. Of course, Trudi and Angus are sitting in the far corner conversing with Mayor Whaley and his wife, and that probably would have ruined her for another year. How in the world are they going to get her over this heartbreak?

Ray and Cousin Willy leave before the dessert. Sis knows they want to get home early to see if Priscilla calls. As for Kitty B., well she seems different somehow. In a good way. Stronger, and Sis wonders what's changed. Maybe it's the wedding or the hormones leveling off. Maybe it's the fact that she signed up for those dog training classes in Charleston, and LeMar gave her his blessing to take them. She took her poodle, Rhetta, two times last week.

"I had a ball," she told Sis when they were making wreaths a few days ago. "I just ran Rhetta round and round that room on a leash, and the instructor said, 'You're in fine form for a pair of beginners.'"

TWENTY-TWO

Ray

Now it's two hours before Katie Rae's wedding, and Ray's setting up the snacks for the groomsmen and bridesmaids in their separate rooms. Kitty B. made her famous California tarts, and Ray made some pimento cheese as well as ham, pepper, and onion finger sandwiches for them to munch on. And they brought ginger ale for those who might come down with a queasy stomach.

"Have you heard from Priscilla?" Sis calls on her way toward the organ.

"Not yet," Ray says. "I'm expecting her to show up any time now."

Ray can't believe she hasn't heard from her daughter. She's called her cell phone eight times with no response. Priscilla and Donovan were supposed to be on the flight from Baltimore this morning, and when Cousin Willy and Justin went to Charleston to pick them up, they were nowhere to be found. Ray is sure there must be some odd little glitch. Perhaps they overslept or they missed their flight, but you'd think she'd have the decency to call and let them know.

The guests are filing in and to Ray's surprise everyone seems nice and well-dressed. She knows there are over two hundred of Roscoe's parishioners who are invited to the wedding, and she half expected them to show up in shackets and stiff baseball caps, but these people are dressed quite well in their suits and ties and Christmas dresses.

Shawna Bennington comes running out of the ladies' room in her sparkly red sweater dress to embrace Ray. She's got these red feathers along the neckline that tickle Ray's chin. "I can't believe what you all have done to the cathedral!"

Ray gives a tight-lipped smile. "Thank you," she says. "It just goes to show that flowers and greenery mean everything to a space."

"Mmm hmm," Shawna nods and waves to a familiar parishioner. "And I hear y'all gussied up Kitty B.'s house too."

"You're going to die when you see it," Ray says as she pictures the way Kitty B.'s looked this afternoon as she oversaw the setup. "It's like a whole new place. And with the tent on the river and the Christmas lights around the live oaks, it is truly—"

"Excuse me, dear," Shawna says. "I see my Aunt Alvina coming. She drove all the way from Arkansas."

"Hurry up and get a bite to eat, girls," Ray says to the bridesmaids after glancing at the clock. "We've got to get your dresses on in just a moment." Ray loves to stay with the bridal party so she stations herself in the girls' dressing room and holds open her tackle box of wedding essentials.

The girls are still in their street clothes, but their faces and hair are all fixed up. Kitty B. treated them all to an afternoon with Sylvia and Trudi Prescott, who sculpted beautiful French twists with fine little curled wisps for everyone with long enough hair.

Katie Rae smiles and laughs on the edge of the gathering. She's managed to keep off most of the weight from her Special K diet, and she's going to be a more beautiful bride than Ray ever imagined. Sylvia fixed her hair down, but she's taken two strands from the front and tied them back with a pearl clasp so that it looks very free and natural. Quite a good choice for her. Oh, what will Ray do about Priscilla's dreadlocks? Surely, she can talk her daughter into cutting them off before her big day.

Ray watches as Katie Rae leans into Froot Loop's cage and pats his head. She doesn't know why in the world Katie Rae insisted that the parrot attend the ceremony, but she's always been a bit off when it comes to animals. Anyhow, Marshall arranged it so that two groomsmen will bring Froot Loop's cage out just before the ceremony, and they will set it in the far corner of the stage so he can have a good view. Thank goodness Marshall didn't ask to bring any reptiles!

Now Ray zips up dress after glorious bridesmaid dress. She guided Katie Rae on the selection, and she was thrilled when she chose the lovely green velvet gown in the window of Berlin's. They are sleeveless with a regal square neckline and floor-length A-line skirt. Also, they have a satin stole that the bridesmaids are to wear around their necks. The stole settles along their shoulder blades and highlights the velvet-covered buttons on the back of the dress. They are remarkably elegant, and Ray has already ordered next season's styles for Priscilla to choose from.

Kitty B. looks beautiful. She's in a gold silk jacket she bought in the boutique section at Steinmart and a black velvet skirt that sweeps the floor. She's wearing her mama's triple strand of pearls and her long white kid gloves, and she's lost at least ten pounds in the last two weeks so that she looks more like Roberta than ever.

Sis pops in to check on everyone. She sports her standard winter concert dress: a sleeveless black velvet top and a red raw silk skirt. She reminds Ray of a china doll or Snow White with her dark hair, ivory skin, and bright red lipstick. How in world has a man not swooped her up by now? That's one of life's greatest mysteries.

"Come on," Ray says, pulling Katie Rae's arm gently away from Froot Loop's cage. "Let's get the bride dressed."

"Okay," she says sheepishly, and the other girls giggle as they check one another's dresses. Vangie's seamstress did a fair job with Kitty B.'s old dress, but it doesn't have Hilda's touch. Hilda could have cut out the puffy sleeves and created a strapless top trimmed with the beading from the old sleeves, but this gal just sewed some new silk trim across the top, and it doesn't quite match the color of the aged dress. Ray hopes to heaven that Hilda will come out before Priscilla's wedding.

Just as she snaps the final button on Katie Rae's dress, the bride turns to Ray, plunks down on the vanity stool, and starts to weep. Kitty B. and Cricket run over and Ray scurries to find a handkerchief in the bridal emergency kit, which she quickly hands to Katie Rae and says, "Heavens, don't let your makeup run!"

"And don't let your mascara get on the dress, darlin'," Kitty B. adds.

Katie Rae wipes her eyes with a handkerchief then turns to look at her reflection. "I just don't know if I can go through with this." She looks up at Kitty B.'s reflection in the vanity mirror. Ray glances at Kitty B. and then back to Katie Ray. *It's thirty minutes before the ceremony*, Ray thinks. *She can't be doing this.*

"Sweetheart, what do you mean?" Kitty B. asks. "Is there something wrong?"

"I'm just scared." Katie Rae spins her engagement ring round and round her finger as her large chest rises and falls dramatically as if she is starting to hyperventilate. For a minute Ray's afraid her bosoms are going to flop right over the top of the beaded trim, but Katie Rae pulls up her top and says, "I mean this is the rest of my life, Mama. And I haven't known Marshall all that long."

Just then Ray's cell phone rings and though she hesitates to answer it, she can't help herself once she sees Priscilla's cell number lighting up the small screen.

"Excuse me just one moment," Ray says to the gals as she takes a few steps back into the bathroom. She knows she should help get Katie Rae settled down, but she just has to find out about the proposal.

"Mama, you're going to die," Priscilla says from the other end of the phone. Though the connection isn't perfect Ray can tell that she's either giddy or drunk.

"What?" Ray says. "Tell me, darling! I've been waiting for this call all day."

"Vegas, baby," a hoarse male voice hollers into the phone. It sounds vaguely familiar, but Ray can't quite place it.

"Who is that?" she asks. "Did Donovan propose? I helped him with the ring. We picked it out at Croghan's. Don't you love it?"

"That's J.K., Mama."

"J.K.?" Ray says as her gut begins to churn. "As in *Knucklehead* J.K.?"

"Yes," she says, giggling. "Stop that," she says to him in a hushed tone. "Mama, we're in Las Vegas."

"Las Vegas? What in the world are you doing there? And with *J.K.?*"

Kitty B. and Sis peer into the open door of the bathroom. Then they start eyeing each other over Ray, and their faces begin to redden with what they're guessing is a kind of panic or fear. Katie Rae still weeps at the vanity, but they've dropped her arm and they're leaning in to listen to Ray's conversation. Ray moves toward a lavender stall and rests her head against its plastic door. There is a laminated poster right at her eye level that reads, "CREATOR," and it has a picture of this grand waterfall spewing over a lush valley.

"What are you saying, Priscilla?" Ray says.

"J.K. and I just tied the knot, Mama!" she says. "When Donovan proposed yesterday, I just couldn't say yes. Something just wouldn't let me do it, you know? It was just too perfect or something. And then I called J.K. and by last night we were on our way to Vegas. We got married in this cheesy little white chapel that was actually in the center of a casino! Isn't that a riot?"

This is a joke, Ray thinks. *Some kind of awful, ugly prank.*

Then Priscilla continues, "This is right for me, Mama. I know it's not the way you would have planned things, but Donovan's proposal made me realize how much I love J.K. It made it crystal clear in my mind, and we wanted to make it official as quickly as we could. We wanted to be whimsical, too, you know?"

Now bile rises in Ray's throat. She scratches her thigh, which causes a three-pronged run in her new Talbots extra-sheer black hose. This cannot be happening. Her heart beats at a rapid pace. She might faint, she thinks. She might collapse. She might die right here before Katie Rae makes it down the aisle. It'll be the second ambulance the purple cathedral will have seen in a twenty-four hour time span.

"We can throw a big party in Jasper whenever you want, Mama," Priscilla says.

"Yeah!" says J.K. "Absolutely, doll!"

"Mama?" says Priscilla. "You can pull out all of the stops like you've always wanted to. It will be great! Mama?"

Ray is speechless. She's still half expecting Donovan to come on the line and say it's all a joke, but she knows deep down it's not.

"Hey there, Mrs. Montgomery," a raspy voice hollers into the phone. "Yesterday was the greatest day of my life," he says. "I love your daughter so much. I thought I had lost her for good."

Before he utters another word, Ray snaps her cell phone closed, bangs it against the wall several times then throws it in the purple plastic trash can in the church bathroom. Sis and Kitty B. rush in and move cautiously around her as though she's a pig trapped in a flower bed and they want to minimize her destruction.

"Poop 2," Ray says as they take a step closer and try to read her eyes. She can't stop the tears of fury from brimming over. "Priscilla flew to Las Vegas last night and married Poop 2."

Sis and Kitty B. shake their heads and move in to pat her back.

"Oh Ray," Kitty B. says. "I'm so sorry."

Then Cricket comes in and says. "Mama, it's ten minutes until the ceremony, and Katie Rae is still upset and refusing to put her veil on."

Well, I've had about enough of Katie Rae's nonsense. Ray walks fast and furious out of the bathroom and grabs the bride firmly by the shoulders. "Hush up, Katie Rae, and get your fanny ready to go down that aisle. That is a good and devoted man out there who wants to pledge his love to you, and you will be lucky to have him, do you hear me? It's time to buck up now."

That seems to be just what Katie Rae needs to hear. She wipes her nose and hands Cricket the veil and as soon as it is fixed, she stands up and grabs LeMar's arm and heads straight down the aisle.

Ray never makes it into the sanctuary. She sits for a moment in the reception area and grits her teeth as she watches Katie Rae descend the aisle from the television monitor above the receptionist's desk. She thinks of all of the time she's put in at the church, and she doesn't know why God allowed this to happen.

How could You? Ray says to her Maker as she stares at the acrylic cross at the center of the altar on the colored screen. *How in the world could You, after all I've worked for? It's unfair. It's painfully unfair.*

And though Ray wants to spit and cry and catch the next flight to Las Vegas to wring Priscilla's rebellious little neck, she doesn't. Tonight is not the night. And she couldn't shirk her Wedding Guild duties any more than she could let a piece of floral tape show in an arrangement.

She simply walks to her car, slips off her heels, and puts on her tennis shoes. Then she drives back down Highway 17 in the cool, clear December night so that she can make her way over to Cottage Hill Island. It's time to put the final touches on Katie Rae's reception. And as usual, she's the one to do it.

TWENTY-THREE

Kitty B.

"The music was ethereal," LeMar says as Kitty B. drives him toward home for the reception. He puts his hand on her round knee and squeezes it tight.

"Yes, it was," she says, marveling at how that Italian trumpeter worked so well with Sis to fill the room with a kind of exuberance and beauty and joy. "There wasn't a dry eye during your solo." She pats the top of LeMar's hand. And it's the truth. LeMar's voice brought tears to everyone's eyes. He has such a gift, and it pleases him so to sing, especially for his baby girl.

Kitty B. smiles at how beautiful the ceremony was. Katie Rae got herself together and said her vows in a manner that was both bold and tender, and Kitty B.'s so proud of her she could just pop.

"Not a bad homily either," LeMar says.

"Mmm hmm." Kitty B. smiles. Roscoe's words really did bring down the house. He talked about adopting Marshall and how he had prayed each night of his life for Marshall's mate and that he realized a few months ago that it was Katie Rae he had been praying for all along.

"I couldn't imagine a better one." LeMar rubs the back of her neck. "And now it's time to celebrate, sweet!"

LeMar's been better to Kitty B. since she had that talk with him. In fact, his spirits have actually lifted. Maybe it's her standing up to him or all the goings-on at the house with the painting and the fixing or the fact that his youngest is finally married off, but he just seems like a man she hasn't known for quite some time now. He's got a spring in his step, and he hasn't complained about how he feels for at least a week. That is a miracle in and of itself, and she hopes it will last.

Kitty B.'s mama was right. Folks really do rise to the occasion when it comes to weddings. They're hardwired that way. At least they are around Jasper, and she smiles when she thinks of her mama as she waves to Miss C., who is decked out with white feathered angel wings and a shimmery gold halo. The statue stands beside the archway of poinsettias and mistletoe that leads to the tent where Kitty B.'s friends and family have gathered to celebrate.

Shawna Bennington comes running over to Kitty B. in her sparkly red sweater dress with the feathered neckline, and Kitty B. would almost be embarrassed by her if she weren't such a sincerely dear person.

"Everything is so pretty!" she says as she takes a big bite of a California tart. "I can't imagine anything more glorious. You and your friends are amazing!"

"Thank you." Kitty B. returns her embrace. "It was a lovely ceremony, Shawna. Roscoe did such a wonderful job."

"Didn't he?" she says. "I was so proud of him."

Kitty B. takes a moment to look around the tent, and everything seems to twinkle like she's in a Christmas dream. Ray and R.L. have set elaborate candelabras along the buffet tables, and there are little silver ones in the center of each sitting table. Fresh, delicate cedar garlands with thick velvet bows outline everything from the buffet to the sitting tables to the very lining of the tent, and there are silver urns overflowing with scarlet roses and calla lilies and magnolias with their

large and shiny green leaves. Even the tall space heaters they rented
are decked with mistletoe and bows. There is candlelight everywhere,
and it glistens in the crystal and the jewelry and the eyes of the guests.
The gals have really outdone themselves with this one. She can't
imagine a more magical reception.

Then she looks back at her home by the river. Vangie's wedding
gift was the painters, and Willy and Angus spent every afternoon over
there for two weeks patching up cracks in the walls and shaving down
old windows and doors that had swelled so much they were hard to
open or close. Even the yard looks beautiful. Ray bought gorgeous
thorny grapevine spun balls that she wrapped in small white
Christmas lights, and she's hung one of those from all of the most
prominent branches of the live oak trees that line the river front.

The band is already in full force, and Marshall leads Katie Rae
onto the floor for their first dance to "How Sweet It Is to Be Loved
by You." LeMar cuts in shortly after and dances with Katie Rae. He
guides her from side to side with a gentle sway and kisses her soft
cheek and pulls her toward him.

The next thing Kitty B. knows, Sis nudges her toward the dance
floor where she joins LeMar while Katie Rae dances again with
Marshall, and Roscoe and Shawna dance beside them. LeMar pauses
for a moment as he tilts one way or the other the way he used to do
when they were courting, back when Kitty B. was in college. He
spins her round and round and then they stop at the end of the song
when the singer announces "Dr. and Mrs. Marshall Bennington" to
the guests. As the applause erupts around Kitty B., and folks come
around LeMar to shake his hand, Sis leans over and whispers, "Well,
gal, not bad, huh?"

"I tell you," Kitty B. says as she puts her arm around her petite
friend and they step back toward the edge of the tent. "It's more
splendid than I ever imagined, Sis." She scans the candlelit tent as
the band kicks into one of their all-time favorites from the watermelon stealing days, "Sugar Pie, Honey Bunch."

Now other couples begin to gather on the dance floor as Kitty B. surveys the room. Wouldn't you know that Angus and Trudi are right up front locked in an embrace.

"Well, I guess it's best that Hilda isn't here. Much as I wish she were," Kitty B. says.

"Yes." Sis nods. "But I sure miss her, and I have the feeling she won't be back anytime soon."

"Wonder how Ray's doing?" Kitty B. says. They spot her over beneath the oak tree wringing her hands and talking to Cousin Willy. He tries to hug her, but she pushes him away, and Kitty B. guesses she's telling him the whole awful news about Priscilla.

Suddenly, Ray furrows her brow over Willy's shoulder as the beef tenderloin carver serves up a fatty portion to a guest. She storms over to the carving station and gives the poor fellow an earful.

"You better tell Ray she can go on home," Sis says. "Vangie and I can handle the rest of the evening."

"You're right." Kitty B. says. "She needs to go punch something for a while, and it can't be the meat carver."

Just as Kitty B. makes her way over, Capers comes up to Ray and says, "I need to talk to you about something."

"What?" Ray gives the tenderloin carver one stern look before she steps away.

Kitty B. notices that Vangie Dreggs is eavesdropping behind the bar. She's so close to one of the bartenders that someone might order a bourbon and water from her.

"Excuse me," Kitty B. says to Capers, but he does not hear her over the music.

He places his hand on Ray's shoulder. "Since you're our senior warden, Ray, and a very influential member in this community, I want to call on you to play a stronger role in the upcoming Healing Prayer Revival Day. Not many folks have signed up, and we've worked so hard to make it a life-changing day for our parishioners."

Ray bristles and her cheeks fill with air. She can't take much more of this day. She looks down at her feet as if to fashion a response. Then Vangie pops out from behind the bartender and begins her plea.

"Oh, Ray," she says. "It would mean so much to me if you made an announcement in church tomorrow and made a few personal calls to invite folks. I have been asking for your help for months now, and the revival day is next week!"

Vangie moves closer and closer toward Ray and shakes her large head with its smooth, round face and helmet of hair. Ray looks ill like she's eaten a bad oyster, and she puts her arm out as if to stave Vangie off. But Vangie keeps coming closer and Capers is right beside her.

"No!" Ray finally says, turning away from them.

"Why not?" Capers tilts his head to the side.

With this Ray swings back around and shouts, "I'm *not* taking part in any Texas, nouveau riche prayer revival where I have to raise my hands or speak in tongues like the kooks on cable TV! Forget it!"

She turns directly to Capers. "You ought to be ashamed of yourself, Capers. Letting our little chapel of ease get mixed up with such come-yuh nonsense."

"Now, Ray," Capers says. He pats her elbow. "That's rather critical, don't you think?"

Vangie gets right back in Ray's space and says, "What do you mean, come-yuh? That sounds like an insult to me. Ray, I don't know what I ever did to you, but I have the feeling you've had something against me all along."

Cousin Willy makes a beeline for the scene. Ray reaches out and covers Vangie's big, round mouth with her hand.

"Just shut up, Vangie," she says. "Don't say another bloomin' word. Ever since you came to town there's been nothing but trouble. You've infected our church with this nonsense and sold our houses to strangers from way off who just want to use them for second homes. Who knows what else you'll destroy"—Ray turns to look at Capers— "and *you* sat right here and didn't do a thing about it."

Her voice cracks as she adds, "Jasper's gone, don't you see?" She points to Vangie and says, "Our children will never come back here, and now we have to surrender our town to the likes of folks like *this*." Ray's eyes fill with tears, and she turns toward Kitty B.

"I'm so sorry." Ray runs out of the tent and through the archway of poinsettias and into her Volvo station wagon, which is blocked in by several other cars along the dirt road. She has to inch this way and that to get out. All the while Justin and Willy chase after her saying, "Whoa there, Ray!" "Settle down now, gal!'" like she's a feral hog on the loose.

Kitty B. runs over to Sis, but she's in a conversation with that trumpeter at one of the tall tables along the side of the tent. Kitty B. hears, "Would you dance with me, Elizabeth?" And then, "Ever since Giuseppe's wedding I have been thinking of you in that blue dress swaying along the seawall."

"Really?" Sis blushes.

"Yes," he says as he takes her hand.

Well, of course, Kitty B.'s not going to ruin a moment like that, even with Ray's meltdown, so she watches as Salvatore leads Sis toward the dance floor and pulls her close while the band plays "Love Me Tender" by Elvis.

Just then R.L. grabs Kitty B. by the elbow. "Time to cut the cake!"

And sure enough, Katie Rae and Marshall and the videographer are already there, and LeMar is licking his chops and motioning for Kitty B. to lean in for the photograph. The band leader announces the cutting of the cake, and he adds that the cake was created by the mother of the bride. That's awfully sweet, Kitty B. thinks. She wonders who told him that.

Then the next thing Kitty B. knows, Katie Rae is feeding Marshall a bite and vice versa, and they're wiping each other's lips with the linen napkins Ray set out beside the cake. Then the guests clap and pictures flash as the couple kisses again before sharing a glass of champagne and the rest of the first slice of Kitty B.'s beautiful raspberry cream cake.

Ray doesn't reappear for the throwing of the bouquet or the beautiful exit in Kitty B.'s brother's old convertible Mustang that he had refurbished just for the occasion. Truth is, Kitty B. doesn't know what has happened to Ray.

Sis and Salvatore dance cheek to cheek until the band stops. Kitty B. wonders if he smells good. He must, she thinks, or Sis wouldn't be dancing so close. She smiles at the thought of this as Salvatore's lips, those lips that blow the heck out of the trumpet, press right down on Sis's again and again while Vangie and R.L. divide up the leftovers and invite Kitty B. over to drink one more glass of champagne on the dock before shutting down the porch lights.

Now Kitty B. waves good-bye to Vangie and the last guests as LeMar unplugs the tent lights from the front porch. When she walks up to join him, LeMar takes the champagne glass out of her hand, sets it down on the freshly painted railing, and pulls her close.

"Time to bed down," he says.

She nods as he follows her into the house and then from room to room as she switches off the lamps and heads for the stairs. Then LeMar does something he hasn't done in ages as they round the second-floor railing. He follows Kitty B. into her bedroom and crawls into her bed as she slips on her nightgown. Then they fall asleep beside each other for the first time in a decade, his chest rising and falling in time with hers beneath her mama's old afghan.

TWENTY-FOUR

Ray

Ray stands on the windy corner of Irving Place and 18th Street in Manhattan. It's five in the afternoon, and she's just ducked into the corner store to get a cup of coffee and a copy of the *New York Times*.

"Can I have some cream and sugar?" she says to the man in the white turban and T-shirt who rang her up.

He shouts something in Arabic to an elderly man sitting in the far corner of the room. The man nods and points to a corner by the fashion magazines, where a rusted decanter of some sort of milk is resting on a newspaper.

"That's all right, I'll try it black this time." She hurries out the door, takes one sip of the stale coffee and discreetly pours it out on the sidewalk.

Now she walks back toward Priscilla's apartment, where she'll sit and pretend to read the paper until her daughter comes home from work.

"Ugh," she thinks as she examines the dirt and grime on the edge of the concrete steps that lead to the apartment. She's in her best tan pants. The ones she bought at Talbots last fall, and she's not about to ruin them, so she pulls out the business section of the paper and sits on it.

It's the Friday after Katie Rae's wedding, and she knows that Priscilla has to be back from Las Vegas by now. Ray refused her calls over the last several days, but last night she saw Priscilla's home number light up on the telephone screen, and she turned to Willy and said, "She's back, and I'm going up there tomorrow to talk some sense into her."

She put Willy to work researching the grounds for an annulment, and she clapped her hands when he pointed to the third ground in one of his legal journals. "Either spouse was under the influence of drugs or alcohol at the time of the marriage."

"That's it!" she said as she slapped her hand down on the kitchen counter. "Willy, you know they were under the influence, and I bet Priscilla is already regretting her decision."

So Ray took the late morning flight out of Charleston, and she's been waiting outside of Priscilla's apartment building for a couple of hours. She suspects J.K. still has his own apartment in the East Village, and she hopes Priscilla will be taking a cab home alone.

She watches a tall and well-dressed elderly woman walking two poodles toward Gramercy Park, and she thinks of her mother. Ray's mama always wanted to visit Manhattan, but it wasn't until her honeymoon with Willy Sr. that she made it to the grand city. She remembers her mama whispering to her as she helped her pack her bags the night before they left, "This is my first time above the Mason-Dixon Line."

"Is it your first trip outside of South Carolina?" Ray had probed.

"Oh no," her mama said. "I grew up all across the south."

"Where?" Ray said. "Where did you grow up, Mama?"

"Can't remember all of the names, Ray," she said. "My daddy was a traveling preacher, you know? Now hand me that pink sweater."

As the elderly woman rounds the corner, Ray wonders why her mama kept so many secrets, and why she didn't try harder to force the truth out of her. Surely, with enough persistence, Carla Jones would have given Ray some clues about her roots. *Persistence is the only way to get what you want*, Ray thinks. It had taken her a while to figure this out, but now it's the creed she lives by. She can't imagine it any other way.

Now Ray paces back and forth. She lifts her head every time an occupied cab barrels down the street. Surely, the next one will be Priscilla. She knows if she can just get her alone for ten minutes, she could talk some sense into her.

At quarter to six, Priscilla rounds the corner. She's got her brief satchel slung over her shoulder, and she's talking on her cell phone. When Ray waves her direction, she snaps the phone shut and comes running towards her.

"Mama!" she says. "What are you doing here?"

She gives her mother such a forceful embrace that her dreadlocks slap the back of Ray's head. Ray does not soften into her daughter's hug. She keeps her back upright and she pulls away as soon as Priscilla gives her the chance.

"We need to talk," she says. "Let's go to your apartment."

"Okay," Priscilla says. "I have so much to show you. Some pictures from the wedding. Oh, and look at this."

She holds out her hand and points to a thin silver band on her slender finger. It looks like it could have come out of a bubble gum machine at K-Mart.

"This is my ring for now," Priscilla says. "We're going to pick one out together as soon as J.K. signs his new contract with *Knucklehead*."

Ray cringes. She pictures the antique set platinum ring that she picked out with Donovan. It had a beautiful diamond in the center and two sapphires on the side.

She wonders what in the world Donovan thinks now, and she hopes it's not too late for Pris to patch things up with him.

Priscilla's apartment is a wreck. There are dirty plates in the sink and a half-empty bottle of champagne on the coffee table. Pictures from Las Vegas are strewn across the sofa. Ray lets her eyes pass over them. She sees J.K. and Priscilla in blue jeans and T-shirts facing each other between some metal arch wrapped in faux vines. Behind them is an overweight man in a royal blue suit with an eerie grin on his face. How could Priscilla go through with it?

"Want something to drink, Mama?" Priscilla asks, grinning from ear to ear. "I can't believe you're here," she continues, unable to wait for her mother's reply. "You haven't been in my apartment for at least a year now, have you? J.K.'s going to move in this weekend. My rent is better than his so we'll stay here until my lease is up, and then we'll find a new place."

Priscilla pulls her dreadlocks back and ties them in a rubber band she finds on the coffee table. "Did you say you wanted something to drink?"

"No, thank you, darling," Ray says. She scoots the pictures over and pats a place next to her for Priscilla to sit.

"What is it?" Priscilla says. "Is Hilda's mom okay?"

"No, she's not okay, but that's not why I'm here." Ray looks her daughter head on. "It's about *you*."

Priscilla squints her eyes as if she's confused. "Oh, do you want to have a party back home? I was hoping you would. I want everyone to meet J.K."

Ray taps her foot firmly on the hardwood floor. "You can't possibly expect me to believe that you are happy with your rash decision to marry J.K."

Priscilla pulls back from her mother and adjusts her posture. "Yes, Mama. I do expect you to believe it."

"Pris, you were just about to become engaged to a bright and wonderful young man. What happened?"

"Donovan is great, but he's not for me, Mama," she says as she pinches her eyebrow. "You know, I've had this thing for J.K. for years now, and when he chased me down in Grand Central Station last week just as I was about to board my train to visit Donovan, I just couldn't get the thought of him out of my mind. And then when Donovan proposed, all I wanted to do was jump off that boat and take the next train back to New York to see J.K. So that's what I did."

"I don't see how you could know such a thing." Ray points to the pictures, which are falling into the cracks of the sofa. "Maybe that one little moment in the train station was like some scene in a romantic movie, but I can't imagine you really believe that you are meant to spend the rest of your life with Poop—um, I mean, J.K."

Priscilla's eyes widen and she starts to heave as she takes in one deep breath after another.

Ray sucks her teeth. "Let me ask you something, Pris. Were you under the influence when you married him?"

"What?" Priscilla says.

Ray picks up the picture of the two in front of the arch and holds it up for Priscilla to see.

"Sure, we had a little champagne in the plane on the way to Las Vegas," Priscilla says, snatching the picture out of her mother's hand. "But when I accepted J.K.'s proposal that night, I was stone-cold sober and so was he."

Ray looks out of the window for a moment. Across the street she sees an open window of another apartment where an older man puffs on a cigar as the nightly news flashes across his television screen.

Ray turns back to Priscilla. "You've made a terrible mistake," she says. "We've got to get this annulled. The champagne on the plane will be enough to do it."

"What are you talking about, Mama?" Pris says. "I don't want to get it *annulled.*"

"Priscilla, don't be an idiot." Ray bites the inside of her cheek. "J.K. is worthless. He's a child who makes his living hurting himself so that other people can laugh at him. Do you think he'll ever grow up?"

Ray snatches another picture of J.K. doing a headstand in some casino lobby and shows it to Priscilla. "This man will *never* mature, much less *provide* for you."

Priscilla stands up and grabs her head with both hands. "That's not true!" she says. "He's a very loving person, Mama. I've got a nice paying job on a new show and so does he. We're going to be fine. I knew you would take this hard, but I never thought you would suggest I break the whole thing off." Priscilla inhales deeply and adds, "As if it never happened."

"I insist that you break it off." Ray stands and takes her daughter by the shoulders. "I've got to save you from yourself, Priscilla. You'll thank me ten years from now. Trust me."

Priscilla begins to weep. She makes these terrible little choking sounds that remind Ray of a small child gasping for air.

"You can't make me, Mama!" she shouts. "You can't make me marry Donovan or move back to South Carolina or join the Wedding Guild of All Saints or who knows what else you have in mind for my life." She pulls Ray's hands off her, steps back, and says, "Now if you can't accept my decision I want you to leave."

"Leave?" Ray says.

Priscilla walks to the door and opens it. "Yes, Mama." Her eyes brim with tears, and she rubs them with her forearm before nodding in the direction of the hallway.

Ray's belly tightens with fury. She's going to talk some sense into her child yet. This is not over. Just as she walks over to slam the door back, a tall, wiry figure comes bounding up the stairs with a bouquet of sunflowers.

"Mrs. Montgomery?" J.K. says. "What are you doing here?"

He runs over to embrace Ray, but he stops short when he sees Priscilla's red and tear-streaked face.

"Everybody okay?" he asks. He gives Priscilla a kiss on the cheek and hands her the flowers. "For you, my bride."

"Thank you," she says, but she doesn't take her eyes off Ray.

J.K. rubs his jeans with the palms of his hands and says to Priscilla, "Should I walk around the block and give you some time?"

"No," Priscilla says, glancing at him. "Mama is welcome to stay, as long as she accepts our marriage."

Ray watches J.K. look back and forth between them. Then he suffles his feet from side to side.

Priscilla raises her eyebrows and says, "It's that simple, Mama. Accept it or leave."

Ray can feel the cramps from the fibroid tumors coming on, and she wants to double over. Nothing about this afternoon has turned out the way she planned. She watches Priscilla grab J.K.'s hand and squeeze it tight, and she knows she has no choice.

"You'll regret this, Priscilla," she says as she walks out the door. "You will for the rest of your days."

Ray weeps all the way to the airport in the cab. The driver reminds her of the gruff cashier in the corner store, and when he offers her some yellowed tissue from a Ziploc bag in his glove compartment, she refuses it. She calls Willy just before she boards the plane. "It went awful."

He sighs. "I'm sorry, Ray, but I can't say I'm surprised. I think we're going to have to come to terms with this one whether we like it or not." *No,* Ray thinks. She's had to come to terms with more than her fair share in this lifetime. She shouldn't have to come to terms with her daughter's foolish mistake.

Just as she is about to hang up he says, "Vangie called to remind you about the revival on Saturday."

"Great," Ray says. "What a way to end the week."

Willy picks her up at the airport and drives her the forty miles home to Jasper. They both collapse in the bed, but Ray can't sleep. Her tumors are flaring up again, and all she sees when she closes her eyes is Priscilla standing there in that doorway as rigid as a steel rod, forcing her to accept her dreadful decision to marry J.K.

Once Willy starts to snore, Ray tiptoes out of bed and goes downstairs to have a glass of wine and a pimento cheese sandwich. Nothing, nothing has turned out the way she planned, and she can't understand why.

She takes a bite of her sandwich and glances over at the schedule on the refrigerator and realizes it was her turn to check in on Hilda tonight.

Shoot. For all I know she could be starving in there.

She grabs a few odds and ends out of the refrigerator and throws on her raincoat and walks down the street to deliver the food.

It must be one in the morning by now, but she can see that a lamp is still lit upstairs in Hilda's bedroom. She knocks on the door and calls up to her. "Hilda," she says, "I brought you a few odds and ends. Some pimento cheese and honey ham and pickled okra. Sorry it's so late."

When no one responds she sits down on the stoop. There is a pen on the bench by the front door, and Ray grabs it and tears off a piece of the paper grocery bag she brought over and begins to write.

Hilda,

This might bring a smile to your face—I'm fit to be tied. Priscilla married Poop 2 in Las Vegas, and I just flew up to New York to see if I could get her to break it off. In fine Priscilla form, she refused.

Then there's Vangie taking over the church with her kooky evangelical agenda, and did you know that some developer from Savannah is going to turn the charming Allston house across the street from me into an apartment building?

Oh, and I threw an out-and-out hissy fit at Katie Rae's wedding, and I'm not even sure if Kitty B. and Sis are talking to me any more. I wouldn't blame them if they aren't. It was practically unforgivable.

Anyway, they both seemed to have changed since you closed yourself in there.

Kitty B.'s signed up for dog training school, of all things, and she drives to Charleston twice a week with one of her mangy dogs for her lessons.

Sis lost it one day and donated her wedding dress to Goodwill after I didn't accept her offer to let Priscilla wear it. Of course, I bought the dress back from Goodwill. I couldn't stand the thought of some stranger getting married in it.

Oh, and my hair seems to be falling out in clumps in the back. Isn't that lovely? And despite the hormone replacement therapy that I'm back on, I still have those awful fibroid tumors, and I'm sure I'll have to have a hysterectomy after all.

I had no control over the first half of my life, Hilda. I know you've figured that much out. But I was hoping things would turn out differently for the second half. I was wrong.

Love,
Ray

Ray slips the note through the door.

"I'm going now," she says. "I'll bring you a better meal to eat tomorrow if I survive the healing prayer revival."

Then she walks beneath the Lady Banksia vines, through the wrought iron gates, up the sidewalk, and home.

The honour of your presence
is requested at the marriage of

Miss Elizabeth Phillips Mims

to

Mr. Salvatore Anatole Giornelli

On Saturday, the twenty-first of April
Two thousand and seven
at six o'clock
12 Third Street
Jasper, South Carolina

TWENTY-FIVE

Sis

Sis knocks on Ray's front door. She and Kitty B. have been summoned over for tea. Ray's been acting strange for months now, and Sis is anxious to hear what she has to say.

She wants to give her plenty of time before she tells them her big news so she twists her engagement ring around so that the diamond faces down and she blots her lips on a napkin as the wide mahogany door opens.

"Hello, Sis," Ray says. "Come on in."

Kitty B. wobbles over and gives Sis an embrace. "We want to hear all about your trip to Italy. Did you get those sandals there?"

"Yes," Sis beams. "At a little leather market in Lucca." She bounces on the balls of her feet and tries hard not to break into a full-fledged grin.

On Ray's side table in the foyer is a stack of brochures for the "Healing Prayer Revival Day."

"So did you patch things up with Capers and Vangie?" Sis asked.

Ray blushes. "Well, yes. You know, no one showed up at that revival day back in January, so I'm helping them coordinate a new one in a few weeks, and I've been handing out fliers left and right.

I'm sure they're going to call on you to help with the music now that you're back."

"I'd be happy to," Sis says. "I'll call Vangie tomorrow."

"Well, come on out on the piazza." Ray points toward the glass doors at the end of her living room. "I've got the tea all set up."

As they take their places around the wicker coffee table, Ray serves them a cup of Earl Grey and some scones and crumpets that she bought from a new bakery in Charleston. In the little silver bowls she inherited from Willy's mother she has fresh raspberries, whipped cream, and lemon curd.

"Ray, this is so nice," Kitty B. says. "You went all out. What's the occasion?"

"Well, go on and serve yourself a cup of tea and I'll tell you." She hands Sis the cream and sugar on a little china tray and nods.

"Are you jet-lagged, Sis?"

"Not really," Sis says. "But I need you all to catch me up on everything. Has anyone heard from Hilda?"

Kitty B. shakes her head and spoons a dollop of whipped cream across her scone.

"We wish," Ray says as she takes her seat and carefully spreads out the linen napkin across her lap. "But there's no news on that front."

"How about Priscilla?" Sis says. "Any news there?"

Ray looks down at her teacup. "No. I kept thinking she would come to her senses, but it looks like I've got to let it go. That's what Willy keeps telling me, anyway."

"I'm sorry." Sis reaches her hand out and pats Ray's elbow.

"Well, enough about that." Ray flaps her hand as if to shoo away a wasp. "I think I better tell y'all what I have on my chest. If I don't, we won't be able to enjoy our tea."

"Go ahead," Kitty B. says as she takes a bite of her scone.

Ray's eyes fill with tears and she looks down into her lap. "Oh, y'all, I'm so sorry about how I behaved at Katie Rae's wedding. Will you ever forgive me?"

Kitty B. and Sis look at each other and laugh.

"Is that what this is about?" Sis says. "You think you need to apologize for *that*?"

Kitty B. laughs so hard that she sneezes. Then she blows her nose into her napkin and says, "Ray, honestly, I think we were all glad to see you're human."

Ray looks up and Sis nods strongly in agreement. She reaches out her hand again. "That was a tough night for you. Probably one of the toughest. You had every right to throw a hissy fit. We would never hold that against you."

"You wouldn't?" Ray looks back and forth at both of the gals as they shake their heads.

"Never," Kitty B. says.

"Y'all are dear friends," Ray says. "I thought you were upset with me about that. I've been worrying over it for the past two months."

They all laugh together and Ray takes a sip of her tea. Then she fans herself. "Hot tea in March. What was I thinking? I can already feel a hot flash coming on."

Kitty B. smiles, takes a sip of her tea, and clears her throat. Then a serious look comes over her face. "I will give you both something to worry about."

"What?" Ray says, as Sis watches three worry lines spread across Kitty B.'s forehead.

Kitty B. pats her eyes with the edge of the napkin. "Y'all, we got some of LeMar's medical tests back yesterday."

Sis can tell by the tone of her voice that something is not right. "New tests? I didn't know anything else was wrong."

Kitty B. swallows hard. "Sis, you missed this, but a few weeks ago LeMar fainted while he was pruning his sweetheart rosebush, and Angus helped me drive him over to MUSC for an MRI. The doctors saw a small mass at the very tip of his brain stem."

"Oh no," Sis covers her mouth with her hand.

"Well, we just found out that it is a malignant tumor."

Ray gasps. "It can't be."

"Not only that, but it's inoperable," Kitty B. says as she wrings her hands. "Poor fellow. He really had been feeling bad—at least this last year or so—and the doctors had missed it." She rubs the back of her head. "It was tucked in good back there, and I am just as sick as I can be about it."

"Well, I just don't understand," Ray says. "I knew he'd had the fall, but I didn't know about the MRI. I thought he'd been feeling better than ever—"

"He has been," Kitty B. says. "He's been up and moving for the first time in a decade. The last couple of months have been the best he's had in years."

Sis jumps up and goes over to embrace Kitty B.

"He says he's going to fight it," Kitty B. says, her chin on Sis's shoulder. "But the doctors at the Hollings Cancer Center are afraid it started in another source, and they want to run more tests this week to see if that's true."

They sit this way for several moments, Sis's arms around Kitty B. and Ray staring in disbelief into her tea.

"We're here for you," Sis says.

"That's right." Ray nods. "Whatever you need, we'll take care of it."

"I know y'all will," Kitty B. says. "Right now I just want to relax with you both and enjoy this tea and scones." So they sit back and pass the teapot and smell the confederate jasmine in between their bits of conversation.

After tea, they send Kitty B. on home and Sis helps Ray clear the plates and wash the dishes. Just as they are drying the last silver spoon, Ray grabs Sis's hand, spins the ring around, and says, "What's this?"

Sis blushes and steps back.

"You're engaged!" Ray squeals. "Oh, my word, Sis!"

Ray pulls Sis over to the kitchen table with her wet hands. "Sit down right now and tell me everything! Oh, I can't believe I didn't figure this out until now." Sis watches Ray wipe her hands on her apron. "I want every detail. Every single one."

"Oh, Ray, he's so wonderful."

"Yes, yes, of course he is," Ray says. "Well, when did he ask you? And how?"

"We were sitting on a park bench sharing a chocolate gelato beside the Romanesque Cathedral in his hometown, Lucca. It's in Tuscany just to the northeast of Pisa. It's a quiet little place with ancient roads and churches and a Puccini museum that LeMar would just flip over. Oh, poor LeMar."

"LeMar is in good hands, Sis." Ray narrows her eyes. "Now tell me more. Were you surprised?"

"Honestly, no," Sis says. "From that first night at Katie Rae's wedding, Salvatore dropped hints about getting married. At first I thought he wanted something from me, my little bit of inheritance or an American citizenship. I didn't know what. But over these last few months I've come to realize that he simply felt something for me that he hadn't felt in a long, long time, and the feeling is mutual!"

"Has he ever been married before?" Ray asks. "Does he have any children?"

"Oh, it's the saddest story," Sis says. "He lost his wife decades ago just before she was to give birth to their first child. He woke up one morning and she was stone still in the bed next to him. She'd had one of those awful embolisms that just gets you out of nowhere, and Salvatore had to lay her and his baby daughter to rest. It took him twenty years to come to grips with it. Don't you know, I could certainly understand that?"

"Yes, you could," Ray says, tears filling her eyes. She pulls one of Cousin Willy's handkerchiefs out of the seersucker jacket hanging on the chair next to her and pats her eyes. "Of course you can. And you love him? You think you are compatible?"

"I know it's only been three months, but it just feels right," Sis says, her eyes wide. "As different and foreign as he is, we have a lot in common. We love music, we love our friends, we love the church, and we love our families." She stands up as if she can't contain herself. "And let me tell you, Ray, this man smells *good*. He smells like tangerines and aftershave and cigarettes and something I can't even put my finger on. Something warm and manly that is just Salvatore, and I just love it. I love him!"

And she knows it's true. She does love him. She couldn't deny it any more than she could the good Lord Himself.

"Well, where are you going to live?" Ray asks.

"We think we can manage to split our time between Jasper and Lucca. Mama wants to give us the old home on Third Street, and Salvatore has a charming little villa by the Cathedral. We will go back and forth every six months, depending on how Mama is feeling and what Salvatore's concert schedule looks like."

"Can you believe it, Sis?" Ray asks. "I'm just so happy for you."

"I really can't believe it," Sis says. "But I'm going to." She sits back down and squeezes Ray's hands. "Now we want the whole wedding to be quiet and quick. We're both in the sunsets of our lives, and we don't need any kind of fuss."

Ray nods steadily and looks off for a moment. Sis can see her wheels spinning. "Ray, I don't want a big to-do."

"I know, I know," she says. "But you will let me plan it, won't you?"

"Of course," Sis says.

"Great!" Ray stands up and embraces her. "You tell me a date and I'll get going. I don't want you to worry about a thing."

Sis lets Ray hold her tight for what seems like whole minutes until Willy comes through the back door and says, "All right, gals. What are y'all blubbering about now?"

TWENTY-SIX

Well, a lot has been going on these last few weeks. Ray stands back for a moment and surveys the preparations going on in her back garden. She nods in satisfaction. This is going to be the best wedding yet. Despite all the drama that has followed her for months now.

After Ray realized there was no way she could talk sense into Priscilla about an annulment, she'd refused to take her calls. Then J.K.'s parents invited her and Willy to Alexandria for a small post-wedding celebration, and Cousin Willy had to pry her into the car and drive her up there by force. She had to admit that J.K.'s parents seemed quite civilized. His father is a banker, and his mother runs an antique shop on King Street in the heart of the historic district. Mrs. Neely had a beautiful dinner for them in their lovely town-home, and J.K. actually behaved as though he had some manners. The gals—except for Hilda, who has remained completely silent for over six months now—are helping Ray plan a wedding celebration for Priscilla and J.K. that will be held in a few weeks.

Then there was the Saturday of the rescheduled Healing Prayer Revival Day at All Saints. When she thinks about it, Ray cannot believe that was the best day she's had in months. It was the sec-

ond week in March, just after Sis had come home from Italy and
announced her engagement.

~ MARCH 11, 2006 ~

Vangie gathered the ushers in the narthex bright and early. "Thank
you all for serving." She frantically checked her file folders and
pulled out the programs and the prayer cards. "Especially you, Ray."

Ray nodded and pointed to the programs. "Want us to hand
those out?"

"Yes," she said, tugging on the gold bangles on her wrist. "I'm nervous as can be about this, y'all. I hope we'll have a turnout this time."

Vangie held up a small index card with "prayer requests" written
at the top and said, "Now tell the participants that this is a day for
their own *personal* healing and revival. If they want prayer for someone else who's on their mind, they should write the person's name
on a pew card and give it to you all. Then I need y'all to turn it into
the prayer ministers we've brought in from some of the churches in
Charleston. They will pray over them."

When Capers opened the door there must have been about thirty
folks lined up in the church yard. Some were All Saints parishioners,
but most were just interested folks from the community.

Ray took her place at the back of the church and ushered folks
into the old family pews for Capers's teaching on the healings in the
New Testament. Then she went up and down the aisles to collect
their prayer requests for loved ones, which she handed to a group
of priests in the back of the room who received the cards and
prayed for them one by one.

During Capers's teaching Ray slipped a prayer card out of the
back pew and put the names of the people who she felt needed it:
Priscilla and J.K.; William and Carson; Laura, the sister she hadn't
seen in four years; and even her daddy, who might still be alive

somewhere out there. She slipped the card to one of the men in the back who nodded and gave her a reassuring smile before he read the names on the card and closed his eyes.

When Capers finished his talk, Ray opened the pews one by one and ushered the participants up to the altar where Vangie and Capers put their hands on them and prayed for their concerns and ailments as Sis played some worship songs softly on the little keyboard Capers had rented for the occasion.

No one fainted or fell down into any strange convulsions when Capers and Vangie prayed for them, much to Ray's relief, but every time a participant walked back down the aisle to their seat after prayer, she noticed they had a different look about them. Ray couldn't tell if it was in their body language or their facial expressions, but it was a look of peace and a quiet strength, and it was a new look for each of the folks she had ushered out of the pews. It was so pronounced in some that she had to stop herself from making her own walk down the aisle when Capers turned to the congregation, opened his hands, and said, "Anyone else?"

After Kitty B. served everyone a delicious chicken salad lunch in the churchyard, Ray helped round everyone up and back into the sanctuary for what Capers called the "Generational Healing Eucharist," which was some kind of unique communion service where, as Capers said, "We will ask God to cut us free from anything negative that has come down our family lines, whether we know about it or not."

Then Vangie told Ray to hand out these little family tree charts for everyone to fill out. "You fill one out too," Vangie said, when Ray took her seat next to her in the back. Well, at first Ray thought about making up things about her family—a little cancer here, a little heart disease there—the way she did in Dr. Arhundati's office. But then when Capers announced that no one would see the charts, she actually turned away from Vangie and put a big question mark up her daddy's side and another up her mama's side.

As they went forward for communion, Ray and all of the participants took their charts and placed them in an offering basket. Next
they followed Capers out to the graveyard and burned the charts as
a symbol of this "cutting free."

Strange thing was, for Ray's whole life she's wanted to know
who her family was. To attach herself to them. She's wanted to
know where she came from, and she's wanted to hitch her wagon
to her ancestors, whoever they were, without stopping to think
that she could be hitching up to something rather awful. Maybe
that's why her mama never elaborated. Maybe she was trying to
protect her.

She realized this as Capers stoked the ashes and some of the participants wept, and she decided to have her first talk with God since
Priscilla's Las Vegas wedding. She turned away from the group and
looked out over all of the weathered, ornate gravestones that stood
like a grand record of the history of Jasper. She was always envious of
the gang who all had family plots around the chapel and a heritage
to point to. "That was Grandmama," one would point. "That was
Great Uncle Rudolph," said another.

Well, God, she says. *Maybe it's for the best. Maybe I don't need to
know about my roots. I've had a blessed life here in Jasper with a loving husband and a place to finally call home, and I might as well let it
go at that.*

As Ray watched the smoke of the singeing family trees waft up
and into the Spanish moss of the live oaks, she let go of the pain in
her heart—the pain she'd carried ever since the night some forty
years ago when Nigel Pringle called her a bastard. Then she
breathed in the sweet smell of the smoke spreading out in the thick
air around her and pictured herself climbing into the back of the
pickup truck the night the pack came calling and how when they
took off, she looked back to find her mama standing on the front
stoop smiling and waving.

When she turned back around in the graveyard on the healing

prayer revival day, most of the participants had filed out of the churchyard, and Vangie was picking up the leftover programs that a few folks had left on the headstones.

Ray came alongside her and picked some up too. Then she patted Vangie's back. "It went real well."

That night when Ray went home, Cousin Willy met her on the back steps with a white wine spritzer and some summer sausage and Triscuits. "How did it go?" he said.

She sat right down on the rocking chair beside him, and they looked out over the garden and she said, "Willy, did you know I never had a father?"

He reached out, put his arm firmly around her shoulders, and took a deep breath. "I figured, sweet."

"You did?" Snippets of their life together flash through her mind. "All this time?"

"Yeah," he said. "Neither you or your mama had much to say about family, and I just assumed—"

"You mean you figured that all along, and it never *bothered* you?"

He turned to face her. "Bothered me? Heck, Ray, the best thing that ever happened to me was you and your move to Jasper. I couldn't have cared less about your family history."

She smiled and rested her head in the nook of his neck.

"There's more," she said. "I wasn't a relative of Mrs. Pringle's on South Battery, Willy. My mama was her housekeeper. We took care of her when she was elderly. That's why she left us some of the inheritance."

Cousin Willy pulled her closer. "It doesn't matter, Ray. That has never mattered to me. The only one it's mattered to is you."

Ray opened her eyes wide and sat up. "Do you think the gals know?"

Willy shrugged and pulled her back close to him. "I don't know, and I don't care."

She settled into his thick chest and breathed in his warmth. She guessed she might have sensed all along that the gals had a hunch about her past. Hilda had always probed her about it, but she thought that was just to get a rise out of her.

"I love you, Ray," Cousin Willy said. "I love you, your gals love you, and the whole town of Jasper would be a wreck without you."

She leaned forward, slapped her knees. "Well, Willy, I think you're right."

"Good," he said.

"And I think we ought to have Sis's wedding right here in our back garden. I'm going to make it glorious. Better than anything the town has ever seen. What do you say? Can I offer it?"

Willy took a sip of her wine spritzer. He winced and said, "I think it's a fine idea. Now you call your gals, and I'm going to get a beer and put a venison loin on the grill."

"You'll help me, won't you?" Ray said to the back of his balding head. "We're going to have to clean the garden up real good, and we might need to repaint the trim of the house."

"'Course." He turned back to grin at her. "'Course, I'll help you, First Lady."

The next day Ray grabbed Sis's old wedding dress—the one she'd bought back from Goodwill the day Sis donated it—and drove over to the fabric store in Savannah where she purchased the most beautiful ivory shade of raw silk you ever saw. Then she went over to Hilda's and rang the doorbell. She had written a letter to Hilda the night before, and she pulled it out of her pocketbook and slipped it through the mail slot.

"Hilda," she called. "I've got a letter for you that will be worth your trip down the stairs. It's about my life before Jasper, which I think you knew all along. But once you get down here to read this, I've got something else for you. It's Sis's old wedding dress and some gorgeous silk from the fabric store. I was hoping you could take the measurements from the old dress to make her a new gown. She'll be marrying that Italian trumpeter next month, you know?"

Ray rested the fabric and the dress on the bench by the front door. She peered through the dining room window, but she couldn't see any sign of Hilda. She cupped her hands and hollered toward the upstairs, where she noticed one window was open just a couple of inches.

"I'm going to keep back checking with you all week, Hilda. If you feel up to making the dress, write me a note. Otherwise, we'll go to town and buy something."

Now on the night before Sis's wedding, Ray really is pulling out all of the stops. It's going to be the most beautiful celebration the town has ever seen. Her gardenias have just started to bloom, and she is using every last one of them for the boutonnieres and the wedding cake and one of the focal points of Sis's spring bouquet. You will never smell a sweeter fragrance in your life!

"Don't you want to save those for Pris's party?" Kitty B. had asked a few days ago when she and Ray went to Charleston to buy the oasis and floral tape.

"No," Ray says. "I don't. I want to use every last one of them for Sis."

Ray even took down her stash of champagne glasses from the shed last week, and she and Richadene washed each of the two hundred glasses by hand for the occasion. When she didn't hear back from Hilda, she took Sis to Charleston where they searched and searched for the right gown. They settled on a two-piece ensemble they found at Saks—a straight satin skirt with a beaded jacket. Ray thought it looked a little like something a mother of the bride would wear, but Sis twirled around in it in front of the dressing room mirror and said,

"This will work fine. Tasteful and age-appropriate. With three weeks to go, I can't be too picky, right?"

Tonight Ray's putting everyone to work for the final touches. She and Kitty B. are cutting the flowers and preparing the oasis for the arrangements while Justin and Willy set out the mosquito zappers beneath the tent in the backyard. Sis even dropped by, and now she's polishing the last few silver trays for the champagne toast.

"Go on home and get some rest." Ray pats Sis's back, looks at her watch, and adds, "It's almost eleven o'clock."

"I'm an old woman, Ray," Sis says. "The last-minute, behind-the-scenes stuff is my favorite part, and I'm not going to miss it."

"I'm spending the night," Kitty B. says. "You can, too, if you want."

Ray laughs. "Of course you can."

"I think I will," she says. "It's thirty-four years later, but I want my prewedding slumber party too."

At midnight, Ray puts the last bits of greenery in some water and says, "Y'all go get ready for bed, and I'll make us a midnight snack."

A few minutes later they are out on the piazza with three shrimp salad sandwiches, a tray of lemon squares, and a bottle of chardonnay, watching the reflection of the moon on the ripples of water moving into Round-O Creek. The heat from the late April day has long since faded, and the air is soft and cool.

"How's LeMar?" Sis asks Kitty B. as she props her feet up on the coffee table.

"Angus took him to the Medical University today," Kitty B. says. "He wanted to hear for himself what the specialist had to stay about the test results, and he'll give me a full report tomorrow."

Kitty B. leans back in the wicker chair, closes her eyes, and breathes in the fresh air. Then she tilts her head to Sis and says,

"But to answer your question, he's hopeful, and that's been a wonderful surprise. Just the other day on our way home from the hospital he said, 'I'm not worried, Kitty B. I think we'll be able to get this under control.'"

Ray hopes LeMar is right and that it will be a long time before they will be coordinating anyone's funeral reception. LeMar has felt ill for over twenty years now, but this cancer has come on so fast it's hard for the gang to take it in. Despite the hot flashes and the bald spots, it's easy to forget that they are all aging. That time will catch up with them sooner or later and that those headstones in the All Saints parish graveyard will have some of their names etched on them in a few short decades.

"Maybe LeMar should come for prayer," Ray says before she even has time to stop herself.

Kitty B. and Sis turn sharply toward her, their eyes widening in disbelief. Ray calmly pats her lips with a napkin and says, "You know, at the church. Capers and Vangie can pray for him."

"You really think he should?" Kitty B. says. "You think that might work?"

"Yes." Ray brushes a crumb off her nightgown and nods her head. "I do."

"Well, then, I'll talk to him about that," Kitty B. says. "I think he just might go, Ray. Thank you for the suggestion."

Sis turns to Kitty B. and winks. Then she reaches out and squeezes Ray's wrist. "It's a wonderful suggestion."

Ray nods her head and looks out over the water. Then she props her legs on the table by Sis.

"I'm just so excited about tomorrow." Kitty B. nudges Sis's elbow. "Aren't you?"

"I am." Sis grins and even in the darkness Ray imagines her cheeks reddening. "I really can't believe it's happening."

"We're just so happy for you," Kitty B. says.

"We are." Ray sits up and looks at the tent and then back to the gals. Her stomach starts to churn the way it usually does before she hosts a big event. "I just hope we haven't forgotten anything, y'all. Is there anything else you can think of?"

"Yes," a quiet voice calls from the dark edge of the garden. "There is one more thing."

Ray leans forward and squints, and she can see a long piece of whiteness moving toward them.

"What's *that*?" Sis says, sitting up in her seat.

"Who's there?" Kitty B. says as she stands.

"She can't get married without this," the figure says as it moves toward the porch, carefully holding the whiteness above the ground.

"Hilda?" Kitty B. takes a step toward the garden and then looks back at Sis and Ray. "Y'all, I think that's her."

"Hush, Kitty B.," the voice says. "Don't make a scene. I'm just coming to drop this wedding gown off."

"It *is* her!" Sis says. She leaps up from her chair and runs out to greet her, and the others follow.

Ray grabs the gown out of her hands and drapes it over the piazza railing and waits her turn to embrace her. In the moonlight Hilda looks better than Ray would ever expect. She's thin but not more so than usual, and she holds her back up straight as a rod with her perfect posture as she blots her painted lips.

Ray smells cigarette smoke and Coco Chanel when she steps toward her. She gives her a firm hug and says, "I'm just so glad to lay eyes on you."

Hilda nods toward the dress. "Go try it on, Sis. I won't be brave enough to come out tomorrow, but I want to see you in it tonight."

Sis takes the dress and Kitty B. follows her upstairs. "We'll back in a minute," she says.

"Thank you," Ray says to Hilda in the darkness of her piazza. "I can't believe you were able to make something in that short amount of time."

Hilda takes a deep breath and looks out over the tidal creek.

"It was my pleasure," she says. "And the least I could do. Y'all have been my lifeline these last few months, and I might just make it because of you."

Ray reaches out and grabs Hilda's hand. "You will," she says. "You just need some time."

Hilda doesn't let go of Ray's hand as Sis comes back down and models the elegant silk gown. It's a silk A-line with a creamy sash and the most delicate cropped jacket with scalloped edges that you have ever seen. Sis looks positively stunning in it.

"I love it, Hilda!" Sis says. "It's more gorgeous than anything I could have imagined, and it fits perfectly. How did you know my measurements?"

Hilda gives Ray's hand a tighter squeeze. "I'm just that good," she says.

Kitty B. claps her hands and Ray pours a glass of wine for Hilda, and they sit on the piazza and tell Hilda all about the plans for tomorrow until she finally says, "I'd better get home now."

They all walk her down Third Street to the corner, Sis lifting her dress as they move along the sidewalk.

"You understand why I can't be there tomorrow?" Hilda says to Sis as she lifts the bottom of her dress when they cross the street.

"Yes," Sis says. "Of course I do."

As they move together through the wrought iron gates of Hilda's home, Ray says, "We want to know something, Hilda."

Hilda pulls out her key and looks back at her as she unlocks the door. "What?"

"Are you going to let us in your house now? So we can see you regularly."

"Probably so," Hilda says as she steps in the doorway, her thin figure like a shadowed mannequin outlined by the soft light from the hall lamp. "But don't stop writing the letters."

They look at one another and smile as Hilda reaches behind the door. "One more thing." She pulls out a miniature lace dress and hands it to Ray. "Here's Miss C.'s ensemble. Can't forget that detail."

Sis reaches out to touch the dress. "Hey, that's the fabric from my old wedding dress," she says. Then she looks at each of them. "Y'all went and bought it back, didn't you?"

They each shrug and look at one another as Sis shakes her head and says, "Y'all are a mess."

"We just like to recycle," Ray says. "Who doesn't like to take some scraps and make something new?"

They all giggle and Hilda says to Sis, "Best wishes, my friend." Then she waves once before gently closing the door.

TWENTY-SEVEN

Ray

Sis's wedding will be the most gorgeous one the town has ever seen. Ray even let Vangie Dreggs in on the action, and she has flown in an ice sculptor from the Four Seasons in Houston who is sculpting a gigantic treble clef as the centerpiece for the shrimp and crab claw table.

Miss C. is a picture herself. Hilda took the bits of Sis's old dress and created a complete ensemble with a full-length dress and a veil. Vangie put a mini organ and a toy trumpet on either side of her that looks adorable. Next to Miss C. is a basket filled with miniature trumpets that Ray found at the dollar store. The guests will play them during the couple's departure.

Ray's garden is a sight. The giant oak trees on the side of the creek are brightened up with pastel painted sap buckets overflowing with flowers: periwinkle and pale green hydrangeas and English roses in yellow and pink. Garlands embellish everything from the piazza to the back porch railing to the rail of the dock. And here's her absolute favorite touch: an old wooden canoe anchored in Round-O Creek overflows with the same flowers as the sap buckets. It floats in the center of the water like a vibrant picture of Lowcountry lushness, and before the guests arrive Ray will light some votives in these little plastic vases and send them gliding out into the creek.

But there is more. At the edge of the creek Willy and Capers created an altar made from hay bales and a grapevine cross. Massive urns on either side of the altar hold the vibrant collection of white roses and gardenias. The wedding programs are lovely, too, with a pressed white pansy in the center and a yellow satin bow. Some of the children in Jasper who take piano lessons from Sis will stand at the edge of the creek in seersucker suits and dresses and hand out the programs.

Then there is the reception tent! Inside there are candelabras draped in green moss. There is an icy caviar and vodka table in honor of Salvatore and a shrimp and grits table and the usual lamb and beef tenderloin stations. The tall, narrow seven-tiered wedding cake is bedecked with gardenias and outlined at the base with votive candles in an array of little crystal vases that belong to Sis's mama.

After Ray makes sure the greeters are in position with the programs, Salvatore arrives, beaming from ear to ear and as handsome as can be in his black tails—a classic! He takes his place at the front of the altar once the guests are seated, and Ray grins at how puffed up he is when the ceremony begins and Cousin Willy walks his bride down the aisle in that raw silk dress Hilda made.

Sis is wearing her mother's double-strand pearls with a rose clasp, and her silky black hair is cut short and falls perfectly around her smiling face. The gardenias in her bouquet smell divine as she makes her way down the casual aisle and to the hay-bale altar. Salvatore squeezes her hand tightly, and they turn to face each other before the altar.

Then Capers lifts his head toward the congregation and begins, "Dearly beloved: We have come together in the presence of God to witness and bless the joining together of this man and this woman in Holy Matrimony. The bond and covenant of marriage was established by God in creation, and our Lord Jesus Christ adorned this manner of life by His presence and first miracle at a wedding in Cana of Galilee. It signifies to us the mystery of the union between Christ and His Church, and Holy Scripture commends it to be honored among all people."

Oh, what a joy! In a sense, it's as though Ray hears these words for the first time. God established marriage. And it symbolizes the mystery of the union between Jesus and His Church. A wedding is the grand celebration of this mystery, and Ray watches intently as Capers prepares the table and makes the Holy Eucharist in her own back garden.

After Sis and Salvatore partake of the body and the blood, Capers invites the congregation to share in the feast. Ray can hardly wait to get down the aisle for another taste of that newfound peace she discovered in the graveyard a few weeks ago.

"The Body of our Lord Jesus Christ keep you in everlasting life, Ray," Capers says as he firmly places the wafer in her hand.

She takes the paper-thin piece and places it on her tongue, and as it dissolves she prays, "Thank you. Thank you, Lord, for keeping me."

Once the reception is under way, Ray gives Vangie and Kitty B. their jobs. Ray's in charge of watching over the food staff, Kitty B. is in charge of the bartenders, and Vangie is in charge of the wrap-up.

Next Sis's mama, Mrs. Mims, hobbles over on her elegant cane, grabs Ray's elbow, and says, "Darling—" Her eyes tear up and she hugs Ray tight. "I can't imagine a more beautiful wedding, and you deserve the credit. Thank you for honoring Sis after all of these years."

"Mrs. Mims," Ray says, patting her back. "There is no one I'd rather do it for."

"Y'all have always been good to each other," she says. "You've always looked after each other, and I know you will long after I'm gone."

"Well, we have to," Ray says. "If we don't, who else will? Certainly not our children, right?"

Mrs. Mims smiles and pats Ray's back. "Bless you," she says. "You're a gift to this community."

Now Ray scans the tent and spots the offspring who have taken the time to show up at the wedding. Cricket and Tommy hold hands by the dock as Marshall and Katie Rae cut a rug on the dance floor beneath the tent. Giuseppe embraces his new Aunt Sis as Salvatore pecks Little Hilda on the cheek. Ray's son and his wife actually made the trip too. They are sitting on a low-lying live oak limb sipping Bellinis from the special batch that one of the uncles in the Giornelli family brought to the wedding.

Priscilla and J.K. did not even take the time to regret the wedding. They didn't send a gift, and no one has heard a word from them in weeks. Well, Ray can't say that she's surprised, but she's not going to let their poor behavior ruin the evening for her. Priscilla knows better. That's all she can say. Maybe one day she'll put all her mama's tried to teach her to use, but Ray's not going to bet on it.

Before long Angus comes over to Ray. "LeMar's report yesterday did not look good. They still haven't located the source, but the cancer has spread to his bones."

"Does Kitty B. know?" she asks.

"I just told her," he says.

"Oh, dear," Ray shakes her head.

Then Kitty B. comes up between them and puts her arms around their waists.

"We're still coming for prayer," she says. "I just talked to Capers about it, and the Benningtons said they want to come and pray for him too. We're not just going to give up, right?" She wrings her soft, wide hands and says, "I better go on home now and see about him. Y'all tell Sis for me."

"All right." Ray nudges Angus. "Walk her to her car, okay?"

Angus nods and puts out his elbow for Kitty B. to take hold of as Vangie comes over to ask Ray a question about storing the table-cloths.

When Vangie sees Ray's face, she leans in and asks, "Is it LeMar?"

Ray nods and pats Vangie's arm. "Let's enjoy the night."

"You're right," Vangie says. "Tomorrow will take care of itself."

Capers ambles up and asks Vangie to dance, and Ray shoos her toward the dance floor and says, "Go on."

Then Ray grabs one of her champagne glasses off one of Mrs. Pringle's silver trays as the waiter passes by. She steps back, takes a sip, and watches Sis and Salvatore embrace as the band kicks in to "L-O-V-E" by Nat King Cole.

Suddenly, Ray feels a warm, wide hand on her back.

"May I have this dance?" Cousin Willy whispers, his plump lips tickling her ears.

When she turns around he smiles with his hands open. Ray slips off her heels so she won't be taller than him, and she puts her hands in his.

As they dance in the fading light of the spring afternoon he says, "You done good, Ray."

"Thank you."

"You know what I was thinking?" he says. "It'll be our thirty-fifth anniversary next summer."

"Will it really?" she says as he closes his eyes and pulls her close. She smells the gardenia on his lapel. Thick perfume.

"How 'bout we renew our vows?"

She pulls back and looks at him, and he opens his deep brown eyes. "You want to?" she says.

"Yes ma'am." He kisses her forehead. "Might as well re-up for another thirty-five." He takes her hand and adds, "I only have one request."

"What's that?"

"It will be very small, and we will get the whole thing catered."

He spins her gently around and pulls her back to him. "We can fly this fellow back in from Houston if you want."

"I don't know." She shakes her head as they sway back and forth. "I wouldn't want it to have a hotel-food feel."

He turns and dips her and as she leans back he says, "You are not going to lift a finger, Ray Montgomery."

"Ray Montgomery," she says as he pulls her back up. She whispers into his ear, "I love that name. I wouldn't change it if I could."

"Good." He squeezes her tight and turns again.

As Ray embraces Cousin Willy, she looks through the tent and out over the water. She can see the votives and the canoe filled with flowers drifting along the edge of the moonlit creek.

She and Willy dance song after song together as Vangie oversees the wrap-up of the reception. Ray can hear her instructing Sis and Salvatore up to the guest room to change, and she watches as Vangie hands out the trumpets at the edge of the piazza for the going-away celebration.

Tomorrow Ray and the gals will count and polish the silver and start cleaning and ironing the linens for Priscilla's reception. She sent the invitations last week, and she's already started to receive responses and a few gifts too.

Now she rests her head on the shoulder of her husband, and she thanks the good Lord for giving her this man so many years ago. What would her life have been like if she didn't let her mama push her out the door that night the gang invited her to come steal a watermelon?

She supposes they might have gotten together sooner or later, but they may not have had that moment. That memory of the warm wheel well in the back of Angus's flatbed, and her future husband patting her back before putting his hand out flat as if he wanted her to give him five. Then his gentle voice filling the black space between them as he said, "I'm Willy, pretty girl."

ACKNOWLEDGMENTS

First I want to thank my dear friend Jenny Dickinson, and my husband, Edward B. Hart, Jr. who gave me the idea during a conversation around the dinner table a few years ago. I'm so glad we decided to compare weddings.

A pregnant writer is no basket of fruit, and I am immensely grateful to my editor, Ami McConnell, and my copy editor, Rachelle Gardner, who kept me (and the story) on track during a long nine months. Their illuminating critiques and wise counsel made all of the difference. Thanks also go to my hometown readers who encouraged me during the early drafts: Lisa Hughes, Amy Watson Smith, and my husband, Edward.

I am indebted to my publicist, Marjory Wentworth, as well as the following South Carolina bookstores: The Cozy Corner on Edisto Island, The Open Book in Greenville, Litchfield Books on Pawleys Island, and the Barnes & Noble booksellers in Mount Pleasant, Hilton Head, and Charleston. The books would never make it into the hands of readers if it weren't for the work of these good folks.

Finally, thanks be to the One from whom all good things come. I am blessed beyond measure to have the opportunity to do what I love.

READING GROUP GUIDE

1. *The Wedding Machine* is written in third person, but each chapter is devoted to different, alternating points of view. What affect do the shifting viewpoints have on the story? Is there one character who forms the emotional core of the book? Discuss.

2. Consider the "watermelon stealing" flashback. Why is the memory of this event significant to each of the four women who form The Wedding Machine? In what ways were their roles and personas established on that summer night so many decades ago?

3. In the prologue, the four gals are described as "young, hopeful virgins promised to their small town sweethearts." In what way is the prospect of marriage promising to each of them? Whose marriage has survived and thrived. Whose hasn't? Why?

4. How is the town of Jasper changing? Who is threatened by this change and why?

5. Ray says that the gals can hardly relate to their offspring. Why do you think this is? What constitutes the chasm between these two generations?

6. Consider the friendships of the foursome. How do they grow and deepen over the course of the story? Does Hilda's "hiding out" contribute to this growth?

7. Why does Sis need to get rid of the wedding dress? How does this contribute to her character's development?

8. Consider Kitty B.'s Thanksgiving confrontation with LeMar. Do you agree with the ultimatum she gave him?

9. What revelation does Ray have at the Healing Prayer Revival Day? How does her conversation with Cousin Willy about her family history bolster this revelation?

10. Do you think Hilda will ever come out of hiding? Imagine how and when this might happen. Describe.

ABOUT THE AUTHOR

Beth Webb Hart, a South Carolina native, holds a B.A. in English Literature from Hollins College and an M.F.A in Creative Writing from Sarah Lawrence College. She lives with her husband, composer Edward Hart, and their family in Charleston.

Author of Two of *Booklist's* Top Ten Fiction Picks for 2006